GRYPHON RIDER ACADEMY

3

STORM FRONT

Flutterbye Trail Press
797 Sam Bass Road #2541
Round Rock, TX 78681

First edition

Editing by Red Loop Editing
Cover Design by Black Bird Book Covers
Chapter Art by Etheric Tales
Map by Reva Design
Printed Interior Design by Enchanting Covers
Published by Flutterbye Trail Press

ISBN: 978-1-954582-14-9 (E-book)
ISBN: 978-1-954582-38-5 (Paperback)
ISBN: 978-1-954582-34-7 (Hardback)

Feedback: Encounter a problem with this book? Let us know at
elisehennessyauthor@gmail.com

BOOKS BY ELISE HENNESSY

Books in the Altare World

GRYPHON RIDER ACADEMY
Second Chance
Chosen
Storm Front
Wild Flight
Gryphon Rider Academy Omnibus 1: Books 1-4

ROYAL SPY INSTITUTE
The Crown Heist
Five & Chance

Also by Elise Hennessy

BLOOD LEGACY SERIES
Dream Walker
The Winter Key
Queen's Return
Court of Illusions

MAP

You can find a full-sized version of this map at: www.
elisehennessy.com/maps

GRYPHON RIDER ACADEMY 3

STORM FRONT

ELISE HENNESSY

CHAPTER 1

TERRITORY DISPUTES

I let Ari think this meeting was my idea. It gave him someone to blame for our early wakeup before the sun rose. Neither of us enjoyed the frigid flight north, toward the distant rocky outcroppings that marked the beginning of wild gryphon territory.

By the time the sun's rays graced the sky, we spotted a trio of beasts waiting for us, a few hours' flight away from Fortress Aerie. They should've been long gone from the human stronghold by this point, but they'd hung back, all for different reasons.

Ari saw from my eyes due to our extra-strong Link since our emotional states were nearly identical. In moments like this when we were at our closest, he was given the miracle of sight by tapping into my senses to escape the darkness of his blindness. Queasy nerves stole through us both, though, and even though we had different reasons for it, the result was the same.

We touched down a safe distance away from the three wild gryphons. The leader was Ari's father, Roshawk, a male with dark brown plumage just a shade away from black. He took a step forward when I dismounted, and I steeled myself.

Though Roshawk had reached out mentally to invite both of us here, I knew he was less than thrilled to see me next to his son.

"You've come." His mind's presence was a growl of power, loud enough to feel like it was vibrating my skull.

The older gryphon's next step included a pronounced limp. A crimson scar spread raised, jagged lines over his flank, wing, and leg, limiting his range of motion. He wore it like it was an honor, the visual reminder that he had killed an eldrafn to defend his flock and survived to lead it further. One of his ears was ripped, nearly torn clean off from a battle long past.

By comparison, his two companions were pristine young things, their feathers vibrant in the dawn light. Sunset and Reyos, newly escaped from Fortress Aerie.

"We have," Ari answered his father. I felt a twinge of his annoyance at my drifting gaze. My sight was an imperfect replacement for the eyes he'd lost in combat almost two years ago, especially when I didn't focus on the gryphon he was speaking with.

When I felt his emotions shift, I looked back at Roshawk, who edged closer cautiously. The wild gryphon watched me with leery yellow eyes, ready with a sharp beak should I try anything he didn't approve of. *"Could you make the human leave?"* he asked, tone laced with awkwardness.

It was an improvement over the vicious glares and accusations of being a "Link thief" from him. *"I don't mind —"* I began to say.

"No," Ari snapped. *"We're just here to say goodbye. You're all heading north, and we're going to war."*

"War," Roshawk echoed, as if the concept was foreign to him.

Reyos clicked his beak for attention, venturing a step forward. *"Skylord, it's a human word for their territory disputes."* The wild gryphon looked bluer than ever in the sunlight, striking with his white beak and talons. His time in captivity had given him a frightfully lean form, however, with missing feathers and tufts of fur marking where the tamers had chained down his wings as part of the taming process.

"Oh." Roshawk bobbed his head, accepting that explanation. It was how I'd finally gotten Reyos to understand why he was kidnapped from the wild and brought to Fortress Aerie in the first place. My people, the Altarians, desperately needed more gryphon riders, but the beasts weren't having hatchlings like they used to.

The practice of stealing wild gryphons from their nests, especially babies, adolescents, and brooding females, resulted in the hostility rolling from Roshawk as he turned to me again. He'd lost his mate, Valtora, and the egg that would become Ari decades ago. His mating Link with Valtora never faded, though, and their separation created a wound that'd never heal as long as they were apart.

"We're leaving in a couple days," I said.

He balked. *"Valtora told me we had a year or more…"*

"I'm sorry. The war has changed everything." I spread my palms, and he turned toward the gesture sharply with his beak parted in warning.

Ari walked past his father, chirping quietly to the third gryphon here, Sunset. Glorious with feathers of red and maroon, she was the former mount of my biggest rival, Victor Callan, until his untimely demise a few months ago. I turned away and let my Link with Ari fade to give him as much privacy as I could.

He wasn't really here for his father, but instead to say goodbye to the female that could've been his mate had she remained a military gryphon. I went to perch on a nearby rock, expecting to be ignored from here. Instead, Reyos came to settle beside me, bunting my knee briefly.

"Sorry again," he whispered, shifting his mental presence to speak with me privately.

The price of his escape with Sunset was the concussion he'd given me on the way out, an unexpected attack that'd distracted the tamers. I reached for him and stroked his neck feathers when he turned his head for it. Despite his choice to return to his flock, it seemed we were still unlikely friends.

"No lasting harm," I said.

The little hairs lining the back of my neck lifted, and I turned to see Roshawk bristling only a foot away. My heart stuttered in my chest. If this wild gryphon decided to attack, there was very little I could do to stop him.

"Don't just ignore me," he growled. *"Explain."*

I gulped a swallow. *"I'd be happy to explain anything you want to hear,"* I promised. Ari, a few paces away, had his beak lifted from where he pressed against Sunset's side. I had the sense he was listening as well.

It was Reyos that disarmed the older gryphon, however. *"Humans aren't so frightening, Skylord. This one's rather good. She's the reason I escaped,"* he said.

The dark feathers across his scarred flank prickled, and Roshawk turned to groom himself for a few moments like an embarrassed cat. He turned in a circle before settling on his undamaged flank and clarifying what he wanted to hear, watching me as I told him all about the Storm Front, where Ari and I would be flying as soon as we graduated in a couple days.

Reyos listened and helped translate certain concepts further for the other gryphon to understand. *"So, let me get this straight. Your Skylord's son was murdered, so you are at war with the group of humans that did it?"* Roshawk asked.

I started to hold up a finger to correct him but thought better of it. Wild gryphons lived more simple lives, so maybe I should let him keep a more basic understanding of the situation. *"Basically,"* I answered.

"Why does he not challenge his rivals personally?"

"Well, our king doesn't fight." The idea of King Cortes holding anything but a ceremonial sword was laughable.

"Which means he sends you and my son to fight in his stead?" he probed.

"Exactly. But not just the two of us. Human wars have hundreds of soldiers on either side, plus dozens of aerial fighters. Ari and I defend the army fighting on land from…" I glanced at Ari, letting him supply mental images of the creatures he'd fought for years, rozash.

Coming in three colors, the sky serpents were monstrous with four wings and two heads, capable of spitting pressurized sand, fire, or acid. Ari's memories were full of different rozash and the devastation they could leave behind if no gryphon riders were there to stop them.

"However, there won't be any rozash up north. Only eldrafn," Ari added for me. He flashed a few memories of the titanic bird of clouds and lightning he and I saw in our dreams, courtesy of the task Mother Nilara had gifted me personally. I still bore a stripe of white hair, a physical sign that I was under her protection until I figured out what, exactly, she wanted from me.

Roshawk shuddered in disgust. *"Sky terrors are bad enough,"* he said, referring to the bird-shaped forces of nature the Rathi had figured out how to tame and ride into combat. *"I don't understand. Why were there humans on the back of those… rozash?"*

His disbelief grew as I explained again that all those glimpses of battlefields ruined by fire or acid were just snippets of the aftermath of combat between Altare and Lithos. *"Barbaric,"* he said, horrified. *"Come with us to the wild. There is no 'war' to worry about there."*

"We can't," Ari answered.

Roshawk ignored him, inching closer to me. *"Forget everything I've said to you before. I will welcome you to my flock like a gryphon if it means my son is safe,"* he said. From the lack of echo in my mind, I had the feeling he was talking to me privately.

"*We can't,*" I repeated. He made a deep, unhappy warble. "*It's our duty to help Altare win. It's everything we've been training for. Besides, Valtora will be there, and she needs us.*"

Bowing his head, he muttered, "*She needs me, too, and the flock we started together.*" He twisted around to look at Ari, still relaxing with Sunset, and a wistful sigh whistled through his beak. "*I can't help but remember the last time we were here. My mate spoke of duty and purpose, two things we don't need to discuss in the wild. Our purpose lies in our flocks and family. Nothing else is more important.*"

"*She still thinks—*"

"*Don't speak for her,*" he interrupted without venom. His tail flipped, betraying his inner agitation. "*She told me herself that I couldn't come with her and she couldn't come with me. The same thing you and Arimus have repeated. Your duty lies elsewhere. I just wonder…*"

Several moments of silence hung between us. When I could take it no longer, I ventured, "*Maybe you would like to come with us?*"

He took a moment to inhale and snarled so viciously Ari sprung to his paws and loped in our direction. "*I would never allow any Link thief on my back!*" Roshawk roared.

I knew I was pressing my luck with what I was about to suggest. I eased to my feet and maneuvered around him, pressing my hands to Ari's shoulders when he closed the distance between us. "*But would you be able to tolerate being around humans if it means you could be with Valtora?*" I asked.

Roshawk's livid breathing had his chest rising and falling like a bellows. His eyes were narrowed to catlike slits as his feathers and fur bristled.

"*Let's go, Sivana,*" Ari said, nudging me away from his father.

"*No, wait.*" With him between Roshawk and me, I felt bold

enough to finish verbalizing the idea. *"If humans could show you they can behave around wild gryphons, if no one tried to touch or tame you, what's stopping you from seeing Valtora? Or for any wild gryphon from seeing their long-lost mates and kids?"*

"It can't be done. Your kind is not to be trusted," the wild gryphon snarled. *"You taunt me with a possibility that can never exist."*

Reyos, standing on the other side of me, scuffed his talons. *"Has it ever been tried before?"* the blue gryphon asked.

"Any gryphon that's tried it has ended up dead or, worse, tame." Roshawk's tone held a sneer. *"You may as well leave, and take your ideas to war with you."*

Ari released a long-suffering sigh. *"Goodbye, Father,"* he said coolly.

"You know where to find me when you come to your senses," he answered.

Ari and I were in the air again less than a minute later. When he calmed down from his protective anger, I told him what he'd missed of my conversation with his father and how I'd felt the yearning that Roshawk had covered with a blast of fury.

The wild Skylord had, at least for a split second, seriously considered returning with us if it meant he could be with Valtora.

CHAPTER 2

STORMS AHEAD

When we swooped through one of the open shutters at the top of Fortress Aerie, I expected to be one of the crowd. Several riders came and went even this early, most the near-elderly men of Final Flight, the air couriers with beasts too old for combat.

With my year group about to be promoted early, many of the messages coming and going from the Academy were coordinating where the thirty-five of us would go. In that bustle, I thought I'd be invisible, but a caretaker seized the front of Ari's reins the moment he landed and folded in his wings.

"Cadet Walker! The Commandant wants you in his office now," he told me.

I cursed under my breath as I dismounted before offering him a nod of thanks when he drew Ari away to get him groomed and fed. My mind raced while I charged down the well-worn stairs toward the Commandant's office on one of the lower floors.

I'd taken Ari out before the sunrise hoping no one would notice our absence. Saying a proper goodbye to Sunset had meant so much to him, but we weren't allowed to leave the fortress whenever we wanted to. Well, *I* couldn't. Gryphons could come and go nearly as they pleased since the psychic Link between beast and rider would ensure they would always return.

However, Ari couldn't fly without me to guide him. Us leaving together must've looked a lot like desertion on the eve of the promotion ceremony when we'd learn where we were assigned on the Storm Front up north. A stern lecture from the Commandant was the least of my worries when he still had control of which combat flight I'd be joining.

My anxiety was stifled when I saw him kneeling next to his gryphon rather than waiting behind his desk like a king summoning me before his court. He gestured for me to close the door, which I did.

The Commandant's image would be in a textbook one day as an example of a man who'd kept himself in peak physical condition his whole, long life. Not an ounce of fat marred the wiry frame clothed today in his formal uniform, Knight-Marshall insignia shining gold on his epaulets. On second glance, though, his shoulders were stooped today, as if the weight of responsibility and exhaustion were too much. Dark half-moons shadowed his eyes.

"Good morning, sir," I said.

"Sit," he responded, eschewing formality. His gryphon, Night, stirred and lifted her head. She nudged her rider with her dark beak before he stood and began to pace the narrow office. From my seat in the uncomfortable chair he kept for cadets, I watched him walk back and forth in a full circuit.

Some men were larger than life, and to me, the Commandant was one of them. I knew something was really wrong to drive the unflappable man to stew in his thoughts rather than sit on the other side of his desk and dress me down for my early morning trip out of the fortress. I nibbled on my lower lip, missing Ari despite just leaving him; he always seemed to have better insight than me in situations like this.

I let the Commandant pace without saying a word. It was my place at the bottom of the military hierarchy to keep my lips shut and wait for orders.

"Cadet Walker, how much do you know about truth serum?" he asked at last.

"I took it once, sir," I said. It'd felt like my head was packed with fluffy candy clouds, all my worries locked away behind a wall of them. I'd smiled overwide with my head lolled to the side as I spoke the truth at Callan's trial, right before his untimely death.

"Are you aware that it's a poison?"

"No, sir," I answered simply. Lord Gadric could've mentioned it, as the Academy's resident Tulari mage, but his class was more geared toward anatomy while my roommate, Ellie, learned his alchemical secrets.

"It's made from the juices of the cabexios leaf. There are seven laws governing the growth and distribution of the plant, plus more around the use of its products against other humans."

I nodded along with his explanation, getting a queasy feeling in my belly from his expression fixed somewhere over my shoulder.

"Even our prisoners of war have three chances to confess their crimes before we force them to take truth serum. I treated the man who attacked you in the stables just like any other prisoner." He finally turned to face me fully. "But from the moment he swallowed the serum, he went into convulsions. He did not confess before he died, Cadet Walker."

My face numbed, frozen in shock. Only a day separated us from the evening the Commandant had taken my would-be killer into his custody and told me he'd take care of it. He'd been Crown Prince Isaac's agent, and I hadn't even known his name, only referring to him as the hooded man. He was the most likely person to have murdered Callan after he was no longer of use to his employer.

I shook my head slowly in denial. With both Callan and the hooded man dead, there was no evidence against the crown prince. Isaac had tried to have me killed, to use me as his martyr so he could ascend the throne to become King of Altare before his father was ready to relinquish it. First through Callan by using a sleight of hand to make it look like his father, King Alonso Cortes, had finally succeeded in removing me as the first female gryphon rider. The hooded man's attempt a couple days ago had been retaliation when I made it clear I was no longer going to let the crown prince manipulate me.

"Lord Gadric has already tested his blood and found evidence of a different serum made from vlorine flower. It is colorless, odorless, and lasts for years in the human body, completely innocuous on its own but deadly when combined with truth serum. His death was no accident," the Commandant said grimly.

I paled to know that was possible. Had the hooded man known he was doomed the moment the truth serum hit his tongue, or had he been unaware that someone had previously slipped him this other serum?

"So now I must involve you further into his investigation, despite my best attempts to shield you. You mentioned this man worked for the crown prince," the Commandant prompted.

"Yes, sir."

Finally, he perched on his seat across his desk from me, picking up a quill. "Tell me everything you know."

"E-Ev-verything, sir?" I echoed, stumbling into my old stutter as nerves shook my hands.

He eyed me sternly, in that way that suggested he was peeling apart my hesitation to see the vulnerable truth underneath. "If it is as serious as I expect, you may have to testify again under truth serum at a later date. However, given the circumstances, I would prefer to believe one of my cadets wouldn't lie about such serious topics as suspected conspiracy and treason."

After hearing about the hooded man's death, I'd prefer to never take truth serum again. So, I gulped a grateful swallow but still didn't say anything. What military investigation could come close to touching the crown prince? If the hooded man's attack had taught me anything, it was that I was vulnerable at any time, while he was not.

Before the silence could become uncomfortable, he added, "If you died on the Storm Front in two weeks' time, would you want what you know to go with you? The Gatekeeper will not bring you back to testify."

Nor would he bring back Callan or the hooded man, two people who could've convinced the king that his son was conspiring against him. I breathed a reluctant sigh. "When I first came to the Gryphon Rider Academy, I owed Crown Prince Isaac a favor for saving Ari's life and allowing me to attend. He told me as much, personally, in Kite Flight's dorm after Yule."

The Commandant's quill scribbled in the wake of my words. "He met with you alone?"

"Yes, sir."

"Tell me what he said."

We ended up in his office for hours as I dredged up every memory of my interactions with the crown prince and what I'd learned secondhand through Princess Odalis and Sunset. His attention seemed so much more sinister with what I knew now. The only thing I left out was my parents' involvement and how they'd been willing to support King Alonso's deposing if it meant I would be safe under Isaac's rule.

His quill paused when I shared Sunset's memory of the hooded man's meeting with Callan. "His gryphon spoke to you?" he asked.

The pendant holding Lord Orion's magic felt hot against my skin. Its chain was tucked under the collar of my flight leathers, hiding my secret with its silvery links, the color of Lady Nilara. I couldn't simply tell anyone I could talk to, and even ride, other peoples' gryphons due to a gift from the god himself, lest it shatter.

It was my biggest frustration, not being able to share the extent of my understanding of the beasts. I was the God of Mankind's mortal Chosen, but only Ari and the gods got to know that. Most days, I wondered why Lord Orion chose such an ordinary person to meet with him personally, but I was sure he would call on me soon to fulfill my duties.

"Of a sort, sir. She wanted to make sure someone knew Cadet Callan was murdered, so she shared the memory with me during her rehabilitation," I said.

He tapped the ragged edges of his quill against his opposite palm, rereading this part of my report. "You have a gift with the gryphons, young lady. It reminds me of someone I used to know." His wistful smile and shaded eyes suggested that was a personal comment, so I didn't think to ask who it was. He gave himself a little shake. "Anyway, I want to commend you for your honesty."

I nodded, still uneasy despite his rare smile. "What happens to the information from here, sir?"

"There is only one man I trust with this knowledge right now. I will be speaking with Paragon Hughes once he arrives for your promotion ceremony." He met my gaze earnestly, like he could steal away all the fear and doubt that rose from me.

If he was going to Knight-Paragon Hughes, that meant my issues had reached the man at the end of the chain of command. The gryphon knight corps only had one Paragon, and he reported directly to the king.

"I should have come to you sooner," I murmured.

From the moment the crown prince showed up unannounced in my dorm to catch me unawares, I should've realized I was completely out of my depth. Despite that, I felt like my story was in good hands between the Commandant and Paragon Hughes. I'd met Hughes twice, each time noticing his genuine warmth next to the king's hostility. If anyone had the charisma to convince King Cortes to look into his shadow for danger, it would be Hughes.

In typical Commandant fashion, he didn't linger on my feelings. With military briskness, he said, "That will be all, Cadet Walker. You're dismissed to rest and prepare for the storms ahead."

CHAPTER 3

SIGNE'S GIFT

My dorm was looking fairly stripped, with our belongings either shipped home or coming with us to the Storm Front. I noticed the letters set aside on one of our tables immediately, and my heart soared to read my name in my mother's handwriting.

"Hey," Ellie said, barely looking up from a textbook. She sat with her feet propped up, her lunch gathering dust next to her as she got lost in what she was reading.

I sat next to her, stealing a piece of cheese off her plate. The men in our flight were probably off having lunch while I tore into this envelope. "When did we get a mail drop?" I asked, distracted.

"Maybe an hour ago?" She shrugged. "Acton was looking for you, too."

I nodded, thinking it was weird that I'd been apart from Ari and Weslecker this long. The former was stuck with me, but the latter chose to stay close to keep me safe.

"He wants to be stuck with you, too." Ari's voice drifted out of nowhere, our Link strong enough for him to pick up my thoughts and chat with me through several levels of solid rock.

I felt my cheeks warm. *"You know I can't start thinking about him like that."*

"Start?" he echoed playfully. *"So you haven't been admiring him lately?"*

"Ari..."

"Besides, he gives nice paw massages." Now that he mentioned it, I noticed a faint thread of happiness coming to me through our Link, like Weslecker was rubbing Ari's paws at that exact moment.

"Fed and groomed me, too. He couldn't find you, so he's waiting with me for you to show up."

"Can you tell him he doesn't have to wait? I have a couple things to do," I said, sharing my plan with him and what he'd missed of my meeting with the Commandant while I scanned Mother's letter.

I read it through a second time before breathing a sigh of relief. She and Rissa had successfully left Kaiamear under the cover of darkness and traveled to a Temple of Nilara in a small town she left unnamed, just in case someone else intercepted this letter. They were safe from possible retaliation from the crown prince, if a little uncomfortable in too-small accommodations and amongst strangers.

There was no return address. I inspected the envelope, my lips quirked to the side. I wouldn't be able to get word back to them before I was shipped out to the Storm Front. This would probably be the only letter I received from them for quite some time.

Ari's voice interrupted my musing. *"He says he's staying with me for now. What's wrong?"*

"Mother and Rissa are okay," I told him. *"But there's still no word from Father and Valtora. They may not be at the Storm Front. I think we're going to be cut off from everyone until the war's over."*

"They will be. Where else could they go?" he asked, sounding perfectly logical.

"Prison," I answered.

It depended on how King Cortes really took my father's resignation. As the former Commander of the First Gryphon Flight, Father had been in charge of the honor flight tasked with keeping the royal family safe. It was a high honor, and members of the flight were usually appointed for life.

Father had resigned to send a message to the king—he couldn't protect the king anymore if King Cortes continued ignoring or causing threats to my life. The only hint of reaction I'd received here at the Academy was Prince Mateo saying his father "seemed shaken" by it. Had he actually accepted this event for what it was, a spit in the face, or had he retaliated by attacking my father in return?

Ari scoffed in my mind. *"You're worrying too much."*

Could he really blame me, though? Nothing was certain except the chaos of war, caused by the crown prince's ambition.

"Um…" I glanced up at the uncertain noise, realizing Ellie had finally put her textbook down and was watching me while wringing her hands. "Is everything okay?" she asked.

I forced a small smile. "I'm not sure right now."

"That's how I feel too," she said in a small voice, showing me the spine of her book, *Principles of Engineering.* "Feels like I've trained for this moment for years, but I still don't think I know enough to be of any help to anyone. I can tell you all about how a magelight works, but not all this other stuff I'm supposed to know."

"You're going to the Storm Front, too?" I asked in surprise, and she bobbed her head. Somehow, in a week of last-minute preparations, I'd missed this detail.

"I'm joining the engineering corps as a full member. No apprenticeship or warning, just the full duties and responsibilities right away," she said.

No wonder Ellie was reading that textbook like her life depended on it. My mousy best friend was a frazzled mess, her eyes bloodshot like she'd been looking over those pages without a wink of rest. "You're going to be amazing, Ellie. No one knows everything when they start their jobs, but that's why you have other people to help you," I said, covering her fretting hands with one of mine.

"Yeah, but how many will be there because they took an academic scholarship at one of the military academies? I'm going to embarrass myself in front of them," she murmured.

I snorted in disbelief. "I sincerely doubt that. I've seen how fast you pick things up and come up with solutions to problems no one else could." A modest blush started to darken her cheeks as I gave her hands a squeeze. "You're going to impress the head engineer so much when he, or she, sees how smart you are firsthand."

"I hope so," she said, squeezing me back. "Thanks, Sivana."

"Let's spend some time together this evening," I suggested. "I just have to talk to someone real quick."

She nodded, and I bid her farewell to head down the Academy's stairs again to the classroom level, where our instructors were having open hours for any last-minute questions or advice. The thrum of many male voices drifted out of each door as I passed them by, heading for Instructor Signe's class.

The elderly Rathi woman had fewer cadets in her room than I expected, her heavily accented voice hushed to talk to the young men ahead of me privately. I waited in line for a chance to speak with her and try one last time to get some insight from her as to how to complete my task from Lady Nilara. After the seemingly positive results of telling the whole truth about my situation to the Commandant, I'd realized I never told Signe why I was suddenly so interested in fighting eldrafn solo.

Signe's voice rasped today, interrupted by wet coughs

every so often. Her ivory Rathi complexion was sallow, her purple-tinted eyes seeming bruised with deep hollows. I eyed her in concern when it was my turn with her. She held her own sort of court on her usual stool, her crippled leg positioned behind one of its spokes.

Her class was my favorite, full of tales of adventure and glory from an unfamiliar culture. Just like the Commandant, though, she wasn't one to mince words. As I wondered if I should mention her health and insist she get her rest, she prompted impatiently, "Yes, girl?"

I cleared my throat and glanced behind me. For the moment, I was alone with her. "Good afternoon, ma'am." She responded with her usual scoff at the formality, and my face split into a smile. "I, uh, know you don't believe in the goddess who gave me this." I pointed to the white streak through my hair, and Signe scowled at it.

"Mother Nilara didn't quite tell me what my task was, but I've been getting the same dream over and over, and I think she wants me to kill an eldrafn." I told her about the gigantic eldrafn who killed Ari and me nearly instantly from the moment it noticed us in said dream.

The Rathi woman's brows rose. "I wouldn't think the soft Altarian goddess had it in her," she muttered. "Eldrafn do not get to the size you described. It would be catastrophic if they did, because they would be a hurricane within a thunderstorm. Anything in their path would be decimated with lighting and gale-force winds."

"Really?" I frowned, wishing anew that the mother goddess deigned to explain her intentions.

"I *suppose* it is possible, in theory. If you combine two storms at peak strength, the result would be massive," she mused. "But we are speaking of living things, and two eldrafn cannot join into one without one of them dying in the process. I do, however, have an idea."

She stooped to pick up her walking cane and unfolded to her feet with a groan. "Instructor…" I said with uncertainty as I watched her shuffle toward the door.

"Come with me. Close the door too," she ordered.

I offered her my arm, and to my surprise, she let me help support her weight as we traveled at a painstaking pace down the hall and a flight of stairs toward her personal quarters. She didn't say a word over the course of the journey, puffing with exertion and muffling a few coughs into her shoulder.

After she unlocked the door, I tried to steer her toward the padded seat in her living room, but she tugged free of me and indicated that I should sit in the chair across from hers. She limped her way from her bedroom and back, setting a wooden box down between us. I recognized it immediately and leaned forward as she lifted the lid.

What seemed like a flat, matte rock was actually a treasure from her past, the heart of her own eldrafn, who'd died decades ago. It was bigger than the cradle of my two palms together, and a purple color shot through with jagged black marks like lightning strikes.

Signe sat heavily and leaned back with a low groan. "Instructor, you should rest," I blurted, thinking of how difficult the return trip would be for her.

She puffed and coughed for a few long moments, her eyes tightly shut. "You are heading north," she murmured.

"Yes, ma'am."

"Take Revna's egg with you," she wheezed.

I inhaled sharply, my gaze turning toward the eldrafn heart. I couldn't possibly take it from her. To me, it was a big, heavy rock, and not even a pretty one. But to her, it was all she had left of a dear companion she'd lost long before I'd been born.

When I opened my mouth to say as much, I noticed her

gaze on me, piercing in its intensity. "Your soft mother goddess may not have explained how it happens, but you will face an eldrafn up north, and when you do, you will need extra help," she said. "Like I've told you before, only the power of a living eldrafn will bring back my beloved Revna. Take the egg. Ride to combat with her in your arms." Her accent thickened with her conviction.

"I can't just… I would probably drop it…" I protested.

"You will not," she said, as if ordering me would change the result of me trying to juggle a shield, combat lance, and Revna's egg in a combat situation while also guiding Ari. I just couldn't see it working.

Her nostrils flared from a frustrated huff. "This is the greatest gift I can give any Altarian. Don't you see? I've held Revna's egg up in the middle of countless thunderstorms, and she's absorbed just as many lightning strikes. Do I seem deaf to you from the crack of thunder? Do I seem scarred from the blasts of power?"

"N-no, ma'am," I said, eyeing the egg anew.

"It is the only way I see you and your gryphon fighting an eldrafn alone and winning. Accept this gift, girl, and do what I could not. Give Revna another chance at life." Her voice cracked at the end, and she turned away, her Rathi pride shuttering the emotional response.

"Okay," I murmured. "But when my Commander sees that I have an eldrafn egg…"

"Keep it a secret, if you can," she replied. "Swaddle her in layers of sheepskin with a copper rod for comfort. She will keep you safe."

I was still doubtful a long-dead eldrafn heart could protect me from a lightning strike, but I still stood to heft it from its box. It was as heavy as pure stone and just as inert. Yet something in me was touched by the veiled desperation that motivated her to ask me to take it. She'd exhausted every other avenue of bringing back Revna, so now it was my turn to try.

"I will do my best, Instructor. You have my word," I vowed.

I'd figure out how to keep it my secret, even if it saved me from the fury of a living eldrafn's lightning. It didn't harm me to make a promise to the elderly woman and watch the hope shine through the violet eyes set in her stoic expression.

CHAPTER 4
TRUE FACES

I PUT the eldrafn egg back in its box and placed it at the foot of my bed with my other items. Hands on hips, I surveyed the saddlebags and small boxes I was taking to the Storm Front. My belongings weren't much, so I decided the extra package could be strapped to Ari's side with the rest.

That done, I went to retrieve my gryphon from the stables, unsurprised to see Weslecker still in the stall. It was cramped with his own gryphon, Ironfeather, sprawled companionably over both his rider and Ari, who attempted to nap while the other gryphon batted playfully at one of his ears.

Weslecker and his gryphon both lit up when they saw me. The gryphon sat up with a noise close to a hatchling's squeak, despite how he was quickly filling out toward adulthood. His voice was young and sweet in my mind as he reached out to say, *"Sivvy! Tell Ari it's too late for a nap."*

"It's a perfect time," Ari grumbled back but stirred with a great yawn and stretch of his front talons.

I smiled to myself, getting a little butterfly flutter in my belly when I met Weslecker's gaze. The two gryphons continued to bicker about naps while the young nobleman stood and brushed off stray bits of hay from his cadet uniform. His hair was freshly cut to a fine velvet of auburn, and I noticed the barbers hadn't let him keep the modest facial hair he'd been trying to cultivate.

"I knew you'd be around if I stayed here long enough," he teased. He had the kind of smooth accent more suitable for sly comments across a lavish king's feast rather than a gryphon stable. It'd caused him no end of teasing from the rest of our flight-mates, but I'd grown to like it as something that was unique to him amongst my friend group.

I glanced left to right, making sure no prying eyes were watching before I opened the stall door and hugged him. He didn't hesitate to fold me into his strong arms; I was the one constantly pulling away from him out of fear of accusations of fraternization. "Everything all right?" he whispered over my hair.

"Just nice to see you," I whispered back.

He hummed, sounding unconvinced, and waited as I roused Ari to bring him back to the dorm with us. As we walked side by side toward the stairs, I chanced a glance at him, just to see him doing the same thing. I felt myself blush.

I didn't think it was fair to tell him what consumed my thoughts from the moment I saw him sitting with the two gryphons. We were leaving the Academy tomorrow, though, and I'd dwelled so long on thoughts of splitting up with him and the rest of our flight that the opposite possibility tied up the threads of my mind. How would things between us change if we were assigned to flights that shared the same camp?

Would anyone care if I slipped my hand into his in the evenings like I wanted to now? When he'd kissed me several months ago, I'd asked him to wait until we were out of the Academy. I'd said after graduation, but tomorrow's promotion ceremony was the next best thing. The king's requirements that I pass my classes and succeed at the Academy were met if I was out fighting his war, so maybe I could finally be with Acton.

I came back to myself when I felt Ari chuckle. *"Don't laugh at me,"* I said defensively.

"I'm not," he replied. *"This is just cute. Alamid never thought so hard about his mate."*

"He's not—I mean, I'm not—" I stuttered.

"Granted, he didn't really have *a mate."* His tone turned fond, wistful even. All my thoughts of Weslecker had tickled his memories, it seemed. I felt his sense of nostalgia over our Link as he thought of the many times his first rider had approached women. Unlike my father, his best friend, who'd married right after graduating from the Academy, Alamid hadn't settled down.

He had been more like an uncle to me than anything. My smile began to shrink as we both began to miss him fiercely.

"Sivana, really, what's wrong?" Weslecker asked. He opened the door back to our dorm, just seeing my reaction without knowing what passed between Ari and me. I forced a new smile just for him.

At this point, the rest of our flight was sprawled in the common area with their gryphons. Restless legs bounced, and several sets of eyes turned our way. I looked over all the familiar faces I'd miss if we were separated by combat flight assignments or the ravages of the war ahead.

Sharde sat beside Ellie now, *Principles of Engineering* tucked into the corner of his chair and away from her grasp. He held her hand, not even a bit afraid of accusations of fraternization with how he looked at her. Across their feet rested Puzzlebox, a petite and fluffy white gryphon with dark speckles along her flanks. She peeped a friendly greeting.

On the floor, Biggs lay with his head on his gryphon Echo's dusky brown wing. He rested his arms under him, but his face was slack with boredom. There was no competition to win here, nothing to keep him occupied until tomorrow.

Actually, I saw variations of this expression on everyone. A day off before we left was like visiting the three hells if we had nothing to do.

"Hey, guys," I said, stroking my chin thoughtfully.

Feyring elbowed Korvic, whispering loudly, "She's got that look on her face."

"She does," Pereyra agreed.

"What look?" I asked. "I was just thinking we need to play a couple rounds of talonball."

The last member of my flight, buff, soft-spoken Credell, stood first. "Yes, ma'am. I'll go get a ball," he drawled in his slow, easy way.

"We just need a team to face—" I began to say, but Sharde was already out the door.

It didn't take long to learn that he'd invited every second-year to join us, flooding the Green with restless gryphons and cadets eager for one last competition. I looked up from the sidelines to see a bare muscled chest go barreling past and stifled a laugh. It was Commander Falirin, our combat instructor, who rapidly turned around a losing score on Harrier Flight's side.

More of our trainers joined in the games, while the Commandant himself arrived last, watching beside me with a hand resting on Night's neck. "This was your idea, wasn't it, Cadet Walker?" he asked.

"Not to this extent, sir."

His lips quirked on one side, like he fought a smile. "All right. Well, make sure everyone's off the Green by nightfall. We still have a ceremony to prepare for."

"Yes, sir," I said to his back, surprised to see him leave just as quickly as he'd arrived.

THE NEXT MORNING, we marched through a Pass in Review with me leading Kite Flight as Cadet-Commander. When we turned to salute the main stage, standing up front to either side of the Commandant were Paragon Hughes and…Crown Prince Isaac. I yelped, nearly tripping over my shoelaces like the greenest of cadets learning how to present arms while marching.

"What's he doing here?" I hissed to Ari, who watched it all through my eyesight.

Ari growled wordlessly, projecting a feel akin to a shrug. *"We'll just have to see. This won't be a usual graduation ceremony, after all."*

He was certainly right about that. There were only two rows of seats this year, since the third-years would not be returning from their squire-ships. They would have a delayed promotion to full gryphon knight status, just like my year group. While the first-years were seated by flight right now, by the end of the ceremony, they'd know their ranks for the first time and sit according to them.

Training at the Academy would go a different direction for the young men that'd remain here, since their gryphons needed time to mature to gain the strength and ability to carry a man and equipment into a combat situation. I knew they were in good hands as I took my seat, assisted by a sergeant with a clipboard.

To my surprise, I'd moved up a space since the last time we'd had our ranks shuffled. I sat in the eighth chair with Ari resting in the grass by my side. *"We've come a long way,"* I said to him, glancing toward either end of the line. Sharde warmed the last seat, the spot I remember being assigned at the end of my first year.

Ari stirred with a sense of discontent. Over our Link, I felt him thinking of the last time he'd been at the Academy. He and Alamid had the extra talent and ability to jockey for the number one spot amongst other similarly talented pairs.

Though we'd proven that a woman and a blind gryphon deserved a chance here, we hadn't ever challenged the two sitting at the other end of our row.

In rank two sat Weslecker with a straight spine and Ironfeather preening proudly next to him. And rank one, our Ace-to-be, was the same young man it always was. Bronze-skinned Prince Mateo, third son of King Cortes, who eyed his brother up on stage with a practiced, neutral expression. Only the slightest pinch of his lips betrayed his thoughts. His gryphon, Mireille, chose to sit beside her twin and nipped him when he moved to sprawl into the grass. With a short yelp, he sat straight like her.

"We should be over there too," he said.

"Maybe we will. We could do something up north that'll move up our rank by the time we return," I suggested.

"Hmm."

A throat cleared, magnified by a magical device to several times its normal volume. Paragon Hughes, white-haired and dignified in a formal uniform shining with medals, stepped forward to speak with us first. He leaned on his walking cane now, rather than holding it like a decoration the last time I'd seen him.

"Good morning, cadets."

"Good morning, sir!" chorused from over seventy throats.

His keen gaze roved over us. "A wise man once said that a victorious army is created during peacetime, from sweat and hard work, training and maintaining their skills while everyone else grows complacent with what they already have. Even before our border with Lithos was attacked six years ago, the leadership at the Gryphon Rider Academy has stood behind this idea and worked to produce the most highly trained fighters to defend Altare's skies.

"You have lived this reality for almost two years, enough time to be honed into fine knights-to-be..."

I felt a prickle that raised the fine hairs on the back of my neck. Hughes delivered a speech that had the young men around me adjusting their shoulders up and nodding along. I was only half listening when I realized the crown prince, standing just a couple steps behind Hughes, was staring directly at me without even a hint of his fake smile.

To say I'd betrayed Crown Prince Isaac was only telling half the story. He was the one who'd smuggled Callan a real combat lance cleverly concealed as a practice one, who'd convinced me I owed him and that debt could be repaid if I helped kick off a massive riot in Kaiamear's trade district.

He was the one who'd gotten his other brother, Prince Valentino, killed in the opening salvo of our war against a coalition of Rathi villages. Another fact I couldn't prove, not without concrete evidence rather than the hearsay that he'd been conducting secret meetings in the Rathi language and offering battle plans and weapons to our enemies.

His fingerprints were off all of these events, his hands clean as an indirect coordinator. It felt like I was one of the only people who knew his true face, with no way to unmask him. The Paragon announced that he was here in the king's place to award us our squire-ships. I'd rather see the look of restrained hostility on the king's face rather than go up there and shake the crown prince's hand.

During his speech, Hughes emphasized the same tired four core tenants of the Academy that were featured in every major speech we heard: courage, loyalty, discipline, and integrity. Then he handed the voice amplifier to Isaac and stepped back. A few of us shifted in our seats, eager to see how this worked.

"We will begin with my talented little brother, Mateo Cortes"—he looked down his nose at Mateo, who was ushered to his feet to come up to the stage—"the rank one cadet of your year group. He and his gryphon, Mireille, have been assigned to the Third Gryphon Flight under the close watch of its Commander. Congratulations."

We applauded politely as Mateo shook the Commandant's hand first and accepted a scroll from him. I watched how it went closely, sighing to myself when he shook his brother's hand last and exchanged a brief word with him.

That meant I'd need to look Isaac in the eye when it was my turn, and no one else got as much recognition from the crown prince when he announced which flight they were assigned to. Weslecker would be joining his best friend in the Third, but as I waited for my turn, the assignments were already switching to different flights. The Fourth took a few squires, and we were into the Sixth when a sergeant gestured for me to stand.

"Rank eight, Sivana Walker." He paused as I climbed onto the stage and came forward to shake the Commandant's hand while accepting the scroll with my squire-ship. "She and her gryphon, Arimus, have been assigned to the Seventh Gryphon Flight."

I noticed he hadn't given me a stately congratulations like the other cadets before me, but I was already reaching out to grasp hands with Paragon Hughes. "Good job, young woman. We are lucky to have you," he whispered.

"Thank you, sir," I said, my heart leaping up to jam in my throat as I turned to get the worst part of this over with. I extended my hand to Isaac, who held the voice amplifier to the side so it didn't pick up our words on stage.

His generous lips pulled into a sneer, and for a moment, I thought he wouldn't shake my hand in plain view of all my peers. Instead of a snub, though, his meaty hand caught mine the moment I started to falter. He jerked his elbow back to throw me off balance. Giving me the fakest smile yet, he whispered, "May Daroche find you on the battlefield, foolish girl."

My mouth hung half-open. Beside me, Ari rumbled an angry growl at the insult, echoing the surge of emotion in my chest.

Sure, most Altarians curse at each other and suggest the Gatekeeper take them early, but only saying the Gatekeeper's real name would draw his attention. His cold, dead gaze was now fixed on this stage from the afterlife, memorizing our faces. It was the worst kind of act, to have a life's worth weighed on the spot. If I had any doubts about Isaac, they were vapor in that moment I had to respond.

And with a sharp inhale, I hissed, "Not if he finds you first."

Scroll crumpled in my fist, I barged past him and flicked my right hand like I'd just touched something slimy. Maybe I was imagining it, but it seemed to take a longer moment for the crown prince to announce the next cadet. Fuming, I snapped the decorative ribbon holding my scroll closed.

I'm sorry for his audacity, Lord Gatekeeper. Please consider mercy, I prayed in my head, bowed over the words concealed within the roll of paper.

"Well, what does it say?" Ari asked tentatively. The spike of my temper had disrupted our Link, leaving him blind next to me. He wasn't nearly as angry as I was, missing some of the significance of speaking the Gatekeeper's name in such a way. I reached down out of habit to smooth his feathers and remind him in his darkness that I was there.

The Academy didn't deliver any important documents at ceremonies like this, so the rumpled paper I struggled to smooth held only a few sentences. *"We are to be apprenticed to Knight-Captain Zachary Cherin and his gryphon, Tempest. He leads Element Bravo within the Seventh."*

He bunted my thigh, coaxing me to scratch into his feathery neck. I calmed myself with a few deep breaths as he considered our placement. *"It's not a bad assignment, if a little beneath us. Alamid and I spent some time with the Seventh."*

Isaac was calling up another cadet. I looked up from my gryphon, a hateful expression on my face. Ari nipped my fingers, saying, *"And if I recall, I met a Tempest during that time. A fine male. Not as fast as me, though."*

I shook myself. No number of dirty looks would clean off the chill lingering on my skin, as if the Gatekeeper had left a sign of his presence to linger after his name was spoken aloud. Sighing, I deflated and buried my hand into Ari's thick double coat of coppery fur. If we weren't in the midst of a formal event, I'd be on the grass holding him for comfort instead.

"No gryphon is as fast as you," I pointed out.

At least in his prime. It'd gotten him a spot in the First as the gryphon used to bait rozash while his flight-mates killed them. He'd lost a lot of muscle after his devastating injury, but now he also carried a stone from the River of Origin in his gizzard and an extra reddish shine in his fur and feathers from the touch of Lord Orion.

"It's still the truth. I know it," he said, lifting his beak.

We would see soon. As soon as the ceremony was over, we were promised a proper graduation in the future. The first-years went chattering back to the Academy, while we huddled up in clusters. Members of Final Flight were waiting to deliver us to the Storm Front, but I was amongst a group of six heading for an unexpected location where the Sixth and Seventh were currently posted: the west coast. I cast a longing glance over where Prince Mateo and Weslecker stood together, part of a much larger group heading to the main fighting front.

Instead of joining their camps, it sounded like I'd be guarding one of the Duke Weslecker's many properties, stationed just off from Port Lindell and the seasonal estate where I'd spent part of the summer. How was that fair?

"Think of it this way. It'll be an uneventful squire-ship," Ari suggested. I hushed him before he could jinx us.

CHAPTER 5

DEADEYE

They gave us thirty minutes to gather our things and say goodbye, enough time to compare notes on where everyone was really going. There were undercurrents of fear and excitement intertwined in every conversation. While we were finally fulfilling the jobs we'd been trained for, most of us realized we were about to see the horrors of war firsthand.

It sounded like every major port was getting reinforced with new squires. Each combat flight not already engaged in fighting Lithos was now spread out across the curve of the northern Altarian coast.

Weslecker practically crushed me when I went to hug him in farewell in our dorm. "Write to me when you can," he said. "I'll send word to the summer estate. If you're right next to Port Lindell, then you can take food and supplies from it at any time. The staff will remember you."

"Really? That will be okay?" I asked. I lingered in his hold perhaps a few moments too long before we drew away.

"I'll make sure of it," he promised.

I wet my lips, and his gaze traced the motion. "I'm going to miss you," I murmured.

"As I will miss you. But it should be temporary." He gave

my shoulder a squeeze. "Who knows when the gods will reunite us?"

He glanced up and cast a quick look around before pressing a kiss to my forehead. Before I could react, he was walking away, joining our other flight-mates. I took the momentary distraction of their goodbyes as an opportunity to scrub the surprised blush from my face. I'd enjoyed the protective gesture and his proximity way too much, considering we were going to be parted for who knew how long.

None of my flight-mates were assigned to the Sixth or Seventh, meaning Ari and I would be amongst rivals at best with the older strangers who made up the combat flights. Ari had already assured me that this was what it was like after graduation anyway. We'd have been lucky to join a flight with one person we knew from our time at the Academy, since new blood tended to be spread out.

Still, I said goodbye with a heavy heart to my friends, and it became harder each time until I ended with a tearful embrace with Ellie. "You're going to do great," I reminded her.

"So will you! I want to hear about everything," she said.

"I'll write," I promised. With my family scattered and hiding, it hadn't occurred to me that I'd be penning letters to my flight instead. At least mail drops would be something to look forward to.

We returned to the Green with our gryphons weighed down with everything we were taking with us. I split off to join the group heading westward, nodding to the one young man I knew best amongst the other five waiting to fly out. He was from Falcon Flight, Hale Barlowe, the two of us in an uneasy truce after Callan's death.

"Walker!"

I turned, fighting a smile when I saw Prince Mateo heading over. Ari and I met him and Mireille halfway, and I spent a moment reading his handsome features. My gryphon poked his side of our Link with a curious hum.

"What?" I asked him, distracted when Mireille pressed her head to my middle with enough force to push me back.

"Nothing," he said innocently.

"Stay safe, Sivvy," Mireille interrupted, her mental voice layering over his. Her mental presence was filling out to represent her as a strong female, and it seemed that Puzzlebox's nickname for me was spreading. *"I promise I will look after my brother, and Mateo and Acton as well."*

"They're in safe wings, then," I said, hardly having to bend my knees to put my arms around her thick neck. She rested her head against mine, the two of us sharing our love for each other over the temporary Link we forged in that moment.

"Things will be awfully boring without you. Who else will tie my rider in knots?" she asked.

"What do you mean?" I had my suspicions when Ari chuckled.

The young man in question cleared his throat. "Mind if I say goodbye to her too?" he asked his gryphon aloud, who backed away from me with a playful twitter.

He came forward with his hand extended for a cordial shake goodbye. Mateo had to be more careful than anyone else here, with his father having eyes everywhere. Our friendship was limited to whispered moments like this one. "I noticed something happened on stage. What did my brother say to you?" he murmured.

My arms felt a chill all over again. "He spoke the Gatekeeper's true name," I whispered back.

Mateo muttered a curse. "I'm sorry. He's playing with fire, knowing that we're onto him."

My situation had been a "we" for longer than I'd known. Before Mateo was comfortable telling me that he was helping me covertly, he'd been a mysterious, nameless friend offering gifts of things I needed most. Now, when his father and eldest brother had established two clear sides that could fracture into civil war, I had decided to pick the third side sponsored by him and his sister, Odalis, which was less a path to Altare's throne and more all of us acting toward what we thought was right.

"It's not your fault," I sighed. "Just…how are we going to prove what he's done while we're stationed across the Storm Front?"

He glanced down at his hands for a moment. "I'm not so worried about that right now. Not when it sounds like he is willing to sink to new lows to have you killed. Do everything you can to stay safe, all right? I wouldn't put it past him to send someone after you," he said.

The goosebumps-raising feeling I had seemed to intensify. I wouldn't put it past him, either, so there had to be a possibility it would happen.

"I will, I promise." But as I said that, I thought of the fact that I would be separated from my flight-mates and the gryphons I'd grown so close to. Fate was unkind with my assigned squire-ship.

Sergeant Kobarn approached us, saying, "All right, you two, break it up. It's time to go."

We parted and were caught up in the process of last-minute saddle checks. I secured my battered training shield last, still showing a toy kite against a blue field. There hadn't been time to paint us new ones with our squire flight's crest when we all could make do with what we already had. The closed gryphon eye that was my personal symbol winked at me with silver paint, still a mysterious mistake that should've been gold for the vibrant color Ari's eyes used to be.

Around us, riders were climbing onto their gryphons, and I took one last look back at those leaving for the main front. I don't know if it was the moment I looked up to see Iron-feather and Mireille becoming distant flying figures, but I came to a realization that had Ari saying to himself, *"Finally."*

I liked Mateo and Acton and would miss them terribly. But...I wasn't sure which one I liked and would miss *more*. Gods help me.

"S*OME FEMALES CLAIM multiple males out in the wild, you know*," Ari said, probing a conversation I really didn't want to have for what felt like the tenth time during our lengthy journey across Altare. It was day two of riding dawn to dusk, after our small group was forced to land and stay in a local inn somewhere in the middle of the country. The elderly gryphon of the Final Flight member who led us west had just assured Ari and me that we were close.

"*That's not how human relationships work*," I pointed out.

"*Maybe it should be. Then you wouldn't be so conflicted.*"

Conflicted. What a nice way to say this problem had consumed most of my thoughts on the long flight west. It distracted me from the soreness we shared over our Link: for me, it was sitting for such a long period of time, and for him, it was the extra-long flight.

At what point had I started seeing both Weslecker and Mateo the same way? Less as fellow cadets, more as men I might have a future with?

The *when it happened*, I decided, could be placed aside for the *what am I going to do about it?* They were best friends; they'd figure out real quick if they both fancied the same girl and she was leading them both on.

Well, if they both fancied me in the first place.

"*I think they do*," Ari put in, trying to be helpful before I spun my thoughts in another circle.

"*That's the problem*," I fretted.

"*Is this something you can fix right this moment?*" he asked.

"Because I don't think you can. Therefore, you have time to decide, and they have time to change their minds."

Sorrow tinged the end of his statement, and a flash of maroon feathers filled his own thoughts. I heaved a sigh, rubbing my hand through his damp neck fur. *"You're right, of course."*

"Of course," he echoed.

"What do you remember of the Seventh?"

He considered as I adjusted my flight goggles, squinting at a shimmering line in the distance. The coastline. Ari thought loud and pointedly that we should have discussed this earlier.

"When we were assigned to the Seventh, it was led by a Commander with a wild-born gryphon that could challenge Valtora for size and strength. His call sign was Wrath."

Call signs were still strange to me. Outside of the First, the flight I was assigned to as caretaker, and the Second, the massive flight that trained and tamed gryphons, combat flights nicknamed a rider and his gryphon as a unit for easy address.

"What was your call sign with Alamid?" I asked.

He heaved a sigh. *"Arrow. Alamid got a tattoo of one when we were reassigned with his promotion to Captain."*

I nodded, not surprised it was a reference to his speed in flight.

"Actually…it was more a reference to how both our names started with 'a.' The guys had Alamid pick from a list of suitable military-related words that also started with it."

"Really?" I snorted.

"If you think downtime at the Academy is bad, wait until you're bored in a military camp. The weirdest things are hilarious," he said.

"I'll take your word for it."

He pulsed a sense of amusement as we circled toward the pointed shapes of tents set up outside the boundaries of Port

Lindell and the distinctive beachfront property of the Weslecker family.

On the other side of the temporary camp, where the coastline curved back toward the water, was a squat naval fort with a platform several gryphon lengths into the ocean. It bristled with cannons and miniature wheeled shapes that Ari identified as Tulari tools with the capability of firing sticky globs of fire magic that burned unnaturally on the ocean's surface even if they missed their intended target.

As we circled in for a landing, I pondered our living situation, thankful for my military training already. The fort was too small to provide for the mixed group we were about to join and was a naval asset, so it was unlikely we'd set foot inside at all. To one side of the camp, the brown and red tents were ground troops, probably fresh recruits, while the tents painted with blue stripes were for the gryphon riders and the empty field behind them designated for the gryphons.

"Do you think Port Lindell will be a target for the Rathi?" I pondered.

Altare's western coastline curved away from the Rathi Islands. If I had my geography right, there were a couple port towns that would be closer targets for the northern raiders.

"Our superiors obviously think so," he replied. He groaned upon a heavy landing, and our Link flashed with the ache in his flight muscles like how my legs burned after a long run. Once I dismounted, he shook himself, impatient with the extra heavy weight of the luggage he'd carried with us.

I was nearly finished removing his saddlebags when I heard someone engaging our Final Flight guide in conversation. "This our allotment of squires?"

"Yes, sir."

"Six of 'em? Bet we'll be returning two back to the Academy. Ha!" I peered behind Ari just in time to see the speaker clap the older man on the shoulder with a sharp bark of laughter.

Thrown off balance, our guide stepped back, saying, "You should not bait the Gatekeeper."

"Lighten your shoulders. It's a joke. I heard we're getting the fancy Nilarite girl everyone's a-gaga for. We'd best return her alive. Ha!"

"That's Commander Wrath," Ari said without a hint of doubt.

When the other rider's expression didn't shade away from disapproval, Commander Wrath pushed a coin purse into his hands and guided him away. "Here's your fee. Your services are needed to lift away a shipment of mail to…"

I tried exchanging a glance with Barlowe, the closest squire now standing next to his heap of belongings. He met my eye with a brief glare before turning away. *"I suppose he's sore about being ranked below us,"* I commented to Ari.

"I thought that was just his face," Ari said, drawing a snort of surprise from me.

The Seventh had claimed the cadets ranked eight through ten, so I turned to look for the other young man assigned alongside Barlowe and me. It was Devos, who was formerly of Harrier Flight and was one of its most boastful hecklers. He jerked his chin in greeting from a casual glance in my direction, currently leaning companionably against his gryphon. We'd had few conversations, and even fewer of them pleasant, so I wasn't looking forward to seeing what would happen if there was a Barlowe-Devos alliance during our time serving the Seventh.

Someone came for the last two cadets who'd be joining the Sixth, and soon Commander Wrath's rough voice preceded him leading a group of men toward us. "…Anyway, here are your greenies. Squires, front and center!"

I lined up with the other two young men at attention, feeling their scrutiny. "*Two* redheads. Aren't you lot supposed to be rare?" Wrath asked. He spoke loud enough to mask the murmuring of his men behind him.

Devos and I barely twitched. Sometimes in training, when someone posed a question to us as a group that wasn't a simple yes or no, we got confused. Were we supposed to state the obvious, or were we just meant to assume it was a rhetorical question? Devos stood in stony silence, his short, orangey hair a different shade from mine, but his fair face was just as touched by a sprinkling of freckles. I imagined he hated that the first thing our new Commander did was compare him to me.

"Yes, sir," I said in a quiet voice.

"I'm your new Commander, call sign Wrath. Welcome to the Seventh Gryphon Flight, a proud heritage flight founded with the beginning of the gryphon knight corps by King Altare himself. We hold our squires to the highest standards. Even in wartime, we expect you to obey your assigned mentor and serve him as his faithful shadow."

There was a meaningful pause, which we filled with a snappy chorus of "yes, sir" when we realized he was waiting for it.

He gave us a fairly lengthy list of rules, almost identical to what was expected of us in the Academy. I tried not to be resentful when he repeated three separate times that there would be no fraternizing, knowing the emphasis was because I was the only female amongst the whole flight.

Finally, he beckoned to me. "At ease, Squire Walker. Come here." Ari paced at my side, letting me guide him with a hand on his wing.

I got my first good look at Wrath, surprised to see a man who looked like he was only a couple years away from retiring to Final Flight. He had an olive complexion and shadows of stubble on his bald head that suggested he wouldn't grow any hair along the top of his scalp if he ever gave it a try. Wrinkles dug deep into his laugh lines, suggesting a jolly demeanor when he wasn't speaking to a new squire. He was only a couple inches taller than me, with a thicker build within his snug flight leathers.

"Your mentor will be none other than this man. I paired you myself. Ha!" He smiled proudly as he gestured to one of the men waiting behind him. "This is Captain Cherin, call sign Deadeye."

The nerves rustling in my stomach soured in unwelcome surprise.

"What kind of name is that?" Ari demanded, a low growl doing little to disguise his displeasure.

Coming forward to shake my hand was a man with an eyepatch where his left eye should be. His skin tone was a rich earthy brown, matching the leather of the patch almost perfectly, and his generous lips were tilted in a serious expression. "A pleasure to meet you, Squire Walker," he said, voice a deep rumble. Unlike Wrath, he towered over me, well over six feet tall.

"Yes, sir," I responded.

"Let me show you where you'll be staying, and then you can retrieve your things." He strode into the camp before I could hear the names of the men Barlowe and Devos were assigned to.

The moment we were out of earshot, my new mentor stopped and touched my shoulder with his fingertips. "I do not expect you to refer to me by call sign. It is Captain Cherin or sir to you, understood?"

"Yes, sir." My shoulders loosened a notch with relief, though Ari's anger still burned hot on the other side of our Link.

A line appeared between Cherin's dark brows. "First lesson: watch your expressions around your superiors. I volunteered to be your mentor, but Wrath likes to test boundaries. If I noticed you flinch at my call sign, he definitely took note of it."

"Yes, sir."

"Do you say anything else?" he sighed. "This isn't the Academy. You can talk to me."

Were I Sharde, I'd definitely answer by repeating myself again. I'd heard him cheekily say "yes, sir" so often it played out in my head, and I smiled. Gods, I missed my flight already.

Cherin's nostrils flared. "Don't take that the wrong way, Walker. We won't be friends. Your tent is this way."

I followed him, thinking he was right. I really did need to work on my expressions around my superiors. And every gryphon rider here except my fellow squires outranked me.

CHAPTER 6

A FINE TRADITION

One benefit of being the only female gryphon rider: I got a tent all to myself. A space meant for two or three people felt luxurious rather than cramped with my things partially unpacked and Ari resting next to me with his wings tucked tightly. We'd been given the rest of the afternoon to settle in.

I contemplated the furs that made up the tent's floor. None of them were sheepskin, but they were weathered and stained like they'd been used as temporary bedding several times too many.

"You're thinking too literally," Ari said.

He knew I was looking at the inert eldrafn egg weighing down my lap. *Swaddle her in layers of sheepskin with a copper rod for comfort,* were Signe's instructions. Yet I had no sheepskin nor any copper. If I were to take the egg into combat wrapped in these furs, its weight would split them with little effort, and there went my promise to keep it safe.

"I bet our arse of a Commander has sheepskins in his tent," I muttered.

"They'd probably frown upon us stealing from him."

"Yeah." Then I sat straighter. *"I'll just ask the Weslecker estate for supplies."* I'd thought about how exactly we'd fly into

combat with the heavy egg and missed Ellie since coming up with working solutions to logistical problems was her strong suit.

My best idea was a sturdy leather sling with a sheepskin interior, something I could attach to Ari's saddle to have it resting within my reach. I'd need help to make such a thing, but it would be worth it if it meant Ari and I became functionally immune to eldrafn lightning.

Ari was about to reply when there was a rustling at the tent's opening. "Walker? You decent?" Barlowe asked.

"One moment," I called. I hid the egg behind a saddlebag before the other squire could lift the flap and see me staring at it.

I came outside with Ari. "Commander Wrath wants to see us before dinner," Barlowe said. Devos was already with him, arms crossed, and their two gryphons shifting impatiently behind them. I glanced up, a little surprised to see the sun low in the sky, kissing the ocean with orange rays. I'd been preoccupied with the eldrafn egg for longer than I thought.

"You've got space for your gryphon in there?" Devos asked. He shoved a flap aside to look into my living space.

"Hey, privacy," I snapped. "You want me going into your tent next?"

"You mean the one I have to *share*?" he replied in the same tone.

Barlowe cleared his throat, looking uncomfortable. "Leave her alone, Devos. We don't want to be late."

I drew back, my brows lifting in surprise. Barlowe was defending me now? We walked in uneasy silence, heading toward the field where I'd seen the Sixth and Seventh's beasts resting. There were less gryphons here now, but enough men waiting to represent a whole flight. When we spotted Commander Wrath, the three of us lined up again at attention, this time with our gryphons striking the proud pose of military beasts next to us. I helped correct the angle of Ari's head mentally with a quick glance at him out of the corner of my eye.

"Good evening to our new squires," Wrath said, stepping forward and rubbing his hands together. A few riders stepped forward, carrying buckets of fish on ice to place before us. "Before you can become a proper member of the Seventh, there is one tradition you must experience. Who wants to go first?"

I tried to sneak a glance at the buckets in front of me, recognizing the Tulari-made pails used to keep ice cold and fish from getting rank. The flights usually didn't get first pick from the catch of the day, so investing in expensive magical tools was the ongoing solution.

Something told me part of this was feeding gryphons. But with the whole flight amassed, I also expected something unpleasant to follow. Still, I stepped forward, hoping it would help earn me some respect. "I volunteer, sir," I said.

"Excellent. Take a bucket, Squire Walker. We here in the Seventh don't want to invest our time and effort into squires who cannot handle gryphons, both on and off the battlefield. We take the phrase 'having a heart of the gryphon' quite literally, even." He turned and inclined his head. From the group of waiting beasts lumbered one of the biggest I've ever had the pleasure of meeting.

She was a muscular white creature with bold black spots spread liberally across her flanks. Her face was free of them, except one that dotted the edge of her beak like a beauty mark and a second one that haloed one of her keen yellow eyes.

"This sweetheart is Skyla, my gryphon," Wrath said, patting her shoulder. To demonstrate her sweetness, the feathers lining her spine lifted, and her beak parted to release an ominous hiss as she glared at us. Behind me, Barlowe loosed an uneasy laugh.

"Every rider of the Seventh will introduce himself and his

gryphon. Your task is to feed one fish to each beast," Wrath told me. I nodded along, knowing I could do this in my sleep. "But if any gryphon refuses, you must eat the fish instead."

Oh. I eyed the contents of my bucket, realizing they held fillets rather than whole fish. "Raw, sir?" I asked.

"We ask our gryphons to eat raw fish all the time. It won't hurt you too much."

My belly gave a sickened churn. "All right, sir. I understand."

Toward the beginning of my training, Father had warned me that each flight had its own traditions. And by "traditions," he clarified, he meant hazing rituals. Eating raw fish was not nearly as bad as some of the things he'd told me about, which had boiled down to pure meanness.

It was a similar tradition amongst the caretakers to stick a new person in the same stall as one of the meanest gryphons. I'd gotten lucky, because in the First, that meant I had a peaceful grooming session with Valtora. When other new folk signed on, I'd quietly pushed them aside and took care of her instead, effectively ending some of the senior caretakers' fun.

As I approached Skyla with a fish fillet in hand, I hoped I had a similar trick up my sleeve. I met her gaze, trying to establish a temporary Link to speak with her directly. "Hello, pretty gryphon. I have your dinner here," I said aloud.

While privately, I was saying, *"Good evening, Skymother."*

She shifted her wings with a rustle of feathers. *"A daring one, aren't you,"* she commented. She had a deep-bodied squawk of a voice. *"How do you know of Skymothers?"*

"From my own Skymother, Valtora."

Skyla assessed me anew with a birdlike cock of her head. *"Hmm. I know a Valtora. Who is she to you?"*

"She's my gryphon's mother and helped raise me as well. It's because of her that I chose to work with gryphons," I told her.

Skyla clicked her beak, turning to inspect the fillet I had offered up to her. But she didn't reply, not as the fish melted slimy water that dripped off my fingers. *"Will you please eat this fish?"* I finally asked.

"What will you do for me in return?"

"Well...I've never heard complaints about my massaging skills." I also spoke the same soothing platitudes aloud that I used to with the First's beasts while trying to coax them into taking a swallow of something they didn't want to stomach.

"Hmph. You'll have to do better to get me to eat bitterfish." It took me a moment to realize she hadn't named a specific fish, which I couldn't identify without a head and the shine of its scales. It was simply...a side of a bitter fish, something Skyla didn't want to gum up her gizzard. Her words held a second layer of meaning, as she was speaking a translation of images, thoughts, and memories like all gryphons communicate.

"I will find you something better at a later date?" I offered.

Tilting her head, she regarded me with a narrowing of her eyes. *"Where do you intend to find something better in a war camp?"*

"Port Lindell."

She whistled a short laugh. *"You know the fishermen there?"*

"Well, no, but the estate there may give me supplies. I'm good friends with one of the Wesleckers."

Skyla parted her beak, stepping forward like she was about to snatch the fish out of my hand. She froze with the point inches from the bitter fish's flesh before taking a swipe at me with her hooked talons. I jumped out of the way just in time with a surprised shout, dropping the fillet in the process. Masculine chuckles filled the air along with the whistle of amusement from Skyla.

"Eat it yourself. If you are of Valtora's flock, then I want no favor from you," she said coolly.

Resigned, I peeled the fillet off the grass and brushed the worst coating of dirt and grass off it.

"Eat it, squire," Commander Wrath ordered, crossing his

arms. "And you will not be leaving to go to Port Lindell any time soon."

I glanced around, as if one of the men or perhaps even a gryphon would save me from this, but all I saw on their faces was anticipation, amusement, and a lack of sympathy. Steeling myself, I tore a reluctant bite out of the slimy flesh and nearly gagged. It *was* bitter, sliding cold and mushy down my throat.

"How's that taste?" Apparently, Skyla wasn't done with me, looking down her beak as the men laughed at my expense. *"Day in, day out, you Link thieves expect your pet gryphons to eat whatever you waft in front of us. I hope this lesson lingers longer than your stay in the Seventh."*

Realization dawned on me as I imagined a different gryphon standing there, staring at me without the careful mask over his hatred. *"You didn't intend to eat this,"* I said.

"I never do."

She had to get her revenge where she could, I supposed. I let my connection with her fade as I struggled with the last bit of fish. There were at least twenty gryphons in the flight. Surely some of them would have some pity and eat the bitter fish from my hand, but I dreaded how many wouldn't when the Skymother and leader amongst them had turned me down.

One by one, I met the flight members and their gryphons. The Captains came first, each the leader of one of the four elements within the Seventh. Cherin introduced me to his gryphon, Tempest, who was a sleek, gray male with white across his belly and the underside of his wings. His mental presence was calm and cordial by comparison to Skyla, and he ate the fillet I offered him without more than a soft twitter of complaint.

Barlowe and Devos were assigned to the Captains of Elements C and D, call signs Bucktooth and Pass. I wondered about the first Captain until I was through the whole ritual and met an older squire who'd been with the Seventh since Yule. He'd flashed me a sympathetic look and scruffed his gryphon when the beast tried to refuse the bitter fish, since by the time this was over, I'd had to stomach four more fillets and thrown up once.

"*Yuck,*" Ari said when I finished up by feeding him last. My empty buckets were whisked away, and Devos started the process all over with Skyla.

Yuck was right. I had a hand over my middle, feeling like I had to be green tinged. Hopefully there would be something left over after the rest of the camp was done with the evening meal, as the sun had long set and the gryphons loosed long yawns waiting for Devos and then Barlowe to offer them fish.

"*Is it funny because they had to do this too?*" I asked, watching the men hoot when Barlowe struggled through his first bite.

He nudged me with his beak. "*It could be worse.*"

"I mean, I just don't get it—"

"*When Alamid joined, it was the same tradition. Except he had to be nude too.*"

"*Good gods!*" I was really grateful something had changed between now and back then.

Once Barlowe was finished, we lined back up. I felt like we'd lost the crisp edges to our postures and neutral bearings. "Well, boys. It seems we have three new squires with a heart of the gryphon. Ha!" Commander Wrath announced to a hail of applause from the rest of the flight.

They ushered us to a fire pit afterward, with a still-bubbling pot of stew for us all to share. A hand landed on my shoulder, and I startled, but it was just Cherin offering forward a silvery canteen. "It's medicine so you don't get parasites," he said gruffly.

My stomach lurched with a violent gurgle from just a sip of the water, which was nearly as bitter as the fish. "Better hold that down. I only bought enough powder for one dose," Cherin said.

"What about…" I glanced to Barlowe perched on a rock nearby, eagerly spooning stew into his mouth.

"The other new squires are Pass and Bucktooth's problem. You're mine," he replied, gesturing for me to scoot to the other side of the bench I'd claimed. This way, his good eye was facing me, narrowed in clear warning while I struggled to hold the medicine down.

He and I sat quietly while it seemed like the rest of his flight came alive with shouting and ribbing, good-natured cursing flying across the fire. I learned a few new turns of phrase in the first ten minutes, until the gritty dregs of the medicine hit my tongue. Cherin pulled the canteen out of my hand and replaced it with a warm bowl of stew, which tasted truly divine after the abuse my taste buds had recently endured.

"You get used to it," he said, and I wasn't sure which "it" I was going to get used to before he was on to a new subject. "As my squire, you are now on gryphon time. You and Arimus will wake just before sunrise every day to join me for PT."

A flask crossed the circle of men, and one of my new flight-mates pushed it into my hand next. "Don't give her that swill," Cherin snapped, stealing it away before I got more than one noxious sniff of the alcohol within it. He knocked back a taste of it instead and gave himself a shake.

"That's no fun, Deadeye," the other man said as he passed the flask to Barlowe.

I had my hand half-raised, a rebuke on my tongue, but it wasn't like I was going to drink anyway. "When she's not my squire, she can drink all she wants," Cherin replied.

"Isn't that my decision, sir?"

"No. I will PT you to death if I catch you drinking any of

Bucktooth's swill or puffing on anyone's pipe. Like I said, you're my responsibility, and I hold you to higher standards than any man here. Understood?" he demanded.

He sounded more like my father than my mentor, but I swallowed my pride. It was better to have someone to hold me accountable rather than the opposite, I thought, so I said without hesitation, "Yes, sir."

The corner of his mouth started to lift. "However, I give you my entire permission to defend yourself against threats with both fists and words, even amongst flight-mates. My wife and I have two girls. I dread either deciding to join the military."

"Oh? How old are they?" I asked curiously.

"Four and six. My eldest just acquired a red-haired doll and a toy gryphon." He gave me a sidelong look, and my shoulders lifted with embarrassment. I knew certain shops were cashing in on selling items that looked like Ari and me, lighting up dreams of gryphon riding in a new generation of girls who wanted to follow me.

It was both mortifying and humbling. I hadn't graduated from the Gryphon Rider Academy yet. Other than saving Ari and Linking with him, I hadn't done enough to deserve the attention I was getting. It was more Crown Prince Isaac's doing, turning me into a "symbol of change," which had moved the hearts of strangers.

"Um, is that why you volunteered…"

"When I said I volunteered to mentor you, it was more a 'voluntold' to pick one of the three of you. You were the highest ranked." He shrugged. "That means you have more promise than those two boys, right?"

"In theory," I replied.

He lifted a brow. "Don't be humble, Squire Walker. The only answer to that question is the same thing you keep saying to me."

It took me a moment to realize what he meant and notice the teasing glimmer in his brown eye. Despite the bitter introduction, perhaps my stay with the Seventh wouldn't be so bad. My mood lifted as I said, "Yes, sir."

CHAPTER 7

BOREDOM AND FIRE

Weeks passed. Nothing happened.

Okay, okay, I got up before the dawn every single day to run alongside half the men of the Seventh, plus Barlowe and sometimes Devos if his mentor remembered to wake up in time. I belted new PT songs at the top of my lungs but whispered the naughty parts since Cherin watched me like a hungry gryphon for any missteps.

Instead of demerits, he assigned me additional PT. Push-ups, lunges, sparring, Altarian burning slides—you name it, I probably had to do it for my afternoon PT sessions. I got used to it and even looked forward to something to do by midday. Soon, I didn't even mind how I baked under the summer sun.

The camp grew restless. We were here in case of an attack, and yet there were no attacks that reached this far west. Word came and went, and I began receiving letters with my old flight-mates, learning that there were full-fledged battles elsewhere that we weren't involved in. Ellie, Sharde, Feyring, Weslecker, they were all fine.

I worried about the people who didn't write, though. Prince Mateo, Princess Odalis, my family. But most of them didn't know where I was. Scattered to the four winds, I hoped they were all safe.

Old copies of *The Kaiamear Gazette* and *Voice of the People* circulated the camp. While having the two newspapers writing about me wasn't new, the odd looks I got from the strangers around me seemed more intense than usual.

"LADY GRYPHON RIDER INCITES RIOT" wrote *The Kaiamear Gazette*, with Miles Glimmerwick as the author. I skimmed the article and nearly crumpled the fragile pages as it painted me as the aggressor trying to get Kaiamear's citizens to revolt when it was part of the crown prince's plan all along.

The message was clear, even from a distance: Isaac had created my identity as Altare's darling with his newspaper, and he would destroy that image with the same tool.

Barlowe wrestled the paper out of my hand. "Read this one instead," he said, handing me a copy of *Voice of the People* published around the same time.

I checked the byline and the name of the paper several times, making sure I hadn't made a mistake. The name wasn't Mother's, but I did recognize it as one of the Nilarite women she worked with in Kaiamear. It was a more honest account of what happened, including that I had tried to calm the crowd after Isaac's men riled them up.

"Since when do I agree with the *Voice* more than the *Gazette*?" I muttered. Very few editions of the newspapers made it this far out of Kaiamear, but after covering the riot, my name faded out of the public's eye, just how I liked it.

In the meantime, I sought any kind of new experience to ward off soul-crushing boredom and the sense that I should be anywhere but here.

After eating that ration of awful fish in front of the Seventh, the adult riders treated me like the other squires. We fetched useless items for them, shined their shoes, and ate last at every meal. But at least it was equal. Also, true to

Commander Wrath's word, I was not permitted to leave the camp, even to visit the Weslecker estate after penning a polite request to them for supplies. In the meantime, one of my new flight-mates, Captain Exquisite, taught me new card games and begrudgingly admitted he'd used that word to his mentor during a squire-ship with the Fourteenth, so now it was his call sign.

He also tried to call me Girl. It took me days to realize it wasn't "girl, come here" but with a capital G. That's what they wanted my call sign to be. Girl.

"I don't answer to that," I'd replied.

That evening, Cherin announced he'd be giving me my call sign when I earned it.

"Should've named you Killjoy," Exquisite called.

"Three hells, you lot wanted to call her Girl," he snapped.

With a grumble, most of the men started calling me Walker again. I was glad Cherin commanded that kind of respect, because many of the stories behind the call signs I heard were uncharacteristically goofy for a hallowed institution like the gryphon knight corps.

Some, like Bucktooth and Deadeye, were just names for obvious features.

Others, like Exquisite and Pass—short for Passing Grade, which he requested from his mentor after causing a huge, undisclosed disaster at the end of his squire-ship—were borne of unique moments with their comrades.

By the sighs I received when I asked about call signs, I figured they felt obligated to explain how they came about. Almost no one chose their own call sign unless they were Commander Wrath, so I had a sense of anticipation as to what mistake I'd be named after.

I spent some of my free time with the flight's gryphons, helping where I could since forty-plus gryphons was a lot to keep up with for the two caretakers assigned to the camp. I'd dodged the sharp beak and wicked talons of Skyla more times than I could count, to the point I had to allow one of the care-takers to see to her instead. But I enjoyed getting to know a few others, like Tempest, who proved he was just as mellow a personality as Ari with the skills to fly circles around him and me.

Cherin and Tempest drilled Ari and me every other day in endurance training. *"The Academy doesn't practice the kind of endurance you'll need in combat,"* Tempest explained. *"It makes sense. You couldn't be in the saddle all day there."*

But as it turned out, we had time to try it now, flying laps over Port Lindell and chasing Tempest in full-fledged sky sprints until Ari was ready to foam from exertion. I had the sense he was embarrassed he couldn't keep up with the other gryphon when he'd always been the fastest male around.

"There's a big difference between short chases and long marathons in the air," I'd said, trying to soothe those feelings. Like everything else, we'd get better at this too.

"Of course. It's just…" He scuffed his talons in the dirt. *"I used to be better, that's all. Some Captain of the Seventh shouldn't have a gryphon who can out-fly me like this."*

"Well, we're here to learn." After our visit to the home of the gods, I thought we'd never find a situation where Ari felt slow and overexerted. But our long trip there had been made at a pace he set, with no competing male in peak condition there to challenge him.

Mercifully, our dreams were free of eldrafn. I slept heavily, mostly carefree with my gryphon cuddled up next to me. We'd discussed what we'd do if a would-be killer paid for by the crown prince's gold appeared. Ari, by far the lighter sleeper of the two of us, was positioned toward the flap of the tent. I'd placed a sizable rock in the entranceway each night to trip anyone sneaking in under the cover of darkness and slept with my cavalry saber by my bedroll every night.

We didn't need the sleeping measures yet, because no one

tried to break into my tent at night. But it was better safe than sorry.

I'd been given my first combat lance and cavalry saber my second day in camp. Both were a little used, but it was the first time I'd been entrusted with the real deal and expected to defend Altare with them.

Eventually, a matronly woman appeared in the camp with a box in hand, asking for me. The Weslecker estate had given up waiting for me to come get the things I'd asked for, so I received a scolding on top of the box.

"Sorry, ma'am," I said, chastened as the objects inside the box weighed down my arms.

"Will you be needing anything else?" she asked, perking up like nothing had happened.

"W-Well, um, I do need to combine these items." I'd asked for sturdy twine and the tools to sew my prototype eldrafn egg sling into existence. But like with most domestic tasks, I was hopeless at sewing.

Cherin gave me leave to take her to my tent, and I unpacked the items and showed her the rough sketches I had in mind. "You want to fly a newborn babe with you or some-thing?" she asked, raising a skeptical brow as she began cutting and stitching a cured hide into the shape of the sling and lined it with a section of plush sheepskin.

"No, ma'am," I said, resisting the urge to show her the eldrafn egg I had hidden in one of my saddlebags. The last thing I needed was to explain myself to someone who could give away its existence as a piece of juicy gossip.

She didn't seem to care that I didn't explain, though. "You had an empty bill to ask for anything. The young lord must adore you," she said in the same kind of tone the grand-mothers of Kaiamear took when planning meetups between their grandkids. A matron could smell young love from a league away, and there was always an opinion to follow.

She reminded me of my own Gramma, gods rest her soul.

"What you're making will help me more than you know," I said.

"Harrumph. You're not using him on a flight of fancy, are you, lass?"

"No, ma'am. I would never."

I'd never really put my Acton verses Mateo debate away in favor of life as a squire and member of the Seventh. I felt that oily doubt creep up again, because what if I *was* using Weslecker? These were high-quality materials that I'd gotten hand-delivered and assembled. This matron was likely being paid extra to sit here and ensure I was happy with the final result.

One thing I knew, though, was that Weslecker had written where Prince Mateo had not. I read his letter every night before bed. He had the kind of penmanship that would make Mother weep with joy, but it was his sign-off that I lingered on.

I miss you dearly. You deserve to be here in the thick of things with the rest of us.

How I wished I was! I clung to the thought that he missed me and held it close through my lonelier evenings. The woman across from me made an approving noise. I'd daydreamed away for a moment and came back to her smiling at me knowingly.

"Well, here's your pouch. Do be careful with the babe, all right?" she said, offering me the finished sling. It had rings at the end of long leather straps to hook into the saddle horn and across the back, to secure the egg under, but next to, my left knee—at least, that was the intention.

She'd whipped this up in a couple hours and rifled through the smaller things left in her delivery before handing me a circular rod that gleamed bright copper. "Didn't know how long you wanted it, so I just grabbed what the blacksmith had on hand," she said with a shrug. It was about a foot long, sure to poke out of the pouch. Maybe that was a good thing. I didn't know what its use would be, after all.

"And you didn't ask for this, but I figured you'd need it." Next, she handed me a few wrapped chocolate bars and sweets and left me with a pat on the head.

I waited until the tent flap settled before devouring one of the chocolate bars and tucking away the rest out of sight. I was rolling a hard candy on my tongue when I hefted the eldrafn egg and placed it inside the new pouch. It was a perfect fit, but the true test was when I stood with both straps in hand and lifted.

The leather made a tightening sound to be used this way the first time, but as I bounced and wiggled it, it held, wrapping itself firmly around the egg inside.

I nodded in approval. When and if Ari and I faced an eldrafn, we now had an advantage at our side.

ARI WAS cross with me for the extra weight, but the sling fit his saddle, and we practiced with the eldrafn egg strapped to him. Ellie would be so proud when I told her how I'd successfully measured out a prototype! Unfortunately, any sharp turns had the hefty egg slapping Ari in the side, so I had to get used to threading my leg under the strap and through the riding harness every time we went into the air to save him from undue pain.

After I stumbled out a half-baked explanation for the extra straps on my saddle to Cherin, though, I hid the egg and its sling and hoped he wouldn't look into the matter further. I hadn't realized my idea would still make its presence on my saddle so noticeable.

A messenger arrived for Commander Wrath not a week later. He was the latest in a series of them, each passing messages along to the leadership in the camp. We knew it had to be serious news, as he called several private meetings over time with the four Captains and left the rest of us sitting around waiting to hear about what happened. This evening was no exception.

"Do you think the Rathi surrendered?" Barlowe asked hopefully while we watched one of the army chefs dropping scraps into a cauldron hanging over a freshly stoked fire to begin one of the pots of evening stew.

Devos scoffed on his other side. "No, you idiot. Did you pay a moment of attention to World Cultures class?"

"Hard to when I couldn't understand the instructor!"

"They won't surrender," I said over Devos's reply. "It's the highest honor for a Rathi warrior to die in battle."

"Right, of course," Barlowe sighed.

"*And*," I added pointedly, because I'd hung on Signe's every word in her class, "Altare has never won a war against the Rathi as a whole because uninvolved tribes always end up piling themselves into ongoing conflicts against us. Every Rathi wants a glorious personal legend, made immortal through others retelling the story of their lives."

"Where'd you learn all that?" he asked. I just slanted him a look.

There was a rustling from the Commander's tent, and out strode the Seventh's leaders. Wrath stood at the threshold with his second, Exquisite, while the other Captains came to retrieve us.

Cherin drew me aside with a hand on the shoulder, away from the curious glances from the rest of our flight. "I volunteered you," he said.

"Err…"

"Don't worry, I volunteered myself as well. A sizable cluster of Rathi vessels were spotted sailing straight for Port Lindell, under the cover of a mid-sized eldrafn. We have three days to prepare, maybe."

My heart leapt to double time. "It's happening, sir? We're flying into combat?"

"Yes, but we're taking on an extra challenge," he said. "High Command is calling for the formation of a few strike teams assembled of the fastest fliers of size to carry a second rider. That means anyone with large male gryphons, like you and me."

My brow drew in confusion. Usually, females were tasked with carrying an additional person, considering their advantages in strength and size.

"A group of pyrojacks will be arriving on the morrow. One will be assigned to you. Our new team is tasked with burning as many Rathi ships as possible before they make landfall."

I wetted my lips and nodded slowly. A pyrojack was a Tulari blessed with fire magic and then trained for military service. It wasn't unheard of to have a gryphon rider carry them into combat, and it felt like an undue honor that I'd been successfully volunteered for such a task.

"But what about the eldrafn?" I asked.

"Not our problem. The rest of our flight and the Sixth will team up to keep it busy." He clapped me on the arm. "Eat up, now. We won't have much time to get used to our new partners."

Uneasily, I returned to the fire pit and looked at the faces of the riders around me. How many would be joining this team as well?

"Whoever they assign us to carry along to battle, I hope they're not heavy," Ari grumbled.

I KNEW the Tulari had arrived the moment Cherin and I returned from a light afternoon session of endurance training. The air felt different. Quieter. Silence was the one thing a camp of soldiers never really had unless it was the dead of night, or apparently amongst the presence of mages.

So, it was to my great surprise as I crossed the camp to notice a robed and hooded figure beside Commander Wrath's tent. He stood like a silent sentinel with a strange beast lying across the ground next to him.

Ordinarily, I would be creeping closer to catch a glimpse of the leonine nightbloom, an eternal companion to one of the Gatekeeper's Mercy. But the sight of its master made me break out into a cold sweat, especially as his hooded head turned in my direction.

A nightbloom was a creature of life and death, a combination of the spirit of an animal with an anchoring of verdant plant life to keep it corporeal. The one flopped out like a bored cat had flower buds lining its front paws and along the thick vines of greenery across its spine. No one but the Mercy knew exactly how they worked, but it was whispered that each blooming flower upon a nightbloom represented a soul it carried, until they could be delivered to the afterlife.

A shout of alarm pierced the silence of the camp, and rushing out of the Commander's tent was a young woman trailing smoke from the bundle she held. She tossed down what looked like two furs being consumed by bright, greedy flames and stamped on them. "Not now, no, stop it," she muttered.

"Do you need help?" I offered. Her sudden appearance had taken the Mercy's attention away from me, and I could've wilted with relief.

"No! I'm totally fine and didn't set those on fire, thank you for asking," the other woman exclaimed, bundling the now-extinguished furs back to her chest like holding a shield between us.

Our gazes met, and I sucked in a small gasp. She had a bright scarlet Tulari circle branded across her cheek, glowing with orange edges like she was actively casting a fire spell.

The effect made one of her brown irises glow orange, so unusual that I didn't realize for a few moments why her face was so striking.

This young woman had Lithosian features, most notable in the softer curves of her face, the bold line of her nose, her up tilted eyes, and a skin tone like golden honey. Her coal-black hair feathered around her jawline, curving out at the very tips in abrupt frizzles that almost looked burnt.

My mouth tightened with reflexive dislike. What was a Lithosian—one of our enemies—doing here, in an Altarian war camp? Was she here to sabotage us? Yet she wore the same kind of bland brown robe I'd seen my little brother returning to Kaiamear with, which were apparently assigned to young Tulari of all specialties…at the Tulari Academy, which only served Altarians.

"Shouldn't you be going back inside?" I asked, conflicted. Maybe she was Altarian and I was just overreacting.

At the same time, she exclaimed, "You're the girl gryphon rider, aren't you?"

While I nodded, she replied to my question with a shrug. "I think I excused myself by rushing out. It happens," she said. I noticed her voice held only a small trace of an accent.

"Okay, then," I said quietly. I stepped aside for Cherin to head into the Commander's tent, leaving an awkward silence between myself, the Lithosian pyrojack, and the Mercy who still had barely moved.

Should I ask where she's from? As if sensing the direction of my thoughts, she ducked her head, scuffing patterns in the trampled grass where she stood.

"Maybe her name first. She sounds Altarian," Ari ventured. He'd sat out of the way of foot traffic behind me.

Cherin poked his head back out of the tent. "Walker, go join the rest of our flight. Tell them to expect a debriefing for the coming fight," he told me.

UNSTABLE

In the gryphon's field, Commander Wrath addressed the Seventh, standing at attention, and a group of Tulari assembled into a gaggle. I stood just behind Cherin and Tempest, trying to catch a glimpse of our promised pyrojacks.

"Try to focus. I can feel your eyes straining," Ari said. He was just as curious as I was, but it was of little use now with the Commander finally briefing us on what he knew.

"Our intelligence reports that a raiding party of six Rathi longships are inbound to Port Lindell under the cover of a mid-sized eldrafn. They are coming with arrows, fire, and volta to take the city. We will meet them in twenty-four hours to cripple them before they make landfall.

"High Command sent us a volunteer force of Tulari pyrojacks that will partner with our fastest fliers. In our flight, Captains Deadeye and Pass, Lieutenant Occasion, and Squires Devos and Walker will form one element of a new strike team assembled to adapt to the threats ahead of us.

"Your Tulari partner will rain fire down upon the enemy and cast shielding spells to protect you from lightning slung from eldrafn and volta alike. Your job is to make passes at the

Rathi longships while the rest of us attack the eldrafn directly. Is that clear?"

"Yes, sir!" I shouted along with the four men who would be in the strike team with me.

"I wonder how many volta they've brought along," I commented to Ari as Wrath addressed the rest of the men about their strategy for either chasing away or killing the protecting eldrafn coming with the Rathi force.

Volta were like Tulari, or so Signe had explained in class. But instead of being touched by a god shortly after birth and carrying the mark of it on their face, the volta fostered their power within them. It was said the goddess Idunn's fury boiled in the hearts of the volta, and only the bravest would embrace it and learn to wield lightning.

As far as I understood it, volta were quite rare. *"Enough to be a threat. We will have to protect ourselves from above and below,"* Ari replied. *"At least volta lightning can miss."* Instead of being directly from a bird-like creature formed of storms, human volta charged lightning in their hands and threw it.

I shifted with unease when Wrath was finished. It sounded like we were a distraction before the main battle. The soldiers were arming up and preparing to defend the city from the Rathi that survived the skirmish with us and made landfall.

"Give it your best, men. The Crown is offering a handsome reward to any rider who takes down one of the enemy eldrafn. Our intelligence reports that there are nine right now—named 'em after some board game pieces. You may know the one. Ha! Soon we face the Earl." Wrath finally cracked a smile and dismissed the flight to prepare, except for the five of us on the new strike team.

A board game. I knew what he was referring to right away—Circles of Power, a strategy game Father loved with nine different pieces, each with a unique method of traversing a checkered board.

Assuming our scouts and spies understood what gave eldrafn size, strength, and power, the Earl would be a smaller, more expendable piece in the game board of war. I assumed the biggest and strongest would be named the King, the Advisor, or the Duchess.

Mid-sized, as the Earl was described, could also name the Chariot and the Mage, or even the Priestess. The pieces I always lost first in a Circles game were the Soldiers and the Knights, meant to fight and die on the front lines without making a full trip around the board.

I was still considering eldrafn sizes and what the military might nickname a tenth one, should another tribe join the Rathi forces, when I looked up to see the Lithosian girl beaming at me. I flashed a reluctant smile back, still unsure of her.

A fully fledged mage was talking in hushed tones with Wrath. His scarlet robe matched the matte color of the mark across his left temple, gaudy and out of place in a military camp, especially since his sleeves and collar had the texture of velvet.

The ten Tulari waiting with us dressed in brown robes like the Lithosian girl's, except at some point, hers had acquired a singe mark at the elbow.

"Why are all of them apprentices?" asked Pass loudly. "Were the adult pyrojacks too busy to help us?"

I bit my lip on pointing out the graying Tulari who was obviously the leader of this group. Something about him screamed that he was an instructor, too old and out of practice to dare climb on a gryphon and set any longships on fire.

"We're volunteers from the Academy. We heard that…you volunteered too…" The Lithosian girl's perky voice faded to a nervous noise when Pass fixed a glare on her.

"Did I ask for you to speak, desert sc—"

"That's enough!" Wrath barked over him.

"Sir," Pass said, so crisp the word could cut.

The scarlet-robed Tulari next to him tutted. "Miss Zaveri is an Altarian citizen, same as you," he said in a scornful tone. "The Tulari as a whole cannot supply endless people to the war machine. Our best warmages of all kinds are already split between two fronts."

Pass deferred to Wrath, asking, "If we could speak privately for a moment, sir?"

Wrath and Pass stepped out of earshot, but I watched the Captain's sharp gestures with a frown. "He's going to un-volunteer himself," Cherin said in an undertone.

"Is that allowed?" I asked.

"He was in on the same briefings as I was. High Command wants volunteers only, so it's up to Wrath to punish him for cold feet," he replied.

Pass clicked his tongue, calling his gryphon to him. They started to walk away, while Wrath returned to address those of us still here.

"I can't believe—he just gets to do that?" I said in disbelief.

Cherin turned his unerring attention on me. In a grave tone, he asked, "Would you like to follow him?"

I knew if I tried to back out, my mentor would make sure there were three hells to pay. As dangerous as it would be to carry an apprentice mage into combat if they didn't know what they were doing, I assumed Cherin had a way of making the rest of my life just as difficult if I answered yes to his question.

"No, sir," I said, resigned.

Maybe these apprentices knew enough magic that it wouldn't be a problem. Wrath gestured to the elder Tulari, who identified his apprentices by their rank. Five of them split off to join the volunteer force from the Sixth, and the higher-ranked pyrojacks were matched to the older gryphon riders. That left Miss Zaveri and two young men when Wrath interceded. "Squire Walker has room in her tent for another. Match her with the other girl."

"Very well. Go get settled," the elder mage said to her.

She bounced on the balls of her feet in happiness. "Five wonders, this is going to be great!" She came forward with her hand extended, shaking mine with a firm grip. I hadn't realized it earlier, but she was a tiny thing, barely scraping five feet tall, with a thin frame hidden under the billows of her robe. Her skin felt like she'd been toasting it next to a fire, hot enough to make my palm sweat. "Zuri Zaveri, at your service. Let me grab my things. I only have a few bags."

She was a few paces away in a blink, so I assumed I didn't need much of an introduction.

"At least she won't weigh much," Ari commented, nudging me. He urged me to glance to the side, where Cherin was talking to his assigned partner, a young man nearly as tall as he was. I could feel his smugness on this side of the Link.

"You're going to be much faster than Tempest," I said, agreeing with his thoughts.

"Walker, be ready to be back in the air within the hour," Cherin said when he noticed me waiting. "We will be practicing a few strafing strategies before the sun sets."

I opened my mouth to reply when I saw Zuri returning with her arms laden with bags, forming a tower that obscured her vision. I jumped forward to take a few from her, and she beamed at me again. "Lead the way! To think I got partnered with *the* Sivana Walker," she said as she trailed me back to my...our tent. "My Academy rivals are going to be so jealous when they hear the news. They're going to wish *they* volunteered."

"Um, right." I tingled with discomfort. She sounded like she'd fit in with the fan group that'd cornered me in Kaiamear one afternoon. Well, despite her Lithosian heritage,

I knew she couldn't be a sympathizer if she held a gryphon rider in such high regard.

I took her to my tent and ducked inside to move around the things that'd migrated to the empty side. As I pushed out the rectangular rock I set behind the tent flaps each night, she stuck her head in the space with narrowed eyes. "Huh. Smells like…gryphon. No offense! Sorry. It's just a little musky. Nothing a little fire won't fix," she said, biting off her stream of words with a little laugh. "Did I say that out loud? I'm not going to burn our tent down, I promise."

"None taken," I replied, cocking an eyebrow at her.

"This one talks a lot," Ari commented, sitting outside the tent with a disgruntled warble as he began to clean his wing.

"It's just, I thought I sensed a super-strong artifact or something in here." She started piling up her bags on her side of the tent. "You wouldn't happen to have something giving off a powerful signature, would you? I know you're not a Tulari, so if you need to use a mage-activated artifact, I'm your girl."

"I'm not sure—"

"Is it in that thing right there?" One of her slender fingers pointed right at the saddlebag where I kept the eldrafn egg hidden.

I glanced toward Ari, who froze mid-preen as we both realized she'd identified the egg within seconds of entering the tent. *"Well, if she's going to be flying with us, she'll see it then,"* he said, with the mental equivalent of a shrug.

"I just don't trust her mouth not to run away with the information," I replied.

"Oh, neat, are you two having a conversation in your heads without me?" she asked. I glanced up, expecting that to be a sarcastic question, but she delivered it with all the earnestness of someone who'd never been around gryphon riders.

I went into the tent and sat down, dragging the egg's sling over to rest next to me. "Zuri," I began.

She sat across from me and held up a finger. "Actually, my friends call me Zizi. Much less of a mouthful than *Zuri Zaveri*, and it's the essence of my name all in one. I'd be really happy if you called me that." The orange-tinged eye above her Tulari mark seemed to sparkle with sincerity.

"Okay. Zizi. I'll show it to you, but you have to keep it a secret," I said. She mimed stitching her lips together and knotting the thread off at the end. "You really sense a…signature? Whatever that is."

"You know how everything has a smell? Well, a magic signature is like…a magic smell. But I feel it more than smell it, if that makes sense."

"Right." I understood well enough, so I took the pouch out of the saddlebag and pulled the egg out of its sheepskin cradle to offer to her. She took it and turned it over, her mouth forming an awed *o*. "It's an eldrafn egg. It hasn't hatched in over fifty years, if I had to guess, so I thought it was dead."

"Dead? This thing is practically vibrating with magic," she gasped. "I bet it could absorb an entire lightning strike if you need it to! And look, you have a lightning rod and everything." She pointed to the copper rod sticking out of the pouch.

"Oh, that's what that's for," I murmured, feeling a little foolish for not guessing sooner. "This is a secret, Zizi. Anyone else would destroy it if they knew about it. But I'm going to take it up into the air with us, so I figured you should know."

"Yeah, sure, of course, but like, what will you do if it actually hatches?" she asked in a frenetic but hushed tone. "I don't think anyone around here would like to see a baby eldrafn, but you know what, I bet it'll be really cute. Still, an egg is a lot easier to hide than the real deal and all."

I sighed, lifting a shoulder. I hadn't thought it through yet, assuming that it wouldn't hatch at all. But if it had a magic signature she'd noticed immediately, there really was a possibility Revna would have a second chance. Maybe if Signe had more time, she'd successfully hatch it if she took it out into a few more storms. "If it hatches, I will need to return her to her original owner somehow."

"A Rathi?" she asked.

"Someone on our side," I replied carefully.

Zizi stilled for a moment, her brow furrowed in thought. "Okay. If it happens, I'll help you if I can. And I'll keep your secret. That's what a good partner and friend would do, and I want to be both things. Maybe I'll tell you a secret in return. How about that?"

"If you want to," I said.

She handed me the egg, and I put it away while she started arranging her things more comfortably, digging out a quilt made with vivid colors and geometric shapes that she draped over her lap. "Don't worry, it's fireproof," she said, flashing her winning smile at me.

"I wasn't worr—"

It turned out, she was just starting to tell me the promised secret. "So, you know how there are different kinds of Tulari mages?" she asked. I didn't answer, because she did a split-second later. "Healers, wizards, and pyromancers, right? Well, there are sub-classes of mages. A wizard trained for combat magic is a warmage, or a pyromancer under the same circumstances is a pyrojack."

"I know some of this. My younger brother is an apprentice wizard," I interjected while she caught a breath. "He's determined to be a crafter, but it doesn't seem like Lord Orion blessed him that much."

"Oh, good, you know what a crafter is. A proper crafter Tulari can regenerate their magic without communing with Lord Orion. I can do that," she confided. "That's my secret."

"You're a crafter?" My brows rose. If she were capable of working magic that strong, she shouldn't be here. Crafters made good money enchanting things like magelights, but my understanding was that with a gift of extra-strong fire magic, she could work enchantments into molten metal to create magical armor and weapons.

"Uh, sort of," she hedged. "It's a long story, so I'll tell you some other time. I'm...not a crafter. I just have too much magic most of the time. Other mages consider me, um, unstable."

My gaze turned to the still-glowing mark on her cheek and the magic that seemed to have taken over one of her eyes with a spark like molten fire. I thought unstable mages didn't exist anymore, not after it became a requirement for everyone with magic to attend the Tulari Academy.

In fundamental school, it was required to learn of King Altare's darker follies alongside his successes in bringing together our country into what it was today. He'd sanctioned and relied on the Laughing Legion, comprised entirely of unstable mages who would overload their bodies with their chosen element and cackle as they left destruction in their wake. A healer with too much magic could will catastrophic damage on another person's body, a wizard could suck all the air out of someone's lungs...

But unstable pyromancers were truly feared, capable of nullifying dragon fire and razing battlefields. Laughing uncontrollably and crazed with power, they usually burned themselves to cinders before the age of twenty. It was out of caution that the Tulari Academy was founded, to impose limits on mages born without them before they matured with the power to repeat history.

"Do you lose your mind when you wield your magic?" I asked quietly.

"I...I do have the laugh," she admitted. "Don't worry, though, I mostly have it under control! My professors at the Academy are proud of my growth. I'm not going to hurt you or Ari. Chances are, if anyone gets burned, it's going to be me. It'll be totally fine."

A brief melody on a horn marked the passing of the hour. We needed to report back to the field and get into the air together, I knew, making to stand. "For the record, if your magic burns you, that's not fine," I said, frowning.

Her smile held an edge as she followed me out into the sunlight. "If you say so," she replied.

CHAPTER 9

STRIKE TEAM THREE

ZIZI ENDED our practice runs with blackened palms. Just like I'd told her about the eldrafn egg because it'd be impossible to hide once I clipped it to Ari's saddle again, I realized she'd mentioned her unstable status for the same reason. She didn't use a wand like the other pyrojacks, which was highly unusual. She also hadn't laughed, but throwing a couple fireballs into the ocean had burned her skin thoroughly.

My understanding of unstable pyromancy didn't go beyond the horror stories of what they were capable of. Its aberrancy was feared, but the sight of Zizi's hands clicked another piece of the truth into place. She wasn't immune to her own magic.

"Don't look at me like that," she said while we waited for dinner. The glow had left her eye after she'd used some of her magic, but her Tulari mark was still an active orange. "Look, any time I hurt myself with my magic, it repairs much faster than anyone else would heal from a burn. See?"

She shoved her hands at me, wiggling them for good measure. Instead of charred, they were the pink color of raw new skin. "Don't worry about me. I've had *much* worse," she assured.

"And that *really* doesn't help me feel better," I replied with the same emphasis she spoke with.

The elder mage who'd dropped off the apprentice pyro-jacks was long gone, so it wasn't like I could appeal to him to take her out of situations where she'd be pressed to use her magic. One of her counterparts was sitting out the coming fight because of Pass leaving the strike team, and I contemplated how exactly to tell Wrath or Cherin that I wanted Zizi to be the one waiting in camp instead.

"*I think she has to use her magic,*" Ari interjected into my thoughts. "*Besides…why deny that part of yourself?*"

"*If it hurts you, that's why!*"

"*Sivana. Sivvy,*" he corrected himself with a chuckle. "*She's lightweight and an accurate shot with her fire magic. She even showed us that if she bothers with a wand, she can cast a shield that'll protect us from lightning strikes. If she can do her job, why complain?*"

"*In doing her job, she might also set us on fire. And we won't heal as quickly as she will,*" I pointed out.

He placed his talons on my knee, his seriousness earnest over our Link. "*She took your secret with far more grace than you've taken hers. I know you don't want to admit it, but you haven't forgotten that she looks Lithosian.*"

"*That has nothing to do with her being unstable,*" I protested.

"*She also promised that she won't hurt us, but you haven't accepted it. Yet you said you were giving a potential baby eldrafn to a Rathi 'friend,' and she just nodded along.*"

"*That doesn't mean she doesn't also have doubts.*" When I glanced over at her, she was wolfing down a serving of stew with such gusto that the chef was offering her a second one. I couldn't help a little laugh, wondering if her magic made her hungry. "*I mean…I'm not wrong, am I? To worry she's going to kill the three of us by accident?*"

"*You or I could also make a mistake that will kill the three of us,"* he said. *"I'm just saying, you've failed to give her any benefit of the doubt, and that's not like you."*

My lips twisted. He was right, I had let my biases shade how I saw her. It was hard to forget that we'd been at war with Lithos for ages, but that wasn't something she was involved in. *"Well, she's our partner for the foreseeable future, and I doubt that's going to change even if I did try to complain. I'll try to be better."*

"There's my rider." He had a sense of pride that had me sliding down to sit beside him in the dirt as I accepted my serving of food for the evening.

Devos raised a brow over at Zizi as she polished off her second bowl. "Good, huh?" he asked.

"I mean, sure. I've had worse," she said, setting it aside and standing. She extended her hands toward our campfire, and wisps of flame broke off from it, flowing toward her.

I watched, keeping my mouth shut since she did this in full view of the rest of the flight and apprentice mages assigned to us. Several men were watching as Devos was the first to ask, "And what are you doing?"

She beamed over at him. "Making sure tomorrow will be memorable. Earning a medal, hopefully. One thing for certain, though, I'll make you regret that I'm not your battle partner."

"Doubtful. You're going to be the one regretting it when you feel how that blind gryphon really flies," he scoffed.

"I already did. If you didn't notice, we just practiced a few strafing runs. He flies just fine. Would you really want folks to talk about you like you're useless if you had a disability?" she countered. "That's right, I didn't think so."

Ari twittered a quiet agreement. He liked her, I realized, the feeling dissonant across our Link since I was still unsure of her. The Link worked best when we were in harmony.

Zizi sat down, turning to look toward something past where Ari and I sat. Her eyes reflected back the flames of the campfire, both of them a subtly glowing amber while her whole Tulari mark was ignited an active orange-yellow. Maybe this was what it looked like when she was full of fire magic.

"Uh, Sivana," she said.

I cast my gaze over Ari's shoulder in time to see a hooded figure emerge from the shadows, alongside the glowing white eyes of a nightbloom. Then, a second Mercy seemed to simply appear, with a dark gray robe draped over a feminine form. Her nightbloom was distinctly avian, hopping behind her with unearthly silence.

Actually, the most noticeable quiet came from the circle of our flight as the two Mercy wordlessly accepted bowls of stew and looked around as if they were trying to find a place to sit. The man pointed at me, and the woman nodded.

This was it. They were here for me. I dropped my bowl on a surge of adrenaline, ready to pop to my feet and bolt. But the man and his cat-like nightbloom were stepping back into the darkness, and the woman knelt to place something close to me before following him.

It was a letter. And on its front, my name was written in Odalis's handwriting. I deflated with a sigh of profound relief. My friend must've asked one of the Mercy to deliver a message to me—but it was possible the female Mercy *was* Odalis. Gatekeeper knew how long it took to train and send off one of his marked followers.

"I thought they were here for my soul," I muttered as I opened the letter.

"Well, then they'd at least have read you your last rites first." Zizi's perky voice had me jumping and dropping the paper before I had a chance to read what it said. She'd slid onto the bench right above where I sat with Ari.

"Do Mercy speak?" I asked her curiously. I'd never had business with one until I'd dropped Odalis off at the Church of Mercy. The princess would probably be okay if she never had to engage in small talk again.

"Of course! But I don't think they do so around us common mortals. Ruins the mystique, you know?" she chattered. "They always hang out in military camps, too. I once went up and challenged one to a Circles game, and you know what? He beat me in less than ten turns. He just said thanks at the end, and that was it."

I raised a brow up at her. "Let me just skip the fact that you had the stones to challenge a Mercy to a board game. You've been in a military camp before?"

"Oh, yeah! I always volunteer. The last time…didn't end so well." Her smile slipped for a moment before replacing itself toothier than ever. "I think the Mercy have to be here to remind us that any life we take is one they have to escort onward. They certainly have a *presence*, don't they?"

"That, they do," I murmured.

"You have a Mercy friend, huh? That could come in handy one day," she said when I returned to reading what Odalis had written.

For the first time, there was no code hidden in her neat script. She still wrote of her day-to-day life, but it was leagues more interesting than the drudgery she was subjected to as a sheltered princess.

"By the time she finishes training, she might be a completely different person," I replied.

Already, Odalis wrote with a more mature voice. She'd seen death's work at the Church of Mercy and was already tending to the seeds of the plants that would become part of her nightbloom. She told me she couldn't tell me more about the process…so there were Mercy secrets taking root as well.

She ended the letter by asking for an update on how I was doing and where I was, "sure that I was having a better adventure than her," and I folded the paper with a small laugh. If only she'd seen how boring camp life was, she'd prefer to be a princess again over it.

"Well, knowing death as the Mercy do, you might be right.

But if she's your friend, she must be a good person, right?" As I got up to go back to my tent, Zizi followed like a faithful shadow.

"You give me entirely too much credit. I saw a young man for over a year who tried to kill me later," I said.

"Oh, no way. What did you do? Did you set his stuff on fire?" she asked. I made a little incredulous noise, and she followed that up by blurting, "Kidding! Totally kidding. Haha."

"I didn't, but there were a few times I wanted to. He, uh, died not too long ago."

"Oh."

"Yeah. It's a long story," I said.

She reached our tent and began to duck inside. "Well, we have all night. I'll be the lantern." She pointed at her glowing cheek, which lent soft light to the inside of our living space. Ari followed her inside, and when I tried to squeeze in, it was obvious we didn't have enough room without him lying on someone.

"We're up at first light to skirmish with the Rathi," I pointed out, lying down on my bedroll. Ari landed on me and twisted around, his paws mashing a few soft points on Zizi and me as he tried to get comfortable between us.

She cleared her throat when one of his back paws pressed against her face. "Uh, not to be a problematic tent mate, but does Arimus need to be in here too?"

"Tell her yes. And don't forget the stone," he said.

He'd managed to orient his beak toward the tent flap. I wiggled out from under his side to push the big rock into place. Anyone who entered in the dead of night would have a surprise, all right—he would fall right on top of a gryphon or an unstable pyrojack. "It's a safety thing," I said, lifting one of his wings to get back into my spot.

"Also, he says you're quite warm," I shared. The gryphon

was already feeling cozy, drifting off with a lazy click of his beak.

After a few moments, she sighed. "At least he's not a rozash. The ruby and emerald ones stink."

"Pyremaw and acidmaw?" I guessed.

"Yes. In Lithos"—she spoke the country's name with a rolling flare—"we know them by how beautifully their scales gleam in the desert sun, not what breath weapon they have."

Huh, that did make sense. Altarians knew the rozash by the type of devastation they could leave behind if left unchecked, just like how the Rathi named their eldrafn but the wild gryphons called them sky terrors as the one creature that could predate upon them.

"Have you ever met a rozash?" I asked, muffling a yawn.

While I was getting sleepy, especially with Ari snoozing between us, she sounded perky as ever. "Oh yeah, my father had a few single-headed rozash in his old business. They're not too bright, but they can learn how to carry things between two cities if they have a roost in both places."

"No riders?"

"Very few rozash get riders. They're usually used for delivery, or as beasts of burden, or on rare occasion as pets. I wanted a ruby one before we had to move," she said. I fluttered my eyelids, realizing she was holding something that put off a little extra light. She had a wand in one hand with runes glimmering around its tip; in her other hand she was rolling a ball of fire no bigger than my pinky nail between her fingers as if she were a street magician about to make it disappear.

"What are you doing?" I murmured, worried she'd drop it and set Ari's feathers alight.

She didn't look up, brow furrowed in concentration. "Reminding my fire who is in charge for tomorrow. You can rest if you want. I'll be up for a while yet."

"All right," I said. A bit of my concern crept into those two words, but it'd been a long day, and tomorrow promised to be worse, so I let myself drift to sleep while she played with her magic.

WHEN THE HORNS played to rouse the whole camp, my side felt cool. In the night, Ari had sprawled over Zizi, practically squashing the smaller girl. *"I see how it is,"* I commented to him.

With a great yawn, he crawled out of the tent first and waited outside while we geared up for battle. *"She's warmer than you,"* he teased.

Despite suggesting that she'd be staying up late, Zizi woke with her usual smile and the kind of pep I wished I had right before daybreak. "We're getting a medal for sure. Walker and Zaveri, the best fighters of Strike Team Three."

"I didn't realize we were in the third team," I commented, stifling a roll of my eyes. She probably didn't know there were no medals until the end of a war unless someone was suitably heroic for the biggest honor, which merited a ceremony at the earliest convenience.

Her shoulders raised. "Oh, yeah, sorry to tell you. The first two teams were further up the coast. We were just…"

"The last to volunteer?" I ventured.

She clicked her fingers, accidentally sending out a shower of sparks. Cursing quietly, she stamped out the smoking grass before it could become a full-fledged fire. "Yeah, something like that!"

I shook my head, hurrying past her to report in with the rest of Strike Team Three in the middle of the Sixth and Seventh beginning to line up at attention. There were nine of us in total alongside our male gryphons, with the pyro-jacks standing around awkwardly while we waited for instructions. Zizi slid in next to me, imitating my stance poorly.

The two Commanders prepared to repeat our strategy for the coming skirmish. Wrath spoke first. "Men, today, Rathi raiders intend to make landfall across much of Altare's coastline. It's almost like they know how stretched our resources are. Ha! Six longships approach Port Lindell as we speak, escorted by the eldrafn we've labeled the Earl. We are all that stands between the Earl decimating the fine city that's hosted us for weeks now. Here is how this will go…"

We'd heard the basics multiple times—the strike team would swoop down close enough for our pyrojacks to attack the incoming Rathi longships with their fire magic. We would be the ones keeping their volta and archers busy, which made my palms sweat.

On the other hand, the rest of our flights would be engaging the Earl directly, drawing its lightning away from us.

Wrath told us, "I've consulted with our mages on how their shields work. Those of you flying with pyrojacks will be able to withstand up to three strikes of volta lightning before you have to retreat, but arrows will fly right through the shield, so you must be fast and careful.

"Anyone engaging the Earl will have one chance to take a hit from its lightning. If you are struck, your orders are to retreat immediately. Am I understood?"

"Yes, sir!"

"We have one pyrojack staying behind. I will carry him into battle so he can wait on the shore closer to us to re-cast a shield on anyone who loses theirs. Our goal is to eliminate the Earl if possible, but if we can deplete its power or drive it back, that's good enough. With it hanging overhead, its lightning is drawn on to charge the volta, and it can stir up a rainstorm to protect its longships.

"Don't be a hero today and get yourself killed. Port

Lindell's coast guard will be following us with a few ships as reinforcements, and the troops are ready should any Rathi make it to land.

"Let's show these Rathi that the sky is ours! For Altare!"

"For Altare!" we shouted back, and the gryphons shrieked agreement. Zizi pumped her fist and yelled along with the rest of us.

EVASIVE MANEUVERS

I CLIPPED the eldrafn egg to Ari's saddle before we were in the air, while Zizi took a satchel that she slung over her shoulder. She opened it to show off a pocket full of stoppered glass bottles and coarse squares of cloth, but the bulk of the satchel was wands. Dozens and dozens of wooden wands.

"You'll see why I have these." Zizi drew a net of runes around Ari with one of her wands, and it flared with heat and cracked dramatically before she could finish the spell. "Five wonders," she muttered in frustration. She tossed it aside and pulled out another from her stash to resume placing the last runes, ending with a dab of the wand tip toward Ari's beak, then my face, and finally hers.

This was the second time she'd cast this spell for us, but this one would see real use. For a moment, an iridescent bubble appeared a few inches above us before fading to invisibility. I swallowed my nerves and helped her onto Ari's back, cinching a riding harness around her calves. She didn't want it too tight so she could lean over my gryphon more than was wise.

"You've carried a pyrojack to battle before, haven't you?" I

asked Ari, who was rather calm, while I was a ball of nerves to be flying into my first real engagement.

"I've done it a few times. But I've gone into battle plenty." He bunted my hip and pressed his head into my middle while I hugged him around his feathery neck. *"You trust me, right?"*

"Without question," I declared.

"Then let's go show them what this trio of misfits can do," he said in amusement. I realized the joke was all too real as I fit myself into the riding harness, the eldrafn egg resting against my leg in its sling. Between a blind gryphon, a female rider, and an unstable pyrojack, we would be the most unlikely team to return safely of those taking wing around us.

I guided Ari to fall in one of the back positions in the V-formation Cherin and Tempest led. A second element formed up of the five riders from the Sixth in our strike team, taking the lead to guide us over the open ocean.

In the hours of flight that followed, Zizi tried to speak once, but the wind snatched away her chatter before I could register that she was trying to tell me something. She pointed downward, toward the bulky shapes of a few ships headed in the same direction as us. Our coast guard reinforcements, since presumably, our depleted navy was all engaged at the main front.

The time was punctuated by the cross-talk of gryphons instead. Tempest reached out to Ari to wish him good luck and share that Cherin wanted to engage with line formation, the four of us moving in at the same time to strafe the enemy.

A female from the Sixth flying several gryphon lengths above us contacted her son to tell him to stay safe. He grumbled in return, but I could tell there was a lot of love there.

A different male, not sneaky enough to do it privately, bragged to a female he was going to show off for. Smothering a laugh, I pulled my mental presence away before I could hear any more of that.

Before too long, we spotted the approaching Rathi by the

murky curtain of rain and a dark shape taking up a portion of the horizon. The wind grew turbulent on approach, blowing straight into our faces. The single-mast ships below the eldrafn skimmed along the churning waves, their sails trimmed just right to take advantage of a favorable breeze.

Zizi leaned to the side, rubbing her hands. "There they are!" she exclaimed.

I wondered if this skirmish was folly as I saw how vicious the rain pounded down upon our longship targets. The sails and wood would be completely saturated with salt water— unlikely to kindle easily unless the pyrojacks had some secret they weren't sharing.

"Strike team, circle around. The Earl will be engaged first," Tempest ordered for Cherin, leading us in a wide arc around the storm while the rest of the Sixth and Seventh charged ahead.

The Earl flapped its wings, displaying an impressive wingspan that had to be at least forty yards wide. Green-tinged electricity veined the dark storm clouds that formed its body, and it opened its beak to roar like the boom of too-close thunder. It seemed to suck in the air around it before releasing the first bolt of lightning with a devastating crack, and I flinched toward covering my ears as I cringed away from the sound.

The afterimage of green lightning had successfully struck the magical shield encasing one of the riders, which shattered into a hundred brilliant shards. I watched the gryphon peel off in a quick roll and double back with haste. The rest of the riders pressed onward, lances brandished.

"Hold your fire," Tempest ordered.

Zizi shifted eagerly as we rounded the end of the storm where the rain came from lingering clouds rather than the eldrafn's presence. It began to wane to a light drizzle as the Earl swept its wings and chased several riders from the Sixth with a woven net of electricity.

I realized the Earl was leaving some of its ships vulnerable, and that's exactly what Cherin was waiting for. "Get ready!" I shouted to Zizi, watching the first rays of sunlight fall upon the ship closest to us. The Rathi below were a hive of activity, more people packed into a longship than I imagined.

By the time we swooped, they would be ready, the last of the rain dripping off arrow tips and the fingertips of volta as they charged balls of electricity.

"This is what I live for!" Zizi exclaimed back. My ears prickled with the sound of fire igniting.

"Line formation, now. Tell your pyrojacks light bombardment only. We're unlikely to do any real damage yet," Tempest shared. Instead of diving, we flew overhead in a quick pass over the enemy ships. Bursts of flame sparked off sails, masts, and decks as our pyrojacks flung fireballs or, in Zizi's case, a steady stream of fire from both palms, aimed at sails and rigging.

"Hehehe." I heard the high-pitched giggle from Zizi and briefly smelled smoke before the wind stole it away. Our team circled around, and I looked at the enemy ships, unsurprised to see that our first pass had barely singed anything.

"Preserve your pyrojack's magic. This next pass, no magic," Tempest ordered.

"Hold your fire," I exclaimed over my shoulder as we circled back around over the heads of the Rathi. I watched them scrambling below like a kicked hive, several arrows and flashes of thin trails of lightning fired at us this time.

I also realized the second element of our strike team was coming in hot behind us, bombarding with the salvo of fire my element was holding. The longships began to separate further, making it a longer flight between them with no chance of a fireball splashing over two vessels.

We made several passes before I noticed the first fire taking root in the rigging of one longship. The rain had waned dramatically with the Earl otherwise engaged, leaving the enemy vulnerable at last. On the next pass, a bright flash struck Ari's wing. He squawked as he drew up, the shield around us rippling with hairline cracks.

"Repair?" I shouted back at Zizi.

"No! More fire!"

Below us, the Rathi screamed in their guttural language. With fire blooming over all six vessels, they were calling to their eldrafn. Their white arms flashed up at the Earl, and my heart lurched when it turned its green-tinted eyes in our direction and roared a boom of outrage.

Under the deafening battle cry came Tempest shouting, *"Evasive maneuvers! Scatter!"*

The massive beast swooped at us, and I was one of a few who screamed in fear the split-second before impact. Lightning cracked, and sideways rain stung my face as I wrenched Ari in a random direction. Our disciplined lines descended into chaos. My goggles were airtight, so I saw the afterimages of a bolt shattering through an already weakened shield and striking a gryphon square in the side a few yards away.

The beast's spread wings skated on the wind for a few seconds before it slumped and dropped into the sea, dragging a rider and apprentice pyrojack into the waves.

Just like that, the Earl cleared the airspace above us, and I panted with fear and shock, trembling from the feeling of water saturating the inside of my riding leathers. In one attack, it'd extinguished all of our progress and the life of a fellow rider in the process.

"We have to keep going," Ari prompted. My hands had stilled on his reins as I imagined what would've happened had that lightning been aimed just a bit to the left.

"Sivana? Let's get a little closer. I'm going to pull out the good stuff," Zizi prompted, shaking my shoulder from behind.

"Regroup on me," Tempest ordered for Cherin, circling around off to my right. *"Walker, move."*

With shaking fingers, I tugged on the reins, pressing my heel into Ari's side to guide him into the line behind Tempest. Devos followed off his wing now, which meant we'd just lost Lieutenant Occasion. Gods, but it'd been fast. I spotted the Earl wheeling around, returning its attention to the much-diminished Sixth and Seventh that continued to needle it.

"Sir, when do we retreat?" I asked Tempest. Many of the riders from the main flights had to make a round trip to the shore for another shield.

"Steel your nerves, Walker, and have your mage patch up your shield." The stern tone from the gryphon definitely sounded like Cherin.

We circled slowly, giving me a chance to pivot in the saddle and look back at Zizi. My already shot nerves zinged. She looked like something that'd crawled from the three hells, with her glowing orange eyes and streaks of soot smeared across her grinning face.

"We're waiting for shields to get patched up," I told her.

Her expression faltered, and just like that, she was a teenager again, the maniacal gleam gone from her eyes. "I, uh, I can't."

"What do you mean, you can't?" I demanded.

She lifted her palms, showing charred skin that flaked off into ash from a harsh gust of air. "I've already used too much magic. But don't worry. You trust me, right?"

It wasn't lost on me that Ari had asked this question earlier, and I hadn't hesitated a moment, not like now. "If the Earl comes back around and hits us, we *die!*" I shouted at her.

With a wince, she reached into her satchel, nearly fumbling the copper rod as she withdrew it and gave it to me. I realized for the first time that it wasn't snug in the eldrafn egg's pouch. "It makes us the first target, but we'll be okay. Look, I can take out a ship all on my own. Just give me a chance." She gingerly touched her palms together, pleading. She had to know my blood boiled to know she'd nicked the rod while I wasn't looking.

"We are supposed to be partners," I said through gritted teeth.

"So trust that I have something the other pyrojacks don't," she replied.

"And what is that?"

She pulled out a square of cloth and one of the bigger stoppered bottles, smiling once again. "Alchemy. Experience. Daring. You pick. How close to the ocean can you fly?"

I communicated her plan to Tempest as she explained and had me crack the seal on the potion just enough for her to stick the cloth into the violently blue liquid.

Cherin seemed skeptical but signaled that we go try it from Tempest's back. *"I want to know why she has not shared her alchemical bombs after this,"* he said. *"And you will explain that extra pouch you have on your gryphon's saddle again."*

"Yes, sir," I murmured, already dreading that coming conversation.

The rest of Strike Team Three flew in for a lower strafe on the closest longship to give us some cover. Ari continued on to the next longship and swooped until we were dangerously close to crashing into the ocean while Zizi ignited the cloth and hurled the potion toward its stern. We leaned into a desperate bank to take us further out to sea as the bomb exploded with a concussion that blasted Ari off balance and into a forward flip that had the tip of my braid dipping into chilly ocean water.

Zizi whooped as we righted ourselves. Arrows plunked into the water around us, fired from the second longship as its back dipped, taking on water rapidly. Ari shrieked, his beak clacking. An arrow quivered in the meaty muscle of his thigh.

"Now *that* is medal worthy!" Zizi exclaimed. "Should I, uh, pull that out?"

"Leave it!" I said immediately.

"Right, sorry."

"None of the other pyrojacks have bombs like yours?" I asked, keeping a leery eye on the shape of the Earl further out to sea now. The other longships were angling toward the one we'd taken out, spreading out the raiders to other vessels.

"No." She sounded almost sheepish. "I kind of, maybe, stole them."

I pinched my brow with my free hand.

"Look, they were going to the main front, but all the good stuff went there. I thought they could share a little. We need supplies too," she added.

We rejoined our line with Cherin and Devos. *"We're letting them regroup,"* Tempest told me. His rider turned his good eye our way and nodded in curt approval.

"We are?" I asked in disbelief. The longship Zizi and I had hit was definitely sinking, and floods of white-haired Rathi were scrambling off of it.

"The extra weight will slow the remaining vessels. Look to your left and send your luck to our other men in the meantime." He nodded toward the ocean, where the coast guard vessels were turning into position. Understated booms followed a volley of cannon fire.

"Keep your wits about you, Walker," Tempest said as I began to smile. *"We haven't won yet."*

The Earl cracked a bolt of green lightning at one of our ships, leaving a blackened hole in the hull. My hope turned to dread in an instant as the massive creature swooped at a second vessel and seized it in its talons of clouds and lightning. A handful of winged forms buzzed behind the Earl like flies, unable to stop it as it flung the ship like a discarded toy further out to sea.

"I see how a single eldrafn could destroy our navy," I murmured to Ari. He made a pained croak in agreement, in no mood to talk with that arrow stuck in his thigh.

We went on into a focused assault on one of the longships which bore the most damage from cannon fire. It soon became obvious that it was taking on water too, so Cherin ordered us into the next pass.

I tried not to watch the Earl, but my gaze kept slipping toward it as the last riders with intact shields circled it, trying to attack its vulnerable heart. From this distance, I could only guess as to who was still in the fray, but the biggest gryphon had to be Skyla. She would be amongst the last untouched by eldrafn lightning.

"*Focus,*" Ari growled.

The remnants of Strike Team Three were beginning to retreat as the other pyrojacks ran out of magic. I checked in with Zizi, whose eyes had lost their orange glow, but her mark still pulsed with life. "A couple more passes," she promised. "Or one big one." She wouldn't show me her hands. The damage she'd done to herself had to be considerable.

After conferring with Tempest, we had our orders. One big one it was, which we were to save as we chased the last three longships as they curved in toward Port Lindell. The sun was setting, and the last stubborn residents were lighting their fires and going about their day as the enemy approached.

The Earl roared victoriously as it flapped its wings behind the longships, helping along tattered sails and the one vessel that'd lost its mast and was now chugging along with the power of dozens of oarsmen.

As the boom of thunder faded from my hearing, another sound drifted on the breeze—a distant blare of horns and the clang of emergency bells to warn anyone who'd missed the Earl's announcement of its presence.

"*One last pass,*" Tempest shared, forming up with two riders from the Sixth whose pyrojacks still had a little magic left. Ari huffed with exertion as he powered forward to join them.

Zizi giggled and said in a sing-song voice, "Which ship shall we sink today? Those oars look like a centipede's legs. I think they shall die next."

"Gods, okay," I muttered. Maybe she *was* some infernal creature, to laugh at a time like this. But I brought the unstable mage low and within range of the damaged longship, sweat breaking out across my back as Zizi held her hands up over her head and created a ball of fire with a distinctive *fwoosh*. Its light shaded from cherry red to as bright white-gold as the sun's core, then she flung the massive orb to splash over several Rathi below us.

Flames and desperate screams broke out below us. I pulled Ari's reins hard, feeling him churn in the air in pain and exhaustion as he struggled to lift us high enough to avoid an answering volley of volta lightning. A bolt hit us, fracturing the shield of magic into diamond fractals. It was barely hanging in there, just like the three of us.

Zizi's slight weight collapsed against my back. Her Tulari mark sizzled, but it'd finally gone a dormant scarlet. Unfortunately, she was out cold.

"Sir, my pyrojack fell unconscious!" I sent immediately to Tempest. He ordered me to come in for an emergency landing, but as full dark descended on us, I struggled to identify where it was safe. Soldiers flowed forward to meet the Rathi by torchlight, the coast erupting into chaos.

Ari came in low over our camp, having me steer him toward the empty field where the gryphons rested. Zizi slumped toward the ground, and I caught her shoulder, breathing a sigh of relief as someone came forward to help me release her from the saddle.

It was one of the caretakers, whose eyes were twice their size as the Earl roared overhead. "That blighter's not dead?" he asked me.

"Not yet. Any chance a healer's around?" I asked, untying myself and inspecting the arrow embedded in Ari's flesh. He murred with displeasure, limping behind me as the caretaker pointed out where our healers were set up for triage.

"You couldn't possibly expect us to go back up," he complained.

I set my jaw. He knew what I was thinking just as well as I did: we had to. It was the dark of night, and few gryphons were confident and healthy enough to remain in the sky.

"Wrath told us not to be heroes." Yet he stood still for a healer to cut the arrow out of him and staunch the bleeding. Despite Ari's near-immunity to healing magic, the Tulari was able to ensure that the wound was clean and partially closed.

For a moment, I hugged my tired gryphon around his sweat-dampened neck, pressing my forehead to his. *"I know. But we're the only ones with an eldrafn egg, and I don't see anyone else who can distract the Earl. Do you?"*

CHAPTER 11

THE BATTLE OF PORT LINDELL

"You owe me so many salmon," Ari said. I'd ditched my shield, for as little good as it'd done us, so he flew unencumbered by extra weight. His flight muscles still ached and protested, but all that endurance training had done us in good stead. He was still going, after all.

"Let's get through this first," I replied. There was no guarantee the eldrafn egg would draw lightning into itself and spare us from being fried in the process. It was entirely possible we were flying straight into the Gatekeeper's embrace, considering the cyclone of debris the Earl had amassed as it rampaged across Port Lindell like the force of nature it was.

We dodged and ducked the biggest pieces of flying matter. Ari had me quiet my mind and navigated in the dark, sensing the shift in the air from incoming debris. For once, I was the blind one, only able to panic at the last moment when I spotted sides of roofing or half a cart coming straight at us before Ari dodged around it.

The Earl was the easiest thing to spot in the sky, with its roiling clouds still threaded with green lightning. It was diminished from the titan we'd first engaged hours ago, but it was still too strong to stop. A handful of gryphon riders continued to circle it in the dark, drawing away some of its electricity by providing additional targets.

Ari didn't ask; he knew the plan I had in mind, such as it was. We were anonymous shadows in the dark, just like the other riders. If we did draw away some of the lightning from the Earl, no one would see it was because of an unauthorized eldrafn egg.

He flew us straight for the Earl's back, where there had to be a rider piloting the creature. It was so big I hadn't spotted anyone, so I was just shouting in the dark as I cupped my hands over my mouth and tried to speak Rathi at this rider, tossing out the few Rathi insults I knew from Signe's lessons.

"You're an insult to your ancestors! Coward!"

The Earl stirred, its bright green eye tilting back over its shoulder to look straight at Ari and me. Emerald electricity danced within its wings as it pivoted.

"It worked. Go, go, go!" I exclaimed, pulling on Ari's reins. He labored to get up to speed even with the eldrafn's static nipping his tail.

Power built behind us with an ominous crackle as we rushed back toward the sea. The Earl seemed to inhale. I thought of my very first ride with Ari, rushing away from an equally deadly beast furious and ready to kill us.

Crack!

Sparkles of magic rained around us as our shield failed. A blinding flash came from my left, leaving me to blink away lances of afterimages.

The copper rod vibrated, glowing with heat as green sparkles danced over the egg's pouch. *"Are you all right?"* I asked Ari.

"Slightly deaf."

"It worked! The egg took a blast of lightning," I exclaimed. The Earl roared a furious boom, perhaps realizing what had happened.

Heat built in the back of my head, though, and Skyla's voice intruded my thoughts. *"Unfamiliar rider, identify yourself."*

"Ari and Squire Walker, ma'am," I answered.

"You've been hit, Walker. Retreat immediately."

"Not yet, ma'am."

A shadowy beak clamped closed close to Ari's heels, and I broke out into a cold sweat. If its electricity couldn't kill us, it could still rend us to pieces if it wanted to.

"I will tolerate no insubordination from you," Skyla snapped. *"Much as I'd like to see you burn, girl of Valtora's flock."*

"We have time for one maneuver," I answered, trying not to let her get under my skin. Not when the Earl was charging its next lightning strike with an ominous inhale. *"Which direction?"*

Skyla paused for a couple crucial seconds as green illumination bloomed behind me. There was a chance she'd let us take the hit rather than confer with Commander Wrath.

"Up. As sharp as possible," she replied.

I dug my heels into Ari's sides, guiding him into the steepest ascent he could make. *"C'mon, Ari. You can do this. You've done it in your sleep,"* I said, throwing my weight back to help as we went vertical.

The Earl's beak snapped in the empty air where we'd just been.

Ari's heart thudded against my legs like a battle drum, deep and rapid. I felt the strain on his wing joints and the shakes that overtook his core as he pushed himself to his limits.

The little hairs on the back of my head lifted as a blast of electricity loosed from the eldrafn. It disappeared into the night sky, flung astray.

A choked noise drifted from the Earl. Its wings shot up stiffly, and I looked down to see a flare of emerald light building from its core.

"Fly faster!" Skyla screamed at us.

The Earl's heart exploded. A shockwave hit first, sending Ari spiraling out of control over the pitch-black ocean. Lacy strands of green lightning surrounded us in all directions, some redirecting around Ari or me and into the copper lightning rod to feed Revna's egg. It would've been a beautiful moment had I not felt the *pop* of one of Ari's wings dislocating and the suffocating wave of pain that followed.

We plummeted into an uncontrolled fall. This time, there was no way to tell the sky from the rapidly approaching water, not until we came to an abrupt stop and my battered eardrums picked up the slap of the waves a few yards below us.

"Thank the gods," I murmured, looking up at the massive female gryphon who'd caught Ari's saddle and back leg in her talons. Moonlight crusted her white feathers and the scornful look she flashed down at us.

"Stupid, reckless squires," she muttered, dropping us into a cold plunge in the ocean. *"Find your own way back."*

"Wait!" I protested, as she flew away. *"Ari's injured!"*

"I'm sure you'll figure something out," she snipped. She ended the mental connection between us, picking up speed back toward Port Lindell.

At least we weren't too far out to see the fires spread across the city. Ari churned his paws, paddling like a puppy toward the distant battle. His dislocated wing dragged behind him, and I felt like I'd make it so much worse if I tried to lift it or jam it back into place myself.

Port Lindell was aflame while our army faced the Rathi on the shore. We had a great view of the devastation from here. *"Feeling like a hero now?"* Ari asked, his speech starting to slur with bone-deep exhaustion.

I thought of Zizi's cackling and the *fwoosh* of fire. The screams of burning Rathi and the boom of thunder from the deceased Earl. How Zizi's unconscious weight had fallen upon my back the moment she spent the last of her considerable reserves of fire magic.

The *pop* of Ari's dislocating wing and the agony that still gripped him as he took us back to shore.

A hero? Gods. If anything, I felt like exactly the opposite.

"I can't believe Commander Wrath left us like this," I muttered rather than answer him.

Ari chugged along, barely keeping his beak up out of the water. He grunted back.

"Sorry, should I stop talking?"

"No, please. Distract me from the pain," he said with effort. *"He left us because…remember there's money to reward anyone with a confirmed eldrafn kill?"*

"It's not like we would've tried to claim it! Or that we can right now."

"Think about it," he huffed.

I did while fitting a drifting plank of wood under his chin in a feeble attempt to help him. The shore was getting closer. Ari had aimed his beak toward the Weslecker estate, which was completely dark. Abandoned, hopefully. For such a rich family, they could afford to evacuate one of their summer homes to protect their servants.

"I guess…we could've tried to get part of the reward since we helped with the kill," I finally said.

"Exactly. Wrath's been around long enough to know the value of getting his story in first. We won't be in the report," he muttered. I untied myself from his saddle as he dragged our sodden selves out of the ocean. He slumped into the saturated sand with an agonized groan.

I could feel that this was as far as he could go. His eyelids flickered over his fake eyes as I knelt and hooked my hands behind his front legs, digging my boots into the sand as I hefted him inch by painstaking inch out of the persistent surf.

He was soon unconscious, and the best I could do for him was tuck his paws and rest his weight on his good wing.

"I don't care about the money," I told his sleeping face as I knelt in the sand next to him. "All I want people to know is that you kept going even though you were exhausted and that it was because of our help the Earl met its end."

The beach was too peaceful here, too secluded to be bothered by the bustle of Port Lindell or the screams and flames of the ongoing battle. I watched the moon drift across the sky and illuminate the distant sails of trade vessels giving Port Lindell a wide berth.

Scrubbing my bleary eyes, I looked again, but there were no ships on the horizon, just debris bobbing in the waves. I tried to stay up and keep watch, but soon I was lying on the beach too, cushioned by sand and just as unconscious as my gryphon.

I wasn't proud of it, but I broke into the Weslecker estate after coming to with the sun beating down on my face. I tracked sandy muck over the pristine tiles as I rummaged for medical supplies and food. Hopefully the servants would forgive me when they returned, as the estate was mostly intact save for the blown-out windows to one side.

Ari stirred and awoke to me splinting his wing, a bowl of dried fish laid out in front of his beak. He gobbled it down hungrily, snipping his beak from the pain of my inexpert job.

"It'll have to do," I sighed.

With that, we began the long trip across the ruins of the city. Fires still sputtered here and there over ruined shopfronts and the skeletons of houses that'd been built too close together. We spotted semi-familiar soldiers helping extinguish fires or move the biggest pieces of debris onto waiting carts to begin the rebuilding process.

"Is that Squire Walker?" a man called. A search party

emerged from the ruins and escorted us back to camp. I didn't ask anyone if we'd won. It was obvious we had, with the absence of Rathi.

When we finally arrived at the camp, no one was still. The same caretaker as last night took Ari's reins from me, and a different team of soldiers grabbed hold of me to help identify a couple bodies.

Numbly, I realized I was looking at Captain Pass and the battered corpse of his gryphon laid out next to him. Even in leaving Strike Team Three, he hadn't escaped the Gatekeeper's gray shroud. Finally, my body had enough abuse. I tore away to be sick behind a tent, bile and tears mixing.

"The worst part is the clean up afterward," Cherin told me when we crossed paths about an hour later. "We won, by the way."

"I can tell, sir," I murmured. Except it didn't feel all that victorious, not like at the Academy, where a win was overcoming the odds and my rivals.

A bonfire ran for days to dispose of the things we had no place for. Teams from Final Flight arrived to carry away our dead for a proper military burial, and at night, we drank and remembered Pass, Occasion, and the four other riders who'd fallen in the engagement with the Earl.

I noticed anonymous, hooded Mercy coming and going from the camp, still hard at work days later. I knew their differences only by their nightblooms, especially the feline and avian ones. They'd been waiting for this battle long before it happened.

Ari remained my grounded and grouchy companion, snipping his beak at Zizi when she joined us the first evening by sitting beside me quietly.

The mark on her face remained a flat red, and pronounced bags were under her eyes. "Are you all right?" I asked.

"Never better," she sighed. The chatter and laughter were gone.

It was a relief for my sleep schedule, and Ari rested atop me that night, shuffling uncomfortably with his bandaged wing. But I worried about Zizi up until an air courier handed Wrath a bundle of letters a few days after the battle.

As Ari had predicted, he'd taken full credit for killing the Earl, arriving back to camp with its green-tinged heart warped around his blackened lance. He hadn't said a word to me since, but continued laughing his way through the more morbid work of clearing out the camp like he had no regrets.

"Walker," he called, beckoning to me with a letter open in one fist.

"Yes, sir," I muttered. I found it difficult to meet his eyes, just to find him frowning from the letter to me.

He turned and called the Final Flight courier back over. "How exactly is she supposed to do this with a grounded bird?" he asked, tilting the letter and stabbing at it with two fingers.

"I suppose she can come back with me, sir," the other man answered.

I glanced between them with a noise of concern escaping my lips. Whatever the Commander was about to say, I knew I wasn't about to like it. He finally let me read the letter as he grumbled, "Guess the king can do what he wants, but the timing."

My eyes widened, and my stomach soured with dread. He hadn't handed me a letter after all, but a royal edict signed by King Cortes himself, summoning me to appear before him at Lord Orion's temple in Kaiamear in two days' time.

CHAPTER 12
SHATTERED

With little time to spare, I was forced to leave Ari to convalesce without me and was rushed to Kaiamear. Still, when my feet set down in front of Lord Orion's temple, trimmed with gold and guarded by the statues of two rearing gryphons, I was seized by a sense of déjà vu.

I felt like I'd been called here by a force more powerful than the king, and the moment I saw my destination, that supernatural presence was satisfied. I could go in now if I wanted, or I could turn around and head for…well…

No, I couldn't leave and go home. There was no home waiting for me here, not with Father leaving his position in the First and Mother and Rissa in hiding. Our apartments were probably already occupied by the new Commander of the First and his family. Plus, the moment I went for a walk around the city, I would be identified and harassed with no escape in the form of flying away on Ari's back.

There was nowhere to go except forward, to face my fate and answer to the king. It'd taken two days to fly here, so in theory, the king was already waiting for me. As I walked inside, I spotted a lack of traffic to and from the temple's inner sanctum, but armored guards were posted and waiting everywhere I looked instead.

I wondered what the king wanted that required such a summons in the middle of wartime. Several things popped to mind at once, as they had on the journey here. For once, I was not too upset to be parted with Ari, not when his absence could save his life from a thoughtless execution order from King Cortes.

One of the men posted at the inner sanctum's doors opened one of them for me, announcing my presence to the figure standing inside with his back to me.

The king's profile was thinner, his balding revealing more shiny scalp than I recalled. What hair that remained on his head was more gray than black, like the ghost of stress had shocked the color right out of it.

"Sivana Walker," his cultured voice said just loud enough to echo through the inner sanctum.

He faced the gilt statue of Lord Orion, a robed figure who listened as the only other witness to this conversation. "Yes, Your Majesty. I have come just as you ordered," I replied.

The silence was suffocating. I began to wonder if I should say something else or just leave him to his thoughts when he turned with a sudden jerk. His bloodshot eyes found mine, his jowls quivering as his face tightened with hatred. "Where is my daughter, girl?" he demanded.

"Why…uh…s-she…"

He took a step closer, finger lifted to jab accusingly at me. His toffee-toned skin reddened with rage. "You know. *Where is she?*" he shouted.

I froze in that moment, going as still as the statue behind him. I thought Odalis had written to him too—but maybe not.

"Before Lord Orion. Tell me the truth." He swept his hand to the statue standing in silent judgment of us both.

"T-The… She's at the Church of Mercy," I answered in a timid tone.

He stopped a few feet away, his finger still pointing at me, nostrils flaring. "And how would you know that," he said in a low, furious voice, "if *you* weren't the one who took her there?"

I bowed my head in quiet guilt. "It was her wish that she be taken there, Your Majesty. I was in no position to refuse her."

"You have no idea what you've done," he hissed. His hands balled to fists, and I wondered if I would see his anger turn violent.

"I helped you, Your Majesty. Do you recall the riot in the trade district not too long ago?" I said quickly, putting my palms up.

"Bah! A distraction from you and your Nilarite friends so you could take my daughter away." His eyes widened, as possessed in that moment as Zizi with a flame in her hand. "I've brought you here to confess your sins to my patron. Come." He beckoned and pointed, having me stand before the statue of Lord Orion.

Help me, I beseeched the god quietly, watching the king like I would a rabid creature, preparing to jump away should he choose to bite.

"I've had enough of your heresy. Kneel, confess, and accept your punishment, as is your due," the king demanded. As the seconds drifted by with agonizing slowness, I realized he truly expected to see a smiting as I lowered myself to my knees.

"Your Majesty, I don't think this will end the way you're hoping—"

"Fine. I shall do it for you. Lord Orion, look down upon this girl who has spat in your face and chosen to ride one of your avatars despite her gender." He stood over me, seeming to swell with the righteousness he felt. "She has persisted in a mission to spread Lady Nilara's softness through the hallowed institution of the Gryphon Rider Academy to further tread on your edicts."

"What if I could prove you wrong, Your Majesty? Will you stop this?" I asked, meeting his eyes with a resigned kind of surety.

There was one way I could show him who I truly was, to keep him from taking this too far and having me murdered as a heretic, as I suspected was the punishment he wanted to inflict for removing Odalis from his stifling control.

My hand flew to the token under my tunic, resting warm against my heart. *My life is worth losing the magic,* I thought, touched by sorrow already at the thought of parting with the ability to talk to my closest gryphon friends.

I'd never hear Puzzlebox call me Sivvy again. Valtora's motherly tones would return to a sensation of words. The love of the twins, Mireille and Ironfeather, would be reduced to a feeling. But I would be alive, if only I could finally reveal how wrong the king was about Lord Orion's opinions of me. I lifted my braid and drew the chain over my head, prepared to hand it to him.

"Your Majesty, look—" I began to say.

"Just look at this token of the Mother she hides in plain sight," the king exclaimed, ignoring me except to grab the chain from me. He ripped it free from my neckline and held out the shining token to the statue like a war prize.

He turned and gaped as it glowed brighter upon being exposed to the air. "Wait, is this—"

"No!" I screamed, reaching for it. It was one thing for me to offer it up willingly and another for him to take it without my consent.

Formed of feathers sealed in gold and glowing from within with runes from Lord Orion himself, it was a beacon in the half-light of the inner sanctum before it shattered and rained to the ground in a fine golden dust. The temple shuddered like it was hit by the aftershocks of one of the god's wrathful earthquakes from the days of old. The king whitened with a wild-eyed expression.

"*No*. Not like this," I gasped, catching some sparkling motes as they sprinkled down into my waiting palms. My vision wavered with tears. Just like he'd warned me, Lord Orion's blessing shattered the moment someone else knew about it.

I stood, dusting off my hands. The magic was gone. Ari and I were as good as doomed since I no longer had the extra strength in my side of the Link to let him see through my eyes. "How could you?" I breathed. "Don't you know Lord Orion himself gave me that?"

"Young lady, I did not mean to—" He backpedaled away from me, fear etched into his expression from what he saw on my face.

Another tear tracked down my cheek, but I was too seized by a lung-shaking mix of fury and sorrow to notice. "Do you go around ripping necklaces off women you hate, Your Majesty? Or just the ones inconvenient to you?" I snapped.

"Lord Orion," he said, clearly still addressing me. With a grunt, he dropped to his knees before me, hands pressed together with the empty chain between them. "Please have mercy! I didn't know. I didn't know she was your Chosen!"

I paused mid-step, just staring at him grovel. How surreal. I wasn't Lord Orion—and as far as I could tell, he hadn't spoken, just let this all play out to its conclusion with the broken token now dust under my boots.

"How did you know?" I asked. Did. Past tense, because without the blessing, I knew I'd lost what favor I had with the god.

King Cortes peeled his eyes open and looked down at himself. He seemed rather surprised he was intact and stood with as much kingly dignity he could muster. With an open palm, he offered my necklace chain back to me. "The legends say only the Chosen receive magic directly from the gods," he murmured, much deflated from his fury. I felt myself wilt too, gazing down at the empty chain, lighter than it should be. "I am truly sorry. What did it do?"

"It let me talk to other gryphons, and Ari could see through my eyes with its magic," I sighed. With the token gone, I figured I was finally clear to talk about the journey. "I traveled for months to ask Lord Orion for help. Anything he could do for Ari. And in return, he gave it to me and said I'd be his Chosen when he was ready to reveal me."

"Consider yourself revealed," he said stiffly.

"I don't think so, Your Majesty." I pointed to the silver streak through my hair. "I'm supposed to hide as a Nilarite until I'm 'older, stronger, and wiser' and no longer in need of protection. Without his blessing, I doubt he'll bother now. I couldn't keep one precious thing safe."

His generous lips pinched, and he glanced left to right. "Should've had them bring in a stool," he muttered. With a weary sigh, he sank to the floor to sit, robes of state and all. He made a quick gesture that I should sit with him, and I did so a cautious distance away.

"I understand now. The gods have sent you to punish me," he said and held up a hand when I started to contend that. "I understand that it's nothing personal on your end, but sometimes the forces that move our world decide to put one person directly in opposition with another. And I angered the gods long ago, when you were just a tot. No wonder they have sent me such a reckoning."

My face pinched as I wound the empty chain around my fingers. Despite how fervently he spoke, it still sounded like nonsense. I was a reckoning against him? What about his son, the one scheming behind his back?

"After Odalis was born, I knew something was coming. I just never expected…this." He made a wide gesture. "You have to understand, I was willing to pay any price to keep a piece of my beloved Jimena, may the Gatekeeper rest her soul. She wanted a daughter so badly she was willing to risk a fourth pregnancy despite what the healers were saying of her health. When Odalis smiled at me for the first time, I knew I'd made the right decision.

"Now, I'm not so sure. The Gatekeeper has taken her anyway." His shoulders slumped, and instead of a king, I just saw a heartbroken man.

"You still had thirteen years with her, Your Majesty," I said, patting his hand awkwardly. "That's far longer than most fathers keep their babes born with the Gatekeeper's mark. In fact...she told me she wanted to leave before any more misfortune befell your family because she was denying her calling."

"Her calling. My only daughter, serving death," he muttered.

I wet my lips. I'd lost Lord Orion's blessing, willing or not, to have this time with the king. I had to make each moment count. "Your Majesty, I am not your enemy, nor do I intend to be a force against you. I'm just a girl who loved a gryphon too much to let him go."

He made a noncommittal noise, but it did seem like he was listening.

"Lord Orion wanted me to be his Chosen because of my love for his beasts and because he feels like his image as the God of Mankind has been twisted out of recognition. He didn't care that I was a female riding one of his gryphons when I met him," I said, meeting his eye. "I feel like you and I could've gotten along better from the start if you knew that."

Sighing, he said, "Well spoken, Chosen of Orion."

"That's not—"

"You speak for him now, no matter...the magical gift." He swept his hand toward my necklace chain. "We will break the news to the Altarian people very slowly. If Lord Orion wants to be the God of Mankind rather than just of men, then perhaps we can change the mind of the people within the rest of my lifetime."

"Um, speaking of your life—"

"Of course, we will need to wait for you to finish your task for Mother Nilara. No one will believe your status if you have a white streak in your hair."

"Your Majesty," I interjected. "We can worry about this later. Can we talk about your son for a moment?"

His expression fell to its usual serious lines. "You're about to tell me that you are being courted by Mateo, aren't you? That would explain a lot."

Heat flushed over me from head to toe. "N-No! I mean your other son, Your Majesty, the crown prince."

"Oh. What of him?"

"Have you looked into his doings lately?" I asked carefully.

Between Mateo and Odalis, he had had plenty of warning that the crown prince was scheming against him. But to hear them tell it, the king was incapable of finding fault in Isaac. I watched his generous mouth twist, several emotions flashing over his expression before he settled on resigned.

"I shall review a few documents that have become buried on my desk," he said slowly. "I only just lost Valentino and Odalis."

"Yes, but—" I cut myself off when he flashed me a look of warning.

That was too far. He *had* just lost two of his children, though one could still come visit him one day; if he had to lose another, Isaac deserved closer scrutiny. I could see that he wasn't willing to face the truth yet, but that it was in the cards.

He was as close to understanding his eldest son's ambitions as I'd ever seen. That was the kind of progress the old king needed to make.

He stood, evidently ready to be finished with this conversation. But he did offer me a hand up and said almost cordially, "I must return to my duties. I will see that you have an appropriate ride back to the Storm Front."

"Thank you, Your Majesty," I replied in the same tone. "I do hope you think on what we talked about today."

"Trust me, Miss Walker. I will not soon forget this day." We started for the door out into the temple proper when he paused, holding up a finger. "Oh, and if you see your father, please let him know he can return to his position in the First at any time. I will not fail him or his family again."

CHAPTER 13

GLORIOUS

The king was swept away in a perfumed cart. I watched him walk right by a shimmering figure who observed the foot traffic in Temple Row with a curious cock of his head from his seat on the stairs.

"Glorium?" I asked in a low voice. It seemed like I was the only one who could see the gryphon, else there would be plenty of passersby admiring his feathers that reflected prismatic colors in the sunshine.

"Good afternoon, little one." His mental voice held a smile as he stood to his full height, easily twice Ari's size. The only reason he didn't tower over me was because I had stopped to stare at him from the top step of the temple.

I looked around, wondering where Lord Orion was. Perhaps he'd come personally, sensing the disturbance caused by his shattered token. I twisted the chain into another loop around my fingers, feeling its loss even more acutely. How would I break the news to Ari? My sight might not be perfect, but it was how he could still see the world. Without it, he would be lost in his darkness again.

My senses prickled, like I had a solid Link to Glorium and

he was inspecting my emotional state. *"It is just me, I'm afraid. Sorry to disappoint you."*

"I'm not—*I would never,"* I stammered.

He whistled a laugh, bobbing his head playfully. *"Come along. I am to be your appropriate ride back to Arimus."*

When he stooped, I saw he wore a simple saddle without a riding harness. Still, I hesitated to climb onto his back. He flashed me a knowing look, saying, *"Why so nervous? I spoke to the gryphon of your Final Flight escort to make sure she knew you were in good wings. She's having quite the pleasant dream right now, but I could wake her if you would prefer."*

"No...it's just, this is unexpected?"

"Is it? Well, I'm glad to be a welcome surprise," he said, not moving until I finally climbed onto his back, sliding my boots into the stirrups set lower than I was used to. With no reins to grasp, I held the saddle horn as he sprang into the sky.

"Oh, blast," I muttered, mostly to myself. "I *forgot* something."

"What was it?"

"Just a copy of the two big newspapers."

"I wouldn't bother. One's been dragging your name through the mud lately. You don't need to read that tripe," he said casually. *"I would get a copy of the* Voice *in a few days, though, if I were you."*

I eyed him with a raised brow, unsure of what to make of that statement. He turned to look at me with one dark eye, and it seemed like he winked. *"I have to have some magical perks after carrying a god for so long."*

"I see," I replied, wetting my lips as I considered how to ask—

"Don't do it," he said. *"Don't ask what Orion thinks. He decided to let you handle that conversation with the king."*

"Was he happy with how it went?" I asked.

He whistled a laugh, carefree. *"Did you hear what I just said? You had the conversation. You handled it. I want to talk to you now."*

With that, he banked toward the sun, refracting rainbows in a stunning display. I barely noticed we were flying, with how smoothly he cut through the sky.

"Well, okay. What do you want to talk about?" I checked the horizon, noting the position of the sun. I was starting to suspect we weren't going straight to Port Lindell, else he'd be tilting his wings further to the west.

"I thought you would be happy to see this," he said, pushing a memory into my mind.

For a few moments, I was back at the River of Origin, watching a glowing figure embrace a familiar red and maroon gryphon. Sunset had her eyes closed, bunting the man who held her. My glimpse of golden Lord Orion wavered, replaced by the smiling, weathered face of Duncan, one of his clergymen who'd been kind to me.

I gasped. *"Sunset made the journey? She's a Skymother now?"*

"She did, and barely needed my help at the end." He sounded much like a proud father. *"Orion adored her as well. He took the face of her former rider and spent quite some time helping her reminisce."*

"That was kind of him. Would you say she's doing okay?" I'd spent most of my limited free time tending to her during my last semester at the Academy, hoping to see her begin to thrive even without her Link with Callan.

"I would, yes. She's quickly carved a place for herself in Skylord Roshawk's flock and even bends his ear occasionally. King Alonso is not the only stubborn male you've begun to change, you know?"

I almost laughed at the idea that I'd ever influence big personalities like the king or Roshawk, but then I recalled how things had gone the last time I'd seen the stubborn wild gryphon.

"Roshawk's flock is unique anyway," Glorium continued. *"Made up almost entirely by the remnants of broken families the Altarian military has left behind. You planted a seed of an idea with them. Now we just have to wait and see if it flourishes."*

"What idea was that?" I asked.

He balked so obviously with a chirrup of comedic dismay that I tittered a giggle. *"Wait and see, little one. I don't want to get your hopes up. Besides, it's about time I told you where we're really going,"* he replied.

I knew it; he wasn't taking me back to Port Lindell. Despite that, I trusted the glimmering gryphon, even as he tilted his wings into a wide, lazy spiral over a rural area. The farms burst with fertile life just in time for harvesting season.

"You're taking me to see Lord Orion," I guessed.

"Wrong god," he chuckled. *"Sometimes the Mother gives me an offer I can't refuse. The chance to get to know you and earn a reward from her? How could I say no?"*

We weren't heading for a field at all, but instead a narrow lane of buildings set an equal distance from all the farms I saw from higher up. One structure had the squat stature of an inn, and the other buildings were even smaller. But even from above, I realized the end of the lane held four buildings, two to each side of the road, painted in familiar colors of white-silver and yellow-gold, brick-red and faded black.

I didn't dare speak my second guess aloud, just in case I jinxed the chance he might be giving me. If Lady Nilara was involved in anything, it was the affairs of Mother and Rissa. As Glorium swept in for a graceful landing, he said, *"Stay as long as you like. I'll be here, even if you'll be the only one who can see me."*

I practically leapt off his back. *"Can I get you anything before I go? Maybe something to eat?"* I suggested.

"I don't have to eat. A compliment wouldn't be amiss, though." He struck a pose, raising his head with a rustle of his iridescent feathers. With them fluffed out, he sprayed a dazzling display around him.

Placing my excitement aside for a moment, I pet his glimmering wing where I could reach it. He bent his massive forepaws so I could scratch him in the sensitive places behind his beak and ears. *"You are a handsome male. The prettiest gryphon to exist."* I bit my lip to contain another laugh when I saw him visibly preen from the praise he'd asked for.

"Thank you. Sometimes I need to hear it. The gods are too used to me by now," he said.

"Are they as grand as they seem?" I asked in genuine curiosity. *"Do you see who they truly are?"*

"Sure. They sparkle and such." He lifted his wings in a gryphon shrug. *"I can't tell you much more than that. I'm considered a demigod, half in their world and half in yours. It gets frustrating sometimes, the secrets I have to keep."*

"I understand," I said. And I did, even if it was just one secret and I hadn't even kept it for a whole year before it was literally ripped from me. I bid him farewell with a hug around the neck, turning toward the rural temples.

The white one was recently painted, well-maintained from the outside. Hanging planters lined the railing of the four stairs leading up to the silver trimmed door, with a bigger pot of flowers flourishing next to it. I opened it, taking in a breath of sweet-scented air and the soft murmur of a few female voices.

"Welcome to the Mother's tem—Sivana?" The slim acolyte waiting just inside to greet visitors gaped at me before rushing forward. I crushed Rissa in a hug.

"You passed your acolyte tests," I murmured, pulling back with my hands on her shoulders, taking in the dove-gray wrap she wore, complete with a silvery pendant of a crescent moon pinning it in place at her hip. She had her platinum hair down around her face in messy waves and no makeup on, unlike the impeccable double she usually made of Mother.

She beamed with perfect white teeth. "I did. By the way, I'm Alyssa right now, and Mother is Tanith. How…how did you find us?" There was a shadow of concern in her leaf-green eyes. Like if I was able to find them, less savory individuals on the crown prince's payroll could follow.

"I'll tell you and, uh, Tanith together," I promised. Nodding, she looped her arm through mine and took me into one of the side rooms, where a handful of women chatted. At first, I didn't spot Mother, not with her hair dyed chestnut brown and cut just under her ears. She must've been wearing magic of some kind, because she looked up and her features were also slightly different, her eyes darker, the angles of her face shifted.

But I'd been looking into that face for over sixteen years, and I recognized my mother all the same and her understated delight when she spotted me.

"Let's just wait for her to be done with her conversation," Rissa said, drawing me to the side so we could talk like any other pair. "Well, you certainly smell like you've just come off a gryphon."

I took a subtle sniff of my flight leathers. Even after a vigorous scrub, I suppose they still smelled like feathers and salt water. "Gee, thanks," I said, elbowing her. "I see you're okay. The Mother blessed me to have a chance to see it for myself."

With my history with the goddess, she must've known I had to see my family to be sure they were safe. "Yeah. How about you? Is everything all right?" Rissa asked quietly.

"Well…I'm still alive." I sighed, which just made her quirk up an eyebrow in concern. "Are there any consultation rooms here?"

Rissa glanced over my shoulder, holding up two fingers, presumably to Mother. "Yeah, I'll take you to one, and Tanith can join us later," she said, leading me out to the hallway and to a door just off from a tiny shrine that served as this temple's inner sanctum. The consultation room was just comfortable enough for the two of us to sit together, and she looked at me expectantly as soon as we were shut in.

In a flood I hadn't realized I'd dammed in, I told her about the battle of Port Lindell and how Ari was resting so he didn't tear his flight muscles after dislocating one of his wings. "So how—" Rissa tried to get in edgewise but quieted again as I told her about the sudden summons from the king.

"So, he knows where we are," she murmured.

"Not quite," I said. "He just…came at me like we're still in the time of the crusades, trying to get me to confess to Lord Orion everything the *Voice of the People* published about me in the last year."

Mother interrupted us with a knock at the door. She and I hugged awkwardly in the confined space, and we squashed in together. I took a deep breath and pulled the silvery chain out of my pocket and gave Mother the short version of what I'd just told Rissa.

"I had a token of magic from Lord Orion, but the king took it from me and shattered it," I shared. It felt like a huge relief to finally talk about everything with my family, even if they would never get to see the beautiful golden token of feathers and magic. "Err. Lord Orion claimed me to be his Chosen and gave it to me so I could have a stronger Link with Ari and, as it turned out, other gryphons too."

Mother interrupted with dozens of questions, and soon Rissa joined in, the two of them wheedling out the full story of how I'd come to meet the god in the first place. "So that's why you were called," Rissa said.

"Yeah. But it's not like it matters anymore. I failed to protect his token, so I'm not Chosen anymore," I said, picking at my fingernails with a sigh.

They exchanged a knowing look. "How did you end up coming here from the capital, Sivana?" Mother asked.

"Lord Orion's gryphon sort of kidnapped me to come here. He said it was a favor to the Mother." I narrowed my eyes when she smiled wider. "What is it?"

"Does Lord Orion's gryphon give just anyone flights to wherever they need to be?"

"Well, no…"

"He has interesting timing," she said, shrugging delicately. "We cannot host you long, I'm afraid. A redheaded woman wearing gryphon rider gear is quite distinctive, you see. But you're here because the gods thought you had to be, so…let's go pray to the Mother together and see if she will answer."

CHAPTER 14

NOBLE ENOUGH

I KNELT before the small silvery statue of Mother Nilara and felt darkness close around me almost immediately. My surroundings shifted to the dim light of early evening and a bottomless sky…which I stood in alone, impossibly balanced on a storm cloud.

Across from me and eating up the horizon was the eldrafn from my dreams, black as pitch and woven with silver bolts of electricity. Its almond-shaped eyes spotted me, narrowing hatefully, but it didn't attack right away.

"I don't understand. Eldrafn don't get this large," I said aloud. Signe had told me so, and I cherished every lesson that Rathi woman had taught me.

I was fishing for the goddess's attention, but my heart leapt when I realized I had it as she appeared next to me. She wore my mother's face as I knew it, with a platinum bun and immaculate white robes billowing behind her. Instead of standing on a cloud, she bobbed next to me as if held aloft by the beating of her invisible wings.

Her eyes, full of blazing silver power, met mine. "You never explained your task," I blurted. "Ari and I die every time we dream of this eldrafn."

"In all things," she said softly, her voice like the ring of a sweet bell. "Life must come from death. The former is my concern, but the latter is yours. A simple misunderstanding. If I told you what your true task is now, you would never achieve it."

Part of me wanted to stamp my foot like an angry tot, but that wasn't how I wanted the goddess to see me. I wet my lips, considering her soft smile, an uncanny echo of my own mother's. "Thank you for protecting my family, Lady Nilara," I said.

"It is my pleasure to shelter them, and to see you all reunited," she replied warmly. "Be welcome in my holy temple."

The vision started to fade, both eldrafn and goddess becoming hazy shapes as the light of day soaked into my vision. "Wait—" I protested. That was it? We'd barely spoken.

"You will no longer see this eldrafn in your dreams. But *I* will see *you* again when you are ready." Her voice drifted off to little more than a whisper, a trailing thought that followed after a long rest. I blinked back to reality, to Rissa and Mother praying next to me.

We couldn't speak our wishes aloud like we could during our visits to the temple in Kaiamear, so as not to draw attention to ourselves, which was all right with me. It had just highlighted how the Mother answered the two of them while she purposefully left me with silence.

I wished Ari was here so we could turn over the goddess's few words for any hidden meaning together. Instead, I had Rissa, who took me to a hidden stair and up to the cramped quarters she shared with Mother during their stay here. To keep suspicions low, Mother went back out to continue working.

"Can we talk about guys for a second?" I asked, noting the sunlight slanting to late afternoon through the tiny circular window they had.

We sat on Rissa's lumpy bed, and she turned to me with a sparkle in her eyes. "That's my favorite subject," she giggled.

"What do you do if you like two of them at the same time?"

She tilted her head thoughtfully. "Is this theoretical?"

"Uh, no."

"Leave it to you to bring me the most interesting problem in weeks." She rubbed her hands together. "Thank the gods, by the way. I don't want my strong, capable big sister becoming a spinster or anything. Okay, I'm ready. No, wait, who is it? That duke's son better be one of them."

"He is."

She nodded in approval. "And the other one?" When I told her it was Prince Mateo, she made a squeak that could've either been happiness or dismay. "I knew you two would fly off into the sunset."

"That's the thing, I don't know if I will. He doesn't seem as interested, but he does have to worry about being watched and monitored all the time," I sighed.

"Oh, mysterious," she cooed.

"Yeah. When we're alone together, I really like him. He's charming and witty." I found myself smiling wistfully for those rare moments when I got to see that side of Mateo. "He makes me feel like I'm important to him. He's really gone out of his way for me."

She found it quite romantic that he'd been my mysterious gift-giving "friend" before he'd felt comfortable enough to reveal that he was helping me secretly. "That was around the time he was helping Victor though, wasn't it?" she asked.

"Yeah." My smile faded a notch. It hurt to remember that he'd been more of a bully than a friend until Callan had met his untimely death. "His father was watching him and receiving reports through Victor, so he had to follow his lead. Mateo didn't want to be involved, but he was…"

Rissa merely made a "hmm" to that.

"…And also forced to write reports about me to his father, something he was quite resentful of. It's in the past, though." I waved like trying to waft away all those bad memories of my hellish first year at the Academy.

"This isn't telling me why you like the man," she snarked.

"Okay, okay. I do really like him. He's got a good head on his shoulders, better than most of the royals," I said. "He really cares for Mireille, his gryphon, who I helped raise. And like you said, he's a little mysterious. Just out of reach right now."

She nodded along. "What about the duke's son, then?"

"His name's Acton, and before we went to war, he and I were together all the time." I smiled to myself again. Those were better times, when the challenges aimed our way weren't so oriented toward life-or-death struggles. "We were in the same training flight and became friends when he started tutoring me on swordplay. At first, he came off really snobby and arrogant. Every conversation with him seemed to come back to the fact that his family is ultra-wealthy and that he had personal tutors rather than going to fundamental school, and that he was raised playing polo and eating meat every night. But eventually, I think we all figured out he just didn't know what else to say. We kind of beat it out of him and once we did, he proved to be kind and loyal, a good friend."

"Okay, we can work with that," she said.

"We can and definitely have. I would say he had a crush on me first." I blushed as I recounted our awkward beach-front kiss, which he'd initiated and caught me completely off guard. "He promised to wait after that since I couldn't date anyone in the Academy anyway. It's just recently that I've realized it might be okay now."

She poked me with several more questions just like the mini-Mother she was, giggling when she got me to admit that

I'd had more opportunities for the small touches, the hugs and the handholding, with Weslecker.

We talked up until the supper bell, and I understood why women came to the temple just to have a listening ear. It was helpful just to have a less biased person listen as I wrung my hands about Acton's obvious interest versus Mateo's secret care.

Both were supportive in their own ways.

And best—or worst—of all, the thought of either young man had me longing to see him again. I missed how Mateo grounded me to reality, but also how Acton seemed to understand and accept even the oddest of my quirks.

"Maybe it doesn't even matter," I said. "Mateo is royalty, after all. And Acton has to consider his status when picking a partner."

Rissa held up a hand. "We have noble blood, though. If it's a love match, they could both make an argument that you're noble enough."

"Right. Noble enough," I echoed with some amusement.

"You think you like them the same, but I think that's not true. When it comes to a partner, they have to be willing to stand beside you, right? And I think only one of the two has so far," she said, palms up in a carefree shrug. "But what do I know? Except that I was totally right about Victor."

I groaned. "You're never going to let me live it down, are you?"

"Nope! I'm going to put my money on one of them, and you can come back after the war to tell me if I'm right." She beamed, bobbing her head until I nodded back.

"I think that helps. Thanks, Rissa." Even if I knew she wouldn't reveal who she was rooting for, I felt less burdened with the decision after simply talking about it.

I spent the night with my family, but all too soon, they were chasing me out of the temple with hugs and promises to stay safe and hidden. Glorium rested right where I left him, cleaning his wing with lazy strokes of his beak. *"Have a nice visit?"* he asked.

"I did, yes."

"Here, for you." He plucked a loose feather and offered it to me. It glittered in the sunlight, and I smiled broadly.

"Thank you! Maybe this could go on my necklace." I fished the chain out and inspected the loop where the token used to be. I could make it work. When he knelt so I could climb into his saddle, I hesitated. *"Any other stops you want to tell me about first?"*

"I intend to take you straight to Ari. Who knows, he might be ready to carry you himself."

I slung myself onto his back, and he took off swiftly. *"Is that a premonition, or a guess?"*

"Every gryphon with a piece of the River of Origin within them heals faster," he told me. It made sense, considering how quickly Ari had gotten up after having his wing broken. Just another reason why my gryphon was exceptional.

We passed some of the flight in companionable silence before I finally said, *"The Mother spoke to me yesterday."*

"She does that sometimes," he twittered.

I rolled my eyes. *"It's only the second time I've ever talked to her."*

"Oh. Good chat?"

"Brief and cryptic, really."

"Yeah, that sounds like Nilara. Before you ask, I probably can't help. Sorry. If you want to send a message to any gryphons, though, I can help with that."

I considered him and his lighthearted tone. *"There are a few gryphons I'd like to contact, then."*

"Okay, who's first? What do you want him or her to know?"

"Will you tell Puzzlebox I love her?" I decided to test this with an easy, short message, not sure what to expect.

"Done. She's looking around for you, hoping to see you... Sivvy," he said.

"Oh, not you too."

"What? It's cute," he laughed. *"Who's next?"*

"Tell Valtora I miss her double after meeting Skyla," I suggested.

"Oh, trust me, she knows."

Together, we went down my mental list of favorite gryphons, checking in with each of them. I was relieved to know they were all alive. Especially Puzzlebox, who I hoped never saw direct combat.

Glorium described these messages as subliminal ideas in the other gryphon's mind rather than direct speech from him. Most of the beasts didn't know who he was and wouldn't take kindly to a stranger intruding into their thoughts. With that in mind, I built up my confidence to contact Roshawk, saying I hoped he was reconsidering tolerating humans if it meant he could see Valtora.

"I think he will need to weigh his hatred against his love," Glorium responded after a few moments' pause. *"But here we are. You can talk to at least one of your gryphon friends yourself."*

Port Lindell approached swiftly. I could see the damage to its buildings even from a distance, but also signs of life, tiny people coming and going. We started descending toward the military camp right outside of its walls.

I swallowed thickly. *"No, I can't, remember? I lost Lord Orion's token."*

Glorium landed with a graceful sweep of his wings, far enough away from the camp that the scouts may not have noticed me arriving on an invisible gryphon. He knelt so I could dismount.

"So?" he asked in a gentle tone.

"What do you mean, so? It was the only reason I could talk to any gryphons other than Ari," I replied. He followed a few paces behind me as I walked toward the camp and the trampled field where the gryphons rested.

My Link with Ari snapped back into place with me closer

to him, to an instant surge of relief between both of us. As nice as it'd been to see Mother and Rissa, my heart had yearned for this moment and the sight of my gryphon raising his head from the grass, turned in my direction.

"You're back!" he exclaimed.

Next to him, a second gryphon pushed to her paws and charged across the field toward me. My mouth dropped open as her golden plumage caught the sunlight before she shoved me onto my back in her enthusiasm.

"There you are. Where have you been?" Valtora demanded.

"Oof—Skymother!" I exclaimed, winding my arms around her stout neck.

I understood her perfectly and felt the wave of her protective love as she nuzzled my face, careful of her hooked beak.

"Your father volunteers us for this new team you're on and rushes us to get here, then you're not even here," she scolded.

Tears pricked the corners of my eyes. *"Sorry, Skymother. I'm here now."*

"What's wrong?" she asked, her tone gentling.

I shook my head, burying my face in her chest fur before easing myself up to a sitting position. *"Nothing's wrong. We can still talk!"*

Her head cocked to one side. *"We've always been able to talk. I taught you back when you were my little featherless hatchling,"* she said affectionately.

"But—"

"Come, now. Don't make Ari wait any longer." She nudged me until I was kneeling in front of Ari, touching the sides of his face so he knew I was there.

His wing was tucked neatly to his side instead of bandaged. I didn't pick up any twinges of pain as he shuffled forward and laid his head in my lap with a content twitter. *"You might as well tell me what's wrong,"* he commented. *"I sense a lot's happened since you left?"*

"So much," I replied.

I turned my gaze toward the field where I'd left Glorium, just to see that he was gone. One simple word from him had shattered my understanding of Lord Orion's intentions just as thoroughly as the king had smashed his magical token.

So?

Valtora spoke to me as clearly as Ari did, and I felt the tingles along my skin that hinted to Ari and I connecting solidly enough for him to see through my eyes. Why were either of these things possible without the magic?

"Tell me as well." Valtora tucked into Ari's back, covering his middle with one of her wings.

I began to do just that when a throat cleared behind me. "I thought so," a familiar voice said. Father stood at the edge of the field, in full uniform.

Years of Academy training kicked in, and I leapt back to my feet, standing at attention and saluting. He returned it quickly, a glimmer of pride in his eyes.

"Hi, Father. You're here?" I asked. It wasn't like I could run up and hug him here in a military camp, but I wanted to upon seeing him healthy and safe.

"A bit of a long story," he replied. "I heard the king summoned you?"

"Also a long story," I admitted.

Valtora shifted with a grumbling warble. *"She was going to tell us first."*

"It may have to wait," he told her before saying to me, "Strike Team Three is relocating to the main front effective immediately. You're just in time to join us with your chatty pyrojack friend."

CHAPTER 15

ENDURANCE IS KEY

Zizi was back to her usual self when I returned to our tent and began packing my things. Her Tulari mark blazed against her cheek with bold orange fire magic. "You wouldn't believe it—your dad is here!" she greeted me, as if I hadn't just reluctantly parted with him to rush to my tent before the rest of the strike team left without Ari and me.

I dug and scattered my things, looking for the eldrafn egg, just for her to pull it out of the pile of things on her side of the tent. She'd clipped it off Ari's saddle and hidden it for me, to my great relief. We pulled it out and flipped it, looking for any sign of life or cracks, as if it were a real egg instead of a heavy stone.

It remained solid and inert, with the same magical signature as before. It seemed the lightning it'd absorbed from the Earl wasn't enough to bring it back to life.

"I'm glad you're okay," I said. She had a sunny smile rather than the sullen expression she'd worn after exhausting all her magic following the big battle.

She displayed her palms, restored from their burnt state. "Fully mended up. Ready for the next battle with new tricks."

She exaggerated a wink. "They, uh, kind of took my bombs away, so I had to improvise."

"Why am I suddenly overcome by a feeling of dread?" I asked lightly, though I wasn't at all joking.

"Don't worry. It's *totally* safe," she assured me.

To my even greater concern, she didn't explain what her improvised "new tricks" would be. Instead, she told me, "The strike team has three new gryphon riders, but two of them are going to be without pyrojacks until the Academy sends replacements. If they do, you know, since, well…"

"If they're reduced to sending apprentices, I'm guessing there aren't many more willing to volunteer," I ventured.

"Ah, they kind of lied about that. I volunteered, but some of the other pyrojacks didn't," she admitted. "Just like I doubt they let you opt not to go to war, right?"

"Right." I thought of Sharde and Puzzlebox, especially, the duo who would've been happier delivering the mail with Final Flight than whatever they were doing as squires to their assigned flight.

Zizi began hauling bags out of our tent, to be split between Ari and one of the gryphons who wouldn't be burdened by a second person. While she bustled, I reached out to Ari to share everything that'd happened.

"*No wonder you were so upset,*" he hissed, furious to see my memory of the king destroying Lord Orion's token. I echoed him, remembering how angry I'd been before he began opening up to me and finally treating me like a person.

"*The magic isn't gone, though. You can see out of my eyes right now, right?*"

He confirmed that he could, making a little remark about the chocolate bars I was deliberating over, trying to decide if I should eat them or pack them at the top of his saddlebags for easy access.

"*And I could still talk to Valtora, too,*" I said, taking a few more minutes to relive the rest of what he'd missed, from

Glorium's sudden appearance to the visit to my family and then the flight here and the gryphon demigod's final word.

It stuck in my head like a catchy tune that wouldn't stop repeating itself. *So? "It's almost like he was saying it wasn't all that important. He didn't care that it was broken."*

Ari went quiet with a thoughtful hum. When I began lugging the heaviest of my luggage out to him, I saw that he had Tempest sitting beside him, and on the other side, a skinny older gryphon who hopped up with a joyful twitter when he saw me.

"Fog?" I laughed, hugging him around the neck when he came over to bunt me square in the chest. "Is all of the First here?"

Fog belonged to the oldest rider of the First, Captain Pierce, due to retire within the next few years. He'd been one of the fifteen gryphons I'd tended to as a caretaker, as familiar as a close friend.

"No, youngling. Just the ones with any sense," he told me.

I sensed Ari notice the connection that'd formed between Fog and me instantly, and he chirped with a knowing twist to his emotions.

"What do you mean?" I asked, stroking down the roughened texture of Fog's coat. He was named for the fuzzy gray edges he had, his fur never quite flat and oiled like most gryphons'.

"When Valtora's rider resigned, my rider and Icestorm's followed," he said, naming another male beast from the First.

I turned to Ari, raising my brow. *"Sounds like a lot's happened that you haven't told me."*

"It's not like I could get a word in edgewise," he teased.

"It was important too!"

Ari began telling me what he knew: that Father and the two men who'd resigned from the First with him had volunteered to fill the three positions open in Strike Team Three.

They'd arrived yesterday with orders in hand for the rest of the strike team to report to the main front.

I took a quick peek around the field while he spoke and spotted Icestorm looking bored next to a trio of chatting men. I went over to say hello to them, just to be waylaid by the gryphon chattering like a hatchling and rolling over for belly rubs.

"There's your girl," gray-haired Captain Pierce said to my father, smiling down at me with both my hands buried in Icestorm's belly fluff.

"Uh, good afternoon, sirs," I said, realizing myself a second too late.

"If it isn't the famous *Squire* Walker," Pierce replied, a grin stretching the whiskers on his upper lip. "Some reintroductions are in order, it seems. I'm going by my old call sign, Howl."

"Yes, sir, Captain Howl," I said crisply.

"Want to know why that's my old call sign? Of course you do." He tilted his head back and imitated a wolf's howl. A few yards away, Fog did the same thing, but his howl was akin to an eerie wail that had goosebumps rising over my arms.

The man next to him, younger and fit with a full head of blond hair combed over in an attractive style, reintroduced himself as Captain Cyclone. "Congratulations on your promotion, sir," I said, knowing him as one of the newer appointees to the First. Newer was relative, however, and he'd been a Lieutenant for most of his career.

"Thank you, Squire Walker. When are you getting your call sign? Your old man here picked out a new one for himself," Cyclone said, slapping my father heartily on the shoulder.

"My mentor said when I've earned one that's not just 'girl,'" I replied, looking to my father curiously.

He cleared his throat and said, "I decided on Arrow."

"And the military damn well doesn't know what to do with us, so they let us come to your strike team. Isn't that great?" Cyclone was saying, but I barely heard him.

"Arrow? Like…" I murmured.

"I thought it was fitting," he replied with a bittersweet smile.

Behind us, Wrath announced himself with a loud, "Look alive, men! Ha! I need Arrow and Deadeye before you leave."

Father stepped forward, trailing Valtora, who rumbled a low growl. Her gaze was focused on the female looming behind Wrath. Skyla glared back with just as much venom, the two of them exuding such malice that I wondered if there would be a fight right then and there. There was definitely bad blood between them.

Wrath spoke in a hushed tone with Father and Cherin while Howl spoke behind his hand to me. "Too many leaders, not enough followers in our element now with three Captains and two Squires. We let Deadeye stay the leader of the element, while Arrow will step in as the strike team's Commander."

I nodded in understanding while watching Valtora and Skyla press nearly beak to beak.

"I heard you dropped my son in the ocean," Valtora rumbled.

"He and his reckless female rider needed to cool off," Skyla snipped. *"Do I have you to thank for teaching the human how to speak to me so boldly?"*

"How dare you!"

"How dare you?" the speckled Skymother countered.

I wet my lips, realizing I hadn't really responded to Howl. "I really appreciate that you are here, sir," I said. "I heard you resigned from the First with my father?"

"That's right. You'll learn when you stay in the service long enough that you always follow the best leaders if you can. Plus"—he flashed a sideways smirk—"Fog and I haven't seen real combat in years. I'd rather be here than wasting away in the capital."

"...*You'll get your chance to protect your precious son and human without my interference. Enjoy the main front,*" Skyla was saying with false sweetness.

The leadership ended their meeting, and Cherin beckoned to me. "We were going to move out tomorrow at first light, but since you're here, the timeline has been moved up." His one good eye roved over me. "You all right?"

"Yes, sir." I realized he was waiting for me to elaborate and added, "The king just wanted to talk about something concerning his daughter's disappearance."

He seemed to relax. "Ah. I'm glad you're back. Don't let me forget, I wanted to show you one of my tricks after watching you and Arimus fight the other day. For now, it's time for us to set off. We're needed quite urgently with the main fighting force."

Before we left, though, I watched the stare-off with the two Skymothers end with an uneasy growl. "*Thank the winds she's not coming with us,*" Valtora said with a regal lift of her beak.

FATHER SET a cautious pace for us as the new leader of our strike team. Over the course of the several days' journey up the coast, following its curve to the northeast, I realized how small my worries were compared to those of who made their livelihoods in this area.

The Rathi had left scars everywhere they'd attacked. It was one thing to know that Port Lindell was one of many targets, but I saw firsthand how Altare's main ports were now in ruins, some still smoking. Through Valtora, Father shared that the Rathi had severely stretched our resources—but we'd held the line, if only just barely.

The second largest eldrafn in the Rathi army, the Advisor, had fallen, and now we were pressing further into the Rathi Islands to prevent any more incursions on our soil.

I shared the story of the king's summons and how he'd destroyed my necklace, which led to the same kind of questions I'd answered with Mother and Rissa. Father was brisk in turning down the king's offhanded invitation to return to the First. *"I think that opportunity has passed,"* Valtora said in the same cool tone that suggested his brewing anger was about to bubble over.

I spoke further with Valtora about what happened to Lord Orion's token, not surprised to hear her scoff when I shared my worries about its magic. *"I don't see why that had to be a big secret,"* she snorted. *"Didn't I just tell you that I taught you to understand me?"*

"Well, yes, but—"

"No buts," she interrupted. *"Maybe this necklace gave you confidence, but you didn't need it. It sounds like it did its job, making the king trust you enough to listen."*

"I did need it, though. Ari wasn't able to see through my eyes before I started wearing it, and I could...can...talk to other gryphons like I talk to him."

She considered for a few moments, leaving me with the sound of wind whistling through my ears. *"Have you ever considered that you're not the only human who can speak the language of gryphons?"*

"No? There are others?"

"I've only met a few, but yes, there are others. Night was rather fond of her rider's son and taught him like I taught you," she shared.

I wondered why this was news to me. Had I really always known the way to talk to gryphons? All those times when I thought I'd *almost* understood Valtora and other gryphons of the First...

Well, it was possible we'd been talking all along and I hadn't realized it until I Linked with Ari and felt what true understanding of the gryphon language was like.

"*Skymother,*" I said, shocked to my core. "*I didn't need the necklace, all this time?*"

"*No, hatchling. Just like I doubt you needed it to forge a stronger Link with Ari. You did that over time, did you not?*" she asked gently. "*You built it out of trust and need, a mutual understanding of each other and your emotions. The shining man tricked you into believing it was his magic when all along, it was your doing.*

"*Well,*" she added, a touch smug. "*Perhaps a little of mine, too.*"

I was still reeling when we made camp that evening and sat around waiting to share a side of wild boar. Our gryphons had hunted a pack of them, and the group's mood was up with the promise of fresh, hot food.

I put my hand in my pocket to withdraw the single feather Glorium had given me and pulled out something hard and solid. In place of the feather was a glimmering stone with etchings of fine filaments. It even had an eyelet to be threaded onto a necklace at the top.

"*Did you feel any magic today?*" I asked Ari. I stared at the former feather before I felt my expression stretch into a big smile.

"*No? It is pretty, though,*" he commented.

It felt like a subtle reward from the gryphon demigod who couldn't quite tell me I'd figured out the secret to the token that'd I'd once had to hide. Now I had its replacement, a piece of the gods to carry with me.

I had my new pendant on the old chain and was tucking it under my collar when Cherin dragged over a tripod stool he'd unpacked and sat next to me. His earthen-toned skin had a kind of glow by firelight. "How are you holding up, Squire Walker?"

I must've looked distracted and distant. It wasn't every day I realized that Valtora had loved me enough that she'd taught me how to talk to her kind when I was very small. That I'd been called to the River of Origin for no other reason than becoming Lord Orion's Chosen and gaining an object that was always intended to break at a time and place of the god's choosing.

"Gods, all right, sir," I said, giving myself a sound shake.

"I know it can be overwhelming, seeing the aftermath of big battles," he said, referencing one of the big port cities we'd skirted, which was razed to the ground. Port Lindell had gotten off easy by comparison.

"At least no rozash were involved." I didn't have to fake my shudder. Ari had shared enough glimpses of that kind of horror.

He nodded in agreement. "I promised you a secret. First, I saw you and Arimus give Wrath an assist with his eldrafn kill."

"That's right." I expected some praise to offset the sting of being denied even a portion of the bounty for killing the creature.

Cherin's mouth set in a cross line. "Your gryphon was exhausted, and his form was inexcusably sloppy. You almost got yourselves killed. Next time you're hit by a blast of eldrafn lightning, instead of baiting it further, you retreat, do you understand?"

"But—" I protested.

"Do you understand?" he repeated more firmly. "Or would you like to explain to me why that extra pouch you and your pyrojack were trying to hide had an eldrafn egg?"

I froze.

"I saw it before she had an opportunity to take it. You used it to survive a lightning strike." His one good eye inspected me as I sweated what he'd say next. "It's clever. I want to know where the egg came from."

I bowed my head and dropped my voice. "Yes, sir. It was a gift from an instructor who wanted to keep me safe. It was her eldrafn, but the egg hasn't hatched in fifty years or more. It's doubtful that it ever will," I said.

He raised a skeptical brow and asked, "What will you do if it does hatch?"

"I...I will have to return her eldrafn to her, sir."

"It is our duty to kill such beasts, not bring them back."

"It's a special case, sir. The rider in question will meet the Gatekeeper soon, if I'm honest. I would like nothing more than to give her the joy of reuniting with her beast before she goes," I said, holding my breath as he turned his face to the fire and considered.

"Find a better place to hide the egg if you're going to use it. If anyone else discovers what you have, they won't look the other way like I'm prepared to. But if it hatches, I want to know, and I want to be involved with what happens to it next. With that said, I want you to have this." He offered me a pouch that vibrated faintly in my hand. I opened it and upended a flat stone carved with an unfamiliar Tulari rune.

"A magestone, sir?" I asked.

"It seems weak, but it will save your life if you use it right. That rune is for endurance. Most riders swear by magestones for speed, but they last for a short burst before breaking. Good for one use or two before your gryphon starts becoming immune to the effect, just like with healing magic."

"That probably won't work on me either, considering I can't be healed anymore," Ari put in.

"As I've tried to teach you, endurance is key to surviving any sustained engagement. Keep that magestone, and use it next time you and your gryphon are at your limits and there are still enemies to face." His hand curled over my fingers, closing them around his gift.

"Thank you, sir," I said. If anything, I could use the stone on myself or place it next to the extra-large healing magestone Prince Mateo gave me after Ari's wing was broken, there for emergencies.

Cherin cleared his throat sternly. "Don't get too complacent. We will continue extra PT and endurance training. This is strictly for last-ditch moments, understood? There to stand in the gap between life and death."

"Of course, sir. A magestone can't replace hard work," I said agreeably. I placed the stone back in its pouch for the moment and committed to never getting into another situation where I might need it.

CHAPTER 16

REUNIONS

I saw the main camp long before we landed. Hundreds of tents dotted the green hills outside the city of Daramaine. Its ports were taken over by a number of massive naval vessels. As we approached, I counted and thought to myself, *This can't be our entire navy.*

A third of Daramaine was flattened, debris strewn everywhere. The death throes of the Advisor eldrafn, Father told me, taken down by riders of the Third.

"Just a warning. Be prepared to be star-struck," he shared through Valtora. *"A number of the big Heroes of Altare are here."*

I shifted in the saddle with an understated burst of enthusiasm. What I really wanted was a few hours in my bedroll without Zizi's chatter, especially before potentially meeting a Hero of Altare. There were only twenty or so alive, all war heroes, brilliant inventors, or peacemakers who were honored by the king himself for their deeds. While I hoped some of the latter were here, trying to make inroads with the Rathi for a truce, I imagined it was mostly the former, assembled to win a decisive victory against the northern raiders.

"Maybe they'll be star-struck by me as well," I suggested.

"Don't get a big head, hatchling," Valtora answered without hesitation.

Ari whistled a hearty laugh at both of us.

We landed in a narrow field behind tents marked with gryphon knight corps blue. Caretakers came forward to help the others dismount and retrieve their bags, but I noticed they avoided Devos and me.

"Welcome to the forward camp, sir." The familiar drawl greeted Howl, and I flashed a tired smile down at my former flight-mate, Credell. His brown eyes met mine with a playful twinkle. "Squires must tend to themselves, I'm afraid."

Ari made a soft squawk when another young man leaned against his shoulder, right beside my leg. "But some of us can take you to the squire puddle," Sharde said. He looked over my shoulder when someone barked his name and glared.

"Already in trouble?" I asked.

"Alas, it follows me. See you soon." He patted my calf and rushed off to help a different rider.

I turned to get Zizi free of her riding harness. The smoldering embers of her eyes were watching Credell and Sharde before she turned her toothy smile my way. "Do I finally get to meet your friends?" she asked.

"I sure hope so." It meant I would see them too, and exchanging letters was nothing compared to chatting in person. I had Zizi help me pile up our bags, and she went to retrieve the extra luggage of hers that another gryphon had to carry here.

The field bustled with squires doing caretaker work, and I waved to a few friendly faces in the crowd while removing Ari's saddle and tending to his coat. It was clean and free of knots and loose feathers when Sharde reappeared, Puzzlebox at his side.

"Sivvy!" she exclaimed, bounding up to me and tapping her front talons in excitement. *"Sivvy, I have something to tell*

you!" She curved her neck around me when I pulled her into a hug.

"Oh, what is it?" I asked, laughing aloud. I'd really missed this.

"I love you." Her beak parted with delight to finally say it, like she'd been saving it ever since I told her that during my flight with Glorium.

"I love you too! And look how fluffy you've gotten while I was gone." I mussed the fur along her neck and chest, which was as puffy and white as a cloud. Since most signs pointed to her having reached her maximum size, it seemed she would replace extra muscle growth with more fur.

I was thrilled to see her happy and alive, two things I feared she'd lose the moment she entered a real combat situation.

"Where have you been?" she asked. Her liquid dark gaze was wide and innocent, showing a peek at the little girl still within her.

"The military sent Ari and me to protect another place, but we're here now," I assured her. She pawed at my thigh, trying to get me to sit so she could rest in my lap. *"I need to get all my stuff moved first, but I promise we can catch up later."*

"Promise?" she repeated.

I smoothed the fur around her catlike ears. *"Promise."*

"Okay, okay, let's go," Sharde said, gently nudging Puzzlebox as he stooped to pick up some of my bags. "I talked to the camp manager and got you and the Tulari a place in the squire puddle."

"Thanks. Why is it called that, though?" We crossed through half the camp before he turned toward a fire pit ringed with dozens of blue-marked tents. A couple extra were waiting to be pitched.

"Well, there are over fifty squires here, so the leadership kind of just...threw us together. Usually, a group of squires is called a puddle, but they've joked that they need a whole lake for us now." He shrugged and glanced around. "That Tulari you're working with, is she Lithosian?"

I glanced over my shoulder, but it seemed we'd left Zizi behind for the moment. "Yeah. I don't know the whole story, but she's an Altarian now. She barely even has an accent."

"Uh huh," he said, raising a brow.

"Give her a chance. Just know that her magic is, uh, different." I almost said *unstable* or *dangerous* but didn't want to speak poorly of her before he'd even met her. "It makes her very talkative."

When we crossed back to the gryphon's field, I found her waiting beside the pile of her things and a lounging Ari. "Sharde, this is Zuri Zaveri—"

She leapt forward and shook his hand as quickly as the flurry of her speech. "You can call me Zizi—all my friends do. And you're Sivana's friend, right? You two definitely seem like you know each other. Did you two meet at the Academy?"

Behind her back, I made a gesture toward her, like asking "See what I mean?" He nodded subtly.

"And Zizi, this is one of my closest friends, Noah Sharde," I finished.

"Just remember the names Walker and Zaveri. We're going to be the next Heroes of Altare together," she said, beaming. He glanced between us and shrugged in his carefree way.

I ushered her across the camp, all three of us lugging baggage now to make it in one more trip. "Where's everyone else?" I asked Sharde. If there really were fifty or so squires here, I reckoned I'd seen about half of them.

"Our higher-ranked fellows are off drilling." He rolled his eyes. "And if you're asking about Ellie, my genius lady is currently meeting with the engineering corps about a new device that might help us overwinter in the Rathi Islands."

I glanced to the sky and back to him. "Why would we

need to do that?" The Rathi Islands were some of the most inhospitable lands at the best of times but famous for the most brutal winters people could survive.

"I guess no one's told you yet. We're launching a counterassault shortly. If the war doesn't end in a couple short months, we will have to sit and freeze on the islands we will conquer between now and then."

"Oh, no wonder they wanted my strike team so urgently," I said to myself.

Sharde sat outside my tent with Puzzlebox and Ari, chatting through the open flap as Zizi and I got our space comfortable. I didn't dare unpack much. We filled him in on what Strike Team Three had done thus far, which led to me sharing news of the Battle of Port Lindell and the Earl's defeat.

"So, we're going to be needed to help what's left of the navy make the journey north," I said.

"Most definitely. We'll all be crossing by ship, and out on the water, the Rathi are at their strongest." Sharde frowned, picking at the fluff between Puzzlebox's wing feathers.

"It'll be their chance to defeat us quickly," I agreed.

Zizi crackled her knuckles, scattering embers from her palm. "Not if I'm there." She muttered a curse when the furs underfoot started catching fire and stamped them out quickly.

"You inspire so much confidence in me," Sharde said dryly.

Next to him, Ari raised his head. *"Come out for a moment."*

I stepped out of the tent in time for a blur to pass by, blowing my stray flyaways to one side. Lowering my goggles, I spotted a formation of gryphons following the first, including one silvery-gray female. It seemed like they were practicing diving skills, as the more experienced gryphons carried away logs of fresh wood from our fire pit while less confident riders pulled up somewhere around the top of the tents.

When Mireille swooped past with a log in her talons, I cheered and applauded the fleeting figure of Mateo on her back. In the split second he was passing by, I swear his face turned our way and his mouth parted in surprise.

Then they were gone, circling around again to place the logs exactly as they'd been before their round trip through the sky. One squire knocked over the whole pile at the last moment and left it like that, so I helped rebuild the stack when the group flew onward.

Sharde elbowed me when I kept watching the sky for any more sign of the other squires. "They'll be done soon. Then you can moon all you like."

"I do not *moon*—"

"Acton's been a mess lately," he interrupted. "Interestingly, it seems he and the princeling got into a serious fight recently."

"Oh? About what?" I asked, trying to keep the dread out of my voice.

He shrugged, flashing his crooked smile. "I was hoping you could figure it out and tell me. You have no idea how boring it's been around here. Turns out the demerits around here get you either caretaker duty or shoveling latrines, and no one gossips there, not like in the Academy kitchens."

I relaxed again, realizing he wasn't implying I was the reason for their fight. "I'll do my best. You know, I didn't think the real army had demerits."

He gave a lazy wave. "I mean, when you're as incompetent as me, such things never go away."

"You don't seem incompetent to me," Zizi said. She pointed toward the tower of fresh wood. "Need a light?" A tiny flame ignited on her fingertip.

Sharde's brows furrowed. "Where's your wand? Isn't it super dangerous to use your magic without one?"

"Yeah, sure, I guess. Wands are tools of restraint and control. I don't need one," she replied while accidentally flicking fire into the grass. I went over to stamp it out.

Sharde kept a leery eye on her for the fifteen or so minutes we sat around chatting before other young men and their gryphons started crowding the squire puddle with us. I stood the moment I heard their voices approaching, spotting Weslecker's auburn head above some other familiar faces.

He'd seen me too, as the next thing I knew, he'd pulled me into a tight hold. "You're really here," he murmured.

"Unhand her, sir. I want to say hi too!" Biggs exclaimed. I was dragged from Weslecker and into backslapping hugs with several of my Academy friends, mostly my peers, but Valentic and Birch came over as well. They'd been here for longer than the rest of us but were still considered squires. It seemed only a fraction of the current pool of squires was defending our southern border against Lithos right now.

Ari sparked with happiness when Birch sat beside him off to the side. I felt him catching up with his friend while they groomed each other casually.

I looked around for one last gryphon rider, turning to Sharde. "Where's Korvic?"

His face fell. It was like dipping the happiness of this moment into ice water as my question rippled out, drawing uneasy glances and frowns, answering it before anyone uttered a word.

Weslecker put his arm over my shoulders, drawing me into his side as he answered, "We lost him a few days ago."

I hid my face in the warm leather stretched over his chest, mustering my expression. I couldn't cry right now, not in front of all these young men, many of whom had tormented me at the Academy without seeing as much as a single tear.

"It was his dream, you know, being a gryphon rider," I said quietly. And he'd died in one of his first engagements. It was the kind of irony Korvic made jokes of.

"I know," Weslecker murmured.

Someone else sniffled. I lifted away from Weslecker, spotting Feyring a few feet away, swiping at his nose and reddening eyes. The two of them had been inseparable, the chatterbox and the sarcastic one who always had a remark ready to bring Feyring's ego back to the ground.

"Well, ah, tell me about it later," I suggested to get attention away from him. "Are you all done with practice already?"

Weslecker cleared his throat, nodding. "We're expecting new orders eventually. Welcome to the squire puddle, where we're the last to know anything."

"There's a lot of waiting around," Sharde said in agreement.

We settled around the fire pit, where individual groups formed from our old Academy flights. The elder squires kept to each other, enforcing some distance from my less-trained peers, making room for a gaggle of loud apprentice Tulari. Weslecker sat as far from Falcon Flight as possible, studiously ignoring Prince Mateo, who caught my eye and inclined his head as if he were summoning me to his side.

I took my time, making it look as casual as I could, drifting away from comforting Feyring, who was uncharacteristically quiet, to the edge of space where the former Kite Flight was split from the former Falcon Flight. Mireille rested her weight over my lap when I sat down. Mateo reached out and squeezed my hand.

"I'm glad you're okay," he said in an undertone.

"I wrote to you." I didn't mean to make it sound like an accusation, but now that his handsome, inscrutable face was turned toward mine, it tumbled out of my mouth with sharp edges.

"And I couldn't reply. My correspondence is watched," he murmured.

That was about what I expected him to say, too. I blew out

a sigh. "Did you know your father summoned me back to Kaiamear?"

His hand tightened over mine. I didn't mind the hold but couldn't turn my hand over with him squeezing the life out of my fingers. "What?" he hissed. "When?"

"A few days ago. Oh, I'm already back. We had…I think we actually had a conversation for the first time."

I'd intended to tell him and Weslecker about what'd happened at the same time, but when I glanced toward the other young man, I noticed him shredding a blade of grass to bits, an unfriendly expression leveled at the prince. He didn't seem all that happy to see me sitting there with Mateo, either. The hostility made me reconsider, so I whispered the short version to Mateo and eventually reclaimed my hand to fold it in my lap.

"That really happened?" He leaned forward. "And you're really Chosen?"

"A secret I expect you to keep," I warned.

He laughed briefly. "Gods, yes. There would be a riot here tonight if they knew…" He cleared his throat. "I mean, I'm happy for you."

"It's just that I'm a woman?" I prompted.

"Well, Lord Orion wanted to make a statement and certainly did. I just don't know if everyone's ready for it."

"That's what your father said as well."

An uneasy silence descended between us. I was more used to Mateo on his own, when he didn't have to watch his words so closely. His smile was stiff now and only slipped to a less formal look toward Mireille when his gryphon wandered from my lap to go inspect her brother and nudge him onto his side. They play-wrestled halfheartedly on the grass. I wondered if Mireille and Ironfeather were in a funk because of their riders.

Mateo slanted a look across the camp and gestured in my

direction as I stood. I bit my tongue, more sure than ever that they'd had some kind of fight because of me.

"Hey hey, Sivana." Zizi's voice burst through my guilty thoughts as she reappeared. She whispered loudly, "Aren't you going to introduce me?" She indicated Mateo with a poorly smothered giggle.

CHAPTER 17

CROSSING OCEANS

IT WAS FULL DARK, with sleeping gryphons all around us when Ellie slipped into the squire puddle. I greeted the slim young woman with all the energy I had left, considering the hours of grief and waiting. Feyring had finally told me about Korvic's death from the battle with the Advisor eldrafn, and we'd remembered his sharp personality together.

I'd never been happier to see my best friend. She'd changed very little from when I'd seen her last, but some of the mousiness had given way to a more confident stance. She settled between Sharde and me, the three of us sharing Puzzlebox when she draped herself over our laps to rest.

"How's life in the engineering corps?" I asked her.

"Gods, busy!" she burst out with a grin. "Problems to solve every day."

"She's been doing great," Sharde interjected. He brushed a lock of bangs out of Ellie's face. For an unguarded moment, he looked at her like she'd hung the moon tonight.

They gazed into each other's eyes, and I shifted my attention to petting Puzzlebox's warm fluff, feeling a little forgotten.

"Wonder what that feels like," Ari commented. I almost apol-

ogized but sensed that he was making a joke. He'd been in a pile of friendly gryphons this whole time, only talking to me now because he was sandwiched between Birch and Iron-feather and both of them were fast asleep.

"Do you think we're getting new orders tonight?" I asked a little dubiously, glancing around the fire pit. Some of my fellow squires were getting restless. *"Or maybe some dinner?"*

"Not tonight for the orders. Moving a group as big and diverse as this army requires planning and time," he said.

Dinner, at least, was served shortly afterward. Ellie and I traded stories, and inevitably, Zizi came around, so I did one last round of introductions as well. It seemed that my assigned pyrojack preferred the company of gryphon riders, as she stayed to chat with the rest of Kite Flight like another honorary member.

She and Feyring hit off a friendship, though, which I was happy to see for his sake. No one would be able to get in a word edgewise with the fast-paced conversation between them.

A set of ranking gryphon riders came around to dismiss us to our bedrolls, confirming Ari's hunch that any orders would come later. We discovered the hard way that our new tent was smaller than the last one, too, with him unable to get enough room to settle comfortably between Zizi and me.

I rested uneasily, between worries that some assassin would sneak in while I rested without my gryphon next to me and thoughts of Weslecker and Mateo. I had not addressed the issue weighing heavily between the three of us. No wonder Mateo had been so stiff, and Weslecker had seemed off as well.

I have to talk to them. It's my fault…

THE BLAST of a horn woke me at daybreak. Soldiers, sailors, and squires swarmed over the camp with military efficiency. Cherin waited at the outskirts of the squire puddle, yanking me away from the worst of the scramble by telling me where in the gryphon's field the strike teams were meeting.

Thirty of us in total, we stood apart from the flights organizing in neat blocks with our pyrojacks filtering in slowly. Father stood apart as our Flight Commander. Looking around, I noted the other strike teams were half squires. Weslecker nodded in my direction from Strike Team One next to Ironfeather, who yawned hugely.

"Good morning, strike teams," Father said. "In a few short days, the might of the Altarian fleet will carry our army north to the island of Inisthwaite, which will become our foothold in the region if we can successfully take it. We are particularly vulnerable during this ocean crossing. The Rathi still have seven healthy eldrafn and the advantage of fighting on their home soil the moment we make landfall. We have the enviable job of keeping our ships safe.

"The crossing will take us two days. Command wants the strike teams to save their fire in the first twenty-four hours. We will be burning enemy ships if they approach during that time, but we will not go picking fights until our pyrojacks can light up their island directly. Unless our supporting flights are decimated by eldrafn lightning, we are not to engage any eldrafn directly, nor is anyone to sacrifice themselves to become a hero."

I felt his gaze on me for a few seconds before he continued, "Is that understood?"

"Yes, sir!"

He shared some welcome news as well. Each vessel would be carrying multiple Tulari of all three specialties. Presumably, some of them would be fully trained, but more importantly, they'd be able to combine their power and protect the ships as well. They would be taking over casting the shields to protect us from eldrafn lightning if we needed them. Fresh supplies of alchemical bombs, much like the ones Zizi had snuck into our first battle, were distributed to our pyrojacks.

"Pack your things. We begin boarding as soon as everyone has had a quick breakfast," Father said. I blinked in shock. We were moving out that fast?

"Fast is relative," Ari said.

I was glad my things were still mostly packed. We waited next to our things for breakfast as the troops were fed first and shown to their ships. The gryphons would land on deck after the troops boarded and each strike team would cover a different third of the fleet.

Not everyone was going, but it sounded like the bulk of our forces would be moving. There were no second chances if the Rathi decided to decimate us with all seven of their eldrafn at the same time.

"Light red for the Duchess," Sharde was saying to Puzzle-box, who watched him attentively.

"Um, green for the Earl," Biggs pitched in. The rest of my flight thought for a moment.

"You guys know the color of the eldrafns?" I asked.

"We were briefed on it once," Biggs said, pointing at Weslecker. "This guy took notes."

The nobleman released a long-suffering sigh. "If you would just write it down too, you'd stop asking me," he muttered. After some digging in his saddlebag, he produced a notebook and rattled off a list of colors.

I went rigid at the end. "Wait, what color did you say the King was?"

He checked his notes again. "Black clouds, silver lightning."

"That's the one we've dreamed about," I said privately to Ari.

"Figures it would be the biggest one," he groused. *"I, for one, am quite pleased the Mother has stopped plaguing us with death every night."*

Life must come from death. The former is my concern, but the latter is yours, she'd said. I felt like I was so close to figuring out the missing piece of information the goddess was withholding.

"Yeah, yeah. More cryptic hints. We'll figure it out when we need to know it," Ari said, reading my thoughts.

As a cold breakfast was finally distributed to us, I made my way to Weslecker's side. "Can we talk? Privately?" I asked quietly.

He looked down at me with the kind of forbidding frown I hadn't seen him make since before we got to know each other. "Hard to find privacy in a military camp," he replied.

"Oh, okay." I shifted uncertainly.

That was as clear a sign as any that he knew what I was going to try to talk about and didn't want to hear it. Most wise girls would try again some other time.

"I just noticed that you seem angry at a certain someone else—"

His responding expression was as brittle as I'd ever seen it, like each word caused him pain. It wasn't the practiced nobleman mask he could put on like he was preparing for a masquerade. I cut myself off abruptly, seeing that it was a mistake to stir this particular pot. "Look, Sivana, that's between him and me. He made me a promise." Weslecker gritted his teeth. "The prince that's always first, that always gets what he wants, said he'd step aside in one case for me. And he hasn't, and I called him out on it. That's all."

"That's all?" I echoed.

"That's all. Let it go until we help get the fleet safely into the Rathi Islands—I don't want to be distracted." He turned his full attention to the plate of food in his lap, as good as dismissing me. I turned my gaze toward Ironfeather, who hid his face under his wing so we couldn't make eye contact.

I barely tasted my own food before volunteering for caretaker duty to get myself away from the restless energy around the squire puddle.

"Gods, I really did make them fight," I said to Ari as I tried to lose myself to grooming out knots and checking over other riders' beasts for any last-minute needs.

"Technically, that's not what he said."

"Sure seemed like it to me," I said with a sigh.

He touched our Link with some humor, trying to bring me some lightheartedness. *"Maybe not everything relates back to you,"* he replied.

"I'd agree if it weren't for Ironfeather." The gryphon had clearly not wanted to get involved.

Ari clicked his beak and shook his head in his best imitation of a human. *"He has a point, though. We have an ocean to cross and a fleet to protect. It might not matter in a couple days."*

He looked up, hearing Ellie approaching before I did. "Hi, Sivana. Noah said you wanted to talk?"

It was so nice to see her at this particular moment. "You have perfect timing. I was hoping you could put your thinker to another problem. I tried to fix it myself, but I didn't do a great job."

With no one around but the gryphons, I felt comfortable enough to show her the eldrafn egg hidden in Ari's saddlebags and the pouch that clicked into place on his saddle. She had dozens of questions about how the eldrafn egg worked and also recognized the copper as a lightning rod on sight.

"You're sure you saw electricity curving around your body to hit the rod instead?" she prompted.

"Yes. It took most of an eldrafn's strike and left Ari and me unharmed," I confirmed.

"If you don't mind me shortening your prototype's straps, I think there's an easy fix," she said with a smile. "By the way —no one knows about this?"

"A very small number. Most everyone here would smash it if they knew, but it's Instructor Signe's egg," I told her.

I ended up telling her the whole story of Revna for the rest of her hour-long break and let her return to her engineering duties with the empty sling in hand while I placed the egg back in the saddlebag for safekeeping.

Once we finally set off from Daramaine, we had twenty-four hours of peace, like command thought. My strike team floated along with the left flank of the fleet, jumping to motion the moment the horizon darkened with an unexpected storm.

Lightning laced the clouds, and I narrowed my eyes. Light red? The Duchess roared and spread its massive wings wide with a display of pink electricity shot through them like veins. The color didn't diminish the fact that it was twice the Earl's size and providing cover for the entire raiding party rowing out to meet us.

I grabbed Zizi's sweltering hands as soon as I had her calves laced into a riding harness on Ari's back. "Promise me you won't push yourself too hard," I said. She'd banked plenty of fire magic by this point, her eyes glowing back at me a flickering orange.

"My magic hurts me from the moment I start using it. You know I can't promise that." She practically laughed.

I wet my lips. I was no expert in Tulari, especially not the unstable variety, but I had noticed her personality shifting with the ebb and flow of magic she had stored within her. "No, that's your magic talking," I said with forced patience. Her expression shifted in surprise. "Don't push yourself too hard. Nothing but a wand can stop you from burning yourself, but you can hold back enough so you don't pass out in the saddle again."

"I have to give it my all," she said.

"And you'll give everything you have if you end up slipping out of the riding harness and to your certain death in the ocean," I replied firmly.

Shifting to a big grin, she slung an arm around me and into an awkward hug. "Aww, you really care about me! Walker and Zaveri, the most skilled pair on Strike Team Three!"

"Don't forget about me," Ari said.

"Ari, Walker, and Zaveri, the most skilled team," I amended for him.

"That's the spirit!" she exclaimed.

Sighing, I climbed into the saddle and led Ari up to the top deck. A team of Tulari had arranged themselves into a miniature gauntlet that we passed through. First came a pair of wizard apprentices who waved their wands, casting one bubble-like shield, and then another over us. "Is this the same spell you used to protect us?" I asked Zizi, watching the magic fade to transparency.

"Yes, exactly the same. It's one of those generic spells that any Tulari mage can cast, and it's not meant to be layered more than once," she told me.

A fully invested wizard in a fraying sapphire-blue robe started sketching a more complicated spell in the air with his wand. "This isn't a generic one," he said.

Zizi hummed, "Oh, that's smart." And I turned in the saddle to see that she seemed to be reading the spell as each rune hovered there like the page of a book being written right before us. "What do we have acting as a lightning arrester?"

The wizard finished his spell and dabbed the point of his wand toward our faces before turning his head up toward the mast. "The magically reinforced lightning rod up top. Consider this your home ship—as long as you're close to it and this spell is active, any lightning will slide right past you and into the rod instead, which will dissipate even an eldrafn's strike into harmless particles. This is still experimental technology, but it was designed by our best wizard crafters. The spell shields are in place for your bombing runs, for anything a volta might throw at you, or if you're caught outside of the range of your home ship by an eldrafn."

"What is the range we're aiming for?" I asked.

His lips pressed together. "Like I said, it's experimental. Early tests show it has an effective radius of twenty yards."

Zizi and I spoke at the same time. I muttered, "That's not very much."

And she exclaimed, "Oh, that's plenty of space!"

We exchanged a glance, and I pointed upward. "That means we can't be more than twenty yards away from the ship in any direction if we want any lightning to go into the rod, according to this new spell."

I thanked the wizard and moved on, grateful for the spell anyway. Ellie was still tinkering with the way I would take Revna's egg into battle secretly, so we needed this extra protection.

Waiting for us next was a healer holding a staff. When she raised it, runes started drawing themselves while she held an expression of heavy concentration. I knew little about Tulari, but the presence of her staff meant something important for the way she used her magic. Once the spell kicked in, I noticed right away too, as it was like she'd taken the magical shields around us and stuffed them full of cotton.

"Muffling enchantment. Move along now." Her voice was distant, but the impatient gesture she made was crystal clear.

"Thank the gods. I didn't want to lose my hearing," I said.

"Hey, I can still hear you just fine, too. We'll communicate better in the air!" Zizi was clearer than ever, like her voice was trapped in the insulation protecting our ears. I was thankful she didn't see the face I pulled. It would be great to talk to her, as long as she didn't distract me with a constant stream of words or, worse, the manic laughter that took over when she was wrist-deep in fire magic.

Our strike team was forming up at the front of the deck. Cherin, Howl, and Devos had already passed the gauntlet and formed the base of our V-formation. My mentor gestured for me to take the back left position behind Howl.

"When did they find you a pyrojack?" I asked Fog. Not only a pyrojack, but one well past apprentice age, though he wore plain clothes rather than an ostentatious robe.

The gryphon projected a feeling akin to a shrug. *"He volunteered, apparently."*

When Cyclone and Icestorm finished our element's formation, I saw that he, too, had a pyrojack, a woman with the beginnings of wrinkles and gray hair hunkered down and quivering like a frightened mouse. I wondered if she "volunteered" too.

Tempest reached out mentally to share instructions from Cherin. *"All right, team. Our orders are to hold our fire until all available flights begin distracting the Duchess. Aim your bombs at the front or back of each Rathi vessel. Our goal is to sink the enemy before they can board our ships. From there, this battle will be decided by endurance. You should have two shields, a muffling spell, and a spell that will redirect lightning if you're close enough to this ship. Should even one of these fail, you are to retreat to have the spell cast upon you again. Understood?"*

"Yes, sir," Ari and I responded together.

I was starting to share the gist of what he'd said aloud to Zizi when I suddenly heard shouts, even through the muffling spell. Ari raised his head, turning to the left with a growl that vibrated through the barrel of his chest. Soldiers and sailors pointed and screamed as a shadow swooped overhead—a second, smaller eldrafn dropping bolts of lightning and a stinging sideways rain from its storm cloud wings.

CHAPTER 18

WISH UPON A COMET

AN ORANGE-TINGED LIGHTNING strike hit the magic-infused rod atop our ship's main sail. Motes and sparks in the same shade erupted up and down the mast in a stunning display of magic that dissipated harmlessly, as promised.

"Get in the air now!" Tempest ordered. Our element shot into the sky, forming up alongside the other team of five led by Father and Valtora. Father turned toward Cherin, and they made a few hand signals before leading the elements in opposite directions.

The Duchess eldrafn seemed to ignore the gryphon riders trying to swarm around it, keeping them at bay with showers of electricity. The Rathi fleet was spread in a wide arc, and each ship sparked with flashes of light from the fingertips of fully charged volta.

"Change in plan. This storm's not budging, but we still have our orders. We will drop our bombs low and fast to disable as many ships as we can," Tempest said.

"Yes, sir." Only Ari responded this time, while I gulped a swallow. We would be within sniping range of their archers with each pass.

"How many bombs do you have?" I called back to Zizi.

"Ten!"

Ten passes, then. Since her alchemical bombs had been confiscated, the military had redistributed the same number of weapons to each rider-pyrojack team. It didn't seem like much, but it was the best we could do until the Duchess stopped hovering its storm directly overhead. I tightened my flight goggles as we entered the worst part of the storm. Angry wind lashed cold talons over us as we were instantly drenched.

Each flap of Ari's wings sent wet arcs off his waterproof feathers. He made the soft croak that signaled he was lost in the air, our Link sharing that he was unpleasantly muffled with rain getting into his face. I guided him carefully, using the reins and signals from my knees and heels to keep us in line with the rest of our element, though all of our gryphons struggled from the onslaught of weather under the eldrafn's wings.

Tempest had us feint a dive over a few of the ships, so they wasted some of their ammunition before our first real bombing run.

"Not enough fire," Zizi muttered as our alchemical bomb exploded toward the middle of our target. Three muted booms joined ours, while the last sent up a splash from the ocean.

For once, I agreed with her. If our weapons weren't alchemy, they'd have no effect at all under this downpour. We circled back out of the storm, and Ari shook his torso with a relieved chirrup, scattering the worst of the rain out of his sodden pelt.

Water dripped over the lenses of my goggles as I turned toward our distant ships and the orange-laced eldrafn swooping over them. I recognized the color of the Mage, one of the smallest eldrafn in the Rathi coalition. With it flying as quick as it was, the fluff of its storm clouds whisked away to reveal the outline of the bird underneath and the thrumming tangerine core that was its heart.

As I watched, the teams of gryphon riders chasing it peeled off, and a beacon lit from the Altarian flagship. Zizi made a choked gasp, and I saw her clutch at her flight leathers behind me. "It's her. She's here," she whispered.

"Are you okay?" I demanded.

"Yeah, yeah. Just fine and never better…"

A massive ball of fire leapt from the deck of our flagship. My mouth dropped open as it streaked across the sky like a comet. Was that the work of a pyrojack?

It flashed past the orange eldrafn's wing, scattering its clouds with a curl of smoke. It might've been meant to explode, if not for the storm it'd passed through. The Mage flapped with a hole in its wing before the rest of its form swarmed in to patch it.

My element pivoted toward the Rathi fleet, and as we braced for another pass through the storm, I had a realization. "You know the Tulari who cast that spell."

"Yeah, she's one of the Heroes of Altare," she replied with clipped bitterness.

I had to focus on flying for our next pass, my hold on the reins tightening as one bolt after another from the volta below hammered at our magical shield. The two enchantments held together but surrounded us with fractals as they cracked dramatically.

"*Captain Cherin, we're hit. Shield's about to break,*" I reported directly to Tempest.

"*Roger that. Return to our home ship with Cyclone for repair.*"

When we circled out of the storm for a reprieve, I peeled off and followed off Icestorm's wing back toward the Altarian fleet. While the Duchess eldrafn seemed unbothered by us still, the Mage struggled to approach our ships between dodging and striking at the gryphon riders swarming it and avoiding another comet streaking up from the flagship like a shooting star.

Icestorm reached out to me as Captain Cyclone made hand gestures from his saddle. *"We need to wait for an opening. The small eldrafn's movements are too chaotic,"* the gryphon said.

I nodded and flashed a thumbs-up in return. We circled and watched the battle unfold, the ships drifting toward each other in what felt like slow motion as the sky buzzed with activity. Another fiery aura lit up the flagship, and I watched with bated breath as the distant Hero of Altare waited for the harried Mage to approach.

The comet flew. "C'mon," I said under my breath. It soared over the flagship in an arc, through the Mage's cloud-formed body, and exploded next to its thumping heart. Its wings flared up, and the heart's glow intensified until it became as bright as a mini sun before detonating.

Ari anticipated the wave of hot air rolling over us, even from here, spreading his wings to soar on the current rather than getting dashed around again. I cheered as the flight protecting our fleet wheeled around to join the fight against the Duchess.

"Five wonders. I can't believe it," I thought I heard Zizi mutter.

Boom! The pink eldrafn's beak was wide open in a furious crash of thunder. It shook the remains of our shield, scattering loose pieces into thin air. Swooping ahead of its ships, it met the extra flight midway to trap them in a storm of rain and a hail of sparks.

"Wait," I called to Icestorm when he tilted his wings toward the fleet. I pointed back behind us, shocked to see the Rathi breaking ranks. *"They're retreating!"*

"Only some. Come, we have to get our shields repaired," he answered.

One in four of their ships were beginning to turn around and row away in coordinated sweeps of their oars. I followed

Icestorm to a hurried landing on our home ship, where the same team of Tulari were waiting with wands and staff at the ready. The main mast seemed charred, but my thoughts were elsewhere as we received a quick repair of our shields and took to the air again.

"Why did part of their navy retreat?" I asked. *"I thought Rathi saw all fights to their bitter end."*

"Are you really complaining now?" Icestorm countered, incredulous.

"It's just not what Instructor Signe taught me."

He didn't respond for a few minutes while we raced toward where we'd left the rest of our element. *"My rider wants to remind you that the Rathi are a coalition, not a country with a proper military. It's possible the village that owned the orange eldrafn also mans those retreating ships."*

"Oh gods. They just watched their might vanish," I said mostly to myself. Signe *had* taught us that eldrafn shifted the balance of power between tribes.

"Don't go feeling sorry for the enemy. Their loss is our gain." Icestorm sounded about as ruthless as his rider, Cyclone. There was a reason they'd climbed the ranks to the First so quickly.

Ari sent out a mental call to Tempest and the rest of our element. We met up over the ocean, only two riders circling while Devos and his gryphon also returned to our fleet for another shield. Tempest shared the plan, and I turned in the saddle toward Zizi. For once, she was still, staring off over my shoulder with molten orange eyes and a downcast expression.

"Hey, buck up," I said, patting her knee. "Our orders are to drop as much fire as possible on their exposed flank while the Duchess is distracted."

Her smile was slow to grow to its usual toothy edge. "Oh yeah? Now you're speaking my language."

THE ALTARIAN NAVY did not stop to fight the Rathi, though some cannon shots were exchanged, and ships were boarded by angry raiders. We kept going to our original target of the main trade island, Inisthwaite, where during peace time, the Rathi traded their furs and uniquely crafted weapons for good Altarian grain and nonperishables to survive the brutal northern winter.

Now, our soldiers and sailors were greeted by those weapons up front and personal while the gryphon riders continued to skirmish with the Duchess. The strike teams joined in to give the main flights relief once we rammed our way past the Rathi navy. Zizi made a few attempts to shoot at the Duchess's heart with her fireballs, but she was not able to reach the same size and force as the Hero of Altare's comets from earlier.

Thus began the most grueling slog where days blurred together after we made landfall. Our element traded shifts with an element in the Third to ensure we had time to rest and recover, as short and tense as those times felt. I slept with one eye open, feeling like I should still be in the air even though I was aching and saddle sore and, over our Link, could feel how exertion was making Ari's old wing injuries ache, especially where the left one had been broken.

While we physically *couldn't* skirmish around the clock, we were in the air more times than not with a full array of spells protecting us from volta and eldrafn alike. Zizi was with us off and on as well, but this time, we were tasked with burning out the Rathi from the dry, thorny underbrush on the island. There were more shrubs than trees, but it still felt like our enemy was hiding behind every corner and under every bush.

"There's going to be nothing left at this rate," I

commented to Zizi as we circled around the thick oblong island.

The sky nipped at our faces with chill autumn air, but below us, huge and blackened patches of earth failed to show the changing of seasons. All of the homes that clustered behind the trade district were now burnt-out skeletons. We'd found them that way, put to the torch by the Rathi before we arrived. If any were left intact, we'd quickly taken care of them.

"Let's just burn the rest and get it over with," Zizi replied. I shot her a look over my shoulder, and she put her hands up. "*Totally* kidding. I totally don't want to be the one to turn the rest of the island into a burned ruin."

Except out of the corner of my eye, Zizi definitely dropped a pinch of sparks toward a yellowing patch of grass and muffled a giggle.

She was running lower on magic this afternoon, only her Tulari mark glowing with an outline of orange fire. This was her most reasonable, I'd learned, a period of stability and clarity with less of a destructive influence from her magic. When her eyes glowed orange and her teeth were bared in a big grin, her priorities would change. She'd raze the whole island if she could.

The best news I had was that I noticed Zizi keeping herself on the knife's edge of that control, only her mark glowing most times we had a shift together—her cackling reduced to fits of giggles, her desire for mayhem a handful of sparks that flickered out of existence upon contact with the air.

The bad news came with my other shifts, where we matched wits against the Duchess. It was of such a considerable size that it made taking the island a miserable, muddy experience for the Altarian troops when it hung overhead, and gryphon riders could barely budge it. It traded off with a unique eldrafn with dove-gray storm clouds and white lightning, appropriately named the Priestess, another mid-sized beast like the Earl.

I knew from World Cultures that eldrafn had to rest and recharge; otherwise, they'd blow themselves away like real storms, dissipating into nothing. So, we fought either the Duchess or the Priestess as they worked in shifts as well.

We didn't kill them, either. The Priestess's rider had considerable aerial skills, which killed more riders than allowed them close enough to pierce its ivory heart. And the Duchess, I feared, was untouchable. They flew further into the Rathi Islands when we took Inisthwaite, but the fear remained in my heart.

I knew they'd be back. And I knew the Rathi still had an eldrafn larger and stronger than them.

CHAPTER 19

TWIN TERRORS

Once we finally took Inisthwaite, it quickly became apparent that it wasn't big enough to host the entire northern Altarian army. But for a single evening, we turned it into a city of tents and crowded around too-small fires while constant gusts of cold, salty breezes rolled over our encampment.

The camp manager had given us a tiny plot of blackened land for the squire puddle; alongside our gryphons, we made three layers around the fire. No one complained. Not when we had an army chef preparing a warm meal in front of us and the gryphons dozing off with bellies full of freshly caught fish. I was stuck in the third ring, furthest away from the fire. Ari slept cuddled to my right hip, while to my left, Sharde was just settling his arm around Ellie's shoulders and murmuring something that drew out her tired laugh.

Loneliness stung like a biting beetle in the dark. Ordinarily in downtime, I was either surrounded by friendly gryphons or my Academy flight-mates, our time marked by masculine laughter and the play wrestling they always seemed to get into. Even Zizi had found another fire to sit by, probably the biggest one in Inisthwaite.

There were only two men I wanted to talk to right now. Weslecker was a couple yards away, stacking burned bits and pebbles into towers and pyramids while firelight cast sinister red lines across his face. I would have to muster my nerve to approach him after we'd left things off. In the meantime, Mateo was also on the outer ring, quietly combing Mireille's fur.

I took in Ari's sleeping face, imagining what he'd say if he heard my thoughts right now. Maybe he'd remind me that wild gryphon females had multiple mates if they wanted them.

I thought of my sister, who'd been sure my heart was already leaning in one decisive direction.

Why am I relying on others to guide me? I asked myself. Neither Rissa nor Ari could make a decision for me, and yet here I was, delaying, wavering between two young men. Letting what could be unravel at the corners.

That's not fair, though. I'd spent two years being told not to tempt or be tempted by the men around me. Ari's very life had hung on my job as a cadet, and anything other than a model performance was inadequate.

It wasn't so serious that it should bring any level of misery upon the three of us. And like Ari had said, maybe the two of them hadn't argued about me in the first place. Swallowing my nerve, I stood and stepped around people and gryphons until I knelt next to Mireille, rubbing her ears and getting a sleepy nuzzle in reply.

"Nice flying today," I blurted to Mateo.

"Oh, you're here," he said at the same time.

I pulled back with an uncertain laugh. "I've been here since the tents…"

And again, at the same time, he answered, "Thanks, you and Ari as…" He laughed and shook his head. "Nice to see you."

Then he smiled at me, and my belly had that wobbly

feeling like it lived for the moment Mateo let down his guard and let me see past his stoic princely facade. He scooted back further into the shadows of the camp and patted the space next to him.

"Is everything all right?" he asked in a hush.

I bobbed my head. "I've prepared for it every night, but no one's tried to break into my tent, and there's been no word from your brother after he spoke the Gatekeeper's name."

His lips pinched. "I still can't believe he did that to you. Well, he's sent me a few letters."

"Oh?" I shivered from a sudden chill, and it wasn't just because of the cold.

"He invited me to leave the Storm Front and come see him as soon as I can. He's rather insistent, in fact." He frowned down at his hands where they hung between his knees. "I think I should go."

"But—"

"I know it could be a trap. But what if it isn't? What if he thinks he can bring me to his side and divulges something important? Without Odalis spying on him, we have no idea what he's planning anymore."

I gestured around us. "He got his martyr and his war."

"But there has to be *more*. I have to know what it is and how I can save our people from a winter war in the Rathi Islands." He put his hand over mine. "I'll go to help protect you, too."

I didn't expect how nice it would feel to have his warmth pressed to my icy skin. My heart jumped from the contact. "Mateo, I…if you do go see him, be careful."

"Always." He gave my hand a squeeze, his fingertips drifting a feather light touch up my arm as he pulled away. We were both holding our breath.

He blew out a sigh. "Maybe there's something else we should talk about."

"What?" Fear ran little fingers down my insides. For all

my daring in the air with Ari, I must be a coward on my own two legs, because I would've rather been deep in aerial combat rather than sitting down for a serious discussion of feelings.

He scooted a little closer. "Maybe not with words. I just want to know what it feels like." With that, he leaned in and pressed a kiss to my lips. No warning, just a gentle slide of soft skin. My eyes closed, and I leaned in just a touch. I knew what he meant, what he was looking for—did we fit together? Was it worth it to pursue any sort of relationship when we both knew it would be challenged and torn down by our peers and his father?

We parted with our answer and a flash of his smile. "I'll see you later, Sivana," he said, getting up and nudging Mireille until she trotted after him with a great yawn.

I touched a couple fingertips to my lips, which still tingled. A huge sense of relief swept some weight off my shoulders, because I had my answer at last with one quick action. I didn't have to worry about making the right choice anymore when there was only one man I was ready to pursue.

The sensation of eyes on me had me glancing up and meeting another person's gaze across the squire puddle. Brows set low, Weslecker stared in my direction. He shook his head and flattened one of his pebble pyramids with a jerk of his hand.

He'd seen Mateo kiss me; there was no other possibility. For the second time, it felt like he'd caught me with Mateo and shown angry disapproval. I felt small and dirty in that moment, even though he didn't know what'd really just passed between Mateo and me.

The flicker of disappointment on Mateo's face before he smiled at me. He knew it.

I knew it too, confirming that, deep inside, I'd already been leaning in the direction I thought was best. There was no spark there, no passion about to leap into an inferno between myself and Weslecker's best friend. I couldn't pick Mateo when Weslecker had always been so kind and patient with me.

But all Weslecker saw was the kiss. *Gods.* He had to be thinking the worst of both of us right now. As dinner was called for the squires, I looked for him in the line, wanting to set things to rights, but it seemed he'd grabbed his bowl and disappeared. I poked at my own meal halfheartedly. Maybe it was for the best that we didn't chat while he was worked up.

Maybe I'd get a chance to tell him how I felt if we survived the next battle Altare sailed toward tomorrow.

I woke up cold and stiff despite sharing a tent with a pyrojack. Word circled the camp about how the cold infiltrated even the most secure tents and leeched comfort from every bedroll.

Morale was low, which was why I think a meeting was called for all present in the camp, from the chefs to the leaders organizing our war strategies. A makeshift stage was erected from empty cargo crates, and on them stood three men and a woman, Heroes of Altare all. I'd only seen their features in stone, as the legendary figures we studied in fundamental school. For once, I felt like Zizi, filled with fizzy excitement even pressed shoulder-to-shoulder with the soldiers around me to be within shouting distance of four of Altare's proven heroes.

I glanced over my shoulder, where Zizi stood staring fiery daggers up at the stage. If looks could kill, hers would have set an unfortunate victim into a conflagration. I made a mental note to ask what had happened to get her so worked up when we had more privacy.

The group hushed as one of the men raised his arms overhead. "Brave soldiers of Altare! Know no fear as we sail to the next island, Manarfell, and claim a proper foothold in the Rathi Islands."

From the murmuring of the soldiers around me, I caught the name "Magnus" being passed around. One of the oldest living Heroes of Altare, Magnus the Grim was one of the people I'd seen immortalized in the vast hall in Kaiamear's palace. I'd sat at the feet of his granite likeness, inspecting the dog-like creatures carved to obediently sit by his sides.

Magnus was a berserker, marked at birth on his back by the God of War, Anrathor, blessed and cursed with a beastly form of rage and mindless bloodthirst. He was also one of the only berserkers who'd tamed two battle beasts to fight alongside him.

They were the bulky dogs sitting at attention on stage, their crimson eyes glaring into the crowd and their heads on line with his elbows. Lengthy fangs dripped the occasional sizzling droplet of drool, and spikes protruded down the line of their backs, currently laid flat with their relaxed hackles.

As fascinated as I'd been with the gods' blessed beasts as a kid, I'd always ranked battle beasts as the scariest, above even the extinct dragons. Even a nightbloom, feared by a Mercy's side, existed to take a soul into the afterlife, but a battle beast would deliver it there violently.

When Linked with a berserker, they became hulks alongside their master when he or she gave in to the battle rage. Fire would leap from their mouth, along their spine, and the blazing pads of their paws. Magnus's battle beasts were at least forty years old, though, and showing signs of age in the graying of their brown muzzles and yellowed fangs.

Magnus himself had thin salt-and-pepper hair, but that hadn't stopped him from maintaining the berserker physique. He was a barrel of a man wearing expensive plate armor, with a deep, booming voice that carried over all of us without the aid a magical device. With a meaty hand, he gestured to the woman and led us in applause for the death of the Mage eldrafn. Soldiers shouted and whistled over the clapping from all of us.

I caught her name, Irene the Fair, and envied her stylish robes of midnight blue with silvery flames stitched into the sleeves. It was cut with slits up to her hips to show the dark pants she wore underneath with fur trimmings. She held a staff nearly as tall as she was. Metal talons at the top of it clutched a rune-etched orb that glowed with an inner red-orange fire.

All four Heroes of Altare had a short speech for us, and word through the crowd confirmed they were all decorated war heroes. Irene was the only one I hadn't known about beforehand, a recent addition to the roster with her rare and powerful grasp on two different forms of magic. She was dual-blessed, both a wizard and a pyrojack. We'd all seen the magical comets she could produce with that staff.

While she shared a word with us, I snuck another glance at Zizi, who watched her with naked hatred. Her curved Lithosian features were pulled back in a sneer, and flames raged white-hot in the brown depths of her gaze.

There was some history there, but I'd need to wait to hear it. When we were dismissed to our flights, I lined up with Strike Team Three and ordered to unpack my lance. The thirty gryphon riders of the three strike teams were amassing into one flight for the crossing. Our goal: to take down both eldrafn sighted waiting for us along our planned travel route. The troops had begun calling these two eldrafn the Twin Terrors, amongst other less flattering names from the two feminine titles.

"They know what we're planning," I said to myself. Doubt wormed its way through my belly. Was it the crown prince's doing? Odalis thought she'd overheard him sharing battle plans and strategies with the Rathi. Had enough time passed that he'd lost contact with the enemy, or was he passing the information along still, sabotaging us from the back?

My unease didn't fade even when Ellie found me with a new prototype sling to take the eldrafn egg into the air. Instead of clipping to the saddle, she'd shortened the straps to wrap around my wrist and finished final adjustments with it weighing down my arm. "So you can hide it behind your shield, since it's made of wood," she said cheerfully. "Just don't put it on your other wrist, where you hold a metal weapon!"

I thanked her and nodded to myself. It'd be much harder to spot the egg now. This innovation might just save lives—it was a wild card even Isaac wouldn't know about, if he was still helping the Rathi fight us.

We boarded and set sail for Manarfell while leaving behind a portion of the army to maintain hold on the ground we'd already claimed. By afternoon, the Priestess and the Duchess descended together without aid from any Rathi ships, raining destruction on the Altarian fleet and the defensive shields our many mages struggled to maintain.

Our leadership needed a few minutes to formulate a new strategy on the fly for fighting two eldrafn at the same time. Eventually, Valtora reached out for Father, saying, *"We are an extra line of defense in fending off the Priestess."* The cobbled-together flight flew in a V-formation with them in the lead. The other flights split in two directions, coordinating assaults on the massive Duchess and the nimble Priestess, with more gryphons going to attack the former.

The latter pulled back from the fleet to engage us in a deadly aerial ballet that proved that eldrafn lightning could strike the same place twice. It seemed its rider had realized we were all shielded, so each bolt of lightning was followed up by another aimed at the same gryphon rider, with a third on its way if they were still in range.

Ari and I splintered off into our element with Tempest and Cherin picking when we would engage. More reckless riders from the other flights charged in first, engaging the Priestess's until we discovered its strategy.

"We need to get in there," I said to Ari, thinking of our eldrafn egg now hiding behind the curves of my kite shield. It was heavy and awkward there, but if we could just disrupt the pattern of lightning strikes, perhaps we'd catch the Priestess off guard. It only took one strike to the heart to end the creature's life, after all.

Ari hesitated to agree, saying, *"If we are always there when an eldrafn dies, it'll be harder to hide that we have extra help. Besides, look at how it's moving."*

I was, which meant he was too. I quietly admired how the sky terror moved like it was a fraction of its size and strength, smoothly rolling away from any rider who got close enough to try striking its heart. It bent and turned its wings to pelt assailants with heavy rain in the crucial moments before a strike to its heart, using all of its advantages.

If the Earl had this kind of talent, Ari and I would've been dead with our stunt to distract it. It was clear, at least from this distance, that there was an ability gap between the riders and eldrafn each Rathi village had lent to fighting us.

"Prepare yourselves," Valtora sent. Father's element charged first, lances out.

Tempest reached out a moment later to count down the seconds before we followed suit. *"Starburst formation. Go."*

Ari and I swung wide, coming at the Priestess more toward the side than straight ahead like Cherin. The creature roared and flashed lightning at Tempest, two quick strikes that had his shield shattering and smoke rising from his form.

"No!" I exclaimed.

Ari tugged urgently on our Link for me to turn back to the eldrafn before he lost control of his trajectory. We swung in an arc toward the heart beating like a white sun within its light gray chest before its almond-shaped eyes turned our way. It made the inhaling sound that promised a lightning strike, and I raised my kite shield.

The first flash fractured the two magical shields layered over Ari and me beyond repair. There was no time to panic before the second bolt struck and light redirected around the kite shield and into Revna's egg.

The Priestess pivoted hard to keep us from a clean lunge that would have my lance piercing its heart. Gryphons shouted all around me, demanding we retreat, while I made eye contact with the woman seated amongst the fluffy clouds of the enemy eldrafn's back.

Snowy braids and brightly dyed scarfs flapped behind her in the breeze. From a distance, her eyes were narrowed to slits and her voice a distant shout of guttural Rathi. The hand gestures she made were clear, though, before the Priestess roared and shot another blast of lightning, which arched around Ari in a blinding burst of light and also got absorbed into the secret egg.

As we peeled off rapidly from there, I swear I heard the Rathi woman shout, "Thief!" after us. So, she knew how we'd survived her attack. Hopefully no one else would ask questions about how we'd withstood a lightning strike with our shields down.

"We should have an explanation ready," Ari murmured.

A gryphon peeled off to come in line with our wings, and my adrenaline-filled heart gave a jump when I instantly recognized Ironfeather and Weslecker leaning toward me, already making simple hand gestures to ask if we were all right.

"Are you okay?" Ironfeather burst out at the same time, sounding panicked.

"We're fine," I promised. I wondered if they'd retreated with full shields to check on us, feeling warm even if their priority had to be fighting the eldrafn.

Weslecker held up three fingers. *"But you took three light-ning strikes!"* Ironfeather exclaimed.

"I promise, we're okay," I said. Hesitation stole over me for a moment before I added. *"Can we talk?"*

There was a pause between the two of them as well. We circled in the safe zone between the two eldrafn fights since the Duchess currently battled above our home ship, pink-tinged lightning flung all around it.

"Acton doesn't want to talk about what he thinks you want to talk about," Ironfeather told me in a lower voice.

"Can you just tell him I'm sorry, then? And that what he saw wasn't what it looked like?" I hoped it would help to hear it from his beloved gryphon. *"I want to talk when he's ready."*

The silence dragged on between us, and we swooped in different directions when the Duchess moved away from the fleet, chasing an element of gryphon riders. Ari touched down, and we had new shields within fifteen minutes, but it felt like I was counting each moment like Ironfeather would reach back out at any second.

He didn't. We returned to the flight with the Priestess in our separate elements, and my mind was occupied by the battle orders from Tempest and Valtora. Well, at least I'd gotten a whisper in his ear and a sign that he still cared, even if he was justifiably angry with me.

In the meantime, I focused on staying alive. The Priestess or its rider seemed hellsbent on killing me any time they noticed I was amongst the gryphon riders again. They shat-tered my magical shields five times before nightfall, and it felt like targeted umbrage. The fighting slowed after dark, until both of the Twin Terrors retreated in the direction we were going to rest and recharge.

Ari gave a relieved sigh when we landed and flexed his aching wing. *"By Glorium, I'm getting old, aren't I?"*

I was about to tease him for replacing the generic "gods" we swore to with the demigod's name when the horizon rumbled with an ominous roll of thunder. Heads turned as a pitch-black eldrafn blocked out the moon's wan light, illuminating its vast wingspan with a lattice of fine silver lightning instead.

"By Glorium," I breathed. "It's the King."

HONOR DUEL

A HEAVILY ACCENTED voice rolled over us in the darkness of the night and the King above us. "Invaders! Halt your advance and listen! The chieftain of the Bloodrapids Clan challenges your strongest warrior to an honor duel."

Murmurs broke out amongst the soldiers and Tulari on deck around me. "An honor duel?"

"What's that?"

Signe had recounted a famous honor duel in one of the many sagas she'd taught us. Two people fought to the death in an honor duel, each representing whole armies or villages. The duel I was recalling had a major bet on the line.

"The honored chieftain offers control of Manarfell if your champion wins," the voice continued. "Send a champion and an equivalent wager by boat at dawn tomorrow. If your ships continue to approach or you fail to reply by daybreak, our greatest eldrafn will turn you all into shark food. Sleep well, invaders."

"Gods, I don't think the King is leaving," I murmured to Ari, looking up. The darkness seemed impenetrable, but at least it wasn't releasing rain and lightning down on us.

Flashes of light came from the flagship, and the sailors

responded to it. We dropped anchor as, I assumed, our leadership discussed what to do next. Lanterns moved around on our deck, and Father approached with one clasped in his hand. I snapped into my best salute, but I was secretly hoping he wasn't about to tell us to get back in the air.

"Go get some rest, kiddo," he said, clapping me on the shoulder. "I'm going to fly over to the flagship."

"Will you tell me what the plan is?" I asked.

"I'll wake you," he promised.

But he didn't. I woke up sore, stiff, and chilled in my hammock with sunlight beginning to drift in from the port hole. In the cramped quarters below deck, it was impossible to sleep through the movement of everyone stirring and sharing that it was dawn.

I woke an equally sore Ari, who followed me up to the quarterdeck alongside a bustle of bodies. We were all looking up. The King's black shadow was gone, replaced by the circling of the Duchess and the Priestess high above our fleet like eager buzzards. They weren't expending any rain or dropping any lightning, but their proximity sent a nervous shudder through my insides.

I didn't spot my father, but Captain Howl and Fog were only a few paces away. I slid in alongside them and scratched behind Fog's ears when he leaned against my side. "Do you know what's going on, sir?" I asked.

Howl smiled over at me. "We've sent Magnus the Grim to the honor duel."

"Gods help them," I said. "What did we wager in return?"

"By their rules, something of equal value. We're betting the island we just took, Inisthwaite."

My expression fell. "But if Magnus loses, that's it."

"There's one island we could fall back to, but it's very small. I know, young lady, I'm worried as well, but we sent a group to witness the duel and ensure it's fair. All we can do now is wait."

"What if this is a trap? They could leave men behind to ambush us as we're disembarking." It sure seemed like a possibility.

"It would be a clever plan," Howl acknowledged. "But not honorable, and they challenged us to an *honor* duel. I assume their champion is also a berserker, as the Rathi revere Anrathor more than we do. They made the challenge thinking they will win and make us reroute our path through their islands. Or worse, they made the challenge knowing they'd lose it and are forfeiting an island that will be a tactical disadvantage to us."

I hummed. "How so?"

"Do you know how hard it is to get an accurate map of the Rathi Islands? We don't know how many there truly are. They become white blobs on most maps with 'don't sail this far north, you'll freeze' written next to them. We know where Manarfell is, but there's some uncertainty about how large it could be or how close it is to other islands which may be more populous or are home to one of the larger villages in the coalition against us.

"Add that to the old adage 'you never bet what you can't afford to lose,' and ask yourself why the Rathi are sticking their necks out on a chance they double our territory gained."

Well, when he put it that way, I had to think he was probably right. Especially if the Rathi were still getting our battle plans from the crown prince, which was still a possibility that I couldn't forget.

"So, what do we do now?" I asked with a sigh.

"What we're paid to do." He had an edge of humor as he said, "Wait impatiently."

I took a few minutes to stretch and warm up my muscles. Soon we were clicking rations of hardtack together like a toast and making small talk. I watched the sky, leery of the King returning and wiping us out. In the dark, we hadn't gotten a true look at its size, but I knew destruction wasn't an empty threat if the King, the Duchess, and the Priestess combined forces to attack us at the same time. We simply didn't have enough gryphon riders for that scenario.

Eventually, Tempest reached out to say, *"Command has relayed our orders, Squire Walker. Strike Team Three will be taking their pyrojacks to battle today if there is one."*

"Roger that," I replied. Come to think of it, I hadn't seen Zizi since before we boarded the ships. I took Ari with me to wind our way through the crowd on the quarterdeck, looking for any sign of the unstable mage.

I found her standing at the railing on the main deck, facing out to sea. She had a wand out and, as I watched, etched runes in the air with it at a painstaking pace. "Zizi?" I asked. Startling, her half-finished spell flared with heat, and her wand split down the middle with a *crack*.

Her usual smile was a displeased grimace. "Yes?"

"Sorry, I just wanted to tell you that—"

An unearthly sound shattered the air, and I turned toward the source with wide eyes. Our vessel was still pointed toward Manarfell, and some creature had howled like a monster straight from the three hells. The sound shattered the air, deep and menacing. If I thought Fog's imitation of a howl was eerie, it was a pale imitation from the rage and volume coming from what had to be a battle beast.

A truly *furious* battle beast.

"Tell me what?" Zizi prompted, looking unaffected.

"T-That," I stammered, shivering from a spray of goose-bumps up my skin. That sound was the last thing a lot of soldiers heard before a berserker or battle beast ended their life. "T-that we will be flying together today."

Zizi frowned up at the sky. "Is that wise, with two eldrafn circling us?"

"I guess it depends on whether Magnus the Grim just won the honor duel," I replied in a hush.

"Five wonders. Do you think he was the one that made that noise?"

"I thought it was one of his battle beasts," I said.

She shrugged. "Hard to say. I can't feel their magic signatures from here, but if I had to bet, it would be that Magnus just went berserker form."

I didn't think a man could make a sound like that, but I just shrugged with her. A winged shape was flying toward the flagship with great haste, and I split my attention between the sky and the flagship.

My first hint for the outcome of the honor duel came when the two eldrafn ended their circling and flew further north. "We won," I breathed.

Light flashed from the flagship, reflected from a couple giant mirrors. A belated cheer went up from the sailors, and soon the whole ship was a mass of celebration as we pulled up anchor and began to sail for Manarfell. I laughed and hugged Zizi, the two of us joining in as the men started singing the Altarian anthem, which transitioned to a set of shanties as we flowed victoriously toward the island we'd gotten with barely any bloodshed.

The quarterdeck was cleared for the gryphon riders and their pyrojacks by the time we were coming up to the island. My good spirits came to a sudden halt when I spotted the broad figure of Magnus the Grim standing on the shore, holding the limp body of one of his battle beasts. He appeared to be covered in blood, crown to boots.

"*I have a bad feeling,*" I confided to Ari. It wasn't like we were close enough to see his expression or read the emotion in his eyes, but I had a queasy knot in my belly that worsened by the moment as Magnus stood there with his companion, like he wanted us all to see what had become of the loyal doglike beast.

"*As do I. Take a look around,*" he urged. Manarfell had a small stand of trees standing resolutely against the chill breezes from the ocean, but a distant column of smoke didn't bode well. The closest buildings and huts were already collapsed and burnt out.

"They set it on fire before they left," I mused. And the closest island further to our north was only separated from Manarfell by a narrow channel of water. Their land was massive by comparison to our new island and a storm that crackled with pink lightning loomed overhead.

Howl was right. They'd given us land but, in the process, made sure they were sitting at our doorstep. The distinctive shapes of Rathi longships were already rowing our way from the other side of the channel.

"People of Altare!" Magnus's voice boomed. "If we are to keep this island, we must be prepared to fight like we've never fought before. Many of you will be called to sacrifice, as I have." His bloodied teeth clenched as he looked up at us up on the railings, waiting to disembark. "It's time we made the Rathi burn for what they've done!"

Around me, men cheered, and Zizi shrieked agreement while I held on to Ari around the neck with a tight expression. They say never to ignore your intuition, and mine was truly uncomfortable about what was to come.

CHAPTER 21

THE ALTARIAN ADVANCE

FIRE WAS Magnus the Grim's favorite weapon. At least, I had to think so, with how many passes the strike teams made at the Rathi holdings, exhausting our pyrojacks day after day. Autumn wrapped its chill fingers around us at night, and we bedded down with one eye open as our encampment was struck by hit-and-run tactics from the eldrafn and enemy troops at all hours.

There were no trees left in Manarfell. Between the Rathi and our needs for firewood, we burnt through it all and looked longingly across the channel, where we'd already burnt down much of the next island under Magnus's orders. The first man had frozen to death in his bedroll overnight, and we knew something had to change and fast, else more of us would follow.

The great general and Hero of Altare was only present for meetings that occurred on the battlefield. With him and his remaining battle beast gone for days at a time, the rest of our leadership teams slowly eased up on the hyper-aggressive strategies that left me too exhausted to speak to anyone at night and Ari complaining every morning that his wing was too achy for a full shift in the air.

We were only able to keep Manarfell because of the gryphon riders, and it felt like we lost one every other evening when we were at our least coordinated. Endurance was key, just like Cherin said, the difference between returning to camp or not returning at all.

Something had to give, and it did one afternoon when Magnus the Grim invited the army to advance to the next island. Some of the Rathi huts were still standing in the heart of the island, but the inhabitants had met a brutal end.

"Is no one going to talk about Magnus?" I asked my father, pointing out that the general had disappeared again, following his battle beast, which had its nose to the ground.

His lips pressed into a tight line. "He is allowed his grief."

"It looks like he killed most of this village on his own," I said in a low voice. "With his *fists*."

"He's going to need our help for the next island over." He grabbed a branch off a cart passing by, laden with scraps of firewood that hadn't already become cinders. Father scratched the rough shape of islands into the dirt. "We've taken Inisthwaite, Manarfell, and now this island. Our rear guard claimed a small, uninhabited island further to the northwest of Inisthwaite that we're calling the Iceberg. Any prisoners of war we take are going there."

I looked around us with a helpless gesture. "What prisoners of war?"

"There have been a few. Women and children, especially the ones not quick enough to evacuate, are all being taken there. But that's not what I wanted to show you," he said. He stabbed the point of the stick toward a chain of islands packed close together he'd sketched. "The Rathi have retreated to Fegravik, the first island in this archipelago. Our scouts have seen the Duchess and the Priestess returning here to roost, but that's not the worst of it. There have been sightings of the King and the smallest eldrafn, the Soldier, over Fegravik's sky."

"They're going to wipe us out," I murmured. We could barely fend off two eldrafn.

His warm hand closed around my shoulder. "No, they're not. The leadership tent is lively with talks of reining in Magnus the Grim and securing this island as our base of operations if we have to overwinter here. Fegravik will take months to secure, especially once the sea turns to ice."

I thought of Prince Mateo, who'd flown south about a week ago. He'd wanted to prevent us from having to spend the winter in the Rathi Islands, but it sounded like we were about to grind to a standstill. It'd also been a long time since we'd had a mail drop, so I had no idea how his meeting with the crown prince was going.

"In summary, we're going to be all right," Father assured me. "Go take some time in the squire puddle. We deserve this short respite."

"We sure do," Ari groused.

When I located the new squire puddle, I sank gratefully to the ground and got to work massaging the pain out of Ari's old wing injury. The unlikely combination of Sharde and Barlowe was digging out a fire pit. We were diminished from the group I'd joined in Daramaine, some fifty-strong. As I gazed around the circle forming as the afternoon wore on, I noticed the faces missing in the former Harrier Flight and the pair from Osprey Flight who were always pushing each other and carrying on down to one person rolling a Circles game piece between his fingers and glaring down at it.

I got up once Ari felt a little better and set up the tent Zizi dragged over. "We're getting another person," she told me.

"Ellie?" I asked hopefully.

"Yes!" Sharde called, looking up from his shovel. "We did a little trading around."

Ellie wasn't the only extra person coming to the squire puddle. Our pyrojacks and a few full-trained men from the flights were getting shuffled over to make room for everyone.

But I whistled a quiet tune as I took one corner of the tent for myself and set up the things I'd managed to hold on to for this long. It was just enough space for three people, so Ari would need to sleep outside, unfortunately, but he would have Birch and Ironfeather for companions.

I decided I was settled after checking Revna's egg front and back for any new signs of life. It'd taken on electricity from both the Priestess and the Duchess at this point but remained as lively as a cool rock. What would it take to hatch Revna?

"What would it take to return Revna to Signe at this point?" Ari pointed out.

"Good point." Only princes, it seemed, had a reason to go back to Altare.

I placed it back in its pouch, hidden under my other things, and returned to the growing crowd resting around the fire pit. I spotted Weslecker grooming Ironfeather and rubbing him down with a towel. It felt like we hadn't talked in ages, and I'd given up trying to approach him with everything else going on. It was hard enough to talk about feelings without exhaustion and lingering fear being the emotions eclipsing everything else.

He met my gaze and beckoned to me. At some point, regulations had become the least pressing thing to enforce, so he had a shaggy fall of auburn hair and a short scruff of a mustache and beard.

"Good afternoon," I said.

"It is good," he agreed. "A moment to rest. And, uh, chat." His head turned away in a rare show of nerves.

I sat on Ironfeather's other side, scratching behind his ears and beak when he twittered a friendly greeting. *"Smile, it's happening,"* he said.

"I know," Weslecker answered, mustering a tense little lift of his lips. For a moment, I thought the gryphon was talking to me, since my insides had locked up the moment Weslecker suggested that we talk.

"Maybe we should go somewhere more private?" I suggested.

"It's a good idea," Ironfeather prompted when he took a few moments to respond.

Weslecker started to stand. "We could go secure the perimeter, as our army friends say."

Ironfeather stood and shook out his mussed feathers before lying on top of Ari, who complained in a low groan. *"We'll secure our spot!"* the younger gryphon assured.

We didn't dare dip out of the village we were claiming as our new base, instead taking the long way around the main bustle of work cleaning out the standing buildings and the worst debris of those burnt or collapsed.

"How've you been?" I asked.

"Worked to the bone," he muttered. "Just like you and everyone else. Feels like I've pushed this off for a month because I didn't know what to say."

"Me too."

His throat worked in a rough swallow. I glanced around with him, making sure no one was in earshot. "You like Mateo, huh?" he asked.

"Not as much as I like you," I answered, trying to catch his eye to show him my sincerity, but he ducked his gaze with a low chuckle.

"I hope you're not saying that because he's not around…"

I sucked in a gasp, brows crashing together. "I'm not that kind of person, and you know it."

"Sure. But Mateo also told me that he didn't know if he could honor his promise to stay away from you. He *knows* how I feel and still kissed you." He turned a blazing glare my way. "I thought you were saving any relationships for after the Academy. You asked me to wait but invited him in instead?"

"That isn't what…"

He took a step closer, all of his bottled-up anger looking ready to explode. He wasn't about to listen. "Mateo, really? He knew his father was paying Callan and barely lifted a finger to help you. Meanwhile, who was it who taught you swordplay? Who was always by your side, ready to defend you?"

"You were," I answered.

"That's right. I was!"

"I didn't deserve it," I said. His brows lifted, caught halfway between either replying or continuing to show how he'd supported me. "I want to own up to it. I'm sorry, Acton. I don't want to take advantage of you or make you think that's what I'm doing."

"I didn't think you were," he said, lowering his voice.

"We haven't communicated well lately. Trying to start something now"—I gestured to the war camp taking root around us—"well, I don't know how well I'd do for you or anyone else. It doesn't feel like I have enough time to be myself sometimes. But if I was going to choose someone, it would be you. Mateo stole a kiss as a test. We knew the moment it was over that it wasn't right."

He began to nod slowly. I took a deep breath, wetting my lips, hoping I said this next part right. "I'm just worried that you've only helped me thus far to get a relationship out of me at the end. I don't think that's healthy."

"Gods," he sighed, reaching for me. I let him take my hands in his, and our gazes met, drawn to each other. "I wasn't doing anything with the expectation of a relationship, and I'm mortified you even thought that. I just like you, Sivana Walker. I like your smile. I like the way your little nose scrunches up when you laugh—"

"It does not," I said, laughing self-consciously.

"—Just like that," he said with a grin. "But I love the way you charged into the Gryphon Rider Academy knowing it would be hard, knowing every possible odd was stacked against you, and yet here you are, a success story. But you didn't do it for yourself. You climbed those odds and got back up every time you were knocked down because of your gryphon. I love the clear passion you have for them. I love that *you* love Ari enough to take on what must have felt like all of Altare at one point.

"Along the way, I helped because I wanted to see you succeed. More than anything." He gave my hands an earnest squeeze.

I wiped my cheek against my sleeve, searching his face for any sign of doubt. Unlike Mateo, he was an open book, clearly believing everything he'd said. I really didn't deserve him.

"I…I like you too," I said, feeling like my tongue was too thick for my mouth. "I wish we weren't in the middle of a war and, even still, that we wouldn't be accused of fraternization."

He held up a finger. "You know, I asked someone to look into this for me. The regulation is back in my notebook, but Noah and Ellie have already used it to get the others off their case."

I tried not to break into a smile right away, but hopeful butterflies were fluttering around my belly. "Yeah? What does it say?"

"The army allows its men and women to date as long as they are not in the same chain of command. Since Ellie is in the engineering corps and Noah is a gryphon rider, it's allowed. Our flights are different; even though we're on strike teams, I'm assigned to the Third, officially, while you're in the Seventh."

"So, it should be all right?" I asked in a buoyant hush.

"We would have precedent on our side. And…" He brushed a bit of hair out of my face. "We can take it slow. I know it's not the best time or place, but I'm starting to wonder, when is?"

"When is," I echoed, shaking my head. "Not while we were at the Academy. But I do want to try and see where it takes us."

His answering smile was practically radiant. I knew I'd have to work hard to convince some of the men around us, especially Cherin and Father, but maybe we'd all be so busy they wouldn't notice for a while. Not much had changed, except we held hands in the dark that evening before the squires were ordered to our bedrolls. He left me tingling after we parted with a simple kiss on the back of my hand.

I'd thought Ari was asleep through most of this, but as I turned to head to my tent, he murmured, *"Finally."*

CHAPTER 22

WINTER WINDS

WE BEGAN new skirmishes with the Rathi that next morning, and no true progress was made as the days turned into weeks and the air chilled further each day. Even Magnus the Grim's wrathful impatience couldn't break the impasse between us.

We were entrenched on either side of a half day's sailing or a couple hour flight. Between attacks initiated by either side, I caught some much-needed rest. After Ari and I finally felt recharged, the feeling was chased by the same boredom that'd taken root when we had first joined the Seventh, waiting for something to happen.

At least this time I had someone who was reliably there for PT in the morning, dueling or endurance training in the afternoon, or ready to sit with me in the evening to catch up in the shadows around the squire puddle's fire pit. I had a lot to tell Weslecker, starting with the magical token from Lord Orion and how I'd lost it.

"You'd think our king would have basic manners," he'd said, scowling.

While I agreed, I was happy to say that it seemed the king had listened after I was uncovered as the Chosen of Orion.

Weslecker patted me on the back, seeming to accept the title the moment I told him about it.

He was a little more incredulous about Revna's egg and where it came from, then downright skeptical when I also pulled out the magestone Cherin had given me. "My mentor said the best magestone to use in emergencies is the speed one," he said.

"Well, Ari can't use it anyway. Why don't you take it? You can use either, depending on the situation," I suggested, giving him the one enchanted for endurance while I kept my healing magestone in case of an emergency.

"My life and training have been downright boring compared to yours," he admitted.

"I think you mean normal," I said. I was happy to lean into his side and listen to his cultured voice as he recounted his training and recruitment into Strike Team One.

He was also around when we finally had a mail drop, and I had two letters from Mateo delivered atop a box from Mother and another lengthy letter from Odalis. *At least she decided not to send it through a Mercy this time*, which my heart thoroughly appreciated, but I was nervous when Weslecker noticed the first two letters and who they were from.

I opened the box first and passed around one of the bags of mallows, enjoying the burst of sweetness after a long diet of rations and fish. Then I opened Mateo's letters and tried to read the first one.

"This is nonsense," I muttered, letting Weslecker have a look. The ink was smeared, making his handwriting look like vague shapes.

"Huh, no. It's a cipher," he said. He lay the second letter flat and found the cipher code hidden within a dull message about how he'd been spending his days helping his father in court.

Weslecker began copying down a new letter from the first one. "Have you two had to do this before?" I asked.

He nodded absently, cross referencing the letters. "Yes. At first, it was for fun, before I realized our tutors were teaching us how to send messages we only wanted the recipient to read."

Eventually, he passed me the hidden message.

Dear Sivana (and hopefully Acton),

I have met with Isaac and convinced him that I would like to remain in Kaiamear to save myself and Mireille from the Storm Front. He is trying to use his invitation here as political leverage against me, like I am only safe because of him.

To continue this ruse and earn his trust, I must pretend that being safe is what I want, when in truth, I am consumed with guilt to be back in the capital while you're still fighting.

At this time, I do not believe he is willing to tell me anything of substance about his plans. As I sit here writing this in Odalis's old room, I hear him speaking in Lithosian to someone else. I cannot help but have a sense of dread that he is coordinating something big.

Father is overjoyed that I have returned and has given me plenty of work to do in the meantime. He has had a change of heart about you, Sivana. It is still strange to hear him speak positively of you. He will not talk to me about Isaac, however. There is some deep-rooted fear in him, like he knows he will not like what he sees if he inspects Isaac's actions too closely. I am trying to guide him gently.

Please write back with news from the front. I fear you will be there through the winter after all, and I worry for you and our friends.

I will continue using this cipher.

Mateo Cortes III

I read it a couple times, my frown deepening with each pass, before giving it back to Weslecker to look over again. "I told him he should've paid more attention to his language lessons," he muttered.

"I'm more worried about the king," I said quietly. "Because he had the same reaction when I mentioned Isaac.

He knows the apple is rotten on one side, but he won't turn it over to see it for himself."

Weslecker released a soft sigh. "That sounds like Mateo's stubborn old man. I hate that Mateo is stuck there, writing inane letters." He flapped another envelope addressed to him in the prince's handwriting. "But at least he can push the king in a way no one else can."

"Will it be fast enough, though?" I asked.

I traced the path of a falling white pinprick, tiny and fluffy, making its way toward the ground after a delicate dance on a breath of wind. It settled a couple feet away, melting slowly into a drop of water.

The snowflakes that followed didn't melt away so easily, sticking together into dirty clumps around the camp and forming icy filigree over tents and unused equipment.

This far north, winter came early and stayed late like an obnoxious house guest. But this season, the Altarians were the ones overstaying their welcome.

Magnus the Grim led each attack on Fegravik, but this one was the largest, with a full complement of air support kitted out and expecting up to four eldrafn joining the fight against us. We hadn't burnt down the island yet—someone must have convinced the furious berserker in charge that we needed the firewood with winter setting in.

Still, he wanted strike teams at the ready to help smoke out the enemy, so I flew with Zizi as we crossed over to the next island and stayed low to the tree line as our soldiers hiked further inland in search of a fight. The chilling howl of either Magnus or his remaining battle beast went up by mid-afternoon, soon followed by orders to begin setting fires around where our scouts had pinpointed one of their camps.

"I smell..." Ari turned his beak to the wind, giving himself a shake, which had Zizi holding fast to the saddle.

Our Link lit up with Valtora's commanding boom. *"Eldrafn sighted! West as the sun sets. Strike teams, do not engage."*

"Yes, Mother," Ari replied.

The Priestess went rushing overhead, pivoting to drop a charged bolt toward the battlefield. Distantly, men shouted and scrambled away from the charred impact point. A team of gryphon riders peeled off to give chase, lances brandished.

"Mother," Ari continued. *"Do you smell rozash?"*

He was trying hard to identify a dry, bitter smell. I could practically taste it, even though it was coming from his heightened senses and his side of the Link. It reminded him strongly of acidmaw venom.

Tempest interrupted, shouting as the Duchess rose from the horizon, swooping down on the gryphon riders chasing its fellow eldrafn and crushing one in its talons of clouds and electricity. It swooped in one direction while the Priestess took on speed and started flying counterclockwise to it.

A third eldrafn joined them, this one a third of the size of the Priestess, practically a baby of their race. The Soldier, I noted, which was about as tall and long across the wings as a gryphon. It lent its winds to what the other two creatures were spinning up.

"Brace!" Valtora ordered. It was the only warning we had time for when, together, the three eldrafn agitated the wind to tear into Ari's feathers, pushing and tugging until we were out of control on a wild zephyr that whipped us in tight circles.

Zizi screamed, holding tight to my middle while we spun in the cyclone and abruptly flung away with the rest of our fellow gryphon riders, sent far from the battlefield.

"Gods, you're right," Valtora said more privately to Ari and

me. We didn't see the rozash, but the shrill screech of the serpentine creatures sounded nearby.

"No. No no no no no," Ari chanted, heart galloping in the drum of his chest to bring us back as quick as possible. Over a dozen of the brightly colored monsters were dumping their breath weapons over our unprotected army as the gryphon riders rushed back into position.

The burn of acid. The feeling of a saddle sliding from Ari's back. Darkness.

Ari tossed his head, caught in an equally deadly whirlwind of his own emotions and memories. They were so strong that I relived the moment Alamid died without him, down to the shrill agony of Ari's original rider Link shattering.

"Ari, we have to form up." I pulled on his reins when he picked up speed to pass by the V-formation Cherin and Tempest were forming.

"Draw your lance," he said in low fury.

I pulled harder to try to slow him down and turn around to join our element. *"I know you want to fight rozash, but—"*

"Do it!"

"Walker, do not engage on your own! That's an order!" Tempest shouted after us.

We were balanced over an aerial battlefield turned to chaos, with eldrafn and rozash trying to navigate around each other and gryphon rider elements rushing in to handle the unexpected threat. Fire mixed with lightning, sand with acid, all falling in a deadly rain over any troops still fighting below. "Uh, Sivana. What are we doing?" Zizi asked. "Because if we're going alone, I really think you should reconsider!"

"C'mon Ari, we can't do this," I said, feeling his pain and the echo of grief from him. How he wanted to rage and scream and rend the wings off of every rozash in the field. But he was coming back to himself, remembering his training, remembering that he was part of a team.

This was only the second time I'd seen a real rozash, and I forgot how quickly they powered themselves forward with their four wings beating in harmony. Movement caught my eye, and I turned, just to see a sandstone-yellow rozash charging across the sky toward us, its two mouths gaping wide.

My gryphon started to flinch toward a dive.

Heart feeling ready to explode, I cried out Ari's name.

Zizi summoned twin fireballs with a powerful *fwoosh*.

And a sudden force knocked us out of the twin streams of pressurized sand that blasted from the rozash's maws. A great roar came from Valtora as she took the brunt of the attack and dropped toward the worst of the aerial battle. Ari screamed in anguish, the moment too fast for words. He tucked his wings and dove after her, dodging the blurred shapes of other rozash and gryphon riders.

When we drew up alongside Valtora, I noticed her saddle flapping, coming loose from her unconscious form. As Father and the mage riding tandem with him reached for us, Ari grabbed a hold of his mother's wing and scruff with a grunt.

Even with Ari straining, he couldn't keep another gryphon and four people airborne. He pulled us away from the battle with all his might, our clumsy shape defended by a swooping element on one end, intercepting a bolt of lightning.

Tempest's orders were surreal from this end. *"Gryphon down! Defend them! We cannot lose Arrow and Walker!"*

On the other side of us rushed a bulky crimson rozash, its two mouths bursting with flame. "I got this!" Zizi exclaimed, her usual manic giggling threaded with panic as she raised her charred palms. I trembled with impotent fear, only able to watch as twin jets of flame washed toward us.

It was like Zizi had put up a barrier that curved around us, but the eager flames still licked at our armor and toward the trembling pyrojack behind my father aiming his wand toward them, rapidly casting runes for a spell even though it was too late. The wall was all her, her arms trembling as she held back the fire with it connected and flowing off her palms.

She laughed and screamed all in one, tears making rivers down her cheeks, before shoving it all away from us to fall harmlessly to the ground.

Gods, we needed a miracle, and it came to us in two parts. Zizi's save bought us a moment and a temporary reprieve as the pyremaw flew away, likely thinking we were already incinerated. The second part came as an unnatural hush to the wind, silent and still. I raised my head, feeling something big was coming.

High above us, the Priestess had its wings spread wide, its ivory heart burning like the core of the sun. Lightning exploded all around it as it finally died, sending out a wave of electricity and superheated air. It buffeted into us, lifting Ari's wings and flinging us further into the heart of the island, where we came to a hard landing against the trunk of an unburnt tree.

Valtora's blood was already staining the frozen ground around us.

CHAPTER 23

STRANDED

THE SHOCK of the moment hadn't passed yet. I stared, seeing Valtora's prone form lying beside a growing semi-circle of pink snow.

The apprentice pyrojack who flew with my father was hauling away their ruined saddle, each leather strap broken into roughened ends. It sank in rapidly that my Skymother was injured, that in essence, she'd sacrificed herself to protect Ari while he was stuck in a memory-fueled rage.

I tore myself out of my riding harness and dropped my weapon and shield, rushing past my father to her side. "Skymother, no!" I cried, dropping to my knees.

A blast of sand had struck her along the side, abrading away the feathers under her wing and the thick fur over her ribs before it'd eaten into her skin and flesh. It was a raw, bloody wound that at first seemed to cover a lot more of her body than it really did.

"We have to staunch the bleeding. Do you have any cloth?" Father asked, pushing me aside to press a blanket over the abrasion. I noticed he went down heavily, his leg similarly wounded.

Ari stumbled beside me, panting heavily. *"This is my fault. I should have never…why did I…"*

"Hold still," I said, launching myself at his saddlebags. The egg around my left wrist smacked into the back of my hand, and I ripped it off to set to the side. I tossed rations and other necessities aside next. At the bottom of the bag glowed the huge healing magestone Prince Mateo gave me last year for Ari's broken wing. I snatched it and pushed it into Valtora's shoulder, just above the wound. The rune etched into its flat stone side started to glow a brighter green.

"Uh, Sivana," Zizi said. She stood beside me, and I turned to glare at her. I didn't have time for her chatter right now. "That's a gradual-release magestone. Class A, definitely great workmanship but designed to release its magic over the course of a few months—"

"We don't have that kind of time!" I snapped. At any moment, the enemy could discover us, and we couldn't relocate with an unconscious, wounded gryphon.

She put her hands up like she was approaching a furious animal foaming and snapping at her, even her voice gentling. "I know. I need you to give it to me."

"Valtora needs it." My voice cracked, tears escaping to form chill lines down my face.

"And I'm going to give her all the energy in it at once. I just need you to trust me." She held out her hand. The skin of it was charred black, cracking and bleeding at the creases.

Not all of the damage to her hands was from her unstable magic. I pictured the moment rozash fire nearly incinerated us, only held back by the unusual and painful method she wielded her magic. I didn't hesitate to extend the magestone to her, and it wasn't just because of necessity.

Despite everything, I'd come to trust her and see her as a partner and friend. "Can you give some of the healing magic to my father as well?" I asked.

"I'll try, but you know I don't do precision well," she said, trapping the magestone between her hands and setting it alight with a bright burst of fire. Father and the other pyro-jack made sounds of alarm, while I tilted my head, hearing shouts in Rathi and the unmistakable howl of a battle beast close to our location. It sounded like they were coming toward us.

Zizi dropped the charred stone, its rune burned off, and extended her palms toward Valtora and my father. Green magic spilled from her, coating the wound my father exposed on Valtora's side and dancing around his injured leg.

"She's been healed many times in her life," he murmured as at first the magic didn't seem to do much. He carefully wiped at the edges of her abrasion. It was pink, partially healed. The best we could ask for right now, especially when her eyelids fluttered and she groaned to wakefulness.

"Sivana, go scout for us," Father ordered.

"Yes, sir." I recognized his chill, disappointed tone. We would be talking about what'd happened later, if we survived.

I crept through the snow-lined forest toward the sounds of battle, discovering a ridge that overlooked the closest line of combatants. I low crawled to peer over the side at what was going on. Five Rathi were squaring off against a pair of blood-soaked furies, Magnus the Grim and his surviving battle beast.

The enemy had their backs to the ridge, shouting and gesturing, taunting the musclebound berserker in his form of mindless battle rage and peak strength. He loomed a head and shoulders taller than the Rathi, and his battle beast sparked flames all around it from its fiery hackles. Its thin brown pelt was split by skin straining to contain the strength it borrowed from its master.

I was sure I was about to witness a slaughter, with the chance to hail Magnus the Grim and gain his assistance to rejoin our army, when a second battle beast shattered the air with its howl. Another berserker appeared, pointing his battleaxe at Magnus in clear challenge. He was much younger, covered in geometric tattoos down his arms and across his face rather than the temporary patterns of blood on Altare's general.

The two berserkers leapt at each other while the other Rathi held back out of respect for their fighter. It was the clash of two titans, striking each other with the kind of force that would level boulders with one blow. The two battle beasts circled and snapped, just as evenly matched for now.

I could sense Ari's swirl of self-loathing on the other side of my Link and tentatively reached out. His feelings were so skewed off from mine that he wasn't looking through my eyes. *"How's she doing?"* I asked.

"She is in a lot of pain, but she will live. There's no way she's flying until her feathers grow out, though," he answered in a glum murmur.

"We may have a bigger problem. I'm watching Magnus the Grim fight another Rathi berserker."

"Is he losing?" I felt the shift in Ari and the focus of his attention.

I was about to say how evenly matched the two seemed when the Rathi berserker turned his axe on Magnus's beast in one savage chop. Bones crunched, and the beast whimpered out its last breath before its fire extinguished permanently.

"He is. Oh, gods," I said, horrified by the intense anguish that pierced Magnus's battle lust to paint his face with grief. It was the moment a Link broke for good, the other half of a soul going silent. *"Ari—he's going to die!"*

Fear flashed from him. *"Don't jump in that fight."*

There wasn't anything I could do for Magnus the Grim anyway, as the moment he flinched, the Rathi berserker and his battle beast ended him just as brutally. I scooted from the ridge as the dog-like beast released a satisfied howl and the Rathi charged away from us, toward the main fighting.

I rushed back to my small group of survivors, breathing a little easier to see Valtora was on her paws but leaning her good side heavily against Ari for support. I told Father and the two pyrojacks everything I'd seen in a stumbling mess.

While the Tulari seemed just as shaken by the news as I felt, Father's expression was a stony mask. "Our side will sound the retreat the moment they realize Magnus is dead. We need to head away from the village where these Rathi were camping and find a safe place to hide."

He turned to me. "Once we're hidden, you and Ari will fly back and lead a rescue team to us."

"Yes, sir," I answered.

We started walking southwest, toward the far shore of the island. Valtora struggled along, but she wasn't the only one limping. I noticed my father also favored his injured leg, not quite healed from the rush of magic earlier.

"Father, there's something else I need to tell you," I said. I'd scooped up the modified sling with Revna's egg and its abused copper rod. The moment I showed him the matte purple rock, his eyes widened dramatically.

"How did—never mind. Any red-blooded Rathi would kill us all to take that." He quickly found a place for us to bury it in a layer of dirt and snow between the roots of a tree.

He also didn't leave the air between us open for long after we were moving again. "Did you not learn anything from two years at the Academy?" he asked me in a low, furious tone. "Charging off on your own like that. That kind of recklessness is exactly how others get injured or killed."

"Sorry, Father," I mumbled. There was no need to point fingers at Ari for what'd happened. He was my gryphon, so I was responsible any time something went wrong.

"I lost control of myself. He should be blaming me, as should you," Ari said.

A sense of static came from Valtora as she said something directly to him. I felt the spike of pain wedged in his heart begin to loosen as he pictured Alamid and responded back to her privately.

"Leave them alone, Nathaniel. We're alive," Valtora interjected.

"Don't you go defending her," he scolded in return. "She's a woman grown and has to stop trying to be a hero. Don't you remember what happened the last time?"

"All too well. Skyla's rider stole from her," she replied.

"Well, yes, the stolen bounty too. But I meant the *almost dying* and *not following orders* part."

I held up a finger, tentatively channeling my inner Ellie even though Father's stare could've made a flower wilt. "Technically, there was no order against going up again to help fight the Earl. You know about me missing out on the bounty?"

He nodded, lips pressed into a thin line. "Your mentor shared that you helped assist but nearly got yourself killed. And Ari told Valtora about his dislocated wing and your swim back to the port. I didn't want to get your hopes up, but I wrote to Paragon Hughes over the matter."

"Hey, not to interrupt," Zizi said.

My father ignored her. "It's the height of dishonor not to share credit where it's due."

She tried to interject again. "As good as it is that you're talking about this—"

"In fact, I wouldn't be surprised if the Seventh—"

The other pyrojack seized Father by the shoulder and pointed. "Rathi," he hissed.

Father released a curse so clever and nasty I shot him a sideways glance before looking ahead of us. Now that they were spotted, a group of a dozen white-haired men and women were coming out from the underbrush. Each bore the same tattoo on their face, a green-tinted bar crossing their cheeks and the bridges of their noses.

They were also all armed, spears and axes pointed in our

direction. The air crackled beside me as Zizi started creating fire from her abused hands. "No," Father said, holding up his arm. He grabbed Valtora's scruff when she hissed through her beak and started puffing out her feathers and fur. "Stop, look around you."

More Rathi came from the shadows behind the sparse forest around us. We were surrounded by at least twenty armed and healthy people. "What do we do?" I whispered to Father.

Slowly, he put his arms up, palms out. "You can't be serious. We can take them," Zizi complained.

"Stand down. That's an order from a Commander," Father snapped.

With reluctant slowness, I mirrored his pose of surrender. His pyrojack stepped forward, hailing the Rathi in their language. I exchanged a glance with Father, who looked as surprised as I was.

"They want us to surrender our weapons," he said, tossing his wand to the ground. I added my shield and lance since my sword was discarded far behind us, and Father dropped his weapons and shield as well. Zizi grumbled as she added a sharp and wickedly curved dagger to the pile alongside the satchel of her many wands.

The butt of a spear jabbed me sharply into motion after a female Rathi patted me down for any concealed weapons. They closed in around us, letting Father and Valtora set the pace since none of them seemed keen to prod the golden, irritable-looking beast.

Father muttered my way out of the corner of his mouth. "I didn't recognize their tribal tattoos. There's a good chance these people aren't part of the coalition we're at war with."

"And your pyrojack?" I whispered back.

"Janrick from one of our port towns. Could be a trader family. I never suspected him for a double agent."

Other than speaking for us, Janrick was being treated the

same way, forced along with the Rathi toward their village further to the north. We'd have blundered right into it if not for being spotted first. Situated beside the ocean was a sizable town, though we only caught a glimpse of Rathi going about their daily lives.

We were forced toward a series of caves that lined the back of the town, many just holes in the side of the steepest sections of ground, dug out and lined with metal bars to contain prisoners of all sorts. A couple were occupied when we walked past them by sallow, purple-eyed criminals who still leered and spat at the sight of Altarians.

They opened three cells for us, and Valtora rumbled low in her throat when she was expected to go into the first one with Ari. "It could be much worse. It's either this or death," Father said.

"We truly have gone soft, haven't we?" she muttered, watching as the Rathi slammed the bars behind her and her son. It seemed Father responded to her mentally, as I picked up on her reply with no context. *"Be that as it may, rescue is unlikely to come soon."*

Father's pyrojack, Janrick, turned to tell us quietly, "We're going into separate cells, men and women split up. Tomorrow morning, they're going to try selling us to the hostile Rathi tribes we've been fighting."

Father nodded. "Just do what they say for now." His piercing gaze skewered me as Zizi and I were herded toward a different cell. "Don't do anything foolish. The military leaves no one behind."

The cell door slammed behind us, and I seized two bars, watching Father and Janrick get ushered away. "I sure feel left behind," Zizi muttered. She had a little flickering fire in her palm, inspecting every short inch of our cage. We were in a scoop of stone with a dirt floor, with a pair of ratty old sheets folded and placed in a shallow alcove carved into the back of the wall.

We spread the sheets across the ground and sat, watching a pair of Rathi walk by, laughing and joking in their own language. "He's right, though. The people who matter watched us go down. A rescue group is going to come looking for us and other survivors and..." I turned toward her. Her Tulari mark was a deep red, with only the smallest of embers flickering along its edges. She was drooping, exhausted and defeated. "Not to get your hopes up, but our gryphons or I could call out for help when they come close enough."

"Then what?" she sighed.

"Well, they can buy us from this Rathi village instead."

CHAPTER 24

ESCAPING FEGRAVIK

CHILL FINGERS of wind caressed us, a breeze straight and salty from the ocean. I trembled, while Zizi sat in heavy silence for a moment, showing no sign that the weather affected her. "What happened out there, for real?" she asked.

Fatigue was setting in for me as well now that the adrenaline of our near-death and capture had started to fade. It was a long story, but it seemed we had all evening, as the sun was approaching the western horizon. I told her of Ari's first rider, Alamid Maros, and how they'd once fought Lithos in the border skirmishes before full-blown war had erupted between Altare and Lithos.

"By the time Alamid and Ari were promoted to a position in the First Gryphon Flight, they'd fought hundreds of rozash and developed a hatred for the messy destruction they leave behind on a battlefield," I shared. "Then a couple years ago, Alamid died when an acidmaw rozash blinded Ari and damaged his saddle with its spit."

"That's horrible," she murmured. "Didn't you two Link because of a rozash?"

"Yeah. One attacked Kaiamear, and Ari came out of his depression in a moment of clarity and defiance. We've seen illusions of rozash since then, but this was the first time a real group of them has appeared since the night we Linked." My lips twisted. I could feel Ari's attention and the regret churning his insides. "He lost control of himself for a few minutes, that's all."

She snorted. "That's all," she echoed. "Like that's not why we're here right now. But tell Ari I can empathize and don't blame him."

"It's okay, I'll blame myself all on my own," he replied without prompting.

"Ari..."

"Stop. My mother is already trying to smother me in love, but I got her seriously hurt, and now we're stuck in a hole in the ground! I barely see how this could get worse when you consider we might be sold to the enemy and tortured or executed tomorrow."

"We just have to wait for rescue. I have faith that it's coming," I replied.

He pressed on the fear lurking within me. *"And if it's a day too late?"*

"Then we lived longer than then Commander Davises and Crown Prince Isaacs of the country thought we would." We shared some of the sad sort of amusement.

Zizi interrupted the mental conversation by asking, "Can I tell you something?"

"Hmm? Of course." I forced a little smile.

"Just in case we don't survive tomorrow..." She took a deep breath, lifting her shoulders. "I just wanted you to know this. What history wrote about unstable mages is wrong, and I've learned it firsthand."

My brows lifted. "Oh? What do you mean?" I asked.

"The Tulari hide their secrets behind sparkles and ceremony. Even at the Tulari Academy, no one's taken me aside and explained why I cast and handle fire magic differently than other pyromancers. It's just assumed that I have a flaw in the rune on my face or that I have some magic disease that eats at my self-control... Anyway, it's not either of those things. My problems really start and end with my nemesis, *Irene*."

It was like she packed years of loathing into the Hero of Altare's name. "I've been meaning to ask why you seem to know her," I said.

She released a bitter laugh. "The honored dual-blessed warmage, Irene Merriweather, and I go back a long ways. I might as well tell you the whole story."

"Please do. It's not like there's anything else happening."

Zizi inspected her hands, peeling at bits of skin that hadn't regenerated yet. "Where do I even start? Well, as you already know, I'm from a Lithosian family. When I was a kid, the Zaveri family headed the most expansive trading company in Lithos. My father was set to inherit the business from my grand-uncle. We had house servants and magelights, to give you an idea of the wealth involved. Well, when I was born, I had the rune of magic starting to form on my face. It started peeling when I was about six."

I gasped. "That's so early. My brother started showing his rune's colors at eleven." He'd clawed at his face, as the process of the top layer of skin peeling away was incredibly itchy. It'd exposed puffy skin marked the wizard blue of his developing magic. We had to send him to learn magic soon after the rune was fully exposed.

"Yeah, I know. And imagine my parents' panic when I would accidentally set myself alight head to toe," she murmured.

In my mind's eye, I saw Rissa when she was six, immediately horrified at the thought of greedy fire anywhere near her soft skin. Zizi's poor parents. "Oh, *gods*."

"Right? They looked everywhere for a cure. Earlier in my life, my mother had fallen very sick. I remember her being bedridden for months, with doctors and nurses coming and going what felt like daily. It was a Tulari healer who eventually gave her permanent relief. But my experience was very similar. Doctors came around promising a miracle cure, and Nilarite women would pray over me. Father banned leech therapy early on because I'd just burn them off me. The best *and* worst treatment was the ice baths. The doctors would submerge me head to toe in icy water. It brought relief if my magic was running high, but there were days when it was unnecessary and probably almost killed me."

She seemed lost to those memories now, her dull gaze years in the past. "I'm sorry, that sounds unpleasant," I said. "What was the cure? Since you don't light yourself on fire like that anymore."

"That's quite the understatement. Well, even our local Tulari healers were stumped and said we needed to consult with Lord Orion himself or a crafter-class healer. We weren't a religious family, so Father paid to send for one of the most gifted healers when we'd exhausted all other avenues. I was eight at this point, for reference, when Irene Merriweather arrived to answer Father's summons. She pretended to be a crafter Tulari, with the grand staff and everything.

"My parents welcomed her with warm Lithosian hospitality even though she was a foreigner and Altarians weren't the most welcome sight with all the border tensions even back then."

"Wait, only crafter Tulari have staffs?" I asked. "Did she pretend she was a healer too?"

Zizi nodded. "Yeah, and I'll tell you why in a minute. She told my father that she was a crafter-class healer, and we all believed her. Her rune was unusual, wizard blue with a green tint, which we thought meant she was dual-blessed."

"Your family should've gone to Lord Orion. He was the one who gave you the magic, after all," I said, having a bad feeling about what Irene did from this moment in the story to inspire such hatred in Zizi.

"It's not like he ever helped me," she snapped before

releasing a tense sigh. "I mean, Irene did help more than he did. She taught me that my magic outbursts were because I was storing heat within my body and that it was unusual I could do this rather than gain a measured dose of magic from regular communion with Lord Orion. I was unconsciously drawing heat from the fires around me and the warm water of my normal baths, and every day, I went outside with the unforgiving sun shining down on me. Any time that heat grew to be too much to contain, my little eyes would glow demon orange and I'd burst into flames soon after. My magic is a living thing. It wants to be used; it wants to burn and destroy, and if I don't use it, it'll attack me."

"I've seen that," I murmured, gesturing to her hands.

"She told me that she could give me relief from my too-strong magic if I just went through a simple ritual with her," she continued. She drew her sheet aside and started drawing something in the dirt. "I didn't know it at the time, but she was taking me through the same steps every crafter-class Tulari goes through to find their corerune. Regular Tulari don't have one. Mine looked a little like this."

In the shadows of early evening, the corerune looked like a spiky sun, with complicated lines within it like extra, miniature runes. "What is this?" I asked.

"Just a poor imitation of the corerune Irene drew out of me. She helped me enchant the orb atop her staff with my rune and clapped me on the shoulder, promising that my magic would be more controllable. She disappeared back to Altare and told my parents that if I still had trouble after her treatment, I was an unstable mage and needed the advanced training that the Altarian Tulari Academy created specifically for my kind.

"Well, obviously, I had more control of myself because I knew how my magic worked, but I still burned myself and overloaded every wand my tutors put in my hand. My parents eventually made the difficult decision to sell their share of the business and move north to Altare before the borders closed. Right before the war." Her lips pressed into a hard line. "I was one of the youngest pupils at the Academy, and they tried to also get me to cast my corerune, suspecting I was a crafter-class pyromancer. It turns out, I *was*, but a corerune can only ever be used once, and it represented my chance to have control over my magic to channel it through a staff rather than a tiny wand."

I put my arm around her for comfort and she leaned against me. "Did you ever tell anyone at the Academy about Irene stealing it?" I asked.

"Oh yeah." She began to speak with a thick Lithosian accent. It made the flowing Altarian words sound hard and unforgiving, with strong emphasis on the consonants. "But when you sound like I did, no one believed it. The ugly side came out of some of my instructors and peers. I was *just* unstable and needed to learn to control myself."

She cleared her throat and the touch of her homeland away. "So, I learned how to talk and act like an Altarian, hoping one day someone in charge would believe that the great Irene the Fair, Hero of Altare, stole the magic she's been so rewarded for. Barring that, I've volunteered for both war efforts now, hoping to take her staff when she's not looking. If I could just destroy the rune at the top, I could reclaim it for myself and stop suffering for my magic. Plus, *Irene* would be exposed for the sham she is."

I snapped my fingers. "That's where you are at night. Trying to get close to Irene."

"Yeah, but she's always surrounded by soldiers and the other Heroes who like sniffing at her skirts," she scoffed. "I don't think she ever expected to see me again.

"But over time, I've realized the legends of the Laughing Legion could be wrong. Why would anyone *want* to be unstable? I wonder if, maybe, stealing corerunes isn't so uncommon."

"I just don't know if Lord Orion would allow that," I said.

"Hah! The only time I ever talked to him, I asked for his help, and he told me there was nothing he could do. It's *his* design that every crafter-class Tulari has one and only ever one corerune on a tool of power. Think of all the great and terrible enchanted weapons you know about. The Sword of Altare, Flamescythe, the Eye of Draconis. All created from a corerune."

"Wait, really?" I hadn't realized that was how it worked. "I thought crafter-class pyromancers made those weapons."

"Not the truly famous ones. I've wondered if the corerunes on them were gifts from elderly Tulari who wanted their legacy to continue, or if they were stolen." She scuffed her arm over the rune she'd drawn in the dirt. "Only thing I know is Irene's named her staff, with *my* rune, Starfall. If I die tomorrow, then Starfall could become a legendary weapon like the rest one day, with no one the wiser."

"Except for me," I murmured, giving her shoulders a squeeze. "I'm sorry this happened to you, Zizi. If—*when*—we escape, I want to help you get Starfall back." I didn't want to promise her anything, but I hoped to get cleverer minds like Sharde and Ellie's on the task of separating a celebrated warmage from her magical weapon.

"Yeah. We'll see, huh." She sounded pretty skeptical. "Well, if worse comes to worst, I could borrow some of your body heat and try to melt the lock on the cage in the dead of night."

I shivered already, wondering how cold such magic would leave me afterward. "Would you be able to do the same to free the men and the gryphons?"

She muffled a yawn into her shoulder. "Probably not."

"What don't you get some rest?" I suggested. "I'll keep watch for a while."

Zizi had no arguments there and wrapped herself tightly in her sheet. She faced the wall and was soon deep asleep, leaving me to stare out into the night. I hadn't told her my own confession, that I was Lord Orion's Chosen, for as little as I'd done with the title. But he'd promised to answer if I called, so I did so in the silence of the dark.

I need your help and guidance more than ever, Lord Orion.

"Quite the predicament you've gotten yourself into," his soft, borrowed voice answered. Lord Orion was there in a blink on the other side of the cage bars, still wearing the visage of one of his clergymen, Duncan. His eyes barely glowed rather than exposing the bonfire of his power in the middle of a sleeping village.

With a flourish of his fingertip, he drew a rune and tapped it in Zizi's direction. A swirl of gold sparkles settled over her. "There. She won't wake from the sound of our voices. You seek guidance, my Chosen?"

I barely knew where to start. "I'm still your Chosen?" I asked to confirm it from him personally.

"I thought you'd accepted the real purpose of the token already," he replied.

And all I could do was smile to myself. That was the patron god I knew. I stood and clasped the cold metal bars between us. "Can you help us escape?" I whispered.

The god smiled in his warm way. "Alas, I am not able to interfere directly in mortal affairs. It is the same thing I had to tell Miss Zaveri, before you ask. I designed corerunes to be a strong Tulari's lasting legacy. It didn't occur to me at the time that they would be abused in such a way."

"You truly won't do anything to help her?" I asked in disbelief.

"There is a fine line between *can't* and *won't* and forces at work I *won't* speak on," he answered. "She has her place in the weave of the universe, as do you, and I see neither of your threads ending anytime soon."

I rattled the bars once. "So, rescue is coming."

"Soon enough that my time with you is limited. Any last questions?" he invited.

"When will I earn the title you've given me?" I asked immediately.

"You already have. You will make something of the title in time. It could be a secret you only share with yourself as you quietly do your part to change the world. Or a big, bold declaration once you have finally finished my wife's task for you." He showed his palms. "I have given you the freedom to represent me because I know you will not abuse that power. When the time comes for you to use it, I will be there by your side, adding an echo of prophesy to your words."

"But—"

"If you would excuse me. It seems it's time," he interrupted. "Farewell, Sivana."

"Goodbye," I said, realizing he was already fading from view, back into the darkness like he'd never been there in the first place. I got it; he really didn't want to tell me what to do. I gnawed on a knot of frustration. It seemed he knew where my life was going but didn't want to share the steps ahead.

In fact, Mother Nilara had been the same way. I repeated to myself in her bell-like voice, *if I told you what your true task is now, you would never achieve it.*

I paced in front of the bars, hoping not to wake Zizi. Something big was coming; I was sure of it. But in the meantime, a mental presence reached out to me, and I nearly collapsed with relief. *"Hi, Sivvy! We're here to save you. Again!"* Ironfeather said cheerfully. *"Acton thought you might be dead, but I told him no way. I would've felt it."*

"My sweet boy!" I exclaimed. *"Who is 'we'?"*

There was a scuffle and a muffled shout somewhere outside my cage. A short shadow came out of the darkness. "Hey, it's me," none other than Ellie whispered. Metal started scraping softly in the lock.

"All of us are here," Ironfeather told me.

Zizi, who could sleep through a whole conversation with a god, popped up immediately. "Wha-huh? What's happening?" she whispered.

"We're getting rescued," I answered, smothering a relieved little laugh.

She brushed aside the sheet and peered out at Ellie. "Are you picking the lock? Allow me." With a brief flash of fire from her palm, it turned into slag on this side of the door and creaked open a few inches.

Ellie opened it further, putting a finger to her lips. "Can you do that one more time?" she asked under her breath.

I caught the flash of Zizi's teeth by the faint glow from her rune-etched cheek. "Yeah."

We crept down the ridge that had all the cave-like jail cells. My eyes bugged wide to see Cherin's muscular outline, currently tying up an unfortunate Rathi while Sharde stuffed a gag in his mouth. Pereyra, one of my quieter friends, was prodding a second Rathi to ensure he was out cold.

We stopped in front of the gryphons' cell. Valtora's fierce golden eyes peered back at me. *"Finally. They did all the fighting without me,"* she complained.

A hand fell upon Zizi and me both. "Before you release the undoubtedly furious mother gryphon, could you tell her we're doing this without killing anyone?" Sharde whispered.

Valtora didn't need me to say anything. She snorted in derision, getting to her paws and nudging Ari awake. *"Humans and their pacifism,"* she huffed.

"This is a neutral village. We don't want them to think we drew first blood. Gods know we don't want more enemies," Cherin added in a gruff mutter.

When I had Valtora's promise to behave, I nodded to Zizi, who melted the lock on their cage too. "This way," a third person said.

"Captain Howl? You too, sir?" I asked. What a surreal moment, to see my mentor and one of my father's friends here. When Ironfeather said "all of us," I'd immediately thought of just my old Kite Flight friends.

His whispered tone held a smile. "This is the most fun I've had in years. We have another team on the other side of the village, freeing the others. Any wounded?"

"Valtora lost most of the feathers under one of her wings. She won't be able to fly," I reported.

"We're ready for that. Anything else?"

"There's something I need to go get out in the woods."

"Should be fine," he said.

He showed us where our weapons, shields, and wands had been discarded in a heap. Once we all were carrying something out, the men ushered us out of the village, past other guards either knocked out or bound and gagged. We were lucky they hadn't entered the gryphons' cage and removed the saddle from Ari's back. He would be flight-worthy once he shook off the dragging film of sleep. I worried about the twist of emotion within him, however.

"Hey, we're getting rescued. Everything is okay," I assured him.

"I'll believe it when we're safe."

Out in the forest, I recognized Ironfeather and Echo, Biggs's gryphon, who sent feelings of greeting and relief to see that we were okay. Tempest and Fog were there as well, and between the four of them, they were rigged with a complicated rope harness designed to carry a fifth gryphon through the air. Valtora recognized it immediately, limping toward it with a warbling grumble that sounded distinctly embarrassed.

I breathed easier when the other group joined us from the far side of the village. Biggs, Credell, Feyring, and Weslecker escorted Father's pyrojack, while Captain Cyclone was at the rear of the group, supporting Father under one of his shoulders.

For a moment, I blinked in wonder. All of us were really

here, coordinating our escape. I rushed forward, throwing my arms around Weslecker, who held me close and pressed a kiss to my crown. "We cannot tarry. Will Ari be able to make the flight off Fegravik?" he asked.

"Yes," I said, breaking away from him with a nod.

I turned and realized my father was staring at the two of us. A flush took me head to toe.

"Something else you want to tell me?" he asked through gritted teeth.

"Uh, I need to go get that egg," I whispered, pointing into the darkness and rushing off to do just that. We hadn't buried it far, but I needed Ari's sensitive nose to pick up the scent of churned earth in the darkness. He helped me dig out the treasure we'd buried, and I slipped it into his saddle. We returned to the group impatiently waiting and ready to go.

Zizi was shuffled to ride tandem with a different gryphon rider to give Ari some relief. He shifted uneasily as I slipped into his saddle, his ears pinned back. *"We're about to get discovered,"* he warned.

We waited for the team of four to coordinate their takeoff so Valtora could be lifted properly. Ari's sharper hearing had picked up the shouts I heard a few moments later. I cursed that we'd left all our weapons behind. His saddlebags had a few essentials but nothing to defend us if the village followed us with volta or arrows.

One such projectile whistled through the dark, hitting a tree trunk with a solid *thunk*. Ari reared, spreading his wings for a cold takeoff as the rest of our friends scrambled into the air. I gave thanks for the dark, as the gryphon chatter reported a few scraped wings, but we were soon over the ocean, navigating to safety by starlight.

CHAPTER 25

ON ICE

"Like old times, huh?" Biggs asked. We were lined up in front of one of the command tents, painted with a blue stripe to denote the gryphon knight corps. The sun was barely peaking over the horizon, and our gryphons were passed out together nearby, except for Valtora, who was waiting to be seen by Tulari healers alongside Father.

I wanted to go face-down amongst the feathery pile of gryphons, feeling the sleepless night keenly. Zizi's story, my conversation with Lord Orion, even our brush with death all felt foggy around the edges like a fever dream.

"Yeah," I said, mustering a smile. Kite Flight all lined up for punishment, though this time, we were down a man and up Ellie, Howl, Cyclone, Cherin, and two pyrojacks. I saw fatigue in almost every face, but pride and defiance too, especially from Sharde and Weslecker.

The only one of us who was still perky and smiling was Zizi. Her Tulari mark had warmed to a merry orange on her cheek. I'd thought it odd that she'd woken up with enough fire magic within her to destroy two metal locks when she'd fallen asleep with her inner flame guttered and her mark dormant. Now that I saw her trying to engage the other pyrojack in conversation, her voice its usual flurry, my suspicions rose that Lord Orion had sprinkled a little extra magic over her last night.

The command tent rustled. Out stepped a uniformed Captain, who called us to attention for the ranking Knight-Marshall. He stepped out next, gray-haired and severe, just like most officers who worked closely with High Command. "At ease," he said. "Who speaks for your group?"

"I do, sir," Cherin said. "Everything you want to hear about started because of my squire."

I felt my face flame as several sets of eyes turned toward me, the Marshall's included. "Very well. I will hear your report first, followed by your squire's, and then the rest," he said, taking Cherin into the command tent with him.

The moment they were gone, Biggs turned back to whisper, "Weslecker and Sharde were gathering us up for Operation Redhead when he dropped in on us with the other two Captains."

I held up a hand. "Wait, did Sharde name it?"

"He insisted," Weslecker said dryly.

The young man in question leaned around Weslecker to give me a thumbs-up. "I knew at least half of your group were redheads. You, your pops, and Ari."

"Must we name everything so literally, though? And Ari isn't a redhead."

"Well, he still mysteriously changed colors around the same time you got your accessory." He pointed toward the Nilarite-white streak in my hair. "Anyway, the name of the operation doesn't even matter! We saved you, and no one got hurt in the process."

Howl, standing at the back of the group, started stroking his jaw and struggling not to smile. "That's because us old guys showed you how it's done," he pitched in.

"We didn't ne—"

Weslecker elbowed him hard and cut him off with an *oof*. "We greatly appreciated your help," he said for Sharde.

"Yes, thank you," Credell drawled. "I, for one, was glad to learn from senior gryphon riders."

"*Anyway*," Biggs snarked, rolling his eyes. "Our scouts had located the village you were taken to and suspected that, if you all were still alive, you might be there. Weslecker's gryphon was really sure you hadn't died."

"Insisted, really. We made the plan while unsure of your group's status. It was such a relief to see that you all survived your crash," Weslecker added.

I nodded in agreement, knowing it could've been much worse. I could've told them how much it meant that they'd all doubled back to rescue me, when Cherin left the command tent and motioned for me to enter next.

The command tent smelled distinctly of musty pelts and body odor, a combination that turned my stomach. It was lit by a single magelight and had a simple table set up with maps and small figurines. A marble set of Circles game pieces were front and center, though several were knocked over on their faces: the Earl, Advisor, Mage, Priestess, and Soldier.

I blinked in surprise. Had the Soldier eldrafn died yesterday alongside the Priestess? I'd been a little too preoccupied to notice. The pieces representing the rest of the eldrafn were painted with their colors: the King, black and silver; the Duchess, gray and pink; the Chariot, slate and yellow; and the Knight, umber and red.

At the back of the tent sat the Marshall, who gestured that I take a seat next to him. Sighing, he muttered, "There's a reason we split up training flights." He began to ask informed questions with Cherin's debrief in front of him and wrote a few extra details down from what I had to say.

"I take full responsibility for breaking rank and causing the mess afterward," I said. Ari was asleep and unable to protest. "My gryphon and the pyrojack riding tandem with us were not to blame."

"Well, then." He tapped his quill on the page a couple times. "Let me tell you what happens next. Your father and his gryphon will remain here to recuperate. Considering your slip-up didn't result in any loss of life, you will receive the same punishment as the rest of your fellow gryphon riders, who defied orders and left camp to rescue you.

"You're all going to the Iceberg and relieving the last set of riders we had to sideline to feed our prisoners of war," he concluded.

"But sir, we're needed here," I argued. "Most of us are on strike teams. What will happen to the pyrojacks used to riding with us?"

"Should I add insubordination to your file as well, Squire Walker?" he asked coolly.

"N-no, sir."

"Your pyrojacks will be reassigned, and we do not need reckless squires on the front lines endangering the rest of us."

I almost opened my mouth to argue against that, except it really sank in a moment later. He wasn't sending Zizi to the Iceberg with us. It would be in her best interests that I didn't dig my heels in and make the situation worse. This way, at least, she could still try to get her corerune back from Irene.

The Marshall watched my expression and nodded to himself. "Maybe some time on ice will help mellow out you and the rest of your training flight. You will all be on the next ship out, so go pack your things."

FATHER FOUND me soon after the conversation with the Marshall. He looked about as rested as I felt, with worry digging lines into his face and dark smudges under his eyes.

Behind him trailed Weslecker, who was looking unusually cowed.

"We need to talk, the three of us," Father said.

Swallowing my nerves, I followed him. Weslecker and I exchanged a few hand signals like we were mid-battle rather than about to "have a talk" with my still-angry father.

I asked what was happening, and Weslecker made a gesture between us and then a motion toward my father's back. Well, I *had* dodged answering the pointed question that'd followed when my first reaction to seeing their group following our jailbreak was to hug Weslecker rather than my father.

He found a quiet spot on the perimeter of the camp and turned back to us. "Explain your intentions toward my daughter," he demanded of Weslecker.

"Well, I..." He cleared his throat. "We have been courting informally. I assure you, we've been too busy to engage in anything untoward."

Father turned to me. "Is this true?"

"Y-yes. Let me explain—"

"Explain why you two have been tiptoeing this around me?" He started to show his teeth in a reserved smile. "Do you know how worried your mother has been that you wouldn't find someone else? Yet you have, in a war camp."

"You're not mad?" I asked hesitantly.

He narrowed his eyes. "Oh, I've got plenty of reasons to be angry at you, but this isn't one of them. When's it going to be a more formal affair?"

"Actually, Commander Walker, I was hoping to send word back home soon. I know my family would love her," Weslecker said. He put an arm around me slowly, and I stepped into his side, letting my father truly see us together.

"I think my family would too, if they got to know him," I said.

"Then it's official to me." He lifted his chin toward

Weslecker. "I'd like to chat a bit more, man to man, before you leave."

"Of course, sir." Both of them turned toward me. "Perhaps you should get some rest?" he suggested gently. I liked that idea more than I dreaded the fact that that they were going to talk without me. I trusted that Weslecker would be fine. My father wasn't unreasonable, for a commanding officer.

THERE WAS at least one small mercy: the next ship out left port twenty-four hours later. It gave us all a chance to catch some rest and say our goodbyes. I was the last awake in the tent I shared with Ellie and Zizi and caught them mid-farewell as I stirred back to awareness.

"What will you do on the Iceberg? I didn't think there was any engineer-y stuff to do there," Zizi was saying.

I cracked my eyes open a slit, curious of this answer as well.

"Probably no engineer-y stuff," Ellie answered. She fidgeted with her fingers.

"Being away from her work is punishment enough," I added, sitting up with a groan as my sore muscles protested. "Why *were* you there too?"

My brainy best friend lifted her chin. "No one else knew how to pick locks. Not that you all ended up needing my skills."

Zizi's grin sparkled. "Sorry." She turned to me, and the brightness of her usual sunny expression dimmed. "I'm really going to miss you. I can't believe they're reassigning me to another rider."

"It's temporary." I hoped. "Before you know it, we're all going to be back to help you get Starfall, if you don't manage to steal it back without us."

Ellie glanced between us, and I could see the wheels turning behind her honey-toned eyes. Zizi took her bottom lip between her teeth. "As long as you're okay with me talking about it?" I added, realizing I could've overstepped by mentioning it.

The pyrojack thought for a few moments before nodding slowly. "I don't mind sharing my story with people you trust. But let me tell the tale, all right? When you all come back. Um, whenever that might be."

"Soon, hopefully," I said.

We eased into our farewell from there. She followed us to the waterline after I went to retrieve Ari, and before we boarded, he turned and nuzzled Zizi goodbye. Her mouth formed a surprised *o*, and she beamed as she pet his wing on his way back to my side. "Well, goodbye to you too!" she exclaimed.

"I'll miss her warmth," he said to me.

I raised a brow. *"Sure. It's not like you didn't like her from the moment we were assigned together."*

"Sometimes you get a good feeling." His tone held a shrug. I felt that he would've lifted his wings the way a gryphon shrugged too, but he was holding them carefully to rest his sore muscles. As I watched the island holding our base camp shrink into the distance, leaning against the railing, he rested his weight against me and watched the sight through my vision.

His emotions had lifted to a sense of hopeful relief. *"What is punishment to you is a break for me,"* he commented. *"No more fighting, no more carrying two humans and all your battle gear on my back. No more chances to make a critical mistake that could cost lives. And I can feel how happy you are to be away from all those people and just spend time with your closest friends."*

"It might be okay," I admitted slowly. After so many long days fighting, I was left with the sense that we should be

doing something or heading for a conflict rather than away from it. I was sure guilt would set in soon.

Another person joined me at the railing. "What did my father want to talk about?" I asked Weslecker. I slid a little closer to him, just enjoying his nearness.

"Just wanted to see if I was serious about you. Which I am, by the way. I did send a letter to my parents about you."

"So, we're officially together?" I could hardly believe it. After fearing fraternization so long, the moment I truly decided to pursue someone, it seemed no one was going to attempt to forbid it.

His hand skimmed my arm, and his expression turned fond. "I'd say so," he said. "I would never hide you anyway."

I simply blushed, not sure how to respond. My belly felt warm, like a simple compliment from him could make me glow from within.

"Why are you still up here, by the way?" Weslecker murmured.

"Just thinking," I answered.

"Not to alarm you, but I've been doing some thinking as well." He smiled with my playful gasp. "Do you still have that letter from Mateo? Because I still have the translation, and I realized something alarming."

He already had his notebook ready and the part he wanted to highlight circled for me.

Mateo's letter and my reply seemed like it happened ages ago. But with Weslecker's emphasis, I realized the secret we'd overlooked. "The crown prince was meeting with Lithosian officials," I said.

"Just like he coordinated the Rathi attack that killed Prince Valentino—Gatekeeper rest his soul—his fingers most likely are in the sudden appearance of rozash. How else would Lithos know we are at war on two fronts?" he asked.

For a few long moments, I just stared at Mateo's words. "This is what I was afraid of. We are still jumping to a conclusion, though. We don't have proof of what the crown prince was really saying. Who knows, maybe he was really working on getting a marriage alliance with the Lithosian princess."

"Who else has the resources and the reason to combine Lithos and the Rathi coalition against us, though?" he pointed out.

"I just…don't understand why he would. What would the goal be?"

"I've given it some thought, and it's not a hard conclusion. Prince Isaac wants us to lose. He wants us to lose *badly*."

Logically, that made sense. "But why?" I asked, leaning in. "What does he stand to gain if Altare is conquered by the Rathi?"

He shook his head. "Not conquered. In a bad spot. He promised these villages something to go to war in the first place, but he also thought he would have unrest and the threat of civil war to weaken the army on the Storm Front."

"But I stopped that," I said. Because of me, there'd been no big riot in Kaiamear protesting the draft.

"And I'm sure he hates you for that. Point stands, he wanted us to lose to get his father up against a wall. We know that he wanted to use the unrest to force his father to step down from the throne. At that point, he would give the Rathi a generous gift for their assistance. Now he's promising Lithos something to risk their cold-blooded rozash up north. What could it possibly be?" he asked like he already knew the answer, like he'd connected these events and formed a full picture from them.

I was stumped, however. "What *could* it possibly be?"

"*Land*, Sivana. Something both countries desperately want from us. Lithos needs water, and the Rathi long for farms of their own. It's the only thing he could promise as a king that he couldn't as a crown prince. I daresay it's the only thing that makes sense. Isaac would give up portions of Altare to be king."

"Yes, but..." I watched his eyes widen, frustrated that I didn't agree immediately. I put my palms up. "I think it's a great theory. Let me add on to it. In this theoretical case, he assumed the Rathi cannot beat us at full strength, so he adds a new bargain with Lithos that also stretches out their forces.

"It's not the crown prince's way to dole out sections of Altare. He invites foreigners onto our land...and then they are vulnerable. What if this story doesn't end with just a knife in his father's back, but also in his so-called allies'?"

Weslecker considered, before lifting his finger. "Technically, he could finish the war with the Rathi and marry the Lithosian princess. In essence, Altare would be every step of land between the coast and the border with the Endoline Empire."

"*Gods,*" I muttered. "We have to write to Mateo again."

DESPITE THE WAY we'd started the voyage, once Weslecker and I wrote out a lengthy coded letter to Mateo, we spent most of our time on more carefree endeavors. I taught him how to play Circles of Power, and when he was still woeful at it after several rounds, we returned the game board to Ellie and watched her trounce the rest of our training flight one by one.

I enjoyed the time with no one expecting us anywhere or keeping tabs on us. Most of it was spent with Weslecker, easing into the idea that we were more than just friends now. It was okay to let my touches linger. To slip my hand into his. Even to kiss him, though I was afraid I was severely out of practice.

He was patient, though, far more so than I deserved. It was one of the things I liked most about him. Little things about him were becoming endearing, like the flecks of brown in his green eyes, or the way his prim composure broke when

I surprised him into a full laugh. The kind of details I'd been too busy to notice until now.

Our bubble of peace burst when we docked at the Iceberg and traded place with a motley crew of gryphon riders from various flights. I supposed that's what we looked like; outside of the Academy, we represented the gamut from elder riders that were former members of the First, to squires from half a dozen different combat flights.

Winter already had its icy talons around the Iceberg, as evidenced by the name. We got the ground tour from a quirky old army Colonel with a lazy eye, who enjoyed his relatively safe post too much, as evidenced by his presence with us. "Yule came early to give me all these fresh new gryphon riders," he'd said.

"When is Yule?" I asked, mostly to myself.

Colonel Gladden shrugged and made a vague gesture. "In a few days, I reckon. Come along now." He didn't have much to actually show us. Over a hundred Rathi lived on the Iceberg, most of them women, children, and the elderly. We were introduced to a few leaders who governed their tribe members, which surprised me most. They were nearly friendly, too. It turned out that, while a crew of armed Altarians guarded the Iceberg and kept these people here, they stayed peaceful amongst themselves in exchange for food and shelter.

This small island was nearly flat, perfect for the prefabricated buildings placed toward its center where the Rathi lived, along with sturdy walls that served double duty as both wind breaks and separating sections of the Iceberg. As we passed by, white-haired Rathi were shoveling the hard earth, busy planting snow pines along the perimeter of their camp. To have something to do, the Colonel told us.

I understood why we could trust these Rathi when we visited the prison next. Violent prisoners of war were locked in small cells within an elongated building. The floor and walls were insulated with rubber, giving my boots a springy step. "Some of you will be helping take care of the volta and the folks that've gotten too punchy," the Colonel told us. "Can't trust 'em out in the internment camp, so we put 'em here."

At this point, we had dozens of true prisoners of war locked up here. There was a host of armed guards at either entrance and a couple leaning against the bars of empty cells, looking bored. The Rathi stared at us as we walked by, a few slinging low insults in their language or spitting at our heels.

"Grounded, vultures? I didn't know there was a dead body here," a woman said in accented Altarian. She sat right before the bars of her cage, her dirty hair restrained in multiple braids and her hands bound in her lap.

"Most of our new friends don't speak our language, but there are a few exceptions. It's best to ignore them," the Colonel said, moving on without acknowledging her.

For some reason, I hesitated. She seemed familiar to me, but I couldn't place why. My friends filtered around me as I met her eyes like dark amethysts set over two dust-streaked tattoos of ivory white fangs that crossed her cheeks.

Weslecker put a hand on my shoulder, motioning that we should go. "Or am I to be the one killed today?" She sneered, meeting my gaze. "Send me to Idunn with a weapon in my hand, then, so I may see my eldrafn again with some honor."

I snapped my fingers as I placed how I knew her. Without the colorful scarves billowing around her and the fierce presence of the Priestess, its rider was much diminished. "No, I'm not here to harm you," I said, taking a step away. "How did you survive the fall?"

She made a contemptuous noise. "I recognize you, girl. How did you steal an egg from my people?"

"I didn't."

"Hmph. Perhaps I didn't really survive, either," she said.

I moved on before anyone else could notice that Weslecker

and I had lagged behind, feeling her glare fixed on my back. We returned to our gryphons, who were resting in an enclosed building with a floor lined in hay. It was warmer with the body heat of the beasts than the barracks we were shown to. I immediately covered my new cot with my bedroll for extra insulation as a cool breeze whistled through an invisible crack or two somewhere unseen.

"Maybe I should room with you," I suggested to Ari.

He flashed an idea over our Link, and I murmured it to Ellie, one of the only other women sharing this side of the barracks. There were very few female soldiers here, I'd already noted. "Technically, they didn't say we couldn't," she said. She shrugged and flopped her bedroll on the ground, and I did the same on Ari's other side.

When it was time for lights out, Ari sent a mental invitation that had Ironfeather and Puzzlebox poking their beaks into the room, startling a woman writing on a pad across from us on her own cot. She watched as Ironfeather squeezed himself between Ari and me, placing his head in my hands for rubs, while Puzzlebox flopped beside Ellie and snuggled into her arms like an oversized teddy bear.

I wasn't supposed to enjoy my time here, but that night brought on the best sleep I'd had in a long time.

CHAPTER 26

DRINK UP

Once we started working our new duties here, I clearly saw why it was punishment. In the morning, I would guide Ari while he held part of a giant net in his talons, coordinating with three other riders as we scooped the ocean for more than a catch of ice chunks. It was wet, smelly, cold work and didn't even feel productive since it was also our duty to throw back anything inedible before repeating the process.

Part of our catches went to feed the Iceberg, and *gods*, I was tired of fish. I hadn't realized it before, but we were also sending forward the lion's share of our bounty to the main front to feed those still fighting. Air couriers flew fish and crustaceans out by the bucketful.

The comings and goings of various Final Flight members also put deliveries in all of our hands faster. Father wrote to me often to update me on Valtora, who was projected to be out of combat for a month or longer. Her newly solidified immunity to healing magic meant the Tulari struggled to stimulate new feather growth. Nature would have to do the job instead.

Other letters and boxes arrived in an avalanche, and I opened mine in the evening as I sat with my friends in the mess hall, the warmest place on the Altarian side of the Iceberg with the combination a blazing hearth and the heat wafting from the kitchens as it cooked for the whole island. The crush of bodies huddled in the room also seemed to help stave off the winter chill.

Weslecker got to translating Prince Mateo's letters, of which there were two, one addressed to either of us. In the meantime, I realized I was opening Yuletide gifts when I started pulling out orange-cranberry crisps and another bag of mallows from Mother. "I don't think I've seen something more welcome," I laughed, rationing out the sweets to the young men and Ellie at the table with me.

"I miss Yule in the capital," Biggs sighed. "But especially the *giant*, crackling bonfire."

"Don't forget the feast." I savored the tart crunch of one of the crisps so I wouldn't salivate at the thought of all the not-fish items prepared for the people of Kaiamear for one evening of fellowship.

"Yeah…" he said dreamily.

I wasn't the only one unpacking gifts from home. Credell smiled wide when he opened one of his packages and passed around slightly battered wishing cones from a generous heap sent from his family down south, plus a few strips of carefully packed jerky. Pereyra received spiced treats and a heap of letters from his own family, which was huge and supportive.

The only one of us with no mail was Sharde, who I noticed was sitting on his hands and shrugging when Ellie looked up from one of her letters to ask him something. I felt bad for him in the midst of the rest of us enjoying such a big mail drop.

Weslecker tapped my arm, passing me the completed translation of Mateo's letter. "Thanks, Acton," I murmured.

Dear Sivana,

I have written to you a few times, but I imagine those letters were lost somewhere in your movement between the main front and the Iceberg. They may find you eventually. I am glad to hear that you were rescued so quickly. Had I been there, I would like to think that I would've been a part of the group that accomplished such a quick extrication.

You and Acton have come up with a theory that I share. My brother's ambitions seem greater than simply sitting the Altarian throne early. Considering how indifferent he is to the suffering and needless deaths he's caused, I <u>hope</u> in some strange way that there is a bigger plan, but either way, I have come to terms with the fact that Isaac has acted monstrously with his power. He should not gain a position with more of it and fewer restraints on how he uses it.

I take tea with him every few days. He is quick to remind me that I owe him for my safety in Kaiamear, when I believe it's my father that's keeping me from fulfilling orders to return to the Storm Front. My father has never been keen to spend his time and attention on me until recently, and I'm starting to feel like I'm filling the roles Valentino and Odalis used to, for advice and some emotional support.

Father has some outstanding spies in his network, and a few of their reports have sat in the bottom of the paperwork piles on his desk. He's allowed certain accounts of Isaac's actions to go unread, like he is afraid of what they might say. I have coaxed him to finally look, and I don't think he likes what he sees. What man would, king or otherwise?

Let us hope to be done with this pointless second war shortly. I look forward to further updates about how you are doing.

Mateo Cortes III

"Mine is a similar message," Weslecker said once I looked up.

I set the paper aside and pressed my teeth to my bottom lip, torn between two thoughts. "Even with the secrecy, Mateo didn't really say anything new."

"There probably isn't anything new yet. It sounds like the king will drag his heels as much as possible." He made a scornful sound.

"Yeah. I mean, I get it. It's his son, his blood." And he told me he felt like he'd lost two children already, devastating for any caring father. "I just wish he could come to terms with it faster, for the good of the rest of Altare."

Sharde turned to us, looking like a question was poised on his tongue, when there was a commotion from one of the other tables filled with weary soldiers. Old Colonel Gladden stood straddled between a precariously leaning chair and the edge of the table, his arm raised for attention.

"Everyone," he cried. "We missed Yule! It was last week!"

A few of the other men muttered, and a wave of shrugs passed through them. Most turned back to their mail, food, or mugs. "No, this will not do," the Colonel proclaimed. "We must do something! We have young folk and first-year recruits here. I say we have ourselves a party tomorrow. It's good for the morale. Wear your least smelly uniform. There will be a grog! Bring something to put in it. And I'll get us some o' that good swill, too."

"It ain't good if it's swill, sir!" shouted a man with a laugh.

The Colonel jerked his chin toward him. "You'll be first to the grog, then, Major." A few of the older soldiers erupted into jeers and slapped the Major on the back.

Colonel Gladden got down from his perch, and the room was warmer with raised voices. "What did he mean, find something to put in the grog?" I asked.

My friends didn't seem to know, but I caught the eye of Howl, who came over to crowd into a spot at our table. I repeated my question to him, and he grinned wolfishly. "Let me tell you about one of the military's great traditions…"

IN HONOR of the upcoming Yule party, Colonel Gladden authorized camp-wide bathing privileges. The seasoned soldiers always liked to remind young folk like me that we were blessed to be surrounded by water, even if it was cold and salty. At least we could splash off the worst odors that they reminisced on from their time on the desert front against Lithos with *way* too descriptive language.

Routine bathing was still a challenge to organize for a tiny, freezing island populated with far too many people. Especially when many of our potentially violent prisoners of war could sling electricity if we unbound their hands. But in the Yule spirit, the Colonel wanted to allow everyone the dignity of being at least a little more clean.

Naturally, as one of few women on the island who knew how to fight, that led to me guarding the women's bath with Ari as the female volta were permitted to go in one at a time. Some of the camp's workers were here as well, coming and going with laundry as in many cases the prisoners' clothes stank worse than they did.

While I was amongst those who thought this was a kind gesture, I was just as nervous as the workers in thinking that this could go horribly wrong, even with armed guards and limited amounts of prisoners out of their cells at the same time. Especially when the Priestess's rider joined the line.

She was four women back, standing out even amongst her fellow Rathi. She had the height of a man and what I assumed to be a lean, muscled form under the bulk of fur-lined leathers. Unlike many of the other prisoners I'd seen today, she must've turned down the warm, plain wool Altare was issuing out. Either that, or no one trusted the steely-eyed Rathi enough to allow her a moment to undress from her flight leathers with her hands unbound.

Her purple gaze found me and narrowed hatefully. In that moment, she reminded me starkly of Roshawk, defiant and wild.

She stepped out of line, jerking her chin at me. "Vulture."

I lifted my sword, pointing it at her neck. "Back in line," I said in my best commanding tone.

Instead, she inched forward again, letting the blade touch the skin right under her jaw. "Oh, how you tempt me," she said in a mere growl. I snatched the weapon away before she could throw herself on it. While I knew very little of the Link between an eldrafn and its rider, any gryphon rider separated from their beast by a mere week would still be on suicide watch. We had given her no such courtesy.

"Back in line," I repeated more gently.

A muscle feathered under her eye as she stared for long enough that Ari tensed and the other female guards started for us. "Only if we may speak," she finally said.

I motioned for the other guards to return to their post, my hand landing on Ari's shoulder both to relax him and ground myself. "About the egg?" I asked on a hunch.

She nodded stiffly. "*Ja.*"

"Perhaps we could trade some information." Mother would be proud of how quickly I saw an opening and identified someone who may know the kind of knowledge I wanted to gather.

"That depends on what the vulture wants to know," she sniffed.

"All right. I didn't steal the egg, I was given it to hatch," I said, lowering my voice.

Her expression tightened with distrust. "By whom?"

She probably thought I stole the egg from one of the five eldrafn the Altarian army had already killed, but that wouldn't be possible. It was common wisdom in the military that fallen eldrafn hearts were to be destroyed immediately.

"You wouldn't know her."

"And you insult me, to think I would forget the name of any honored eldrafn rider." She puffed up with offense. "Unless you scavenged it from a corpse like a true vulture."

I pinched the ridge of my brow. "No, I…look, I only know her first name and it's Signe."

"Signe," she repeated, gaze drifting thoughtfully. "Signe of the Bear River Clan?"

"I couldn't tell you," I said honestly.

"Mmm. She is very old?"

"Yes."

She nodded. "Then she is Signe the Lost. I am not surprised she would not share her disgraced name with an outsider. The winds know her story and how she dishonored the Bear River Clan with the death of her eldrafn—"

"Revna," I supplied with a nod.

She nodded as well, beginning to relax as we moved up one spot as another female volta finished her bath. "Idunn has not forgotten Signe the Lost or the death of sacred Revna. Her name is in the Eldrafn Saga, as will mine be, in the verses of the lost, the failed, and the disgraced."

"Because you're here?" I asked.

With a bitter laugh, she said, "No, because I survived. A fool serpent rider caught me when Hvitorden lost his life. All honored riders die with their beasts or ensure they rise again to take a new rider. I will be unable to do either.

"Don't look at me like that, outsider. You would never understand. I came to fight your people representing my people, the Icefang, to show Altare the bitter bite of the true north, where the sun rarely rises for half the year. Now that Hvitorden has died, the Icefang are vulnerable to raids from other, stronger Rathi. I can never show my face there again." Her face set with stoic suffering, and I locked my jaw so my expression wouldn't give away any more of my thoughts.

"I know a place where you could be welcome—" I started to offer.

"No." She answered quick and sharp. "As much as I admire that you are willing to help Signe the Lost, I do not wish to join her. Now what is it you want to know from me?"

"Well, first, I'm Sivana. What is your name?" I asked.

She scoffed. "Solfrid, formerly of the Icefang Clan."

"How do you know Altarian, Solfrid?" Since she'd said she was from even farther north, I wasn't sure how exactly she'd managed to learn the language in the first place.

"I spent my youth on my father's ship, trading with your people. When he became Chieftain, I was first to place my hand on Hvitorden's egg after his last rider died, so I became a messenger of sorts when I wasn't chasing off foreign eldrafn from Icefang land." She lifted an ivory brow at me. "You just want to know about me? Is this how you flirt, shy vulture?"

I flushed in surprise, especially when I noticed a fleeting flicker of interest in her eyes. *She's just toying with me*, I thought.

Ari made a sound of disagreement over our Link.

"W-What? N-no. I'm getting there," I stammered. "Also, stop calling me that." *Vulture* was starting to get under my skin like *Link thief* always did.

Solfrid smirked. "There are less flattering names for your kind in the Rathi tongue, if you prefer."

We moved up again. Soon she'd be taking her quick bath and heading back to her jail cell, so I needed to hurry to the point of this line of questioning anyway. "Have you or anyone you know talked to Altare's crown prince, Isaac?"

The good humor erased from her expression, which tightened to a sneer. "Oh, yes, I have spoken with your liar prince."

"What did he promise you and your people?" I asked.

"Hmph. What is it to you?" she countered. "He promised my people much and delivered nothing."

For a few moments, we stared at each other in mutual stubbornness. I'd already reached the limits of what she wanted to share, but I needed to know what he'd truly said to the Rathi to kick off this war in the first place.

"Did he promise you land?" I asked in a low voice.

"I liked you more when we were discussing eldrafn," she replied cuttingly. "If you can give me back my Hvitorden or the scarves my mother lovingly dyed for me, which were torn from my neck and discarded by your fellow Altarians, perhaps I will tell you how your prince betrayed all of us."

Two impossible things, I thought, imagining how easily the scarves in question would be trampled on a battlefield. "Why such a steep price for your information?" I asked.

"Because"—Solfrid leaned in closer, looming over me—"we are not friends, vulture. I owe you nothing."

She shouldered past me, heading for the bath awaiting her. I scrubbed at my face, taking my position watching the line again. *"Well, that was a waste of time,"* I muttered to Ari.

"Perhaps not," he said. *"At least now you know the name and face of at least one Rathi who spoke to the crown prince before the war. She could talk, with sufficient motivation."*

"Are you suggesting torture? Because her eldrafn's heart would've been destroyed, and the scarves must be gone."

"Yes, it could be an option. However, there's always some arse in a war camp who takes prizes from the enemy. Perhaps they weren't discarded like she thinks," he said. *"Imagine how valuable a genuine, pretty piece of Rathi clothing could be."*

"I hate that you're probably right," I grumbled. The first thing I did when I got off duty was write an extra letter to Father, asking if a particular set of colorful scarves had made an appearance in the main war camp.

In the slim chance someone cared enough to read this letter, I didn't quite tell him why I needed to get them back. But I was well aware that Father might still be unhappy with me, so I didn't want him to think I just wanted them for myself. So, I settled for a PS. *The original owner may share important information in exchange for having them back.*

My best uniform had seen better days, but the camp workers had it freshly laundered and free of excessive wrinkles by the time I donned it and headed to the Yule party in the mess hall on Weslecker's arm.

He had his chest lifted proudly as we sauntered in, flanked by Ari, who leaned on Ironfeather for guidance. Both of them were freshly cleaned and groomed by Weslecker himself, who took care of it while I was composing my letter and letting Ellie try to brush out my stubborn mane. Ari had playfully complained that Weslecker missed a few spots, but that was my man for you, who'd never quite become proficient in his gryphon care classes.

We toured to the far wall, where everyone was adding to the grog and talking briefly with Colonel Gladden. He was grinning broadly, like he was delighted to finally have a reason to throw a party on the Iceberg. Either that, or he was marveling at how disgusting the grog was already.

Howl had told us that the grog was a monster child of several different kind of alcohols mixed with ingredients donated by the soldiers, which were supposed to have personal meaning. Grogs down south were gritty with sand, for example, and this one would be cold and diluted with all the snow Sharde had hauled in to drop into it. By the time I parted from Weslecker's side, there were floating bits of cooked white fish, icy chunks, soggy bits of bread and other things turned unrecognizable in the amber-red liquid.

"Whatcha got me for me, lass?" the Colonel asked. It seemed his good eye was focused on me, while the lazy one drifted to where Weslecker still stood with his hand hovering over my lower back.

"Some mallows from home, sir," I said, sprinkling a dusty handful into the mixture. They'd become bloated and soft in the grog, so I really was just making the drinking experience worse. Hopefully this didn't ruin my favorite treat for me.

"Finally, something interesting." He laughed, patting my

shoulder. "Go enjoy the feast, then. I heard they did something special to the fish tonight!"

They could set the fish on fire right in front of me at this point and I wouldn't be impressed, but I still smiled politely and scooted aside a few inches for Weslecker to reluctantly add crumbles of the cubed cheese his family sent him recently. We soon shuffled to where the kitchen staff had set out a buffet.

It was mostly fish, as I feared, but they had made a valiant effort to give us some variety in cooking styles and presentation. If we had to eat seafood, at least we could have it grilled, blackened, sautéed, or poached, with a couple different herbs used lightly here and there. I filled my plate with a modest amount and added a side of roast seaweed before joining my training flight at the table we'd claimed each evening.

Howl, Cyclone, and Cherin dragged over a second table and fit themselves in with us. The three of them were practically honorary members of Kite Flight at this point. My mentor gave us a stern look. "Other than the grog, no alcohol for you all," he stated.

"We're going sober too," Cyclone added, raising a cup of water before taking a sip.

"Surely the whole 'impaired squire judgment' thing doesn't extend to Yule," Sharde complained.

Cherin had imposed the same rules on my friends as I had under him. PT every day it was possible, no funny business, and no odd substances either. I hadn't realized it, but Sharde and Feyring had picked up the bottle while I wasn't around, so the Iceberg and Cherin's strict rules made for a difficult transition.

He narrowed his good eye at Sharde. "Show me you have good judgment first. I don't want to be the one explaining to your mentor why I've allowed you to fly drunk."

Sharde rolled his eyes. "That was just one time, sir!"

Puzzlebox popped her head up next to his elbow,

distracting him when she tried to drag away his plate. The cold weather had brought out more of her fur at this point, giving her a long white mane around her head and chest which her rider maintained faithfully. He relaxed and rubbed the back of her head, feeding her bits of spiced fish he must've taken for her.

"Your fluff ball of a gryphon doesn't deserve to be steered into the ocean, so it's one time too many, squire," Cherin replied.

There were noises of agreement around the table, and Puzzlebox perked up from the attention. "That's fair, sir," Sharde said more mildly.

He scooted over to make room at the table for his gryphon, who draped her front paws over the seat and held her head at shoulder height between him and Ellie, looking around with her beak parted. It was the happiest I'd seen her since we'd come to the Storm Front, surrounded by her friends with no enemies to fight.

A fork struck against the side of a glass silenced us with a *ding ding ding* that rung through the room. Colonel Gladden stood beside the grog with a small empty glass in hand. "A fine late Yule to you all," he announced. "The grog is ready for your entertainment. As promised, we know who's drinking first."

The Major who spoke up yesterday got to his feet with a shrug while his friends laughed and clapped. Gladden produced a second glass, filling them both partially with a ladle-full of the grog mixture. They clinked their glasses together, and the Major drank first, followed by Gladden himself, to cheers and applause from many of the older soldiers.

I watched with a sense of bafflement as the two men shook themselves with a shudder at the taste. "It builds a sense of camaraderie," Howl had explained yesterday. "If you *don't* drink the grog while everyone else does, you're not part of the crowd. They'll ask what's wrong with you. It's just good fun."

And so that became our entertainment for the evening, watching folks stand and call up their friends to drink the grog. Reasons ran the gamut from "he looked at me funny this morning" to "she fell asleep at her post three weeks ago," but the end result was nearly everyone who'd been here longer than us came up to the grog. And though it was disgusting, they all drank to the cheers of those watching.

Woven into the soldiers were my friends also going up to drink. Howl picked on Sharde for being ungrateful, then Sharde boldly called up Cherin for taking on a mentorship role for all the squires sent with him. Eventually, Colonel Gladden's pointed between Weslecker and me. "These two youngin's next, together. For sitting together," he cackled.

I suppose he could've joked about fraternization instead, but I swallowed nervously as I felt eyes on me the whole walk to the grog. "Drink up," Gladden said, handing me a cup full of goopy grog.

"Cheers," Weslecker chuckled, clinking his glass to mine.

We tilted our drinks up at the same time, and I gagged something fierce with the burn of alcohol lancing straight down to my belly. Gladden walloped me on the back, and the mess hall was full of laughter, but I kept it down. Howl was right; I did feel a sense of closeness with everyone else who had to drink that vile mixture. This moment of peace and merriment in the midst of war was exactly what Yule was about, after all.

CHAPTER 27

AN UNEXPECTED LOSS

Before Father could send a reply to my request, the air couriers mysteriously missed a few days of deliveries. We knew something was wrong elsewhere in the world, so I wasn't the only one watching the skies for any sign of news outside the calm on the Iceberg.

Colonel Gladden was the first to receive anything by way of Final Flight, delivered and read privately. He spoke to us in his favorite spot in the mess hall that evening, his usual good cheer diminished. "Our people on the main front have suffered a defeat. A joint force of Rathi and Lithosian rozash riders destroyed most of our forward base, and the casualties are still being tallied.

"We've been pushed back to Manarfell Island, and for those of you who've been that far, it's like the Iceberg, no place to set up a permanent camp. We have to win the next engagement, so the gryphon knight corps' High Command is scraping its reserves, and the army is doing the same. Most of you will be shipping out to the main front at daybreak tomorrow."

I barely slept that evening, since no one knew yet whether Father was amongst those who'd fallen after the devastating loss. True to the Colonel's word, though, a ship was waiting at port to take us back to Manarfell, with a small team of Tulari to help manipulate water currents and wind direction to get us there as fast as possible, plus a true pyromancer standing at the front of the ship to help us cut through any ice standing in the way.

I supposed I should feel grateful that my punishment was over so quickly when some of the soldiers especially had been on the Iceberg for months. Most of them were amongst the men and women around me as we set sail, leaving behind the smallest crew possible to maintain order on the island.

Weslecker kept an arm around me as I stood at the railing, watching the island grow smaller on the horizon. "This feels like a last stand," I said to him quietly. "Calling all our reserves in, pinned on an island with very little resources."

"It very well may be," he sighed. "Either that, or we retreat to Inisthwaite and face the possibility of losing the war completely. It sounds like the Rathi are throwing everything they have at us as well. All four remaining eldrafn dominating the airspace, leaving the army susceptible to rozash attacks. They may not have much left if we can manage to defeat them instead."

I shifted uncomfortably at the idea of the King finally taking the field. "Promise me you'll be careful," I said, grasping his free hand between mine.

"Of course. I have to come back to you." He pulled me closer, claiming my lips and the breathy sound I made. We kissed until someone catcalled, which had me breaking away first with a flush to my cheeks.

Things were comfortable until we reached Inisthwaite, where a familiar group of gryphon riders boarded along with the reserves posted on the island. "Keeping our squires alive, Deadeye? Ha!" The hair on the back of my neck rose at the sharp laugh from none other than Commander Wrath, at the back of the Sixth and Seventh alongside his fellow Commander and big, brutish Skyla.

Cherin saluted crisply, not even batting his eye in surprise. "Good to see you again, sir."

"What are they doing here?" I muttered to Ari.

"No need to defend the coast anymore." He lifted his wings in a shrug. *"Don't make eye contact with Skyla. I can feel how ready she is for a fight from here."*

I could feel her hostile attention too, but Wrath's boots were stomping in my direction. I saluted him crisply with a bland greeting. "Squire Walker, so glad you're still around." He slapped my shoulder hard enough to stagger. "Look, uh, I need to give you this." While I was still recovering my footing, he was pushing something leathery in my hand and moving on.

It was a leather coin purse about as big as my fist, and within glowed gold and silver clorets, the Altarian currency, each stamped with the likeness of the late queen, Jimena Cortes, on one side and the rearing gryphon rampant of Altare on the other face. A slip of paper stuck out in the middle of the coins, and I tied up the purse both to read it and not flash the sight of more money than I'd likely made in my lifetime.

"The portion of the bounty on the Earl that you are owed. Don't worry, after the war, I will be disciplining your Commander if he is found guilty of dishonorable conduct," I read to Ari. *"Signed, Paragon Hughes."* Suddenly, the swaying deck seemed to pitch around me until my gryphon pressed in to keep me steady. *"Ari, do you see how big this is? The Paragon himself interceded."*

"I recall your father writing to him. Is this so surprising?" he asked.

"Well, sure. He basically acted without any doubt to give me all these clorets and embarrassed Commander Wrath by making him give them to me." As a matter of fact, I bet he was expected to

apologize. It wasn't too surprising that hadn't happened, though, given the man's pride.

Ari murred and nudged my hip. *"Is it such a shock that he might want to support you, then?"*

"I suppose not, but—"

I was looking out toward Altare in the south, spotting a lone gryphon rider heading straight for us. Most can't identify the beasts from that far out, but my heart knew the moment she was close enough to Link with.

"Mireille," I breathed, which meant that was Mateo leaning forward over her neck. She skidded to a landing on deck, flopping into a heap and panting heavily from exertion while Mateo slung himself off her back.

Ironfeather inched forward, nudging his sister in concern, while my gaze flashed from her to the dark circles under Mateo's eyes as he shook himself off and crossed the deck to Wrath to salute him. "Commander, I am Squire Cortes, reporting for reserve duty. My mentor was of the Third, and I received word recently of his death."

Wrath returned his salute with a low whistle. "Welcome aboard, Squire Cortes. You're just in time," he replied.

"I'd say so as well," the prince replied primly.

Ari and I went over to check on Mireille, and I adjusted her limbs to sit more comfortably when I felt how spent she was.

"Too much time lying around. I've gone soft already," she said. She flicked her ears in clear request, and I gave her a good scratch behind them and into her damp coat.

"I thought you and your rider wouldn't be coming back," Ari said to her.

She growled low in her throat, talons curling into deadly points. *"We couldn't let you fight all our battles. Besides, Mateo wanted to deliver his next message in person."*

Did he now? I glanced over my shoulder, to where Mateo and Weslecker were deep in conversation. Out of seemingly nowhere, Sharde leaned down with a set of towels, removing Mireille's saddle and drying her off briskly. "Stop mooning," he whispered to me.

"I'm only mooning at Acton," I whispered back.

"I'm aware, but does the princeling know that? It's not the time to do the relationship stuff right now," he said.

"Whatever, Sharde," I muttered. He was probably right. The ship was going to continue on through the night, delivering us to Manarfell by dawn so we could be put to work immediately. The Tulari team would be exhausted, but hopefully the rest of us would catch some rest beforehand.

"However, you could come clean about whatever else is going on," he continued. "Don't think I don't see you and Acton acting weird any time a message comes in from the princeling. And now he's here?"

"That's a long story," I hedged.

"We have plenty of time," he countered.

"Okay, but…" Before the king started to come around to the truth about Isaac, I would say it was treasonous, and that's why I hadn't included the rest of my friends in the conspiracy that had tied itself around me. But depending on what news Mateo was here to deliver, it might not even matter anymore. "Let me talk to the prince first, all right?"

"Uh huh," he said, raising a skeptical brow.

I let him tend to Mireille and went over to the two young men conferring quietly. My heart didn't even leap when Mateo smiled in that charming way of his, like nothing had changed between us. I suppose with him gone, nothing had, but instead, my relationship with Weslecker had grown around it.

"You came here to give us some news?" I asked.

"Well, hello to you too," Mateo said.

"Sorry, Mireille was saying it's urgent."

His smile faded, and he seemed to deflate. "We flew day and night to get here in time, so yes, I would say it's urgent too. My brother approached my father with his ultimatum much earlier than I expected."

"Surrender the throne, and he will get the Rathi to stand down," Weslecker supplied.

"And my father said *no*," Mateo replied, his voice dropping. "That there was no way Isaac has a way to stop the momentum of the battle about to take place over Manarfell. My stubborn old man said that Isaac would regret the weight of the crown and countered with an ultimatum of his own."

He glanced at Weslecker, who intoned seriously, "Get the Rathi to stand down, or surrender the crown prince role to Mateo."

"No kidding?" I breathed. I could see this happening, but only if the king had finally let himself accept that Isaac has been plotting against him.

"Isaac appeared to accept this with grace, but in private told me that our father would regret not taking his deal. His trust in me extended far enough for him to say, 'a great storm is on the horizon, waiting to crown a new king. Leave so you do not get swept up in it too.'"

"Ominous," I murmured.

"So here I am, having left the capital," Mateo said, gesturing to himself. "I slipped a warning to the king, hoping he will evacuate Kaiamear, but I imagine one remark from Isaac will not warrant that much caution. At most, he may evacuate himself and his court, especially if bad news comes from Manarfell."

"Our first goal is to make sure no bad news comes from Manarfell," I said in echo to him. "But Sharde just had a good point. I think it's time we told our friends what's going on."

"Good idea," Weslecker said while Mateo pulled a skeptical face.

THE SHIP WAS PACKED with too many people *just* to tell my training flight what we knew. I was mid-sentence when I realized Cherin, Howl, and Cyclone had joined our group below decks and were listening in with arms crossed.

So, Mateo, Weslecker, and I told them the whole story, starting with the moment the crown prince appeared in my dorm after Yule to tell me that I owed him a favor of his choosing. The air grew tense as I realized all these men were angry on my behalf around the time I shared that the crown prince tried to have me killed for his cause.

Ellie fidgeted with her hands, listening with growing concern. Her hand was up like we were in a lecture by the time we'd told the whole story. "Doesn't this sound like the crown prince knows something we don't about the coming battle? Like he's expecting us to lose and a figurative storm to loom over Altare in the form of the Rathi." She spoke like it was the most logical conclusion.

"Sounds that way," Cherin rumbled. His good eye flicked to the other two Captains. "Where does the First evacuate the court to nowadays?"

Howl stroked his beard thoughtfully. "Unless it's been changed recently, they'll be heading for Caershire."

Considering I hadn't heard of a Caershire before, it was likely an ideal place for the king to hunker down. "Where is that?" I asked.

"It's one of those towns that live in the Church of Mercy's shadow. Nothing but graveyard to the east and rolling green hills to the northwest. Odd folk that live there, but none of them questioned a private group digging out a bunker," Cyclone said. "A few locals offered to help bury the bodies when the army first broke ground, if I recall."

Oh, yeah. No one would want to go there willingly.

"All I have to say is this is above all of our pay grades," Howl added. "A trio of squires should've reported this up the chain of command a lot sooner."

"That's why the king is aware of it now," Mateo said coolly.

"And you all are as well," I added, putting a cheerful twist to it.

"Why didn't you tell me all this high treason *earlier*?" Feyring demanded. He'd definitely been amongst the ones most intrigued by the whole tale.

I was opening my mouth to reply, but it seemed fate wanted to intervene and leave our conversation unfinished. The boat rocked, and a high-pitched bell clanged above us. "Aerial attack? Now?" Cherin demanded, recognizing the ringing pattern. We charged above deck with our gryphons, only about half of which were saddled and ready to ride.

The setting sun backlit the canvas wings of three rozash circling toward out ship, announcing themselves with hisses and shrieks when they realized they'd been spotted.

Smoothly, our Captains transitioned to businesslike calm as they coordinated us into three rough elements. I went below decks again to grab cavalry swords and lances, quickly assisted by a group of soldiers passing weapons and saddles hand over hand up to my waiting friends.

The Sixth and Seventh were already in the air when Ari and I took off, flying just off Tempest's wing with a motley element of Sharde, Feyring, and Biggs. *"Just like you practiced in the Academy. Aim for their weak points, the spine and wing joints,"* Tempest instructed.

The gryphons made various croaks and cries in reply. I could sense some discomfort from Puzzlebox and Echo to be flying so close to full dark. We were lucky the rozash hadn't waited to attack after the sun set, though I found it suspicious that they'd been here over the open ocean, waiting to intercept us.

There were two pyremaws and an acidmaw, all of them with two heads and four swift wings, already twisting midair trying to aim their breath weapons around us to disable our ship.

"They probably weren't expecting this many gryphon riders," I commented to Ari, trying to retrieve him from the burning rage threatening to consume his headspace.

He grunted back but followed Tempest's instructions as we lined up on one of the pyremaws. I held my lance over his wing, aiming for one of the monster's wings as we dove as an element. The Lithosian rider standing on a platform between the rozash's necks saw us, though, and our target twisted out of the way sinuously.

It doubled back, both mouths glowing from their throats before Ari and I banked hard, away from the closer super-heated jet of flame. Under the pulse of Ari's anger came a sense of panic from a couple of the other gryphons close to us. I saw Biggs and Feyring struggling to get their gryphons back in line. It may be the first time either of them was in close combat with a real rozash.

Crack! Tempest surged forward and smashed Cherin's lance into one of the creature's wings. It fluttered uselessly while a scream of agony bellowed from two ember-lined mouths. Turning sharply, Tempest put on a burst of speed, and soon the rozash was giving chase around every turn and bend the gryphon led it through.

Meanwhile, Cherin gave us orders through his gryphon, and we clumsily made the proper formation. Puzzlebox twittered unhappily, projecting a desire to be anywhere else, and the other two gryphons weren't much different. I lined myself up on the second wing to the rozash's left side, which would spell its doom if broken. I wasn't sure if the rest of my friends would be able to score a direct hit.

We dove. Ari lined up with the precision of long experience, and I lost my lance, embedded in the scaly joint where the pyremaw's ruby scales melded into its serpentine body.

The shattering of its bones filled my ears before it was free-falling alongside our diving gryphons.

What I didn't expect was for the dying rozash to swing its body all the way around, one of its mouths closing around the closest gryphon with the *crunch* of wing bones smashing against its fangs. Ari was just coming out of his dive, leaving me nearly face-to-face with Feyring as his gryphon released an agonized, panicked scream. Flames were already licking the underside of her belly as the pyremaw prepared to breathe out for the last time.

Face white with terror, Feyring saluted before Ari peeled away desperately so we weren't incinerated in the same blast that consumed our flight-mate. The rozash hit the ocean with a harsh smack a few moments later, its body broken by the hard impact and soon sinking below the waves.

I dropped Ari's reins, my sight clouding over immediately. That didn't happen—that couldn't have happened! But I could already sense the empty space where Feyring's gryphon had been, a broken Link in and of herself with the echoes of her death rippling grief into every other beast in range to feel the aftershocks of her death.

It was so much worse when Lieutenant Occasion died in front of me while fighting the Earl. His death had been instant, a snap of the fingers between the Earl's attention and the strike of its lightning. But Feyring, he'd had enough time to be afraid, knowing there was nothing that could save him.

I didn't know if I could go on with the image of him in my head. There was only one rozash left, the other two food for the fish, and the other flights could take care of it. I nudged Ari toward the ship, but he stayed stubbornly circling in place. *"Wipe your face and look at the horizon,"* he said.

A horizon shrouded in storm clouds and distant streaks of lightning. *"Manarfell is already under attack,"* he said grimly.

CHAPTER 28

REINFORCEMENTS

"We could make the flight in a couple hours, I reckon," Fog said for Howl as we circled over the ship. I wasn't supposed to hear our leadership plan outright, but I could do little else as I sat on Ari's back limply, trying to keep myself together.

"And if the ship comes under attack and there are no gryphon riders left to defend her?" Skyla demanded in her harsh squawk.

"I volunteer the Sixth to stay behind. Everyone else can go," said an unfamiliar female gryphon, speaking for the Sixth's Commander.

"So noble," Skyla snipped.

"Just go, and hurry. They need us all to get there safely."

A few moments passed before Tempest reached out. *"We're flying ahead of the ship to join the battle ahead. Are you and your rider healthy enough to make the journey?"*

"Yes, sir," Ari responded.

There was one note of hesitation, from Mireille. A few gryphons ordered Mateo and his gryphon to land and get a bit of rest, but the rest of the remaining squires formed up and followed the Seventh toward the sight of lightning on the horizon. Ironfeather flew alongside Ari, with Weslecker making hand gestures toward me in the dark that I wasn't able to see.

"*Are you okay?*" Ironfeather burst out for him.

"*Not really. Feyring died. I…I saw it,*" I answered.

"*Gods, we've barely lost anyone compared to the other flights,*" he murmured. "*Sorry, Sivvy. We can remember him when we're safe.*"

"*And we will be safe,*" Ari interjected. "*We'll get through this.*"

I made a soft sound of disagreement. The only thing I'd learned about the so-called glorious deaths that happened at war was that they were often unexpected and swift. Things could be going our way, then the rider to your left could get struck by eldrafn lightning or consumed in rozash fire.

"*Tell that to Feyring,*" I muttered.

We powered onward in silence from there. I held the hilt of my sword, prepared to use it since my lance was floating somewhere underwater with the monster it'd helped kill. We could take on more rozash this way. From our angle of approach, I could tell at least two eldrafn were circling over Manarfell, flashing silver and red while they blotted out the stars with their black clouds. The King and the Knight, two eldrafn Ari and I hadn't had the displeasure of fighting yet.

Tempest reached out to convey orders. We were to fly in low to both get an idea of what was happening below—if we could see—and try to locate the team of Tulari that were undoubtedly on standby to cast shields and muffling spells on the gryphon riders. It seemed like an impossible task when we passed into the pitch-black space under the eldrafn's wings, but there were flashes below. Volta lightning and the sudden burst of flame off a giant fireball that had to be from Irene wielding Starfall. Despite the pouring rain, it still splashed into a burst bright enough for me to spot fighting figures on the shore and the outline of several longships.

A rozash screeched somewhere nearby, and I cursed. They

didn't need to see to find gryphon riders—relying on pits in their faces which sensed heat like true snakes. Thanks, Anatomy and Physiology class. The freezing, driving rain had to be awful for them, though, the only advantage we had would be for the cold-blooded creatures to slow down from the onslaught of weather from their would-be allies.

"*I see a beacon,*" Tempest said, giving us instructions until we could spot it too. A cluster of magelights shone as brightly as possible from the middle of the island, marking a safe place to land.

Ari's talons squelched in the mud as a few figures stepped out from under the magelights. "Reinforcements? Thank the gods," said one of them. Shields started weaving into place over Ari and the other gryphons who'd come in for a safe landing.

"Any directions you can give us?" Cherin asked gruffly from somewhere nearby.

"Stay alive." I recognized the voice of the curt healer who always cast her magic with a staff. I now knew that meant she was crafter-class, gifted enough to need a larger tool to channel her power into. "The low visibility is a handicap for all of us. We just have to survive until sunrise, then the true fighting begins."

"I know what to do, then," he replied.

As soon as we were in the air, Cherin gathered as many of us around him as he could and had us follow as he and Tempest baited a rozash into chasing them. The creature was eager to escape the freezing rain, so it flew after them longer than most rozash would take a gryphon's bait, until starlight glazed its tan scales and the crust of ice it shook off itself and its single head.

Considering none of us were at our best, we had a prolonged battle with this rozash, but eventually, it tumbled out of the sky from one final strike from Cyclone into its bleeding neck. *"Good. Again,"* Tempest said simply.

There was no way of telling how many rozash circled above the Altarian forces, but we killed three more under Cherin's leadership before the sun rose and the eldrafn stirred. They pulled back to reveal a battlefield covered in frozen blood and bodies from both sides and left us to pick up after the devastation they'd left behind. The Rathi rowed away on their longships, and the few rozash left circled over them, hissing and screeching.

"Maybe the crown prince was right. We are about to lose," I said to Ari, numb and chilled to the bone by the time we landed again.

I joined a team helping the wounded to the triage tents, searching each face for any sign of my father or Valtora. I found Zizi instead, using her magic to keep the tents warm as the team of healers saved those they could.

"Sivana? Five wonders, you're back!" she exclaimed, coming forward in a whirlwind to hug me and then Ari around his neck. "Did you hear the news? We might be retreating."

"Already?" I asked, my brows lifting. "Well…we always knew Manarfell is poorly positioned to defend." But if we fell back, we'd only hold two islands, Inisthwaite and the Iceberg, and I'd already come from that direction.

"If we do, you know what our job will be, right?" she asked, perking up. "Since you're here, I'll reassign myself to you! The guy they have carrying me into battle is a total creep."

"I don't think you can just—"

"Hey, you've bent the rules before! It's for the good of Altare," she exclaimed.

"I've found Valtora," Ari said.

Actually, it looked like she'd found him. Outside the triage tents, the golden gryphon clucked over him and groomed his neck while he grumbled. She was saddled, and the underside of her wing clearly hadn't grown its feathers back past a prickly texture of new quills. Father stood behind her, setting his sword aside. He forewent military decorum and hugged me briefly.

"Hi, kiddo," he murmured. "Look." He pointed to the horizon, which flashed with pink lightning. An answering streak of yellow laced with it, and my stomach dropped with dread.

"They're attacking us again?" I asked.

"I was just in the command tent. We think they kept some of their men in reserve for a second wave, assisted by their two fresh eldrafn," he said grimly. He still had his hand around my shoulder, which he squeezed. "I know you must be exhausted—we all are—but you're about to be summoned to get back into the air."

I was aware of Tempest reaching out. *"Calling the original Strike Team Three,"* he said.

I nodded, matching serious expressions with my father. "Be safe. No heroics. That's an order from a Commander," he said.

"Yes, sir," I replied. Mist filmed my eyes despite my best efforts. I was just so tired, and we hadn't even had more than a moment to grieve the losses piling up around us. "We lost Feyring on the way here."

His lips pressed to a thinner line. "I'm sorry, kiddo."

"I...I have to go," I added, turning to Zizi. "Strike Team Three is needed in the air as soon as possible."

Her mark was glowing, but not her eyes. Just enough fire for a short engagement, I hoped. "I told you, I was born for this," she said, flashing her teeth.

I made the needed adjustments to Ari's saddle, and soon we were covered in enchantments and in the air with Zizi, much to his grumbling about the extra weight. Howl was moved to the other element to lead it, and I counted eight riders total, four in one element and four in the other with Howl's addition. The other two strike teams were also diminished, but I noticed Mireille and Mateo had fit themselves into the same element as Ironfeather and Weslecker, each now carrying a pyrojack as well.

"All right, team. The Rathi were spotted turning their longships around," Tempest said. His voice was heavy with fatigue. *"We suspect a crew of rested reinforcements are now rowing them back our way slowly, biding their time for the Duchess and the Chariot to make the flight from Fegravik. Our goal is to disable as many of their vessels as possible while also not succumbing to our own sloppiness."*

"Yes, sir," answered Ari and the other gryphons around us.

"This is the make-or-break moment, men. If we cannot reduce the Rathi forces to a manageable number, we lose this war. We cannot fail here!" he said fiercely.

I joined in on the war cry lifting from gryphon and rider alike. Zizi cupped her lips and screamed. "For Altare!" we called together.

Over my shoulder, I said more quietly, "I sure hope you have some bombs."

"I have, uh…" She delved into the satchel she kept slung over her shoulder. "Three!"

"Gods," I muttered. We'd just have to make sure each one counted.

The channel separating Manarfell from the next island was short enough to make for a brief battle. We barely had time for three passes with the Rathi suddenly hurrying to avoid a watery grave courtesy of our bombs and more rozash making an appearance to fend us off with acid, sand, and fire.

I watched from above with a squirm of dread as the Rathi made landfall and engaged our forces on the already ravaged shoreline. We'd done our part, but I just hoped it was enough.

Tempest forced us to land for me to pick up a new lance, but Zizi remained behind me, aiming fireballs at passing rozash as long as they weren't red and thus immune to fire.

We were able to do this until the two eldrafn arrived and extinguished most of her efforts with driving rain from their swollen clouds. Even with reinforcements, the surviving gryphon riders were spread thin between the two lightning birds and the seemingly endless sky serpents.

"Not endless," Ari said with effort as we dodged the spit from an acidmaw and lunged in to wound its side with a strike from my lance and a muted fireball from Zizi. *"Just like we're running out of gryphon riders, they have to be on their last rozash."*

It sounded like hopeful thinking to me, but I tried to keep that thought buried as we struggled. Zizi's presence kept ice from forming on Ari's wings and coat, which he was grateful for as the rozash slowed dramatically from prolonged exposure to the elements.

I heard gryphon screeches in the distance and paid it little mind until Ari angled his head to one side. *"Impossible,"* he breathed.

Zizi cried out wordlessly and pointed over my shoulder. The core of the Chariot was flaring brighter, like the sun it blocked. Its explosion was quick and unexpected, blowing hot air over the battlefield in the wake of its sudden demise. As soon as Ari had a handle on the air currents, I pumped my fist and cheered along with the other fatigued gryphon riders around me.

That was just the kind of lucky strike we needed to take back control of the air, though the influx of warmth had made the rozash more quick and lively.

"Sivana, you don't understand. That was my father!" Ari opened his beak to scream. Dozens of gryphons cried out in echo to him. *"And he brought help!"*

I felt his desire for me to look into the lacey lightning that streaked the sky in the wake of the Chariot's death and spotted a dark figure dropping steadily toward the ground.

The battle cry of several unfamiliar gryphons surrounded us in the next moment, and they swooped in, clawing and biting and pulling on rozash wings, tearing at their throats. For several heartbeats, I didn't know what to make of it, my mouth hanging open in awe. Roshawk's help couldn't have come at a more needed time. These gryphons may just save us all.

Two of them fell in at Ari's wings. The silvery-blue male cawed in greeting. *"Hello again, Sivana. We're here to help with your territory dispute,"* said Reyos.

"We're here to help you," Sunset corrected, though it sounded like she was speaking to Ari. She was now the size of a fully grown Skymother, her feathers capturing the orange-yellow of a true sunset at the tips, giving her a bold profile against the drab white of the frozen island below us.

"Reyos? Sunset? What's going on?" Ari asked.

Our new reinforcements were riding into battle without saddle or rider. These were truly *wild* gryphons flying in to our rescue, soon clearing the sky completely of rozash. They choked the sky with their wings and screams of victory from blood-stained beaks.

The tide of battle was turning below us, many Rathi getting cut down in the wake of the show of gryphon force. *"Just what Reyos said. We're here to help you win this war,"* Sunset supplied. *"We don't know which humans to attack, but we definitely can hold the sky."*

As she spoke, I got a glimpse of the most welcome sight. The trained riders had all turned their attention on the Duchess, finally piercing its heart after the long months of it harassing us. Its explosion was a pillar of lightning unlike anything I'd ever seen, so massive it could not go out quietly.

"I can't believe I'm saying this, but any bombs remaining need to be dropped on the Rathi forces before all hands are needed on the

ground," Tempest said, echoing the astonishment Cherin must be feeling. "*If you are not fit for ground combat, then support the wounded.*"

While I thought I was fit to fight, Ari tugged me in a different direction, toward the triage tent. We landed with the two wild gryphons, and I encouraged Zizi to dismount before doing the same, guiding Ari with a hand on his wing toward a trail of burned feathers and blood dragged up the rocky rise toward the tent.

Roshawk, still somehow conscious but burning from several lightning-shaped wounds, dragged himself talon over talon. He snapped his beak weakly at a team of wounded soldiers who braved his anger to smother his wounds with damp towels.

"*Stop! I don't need your help!*" he raged, but his voice was also fading with his strength.

Valtora's head appeared from one of the triage tents. She had a badly wounded man propped on her back that a pair of healers was helping out of her saddle. "*I thought I felt you here,*" she said. She spoke tenderly and crossed the rest of the distance to her mate, lowering herself. Roshawk stopped dragging his body as soon as their beaks touched.

"*My love,*" he said with effort. "*I came…as soon as I could.*"

"*Shh. Save your strength,*" she murmured.

Stubbornly, he lifted his talons to cover hers, pressing closer to nuzzle her cheek. "*I felt your strength…and pain. So did the rest of us…for their mates, sires, brothers…*"

"*You led them here?*"

"*I did. Many are of my flock…but others…they found me when I went looking for family of the tamed gryphons.*" He twitched involuntarily from a lingering spark of electricity in his wounds. His groan afterward was faint. "*I gathered them for you…so I could see you again, save you from this…this duty. For my duty was and always is to you, my love, my heart.*"

"*Hold on a little longer, and we can talk later.*"

"Later?" he asked on a breathy whistle.

"Yes, later, when I can show you how much this means to me. You're going to be okay. There's a human with magic approaching us, and you will let her heal you," Valtora said. Her golden gaze was fully on her mate, but her ear was cocked toward a healer tiptoeing toward them.

Roshawk make a low sound. *"If I must."*

She turned her talons over, clenching them around his. He seemed to draw on her steady strength when he spotted the Tulari drawing the first runes of a spell aimed his way. His beak was parted mid-hiss when the magic hit him, knocking him unconscious.

"Sivana." Valtora's beak lifted, her tone as regal and commanding as a queen's. *"Inform the healers that I will be overseeing my mate's care personally."*

CHAPTER 29
BEFITTING A MATRIARCH

Valtora did not leave Roshawk's side, just like how Sunset shadowed Ari and me as we helped where we could with identifying and transporting the wounded. There was no great divide in time from the drudgery of helping the healers into the drudgery of simply cleaning up in the wake of our victory against near-impossible odds.

The only difference from this clean up and the last after the Battle of Port Lindell was the gryphons. They filled the silence of our work with the chattering back and forth of deep conversation. Mates sat together where there was space, one saddled, the other not. Pairs of wild gryphons cooed over their fully grown babies, many of whom were battle-hardened, proud Altarian mounts, and said beasts ate it all up.

I just wanted to stop and take it in. These moments were one of a kind. Everywhere I looked, there was a reunion taking place, flashes of joy and reminiscing passing over my mind as I heard snippets of their conversations.

Plenty of our beasts were still working, too, helping haul supplies and the wounded, but often accompanied by a wild family member. Their happiness started drawing a smile out of me, despite everything.

We'd won. We'd survived. But what was next? I worried that the appearance of all these untamed gryphons would cause strife somewhere, so eventually, I took Ari and Sunset on a walk—I mean, *securing the perimeter*—and spoke to a few soldiers who seemed to be eyeing our new companions.

"These are wild gryphons who trusted us enough to fly to our defense," I found myself repeating. "They're not used to humans and don't particularly like us. Don't go trying to pet or socialize one."

I discovered someone hauling out a dusty saddle and approaching a cluster of elder gryphons reminiscing together. I inserted myself in the way, holding my arms out. "That's a bad idea," I said, meeting his gaze. He was a younger man, probably a draftee, in an ill-fitting uniform but also wearing a hopeful expression. "Leave the wild gryphons alone."

All at once, his face shifted to one of fear. "Uh, y-yes, ma'am," he mumbled, dropping the saddle at my feet.

The next few who tried only took one look at me before abandoning the idea. I soon realized I wasn't the only one dissuading young soldiers from trying to take a wild gryphon for a joyride.

"You heard Lord Orion's Chosen. The wild gryphons are off-limits," Mateo was mid-sentence to another young man, who startled away when he caught sight of me.

I turned an incredulous look at him. "We're supposed to keep that quiet."

"Was it a secret?" He lifted a royal brow my way. "Because the troops are starting to talk about you, and it's really not subtle."

I wet my lips, feeling the attention of dozens of eyes on me all of a sudden. "W-What's not subtle?" I asked more quietly.

He was looking past me, smiling to Sunset, who had taken my momentary pause to start grooming Ari's wing feathers. "Is that you, Sunset?"

She clucked back, tilting her head and lowering it when he

came over, letting him scratch her behind the ears and beak. "Tell me I'm not seeing things. Sivana, say something about leaving the wild gryphons alone," he instructed.

"Leave the wild gryphons alone," I echoed, now puzzled.

"See?" he said. She bobbed her head in agreement.

"Your eyes are glowing," she explained, pushing a mental image into my head. Gods, I'd seen better days. My hair was half-down from its braid, tangled behind my head, and dark hollows under my eyes marked how long it'd been since I had a restful night. My freckled face was pale and dry from the cold, but my eyes...

They were eerie, not what I saw every time I peered into the mirror. A refraction of gold caught the light, sparking to life when I talked about the wild gryphons. Unsubtle to anyone but me since I didn't feel any different.

"But yes, Father told me. You really made an impression on him when you did the eye thing in Lord Orion's temple," he said.

Fingers of panic threaded up my throat. I'd flashed my patron's gold magic to the king? That fateful meeting was months ago at this point. How often had this happened without my knowledge? And why hadn't anyone pointed it out before now?

"It sounds like he's just lending you a bit of help," Ari ventured, coming forward to press himself to my side.

"Relax, Walker. You just shared that Lord Orion wants these new gryphons to be safe from any clumsy attempts to tame them." Mateo clapped my free shoulder with a brief smile. "No need to panic."

"Okay. No panicking. Except you're telling everyone I'm his Chosen," I said with a sigh. "I don't want to be branded a heretic by evening."

He scowled, his touch lingering. "No one's going to harm you, nor are they going to touch the God of Mankind's beasts. Yes, my father mentioned the change of status too. He...

believes I will be the one to assist you in spreading the message."

"Well, I appreciate your help. Any assistance you can give me, even," I said before muffling a yawn. We parted ways from there, with plenty more work to be done before anyone got to rest.

Our leadership team decided that we were going to remain on Manarfell upon receiving classified reports from our scouts and spies about the state of the Rathi after their defeat. That didn't stop rumors from rolling around the camp, but I heard relatively few of them when nightfall came around and a soldier handed me a tent and a field stool.

I ended up sitting on the stool beside the triage area and giving the tent to Ellie to go find us a place to pitch it. I just… didn't really get up from there. The air chilled, and the wind stirred with the sound of rustling feathers. Ari rested to my right, with Sunset practically lying on him, while to my left sat Reyos. He'd cuddled up to my thigh and promised it was only because of the cold.

That may explain why dozens of wild gryphons arranged themselves around us, forming feathery piles to ward off the frozen night air together. Beasts I'd never met before lay behind me, touching my back lightly to share body heat. I knew it was practical, but I felt truly special at their proximity.

"*By the way…*" I projected to Sunset before I forgot again. She blinked over at me sleepily. "*Congratulations on becoming a Skymother.*"

"*Oh, thank you,*" she murmured. "*I felt the call even before I left you and Ari at the Academy. I went to impress him, though, and to become more his equal.*"

"*Did you now?*" I asked with the same infusion of intrigue my friends used when I spoke of Weslecker.

She clicked her beak. "*Yes, and it is that serious for me. I hope when all this settles…maybe we can find a space to be together. I don't want to follow in the Skylord's flight path, though. If this only works if we are both tame, then I will take a new rider."*

My mouth formed a "wow" silently. I rubbed Ari's wing as a smile threatened to crack my face. He was out cold, a state I wanted to be in with him soon, but that meant he was missing this confession. *"He missed you too, while you were gone,"* I said.

"Being away from him was one of the hardest things I've ever done," she sighed. *"My new flock is not bad, but it took significant work to get them here."* She lifted a wing to encompass the "here" she spoke of.

I invited her to tell me about it, feeling myself sink into the furry side of the gryphon behind me. *"Well, I had to prove myself to them, that I was not just any tame beast,"* she began. *"Roshawk, especially, was suspicious of me when I told him I didn't think all humans were Link thieves. He only listened when I passed his three tests to become one of his lieutenants, after returning to the flock a skymother.*

"I told them all about you and the goodness I saw in other cadets at the Academy. How most gryphon riders don't realize where their beasts come from or the state of the families they leave behind in the wild."

I began to drift off with her soft, calm voice soothing my mind. *"I told them not to let their hatred for human mistakes overcome their love for their lost family members. Skylord Roshawk listened first, and the rest of us followed him here..."*

I HAD A LEISURELY WAKE-UP, face-down in the fluff of a wild gryphon. I pulled away from him with slow caution, but there was no hostility there, and he introduced himself as Echo's father with a yawn and a long stretch. He was the same soft brown color as his daughter, with a similar chipper way about him.

Most of the wild gryphons had spread out to bask in the watery sunlight, but they hadn't ranged too far from the healers' tent. I had a feeling why when I bid Echo's father farewell and ventured inside.

The crafter-class healer pointed her staff toward a section they'd curtained off in the far corner. A low growl rose from Valtora's throat when I pulled it back a sliver to check on them. *"Oh, hello, Sivana,"* she said.

One of her wings was curled around Roshawk protectively. His eyes were open but glazed, like he was coming back from a hefty dose of magic. The feeling was like the slow flow of cold honey, something I was well familiar with.

"How's he doing?" I asked. Bandages seemed to cover him everywhere her wing did not.

"Healing magic can work miracles if you've never been exposed to it before," she replied. Carefully, she tweezed one of the bandages in her beak and pulled it up, revealing a line of pink skin where there'd been a jagged wound yesterday.

"That's great news," I said. *"I think his flock is waiting for his leadership. They're all outside."*

She tilted her head thoughtfully. *"Then he will speak with them when he is up to it. First, I would like some time with him."* Her golden gaze flashed with meaning.

Right. Also without me. *"Take all the time you need,"* I said, closing the curtain for them.

I shared the news with Sunset and Reyos, who took control of the flock in the meantime. Now what to do? Ari was still snoozing, and I wanted to give him more time to rest up. I could join one of the teams working to clear the island, but when I went to do so, wary expressions followed me, and odd glances from complete strangers. Discomfort had goosebumps rising up my arms and I avoided talking to anyone after all.

Eventually, my father found me. "Valtora reminded me that I have something to give you," he said. We wandered through the tent city, to where his was set up. He retrieved a battered wooden box from his things and handed it to me. "One of the soldiers was about to send it home to his sweetheart."

Within were three woolen scarves dyed in bright bands of color, a little worse for wear at this point. "Gods, I forgot I asked you for these."

"Want to share why I needed to spend a king's ransom to get them for you?" he asked dryly.

I closed the box and held it to my chest, telling him about my brief conversation with Solfrid. "I believe she knows something of what the crown prince promised the Rathi."

He frowned through my explanation. "I see your logic, kiddo, but it's unlikely to be anything substantial enough to warrant the effort."

"But what if it was?" I dropped my voice. "Enough to prove his plot. I think a few scarves would be worth it."

Father put his arm around my shoulders, turning me to look to the charred husk of the island we'd lost to the Rathi. "Know what our command thinks?" he said just as quietly. "We're going to see a group of Rathi on the other side of the channel any minute, waving a white flag."

"But they never surrender," I gasped.

"Yesterday, we broke the spine of their army. Our scouts report that the remaining rozash riders have fled, and they are second-guessing fielding their last two eldrafn when we killed the Duchess and the Chariot in the same engagement. Either they surrender now, or we crush the remains of their army once we've regained our footing."

It sounded like he was fairly confident the war was over. I dared to begin feeling a kernel of hope at the prospect. "We could go home for an Altarian winter rather than freeze up here," I said.

"We can gather up the rest of our family and have a proper Yule dinner by the fire." He smiled wistfully. "I miss your mother's cooking."

"I just miss Mother."

He nudged me with a laugh. "Listen to you. A little time on the Storm Front, and you're cured of your teenager phase."

"It's not like that," I said defensively.

His smile was just growing wider. "She's been waiting *years* for you to admit something like that. Oh, if only I had a memory orb! I'd record what you just said, and she could replay it any time she wanted."

I was probably *really* lucky memory orbs were in the same magical classification as magelights and thus not the kind of thing Father toted around, waiting to immortalize something I said.

"Well, I'll tell her myself when we go retrieve her and Rissa from their rural temple." And I was looking forward to it, too.

"While I have you here, can you explain to me why the troops are talking about you like you've turned into some kind of supernatural?" he asked.

"Oh, err, you know how the king said it would take the people a while to get used to me being Chosen?" I began. He let me talk but led me to a fire pit where a warm breakfast was being served. A new squire puddle, I realized, with a few of my friends still eating.

Father patted my shoulder proudly. "There's no better time for you to protect gryphon-kind. I'm proud of you, kiddo."

"Thanks, Father." I bubbled from within when a few of the listening squires pitched in their agreement. There would be no hiding my status anymore, but maybe that would be okay.

AT DAWN THE NEXT MORNING, the Rathi flew a white flag of surrender and boarded an armed Altarian vessel to negotiate with our commanders. I sat outside the healers' tent, sandwiched between Ari and Valtora. She was leaning against Roshawk, who was significantly mellowed from a second blast of healing magic, which was allowing his feathers and fur to grow more quickly.

"I'm not sure we can stay here for long," he said. *"Not because of you or the exceptional human or two that loves my kind. There are many that would want to continue stealing Links and we've presented them with their choice of gryphon."*

"There are more humans that will support us than you think," I said. I reached out to brush my fingers over a wild gryphon's shoulder when he came forward for a skittish hello. In a way, I wondered if some of these beasts had met a friendly human before or if I just had special privilege by Valtora's side.

The moment Roshawk was well enough to walk on his own four paws, he'd gathered his flock around and proclaimed Valtora their Matriarch. I think they woke most of the camp with a cacophony of celebratory screeches.

"And I built our flock from the moment you left," Roshawk had said more privately to his mate. *"So it would be befitting a Matriarch."*

He was being bold, giving Valtora the title he'd long been denied as a male flock leader. In the wild, a Matriarch protected her flock for decades and claimed the best territory to help them thrive. *He* had done that instead, but in one swift move, he'd handed Valtora all the power and control he'd cultivated, and she accepted it gracefully.

I reaped the rewards of Matriarch Valtora's approval in these little touches and greetings. I was their first human, perhaps the only human that'd be a part of their flock.

"I believe we can keep everyone else in line," I said, adding on to my previous thought. *"I have a question for you, Roshawk."*

"Mmm?" he asked with a touch of his usual gruffness.

"How, exactly, have you singlehandedly killed two sky terrors? Everyone else thinks it's impossible," I burst out.

He whistled out in surprise. *"It's not a big secret, and it's definitely not impossible."*

"How is it done? We've lost plenty of good gryphon riders trying to kill a terror as a team," Ari said.

"When I was younger, I noticed something about them. Their heads aren't set above their shoulders, like ours," he said. He hunched his shoulders up, which spread his wings out a couple feet, but allowed him to rest his head closer to his paws. *"It's hard to see under all the clouds they wrap around themselves."*

"And they call gryphon riders vultures," I muttered. While he held the stance, he looked a lot more like a carrion bird that'd scented a fresh kill.

"This hunch creates a weakness, a blind spot. If you swoop in at a sky terror from above and behind it, it's highly unlikely it will see you before you have your talons around its heart." And just like that, Roshawk blew my mind. How had we not noticed this in the long months of being *terrorized*, if the pun is excused, by eldrafn? *"I was young and fit when I killed my first terror. As you can tell, I lost my edge for the second and nearly died for it,"* he grumbled and preened his wing self-consciously.

"You still killed it when we needed the relief most. Thank you again," I said earnestly.

Valtora leaned over and helped him preen. *"My handsome, brave mate,"* she cooed. Roshawk nuzzled her neck with an affectionate murr.

Ari shuddered next to me. *"Must they act like they're newly mated?"* he whispered to me privately.

"In a way, they are," I whispered back.

"You're not helping."

I just grinned, reminded all too clearly of every moment he pointed out how much both Mateo and Weslecker seemed to like me.

"That's entirely different," he complained.

Maybe it was irresponsible, but I rested there with them, playfully bickering with Ari and just enjoying the wild gryphons' company for longer than I should have. The camp was mostly clear at this point, and peace was on the horizon. It felt like an ideal moment to finally catch my breath.

That was, until Tempest reached out mentally. *"Calling all members of Strike Team Three."* Ari and I both went rigid. *"The last two enemy eldrafn have been spotted heading straight for us. Command wants us in the air with our pyrojacks as soon as possible. It seems the Rathi aren't surrendering after all."*

CHAPTER 30
KINGMAKER

"I KNEW it was too good to be true," I said to Zizi as we circled higher over the water, watching for any ships headed our way. We were fully kitted out with shielding and muffling spells. She had a new set of alchemical bombs, and I was carrying my wooden shield and the eldrafn egg around my wrist along with my usual weapons.

"I don't know. It seems quiet to me. *Too* quiet." She tittered a laugh as she wound two small fireballs between her fingers.

"They might be waiting for their eldrafn to hit first this time," Ari ventured. The sunny morning was spoiled by a pitch-black storm heading our way, laced with silver and crimson strikes of electricity.

The gryphon knight corps had shown up in force for the coming threat. Combined with the wild gryphons who'd followed Ari and me into the air, we formed a cloud of wings, bristling with weapons, magic, and talons. But as the moments passed, it seemed we'd formed up just to stare at the horizon.

No attack came. But the red-laced Knight eldrafn passed above our heads with such a buffet of wind that every gryphon was thrown around and, in some cases, into each other with cries of pain and disorientation. I steered Ari as best as I could, with Zizi clinging to my middle while we were tossed by invisible air currents.

It was even worse when the King followed, smacking a second wave of chilled air over us. Many went in for emergency landings. Beaks turned in the wake of both eldrafn, and the angry calls of gryphons turned to puzzlement.

"I don't trust this, team. I want my element in pursuit," Tempest said for Cherin. The sleek male wove his way around several disoriented beasts and was already picking up speed when I got Ari into position off his left flank.

We weren't the only team flapping hard to keep eyes on the two storm-forged birds, but as we gained altitude, I noticed shifts in the patterns of their lightning. "They're zigzagging," I told Zizi.

"They're also not heading for Inisthwaite," Ari added.

"Then it's a chase, and it looks like the bigger one is also faster," Zizi said.

She had a sharp eye. Since the eldrafn were pulling ahead of us, even with Tempest leading our element at top speed, all I could see was their general movements. Still, it made logical sense—the Knight was the one zigzagging, and the King appeared to be lunging at it. The only one under attack here was the smaller eldrafn, but why?

"My guess is some argument between their riders." Ari answered my unspoken thought.

I wet my chapped lips and sent a thought to Tempest. *"Sir, it doesn't seem like this concerns us."*

"Maybe not, but I still want to see how this plays out," he said. *"By the way, Squire Walker, I've finally decided on your call sign."*

"Oh?" That was unexpected.

"Consider it easy because of all your new friends. I dub you call sign Wild." Tempest sounded like he was smiling.

"Thank you, sir. That's so much better than Girl," I said, relieved he hadn't named me after the novelty of my gender. I

still hoped there would be more female gryphon riders to come, especially since King Cortes finally seemed to accept me.

"I wholeheartedly agree."

It seemed he was going to say more when the King lunged once again with a distant rumble of thunder rising from it. The wind shifted around us, and Tempest suddenly balked, as did Cyclone and his beast, Icestorm. I didn't have the same reflexes as the older gryphon riders, so Ari and I went flashing past them.

The King had succeeded in its quest. I caught sight of its beak throwing a glowing ruby ball high above it—the Knight's heart. Panicking, I dug my heels into Ari's sides, and we turned into a hard left bank, expecting an explosion at any moment.

The King closed its mouth around the heart, swallowing it in one gulp. If there was an explosion, it happened from within its body of mist and storm. Hostile turbulence surrounded us as the black wings of the eldrafn expanded rapidly, its lightning making thicker, more prominent lattices over its whole body.

It grew bigger. And bigger. And *bigger*, until it towered over the sky and its roar shook loose some of the muffling spell over Ari. Zizi and I cringed together.

"That's it. The eldrafn from our dreams," I told Ari, pressing him to follow. Massive, black clouds, and silver lightning primed and ready. Even from behind, I knew it on sight as the monster that'd killed us countless times in a shared dream.

"Team, that monster is heading due south for Altare. Don't give chase—you will not make the ocean crossing or catch it," Tempest said.

"Sir, I have to try," I replied.

"More insubordination, Squire Wild?"

"Five wonders. Are we chasing it? I have an idea," Zizi was saying. She turned herself around in the saddle, twisting her riding harness around her ankles in what had to be a painful way. The eldrafn was gaining speed, heading for Altare with the kind of swiftness a gryphon could never achieve.

"Give me a chance, sir. The Mother gave me this task." I looked over my shoulder to where Tempest was just off our wing now.

Though I wore the streak in my hair, I'd never spoken to my mentor of Lady Nilara's task, nor did he ask. I hoped that, if the time ever came, he would step aside if it was truly vital to completing what I was called to do.

The Mother never truly explained the dream of this eldrafn, but the feeling of powerlessness was still fresh in my memories. The same feeling countless Altarians would have when they saw this gigantic storm bearing down on them.

"I thought you were Lord Orion's Chosen," Tempest replied.

"Well, sir, it's complicated."

"The affairs of the gods often are. If you die, it's my head on the line. Don't do anything stupid chasing a god's task," he said stiffly. It was the closest thing I'd get to permission, and I was taking it.

"I'm open to ideas," I called back to Zizi. She had her head lowered, positioning her hands and seeming to hesitate before shifting where she held them.

"Well, here goes nothing!" She drew her arms back before thrusting them forward with a big burst of flame on either palm. Ari squawked in alarm as she propelled him from behind, pushing him through a stubborn air current. He flapped rapidly before spreading his wings to soar for the minute she maintained the spell.

It felt like we gained on the dark storm until Zizi had to cut the magic off, panting heavily. "Great idea!" I called to her. "Can you do it again?"

"Yeah!" She choked on an ill-timed laugh that turned into

a coughing fit. "That was nothing. I'll get us across the whole ocean! No crashing and drowning for us!"

Gods, Zizi, don't remind me that's possible. I was already on edge, seeing only blue water and black storm clouds everywhere I looked. The other gryphon riders were distant specks now, most turning around rather than facing the prospect of crossing the ocean between the Rathi Islands and mainland Altare. It'd taken our military vessels two days to pass the same amount of water.

But the monstrous eldrafn was skimming that water, drawing from it to gain even more size and strength in smaller increments than its sudden explosion from consuming the Knight. "Okay, here we go!" Zizi exclaimed, interrupting my thoughts. This time, Ari was prepared, and we skimmed along the sky at double-time for another heart-lurching minute.

She swiped at her face with the back of her hands. "It's not too late. You don't have to do this," I said, hesitating only when I noticed how her golden skin was sheened with sweat. She'd pushed the limits of her magic in the last few days, facing the Rathi in the last battle and even earlier. It couldn't be healthy for her.

"No, we have to. We can't turn around now," she said, flashing me a strained version of her usual grin. "If we don't, who will? And we can't let this storm destroy Altare."

Still, we paced out the bursts of magic. Ari seemed deep in thought while navigating the air currents with each push. *"It's not going to destroy all of Altare. I think it's a targeted attack, actually."*

"Oh?" I frowned.

"I was searching my memories for any hints. Remember when Mateo told you about the crown prince trying to corner the king and convince him to step down?"

I did remember that. Mateo had rejoined us less than a

week ago, but it felt like an eternity had passed since that conversation.

"Do you remember what the crown prince said that had Mateo coming back to the Storm Front, though?"

My brow furrowed, so he helped me. Mateo had shared that Isaac said…*a great storm is on the horizon, waiting to crown a new king. Leave so you do not get swept up in it too.* And he'd tried to convince the king to evacuate Kaiamear from that ominous statement. It was hard to forget, but now that I was staring down a great storm, I realized how literally Isaac had been speaking.

"How could he possibly know this was going to happen?" I demanded.

"The only thing that makes sense to me is that this was already planned. If all of Isaac's plans failed, he had one last secret up his sleeve. Who was he meeting with before the war? It could've been the King's rider."

"And he cut the rider a different deal. Leading to him murdering the Knight and its rider to achieve this level of size and strength," I added.

"Exactly."

"Which means we're not heading for Kaiamear. The crown prince would've told him about the king and court evacuating to Caershire." I swallowed past a thick stone of fear stuck in my throat. *"Isaac really did help Mateo by telling him to leave. So the king wouldn't insist on evacuating him along with the rest of the court."* A moment of brotherly trust and love that'd given us a hint of the plan…

"No. It was a manipulation too. The king and court will be evacuated already because he knew Mateo would warn their father," Ari interrupted.

Gatekeeper take that man. In the courtly game, the real Circles of Power, we were three moves behind, with the King bearing down for a final victory. *"No, that thing isn't the King anymore,"* I decided. *"It's the Kingmaker."*

Zizi rested her back against mine as the day shaded to afternoon, and then evening. Her Tulari mark was beginning to gutter to a flat red color when we first caught sight of land. "Thank the gods," I muttered. My understanding was, like a real storm, it would begin to slow down and diminish with no ocean water to draw from.

My happiness was fleeting, however. The gale-force winds and hurricane strength rain from the Kingmaker left a swath of devastation behind it from the moment it made landfall. It wouldn't be a hard target to follow, even as its clouds began to blend in with the plum tones of early evening.

Zizi's slight weight reminded me too keenly of the time she'd passed out behind me. I was all too aware, as well, of Ari pushing the limits of his natural speed and endurance after flying all day, even with the extra magical help. I was bleary-eyed and saddle sore, my muscles threatening to lock up from the constant onslaught of cold air.

"We're not going to make it," I said, despairing.

Zizi breathed a tired giggle. "Sure you are. But you're going to have to land a moment to drop me off."

"Huh?"

"Face it, Sivana. When I run out of magic, I'm just dead weight. If you stop for a moment, I'll take the saddlebags too and Ari can fly as unencumbered as possible."

"Yes, but I don't think he'd get back up off the ground if we landed," I said.

He snapped his beak. *Speak for yourself. I can do it.*

I didn't have to say my other thoughts aloud. He read my misgivings off our Link, how I could feel him tiring, and how I doubted we'd catch the Kingmaker if it hadn't been possible with Zizi's help. Even with it slowing over land, it would reach Caershire before we intercepted it at the pace we were going.

"Don't count me out yet. We've come a long way just to give up now, don't you think?" he pointed out.

We circled in for a quick landing while there was still visibility. "Don't worry about me, I'll find my way to somewhere safe," Zizi promised. She staggered like a drunkard when she was free of the saddle but had me stay mounted as she unclipped Ari's saddle bags.

I tossed my cavalry saber down next to her. "Use that if you need. It'll fetch a good price if you need coin, too," I said.

"Okay. Good luck. You need to go." She flashed a tired smile.

I reached out and clasped her thin shoulder. "Thank you for everything."

Ari flexed his wings, turning and taking a step away with his urgency to get back in the air. Zizi cupped her hands to shout after us, "Remember to use the egg! Stay safe!"

I helped navigate Ari into a running leap, and he groaned as the wind caught his sore wings. Only when we were steady did I look down, returning a wave to the distant shape of the young woman below us.

Then we set our sights on the rumbling storm ahead of us, painting the horizon with black clouds and rivaling the emerging stars with flashes of silver lightning.

CHAPTER 31

GREATEST NEED

ENDURANCE IS KEY, a talented gryphon rider once told me. Cherin had handed me a magestone etched with an endurance rune, meant to push a gryphon to the very lengths of what their body could handle.

I'd given that magestone to Weslecker, knowing Ironfeather wasn't already immune to the effects of body-augmenting magic, healing or otherwise. How I wished I'd kept it now so I could press it to Ari's neck and pray it still helped him, even a little bit.

Instead, we had nothing extra to help us. I could only lean so far to reduce our drag, but Zizi was gone, as was the extra weight of the provisions in our saddlebags. Ari himself would be the difference between catching the Kingmaker and arriving just in time to see a ruined Caershire with the king presumably buried under the debris.

Tomorrow, we could have a new man as king, someone willing to use anyone else as a stepping stone to the stairs up to the largest throne in Altare. Pure spite for that thought kept me going, while Ari was locked in a mindset of pure determination.

On his side of the Link, he relived every slight for his

blindness, every moment someone doubted he could achieve the same feats as an able-bodied beast. He pushed to the very ends of what he could do, despite the pain in his wing and the fatigue threatening to claw him out of the sky. In Ari's mind, we were catching that storm. There was no other way this ended.

If only my fellow gryphon riders saw Ari now and felt as he did. Within his heart was every core tenant of the Academy. Here was their courage, loyalty, discipline, and integrity, speeding along to be someone else's miracle.

"We're not going to make it. Not on our own," Ari gritted out. No matter how determined he felt, he also could feel his strength flagging and our altitude dropping despite his best efforts.

"You tried. Ari, you did the best you can. If we won't make it, let's not push you any harder." I stroked the back of his damp neck, feeling the shudders beginning to wrack him as sweat turned to frost in the brutal chill of this winter night.

"No. If the gods intended for us to finish this task, I won't give up. But I will demand their help!" He released a sharp cry into the dark, to the cold stars shining down on us. The wind slapped away the mist from his beak.

Nothing happened. He hadn't evoked a specific god, I thought—

"Glorium. I was calling to him," he interrupted.

"Glorium?" I echoed, confused. But that feeling melted away when something glittered out of the corner of my eye.

The massive gryphon swooped out of nowhere and left an easier current for Ari to glide upon off his right wing. His heart started to come down from its frantic thumping as he had a moment to catch his breath. *"Yes. Glorium! Demigod of gryphons!"* he exclaimed.

"Hello again, little ones," Glorium said, sounding entirely too proud. *"You've called, and I've answered in your moment of greatest need."*

In a private whisper, Ari said to me, *"Every human calls to the gods. They ask and beg and tug, even in casual conversation. Me, me, me, pay attention to me. How many even know of Glorium or think to call to him? Plus, he's a demigod. Maybe he'll be able to meddle in mortal affairs a little."*

"You're brilliant," I murmured. I'd only stolen moments with Lady Nilara, and despite being Lord Orion's Chosen, our conversations had been equally fleeting. But who'd had the time to fly me across Altare?

Glorium, who'd also been so lonely that a nice compliment had puffed out those magnificent feathers of his. The moment Ari wanted him, he'd arrived. *"Glorium, you're a sight for sore eyes,"* I said.

"Thank you, I know."

Gods, he was also a little too smug. But I wasn't going to point it out.

"So, I also know you're very close to an important moment, but did you know someone's been chasing you all this time?" he said.

I turned my neck stiffly to look over my shoulder, like I'd be able to spot them in the dark. *"Really? Who?"*

"I'll give you three guesses."

If my face wasn't frozen in a grimace, I'd have made a more annoyed expression. Were we really playing kid's games *right now*?

"Weslecker?" I sighed.

"Hey, you only needed one guess! That's right! He had his pyro-jack fumble out a spell to mimic what yours did. You've been out of hailing range, but I can fix that."

"Wait, we need—" The glimmering gryphon disappeared, and Ari grunted as he had to push himself to stay in the air without Glorium's tailwind. *"—your help. We needed his help,"* I finished.

The Kingmaker pulled ahead of us again, and there was nothing we could do. It must've only been a few minutes later, but Ironfeather's voice was suddenly in my head, shouting loud and hoarse. *"Sivana! Arimus! Wait for us!"*

"What are you doing?" I countered. *"You didn't have to follow us!"*

"Yes, we did!" he argued. Our connection strengthened as, presumably, Glorium led him to gain on us rapidly. The demigod passed Ari again soon after, with a shadow clinging to his left wing. *"We're here to save you!"*

"We don't need saving, youngling," Ari replied, huffing with relief when he returned to the tailwind off Glorium's right wing. *"We're doing the saving."*

"Great, so are we. What's the plan?" Ironfeather asked. Despite sounding just as exhausted as Ari and I felt, there was still a cheerful twinkle to his tone.

"Remember how a wild gryphon killed the Chariot eldrafn out of nowhere?" I asked. *"We're doing that to this one, because he taught us the secret."*

"What I remember is that gryphon nearly died from his injuries," Ironfeather answered, though I heard Weslecker's prim disapproval in his phrasing.

"Ari and I think this eldrafn will kill the king and his court unless it can be stopped. We're doing this," I said.

"Mmm. Remember the way the Duchess exploded everywhere when it died? The man who got the killing blow died to take it out. And the Duchess was a fraction of the size of this monstrosity we're chasing."

"I have Revna's egg. It'll be different."

"No, Sivana. I doubt it can absorb that much energy—and remember, the king is huddling in a bunker as we speak. He has one in Kaiamear and another in Caershire if that's where we're going. He's going to be fine!" he exclaimed.

"You're not saying anything I haven't thought of. Look, Acton. I have to do this."

I peered across the sky, trying to catch a glimpse of the young man who'd done everything in his power to follow me and pull me out of danger. His devotion put a knot in my chest. We'd barely had a chance to be together before destiny called—because that's what pushed me onward. The knowledge that this eldrafn was meant to die by my hand, and Lady Nilara had known it ever since she kissed my brow.

"It's my task, and I have to do it. My whole life has led up to this moment," I continued. *"If I die in the process..."* I swallowed painfully on the thought. Ari and I hadn't faced the prospect, but now I had Acton and Ironfeather to answer to, and it was nearly too much. *"...then it's what the Mother intended for me."*

Life must come from death. The former is my concern, but the latter is yours. She'd even said it herself. She and Lord Orion had been mute about my future, knowing how this task ended.

Ari and I couldn't fear it. If it was our destiny, we would leave this world the heroes who'd slain the Kingmaker. We'd proven a blind gryphon deserved a second chance. And, hopefully, that women deserved to Link with and ride gryphons with the blessing of the God of Mankind.

"How can we help, then?" asked Ironfeather sorrowfully. *"If you must do it, then you don't have to alone."*

"But you don't—"

"Stop arguing," Ironfeather interrupted. *"We love you. Let us help you."*

I wiped at my face with shaking fingers, swiping at the tears leaking into my flight goggles. *"I love you too."* Ari made a soft croak. *"We love you too,"* I corrected. *"Give me a status report, then. Do you have shields?"*

"Both shields and a muffling spell intact. Acton feels frozen to the saddle, and I'm fine," Ironfeather answered. *"He says the endurance rune you gave him is starting to dim. Once it goes out, we'll have to land and I'll go to sleep for a long time to recover, probably for a few days."*

That sounded about right. *"Does he know about how much longer you have?"* I asked.

"A couple hours at most."

"Ari's basically spent. He called to…wait, can you see the giant gryphon?" I wondered why he hadn't mentioned getting fetched by a demigod gryphon.

"I thought we might have more pressing matters. But yes, we see him. Who is he?"

"That's Glorium. Remember that book we read that suggested Lord Orion had a mount of his own?"

"Gods, all right. Leave it to you to get help from a living legend," he replied.

"It was Ari's idea. But anyway, we have to swoop down on the eldrafn to kill it, and it's moving too quickly for us. I'm worried its heart will move out of range mid-dive at the speed it's traveling at," I said. I recognized I was about to ask the impossible of him, the idea only half-formed. *"If it was distracted even for a few moments, we wouldn't have that problem. But I don't know how it'd even see you, considering its size."*

Weslecker and Ironfeather were quiet for several long moments. I counted the space between lightning strikes from the living storm ahead of us. We were gaining ground at last, but the biggest challenge of all would be getting Ari above the eldrafn to make it possible to swoop down on its heart.

"I have an idea. Do you think there's still a rider on that thing somewhere?" Ironfeather finally asked.

"Presumably around its hulking shoulders," I said.

"We're going to attack him. That'll get the eldrafn's attention."

He wasn't wrong, but I also thought that would be the easiest way to get smote by several lightning bolts at the same time.

"I don't know…"

There was a shift in Ironfeather's mental presence, as if he were turning to the glimmering gryphon between us to ask,

"Lord Glorium, would it be possible for you to take us higher? Above the giant eldrafn, perhaps?"

"Of course," he replied warmly. His feathers brushed out and glimmered the moment Ironfeather called him "Lord," I noticed.

"If he can get us above it, maybe you won't need to attack the rider," I said, still trying to hedge a situation where they weren't also heading into the maw of danger.

"Do you have a better idea? We're about the size of flies to the thing," Ironfeather replied. *"So it probably wouldn't bother with me otherwise."*

"I'm thinking," I said.

I noticed a flicker of faint light from them. Weslecker peered at something he held against Ironfeather's neck as the gryphon seemed to go limp for a split-second before shaking his head and righting himself. *"Think faster. The rune just flickered."*

"Maybe you should land, make sure it doesn't fail at the wrong moment—"

"No, we're doing this. If you have to, so do we, and that's that," he replied stubbornly.

"Hate to interrupt," Glorium interjected. *"I wanted to let you know our unfriendly storm will be above Caershire in thirty minutes."*

Suddenly, the impossibly swift pace behind the giant gryphon's wings seemed akin to a snail's. We were climbing sharply behind him, ascending past comfortable airspace for a human rider. My hand was going to freeze solid around the lance I held in a death grip, and frost crystals began creeping down my scalp in a chilly ripple.

"We have to make it," I murmured.

"We will. But I figured you might want to say your goodbyes," he replied, and his serious tone cut like the chill wind.

"Wes—Acton, I..." I stammered. We were nearly brushing the giant storm's tail feathers, and for the first time, I caught

sight of the bloated heart pounding away within the confines of its black clouds. An eerie half-light gave me the chance to look over and meet Acton's gaze across the wingspan of the demigod we followed. *"I hope you have a long, heroic future ahead of you, with all the sword fights you could possibly want. I hope you come back to the Academy someday to teach the cadets everything you know, just like you wanted. If I'm to die, it's my wish that you tell everyone that you slayed the Kingmaker so you get the reward and the recognition for vanquishing it."*

He shook his head, his auburn hair stiff with ice. *"If you're to die, then I will have you immortalized as a Hero of Altare and will accept no less. But if the Goddess of Life has decided you are doing this, then she had best preserve you. If she won't, then instead...I would not mind joining you. Wherever we go next, I hope it's a place without war where we can settle forever."*

Gods, he was going to make me cry again. I couldn't feel my face, though, and managed to keep my goggles from fogging as we kept ascending. *"I hope so too,"* I murmured.

Ironfeather's tone held a smile for both of us. *"I think we can take it from here. Good luck."*

"Good luck," I echoed, raising a gloved hand to salute. Weslecker returned the gesture before peeling off, speeding along the curve of the eldrafn's wing as he pushed Ironfeather into a full-blown sprint.

Just a little more, and we would be in position as well. I panted for breath in the thin air, seeing dark spots creep in from the corners of my vision. I blinked rapidly, struggling to stay focused on the curve of the eldrafn's body. Glorium successfully led us to hover atop it and angled his body to give us a dip of his head.

A sudden explosion of sound rumbled like the aftermath of a hundred lightning strikes. The eldrafn's smooth flying ended with an angry jerk. *"It's time!"* I shouted and dug my heels into Ari's side. He folded his wings and dove, blinding me as we surged through a bank of black mist.

Ari didn't truly commit to the dive until I had eyes on the heart. It was not the smooth core we'd seen within other eldrafn, bearing a lump like the Knight's heart was fused to its side. My gryphon tucked his wings in tightly, aligning the tip of my lance square on our target. Its throbbing sent rivers of electricity from it, starting to wear away our magical shields as we approached.

The nearly empty chest cavity we crossed was warm and still, just like a storm's eye. If the living storm was still in motion, the heart was too big and unwieldy to move out of our trajectory in time. Our impact had the lance piercing it all the way to the tapered hilt of the weapon, jarring Ari's exhausted body.

Our dive turned into a desperate freefall as silvery-white light erupted behind us, along with the heat of a too-close sun on our back. In one last motion, I held Revna's egg overhead like it could shield us from the explosion that turned my vision white.

CHAPTER 32

THE CROSSROADS OF FATE

DEATH WAS a white room with no walls, just an endless expanse of nothing except the debris at my feet. My left hand was still stretched above me, but the pouch on my wrist was empty.

"No," I whispered, falling to my knees. This wasn't debris at all, but flakes and shards of stone turned to purple-veined glass. The pile was the right size to be the remains of Revna's egg. I'd failed to hatch it. It was destroyed along with Ari and me in the Kingmaker's explosion.

Instructor Signe had trusted me with it. After fifty years of dormancy, I'd managed to take it to the realm beyond with me, shattered like broken dreams. I cast a desperate gaze around for any sign of Ari, or Weslecker, or Ironfeather. Why was I alone with Revna's remains? My heart lurched when a hooded figure approached, emerging from curls of silvery mist.

She was slim, clothed in the dark gray of a Mercy, and approached me with an elegant hand extended. "D-don't be afraid," she said in an unsteady voice, and sniffled. "Death, uh, comes for us all. It finds the young and foolish just as easily as the old and infirm. No one hides from the Lord Gate-keeper for long."

"Odalis?" I breathed, placing my palm in hers. A surge of electricity leapt to bite into our skin, drawing a wince from us both.

She swept the hood down, revealing her young, aristo-cratic features and a trembling lower lip. Her pin-straight black hair was cut to her shoulders, just long enough to slip around and frame her teary face. "When the Lord Gatekeeper said I was claiming my first strong soul this evening, he didn't say it would be yours!" she burst out.

"It's okay," I said, layering my other hand under hers when I felt how it was chilled. "I'm glad he sent you. Do you know where my gryphon is? Did he survive the explosion?"

Her eyelids batted rapidly. "I...I don't know." She squeezed my hand and tugged me to my feet. "You don't feel like a loose soul."

I opened my mouth to ask what a loose soul felt like when someone cleared their throat. I jumped, not expecting more company, especially not for a flash of power to come our way. An impossibly vast form wound out of the mist, made of starlight and dark matter.

I blinked, and a glowing, silver-skinned woman towered there instead, her power contained to an eight-foot frame with a pair of magnificent wings flowing behind her. Moon-stones and pearls glowed over her gown of white silk. Her face was sculpted perfection, cheekbones shimmering with moon dust and framed by hair made of spun moonlight. It was hard to look at her for longer than a few moments and when I finally turned away, my glimpse of the Mother was just a memory, as she'd taken her usual form as my actual mother with eyes blazing full of power.

"That's because she's not dead, sweet Mercy," said Lady Nilara. Her bell-like tone sounded like the twinkling of a thousand stars in harmony here in this white void, sweet yet vast. My head ached.

"Thank the gods," Odalis murmured.

"Where are we, then, my lady?" I asked.

She held up her hand before turning to look over her shoulder. Her voice took on the chill of a frosty, moonlit night. "Where is my son?" she asked.

"He entrusted me to speak for the both of us," answered an accented voice.

I glanced to Odalis with disbelief when a second goddess joined us. She had Solfrid's tall, stocky build, except a heavy winged helm obscured most of her face behind a silvery visor and her furs were dyed a storm cloud gray. Solfrid also didn't carry a broadsword that glowed with Anrathor's blood-red magic slung across her shoulders.

Lady Idunn tilted her head up, like she was meeting the gaze of the goddess wearing my mother's guise. "Besides, this concerns my magic and blessed beasts. Let us get on with it," she said impatiently. Her voice was huskier than Solfrid's, with a jagged edge of danger befitting of a warrior who'd impressed and wed the God of War. She swung his weapon from her shoulders, putting it point-down in the white space between her boots.

"Idunn, these two mortals are here representing Orion and Daroche. You may recall that my husband selected a Chosen. This is her, Sivana Walker. She will be instrumental to your new duty." Lady Nilara gestured to me, and for a moment, the other goddess's attention skimmed over me. I had the distinct feeling that she wasn't impressed with what she saw. I was just trying not to flinch from the casual usage of the Gatekeeper's name. "And standing in for Daroche, one of his newest Mercy, former princess Odalis Cortes."

"Hmph. It's just like him to avoid coming in person," Idunn said sharply. "Have you called me here to waste my time, or has the moment happened?"

I exchanged a glance with Odalis, who looked just as worried and lost as I felt. "What moment?" she whispered.

"One of your mistakes is dead, yes," Nilara answered.

"Watch your phrasing around the mortals," the other goddess snapped. Purple-tinged lightning danced over the hilt where she held her husband's broadsword.

"They should know why they are here, Idunn." She turned a kind expression toward Odalis and me. "When she ascended and married my son, I offered Lady Idunn the chance to have a blessed beast created in her name. Though I had my misgivings, I created eldrafn as you know them today at her description and request."

"And they were a failure," Idunn interrupted irritably. "Killing most mortals who approach them, with a life cycle too unpredictable to rely on. They made my people's lots in life worse by their existence and may have just destabilized the weather in a massive section of our continent, which led to this moment and my new duty."

I wet my lips but squared my shoulders. If I was going to represent Lord Orion, I couldn't let her manner intimidate me. "I thought eldrafn existed before you became a goddess, Lady Idunn."

She scoffed and waved dismissively. "Many tales are exaggerated."

"We are at a crossroads of fate," Nilara added. "You achieved part of my task for you at last, Sivana. The death of the eldrafn you dubbed the Kingmaker happened just in the nick of time, releasing a more natural weather event to wash Altare on down to Lithos in a shower of cold water. His passing also marks the death of the last tame eldrafn. Many still haunt the wild spaces of our world, but that is not a problem to address right now.

"Like I told you, death is your concern, and life is mine. You carried a piece of ten of Idunn's creatures to us." She turned to the other goddess. "Are you ready?"

"My power is yours to use," she replied stiffly.

"Kneel with me, Sivana. This is as much your moment as ours," Nilara said. I rested my weight on my knees, careful not to crush any of the remains of Revna's egg. "Purple is Idunn's chosen color. Revna was a lovely lavender storm, born with too much power and a body too small and unstable to handle it."

I pictured Zizi as she spoke of instability and nodded sadly. "Her rider has tried for fifty years to revive her from this state."

"Indeed. And for her troubles, the egg absorbed more and more energy with no sign of life. It even took some magic from…" She spoke a foreign-sounding name that barely registered past my gasp. After rooting through the glassy debris, a plump egg the size of my fist appeared in her hand. She gave it to me, and I turned it over with wonder.

Emerald green patterns danced over its shell, intertwined with the unique gray of the Earl's storm clouds. "And with my blessing shall he be reborn," Idunn intoned. She named each egg as Nilara dug them from Revna's remains. One by one, in the order of their deaths. The Earl, the Advisor, and the Mage first, each of their shells glimmering like gemstones.

I recognized the name Hvitorden and the ivory and cream shell that enclosed his new life. "They're so much smaller," I murmured.

"That's because they are not eldrafn anymore," Idunn answered. "They are something new."

"Something new," I echoed, my jaw hanging. I wasn't just representing my patron here as the one who killed the King-maker, but also witnessing the birth of a new race of blessed beasts.

Nilara slowed as she created the Duchess's pink egg and laid it out with the rest. She stirred through some sand-like remains with a sigh. "She did not absorb any energy from the eldrafn you knew as the Knight. However, the explosion that destroyed this egg did include a hint of its energy, if I can just get a hold of it…"

She placed a crimson-and-black egg out next. "Anrathor would like that one," Idunn commented.

"It has to return to the mortal world," Nilara replied. "Ten souls barely make a stable species as is."

Idunn huffed quietly in reply while the King's black and silver egg was lined up with the rest. Though she'd said ten, I only saw the nine that the Rathi coalition had ridden to war and lost. But she was not done, this time crushing the last of Revna's old egg together and reaching for me again. She curved my fingers around a warm, solid shell and left me smiling down at a new egg.

It had the same patterns as the rocky heart Ari and I had lugged around for months, but something was shifting within, pushing at its boundaries like it would explode out at any moment. My gaze flicked up for a moment as I realized Idunn was drawing Odalis aside to speak with her in quiet tones.

"Your task for me is nearly complete," Nilara said, pulling my attention back to her and the egg that pulsed in my hand like a heartbeat. "Sivana Walker, you are older, stronger, and wiser than when we last spoke at length. Your service to my husband is only beginning, so it is fitting for you to lose the sign of my protection as this chapter of your life comes to a close."

"Already?" I didn't mean to sound like a little girl, but this goddess was still a connection to my family. As incredible as it was to witness her magic firsthand and hold a newly created life in my palm, I didn't know if I could stand it if this was the last time we met.

The goddess smiled kindly, like she knew exactly where my fears went. "This isn't goodbye by any means. I still love your family, especially dear Talase and Clarissa. I still love you, Sivana, and that you have found a path to walk and a cause to live and die for. We will meet again."

I pressed my lips together to keep my composure. "I look forward to the day," I said.

"Until then, your task is thus. Deliver the eggs to a trusted friend. Idunn's newest race of blessed beasts will need a champion—a Chosen not already devoted elsewhere. Whomever Revna chooses as her new rider will be that person, and you will help find them." She glanced over her shoulder for a moment and lowered her voice. "Idunn's power wanes. She must have a representative who will not only be dedicated to her beasts, but also to helping her find her place in the world as more than a second god of war. Choose wisely, for her sake."

"After her Chosen is picked, that's when this will fade?" I asked, pointed to the white streak in my hair.

She shook her head. "When the eggs leave your control. My husband has arranged for you to be teleported to a safe location that will make the decision of who to entrust them to easy to make," she said.

"Teleported. Oh," I murmured. He must've reached down and plucked Ari and me out of the explosion from the King-maker's death.

"Did I fail to mention that earlier? Well, you are between moments now, in my realm." For a moment, her skin twinkled with silver starlight. "When I release my hold on you and Odalis, you will open your eyes on the other side of the teleporting spell." She patted my hand, leaving behind a ripple of goosebumps on my skin. "In fact, it's time."

RISE AGAIN

Bright magic flared around us, and all my mortal aches and pains returned, especially the awful chill permeating my whole body. Ari squawked in surprise as I pulled on the reins, both of us eyeing the stone fortress that we'd nearly dove into.

Fortress Aerie and the Gryphon Rider Academy. One of the shutters was open at the top, letting us come for a landing in the stables. My hand glimmered as the darkness of the enclosed walls fell on us, and I peeled off my glove, gaping as a small shower of moon dust sprinkled out of the leather.

"We're alive?" Ari asked. His limbs failed to hold up upright for long, and he collapsed where he'd landed.

"Oh, Sivana, thank the gods. Where are we?" Odalis asked, startling me by appearing out of thin air next to me. Perhaps she had…teleported here as well.

"Why do I feel like I missed something?" Ari asked, sounding too tired to be irritated about it. In fact, his words slurred together hard enough that I knew why the Mother had touched my hand.

She'd given me some of her magic to use. A true Nilarite channeled Lady Nilara's healing magic with enough regularity that they didn't stare at their glowing hands as I was still doing.

"Just stay awake a little longer, and I'll tell you," I promised, and rubbed the back of his head and neck.

All my bruises, aches, and frostbitten skin would heal in time, but I worried Ari had pushed himself too far without an intervention. I exhaled and closed my eyes, willing the goddess's power to flow through me. I just hoped he wasn't too immune not to gain some benefit from the touch of gentle, healing moonlight.

"That feels nice," he said faintly. When I opened my eyes again, my fingers were trembling and pale against his neck, where I'd left a handprint of moon dust. I freed myself from my riding harness and flashed Odalis a brief smile before looking him over in concern.

"I'm going to be fine. Don't worry over me like my mother." He shook himself and rose with a groan before pressing his head into my middle. I hugged him around the neck, breathing out with relief. It seemed he would be okay, but he was still cold and wet with melting frost.

"Hey, Odalis. I'm going to find Ari a place to rest, and then I'll show you around," I promised. She followed me like a faithful shadow as Ari and I walked at a painstaking pace to his old stall, which was empty except for a layer of hay. While I moved swiftly to remove his saddle and dry him off, she stood back at a polite distance, humming a quiet tune to herself.

When I was sure Ari would be okay to take a long rest, I turned the towels on myself and dried off as best as I could to help my circulation. My fingers felt less stiff by the time I was finished and inspecting the saddle with a curious hum. Hooked to its old spot was the pouch that'd once held Revna's egg, but it'd been stretched to accommodate multiple eggs that glimmered up at me in a rainbow of shells.

On the very top, the purple one quivered. I picked it up

reverently between my hands, feeling something turning within it. "We have to get this to Instructor Signe right away," I said.

Odalis gasped. "Oh, that's the name of the person Lady Idunn wanted me to pass a message to!"

I unclipped the pouch from the saddle. Signe would be an excellent choice to keep every one of these eggs safe, actually, and that's probably what the goddesses intended. I checked on Ari, intending to tell him about the fateful meeting, but he was already fast asleep and about as receptive to the world as a stone.

"What was the message?" I asked, turning back to Odalis. My heart leapt to my throat, as she'd drawn her hood back over her head. This far from one of the lanterns, she was a faceless Mercy again. "I-If, uh, you can tell me."

"Lead on," she suggested and hooked her arm through mine like we were friends on a stroll through the queen's garden. I took her toward the worn stairwell while she spoke quietly. "Lady Idunn wanted Signe to know she is no longer lost, and she is saving a space at her table for her once she successfully finds a rider for Revna. She's made a deal with Lord Dar—" When I hissed in a breath, she cut herself off abruptly. "Sorry, the Lord Gatekeeper, so she can see the task through."

"Lady Nilara suggested that Revna's new rider would also become Lady Idunn's Chosen. It sounds like that person has a hard task ahead of them." I didn't envy that the new rider would have to endure the goddess's prickly personality, too.

My mind was fogging over, and were I not holding an egg that felt like it'd hatch at any moment, I'd be cuddled up to Ari and equally unconscious. Unfortunately, that meant I forgot there were a few drill sergeants watching the stairs just in case a cadet tried to sneak out of their dorm after lights out to cause mischief.

"You there!" one shouted unexpectedly when we were on the tenth floor. "What do you think you're—"

I startled so hard it was a wonder Odalis didn't need to scoop up my soul and escort it to the next life. But approaching us with his hand already poised into a blade to point at us accusingly was Sergeant Kobarn, Ellie's father. We made eye contact, and he froze.

"Good evening, Sarge," I said. "I'm alive, and everything is fine, but I need to see Instructor Signe right away."

He dropped his tone to the quietest it'd ever been. "Is the Mercy here for her?"

"No. I'll explain later," I said while also having zero intention of unpacking everything that'd led to this moment.

Odalis had drawn herself up and pulled her arm away from mine. "It is urgent," she said.

"Then I'll escort you!" he declared. He charged ahead of us and only paused when he must've realized my tired trudge would never keep up with him.

"Ellie is doing great in the engineering corps," I told him as we made our way down to the level where the instructors resided. "She was safe and healthy the last time I saw her." At this point, I didn't even know how long that'd been.

He breathed a relived sigh. "I'm glad to hear that."

"She'd tell you the worst experience of going to war was the Iceberg, where we were sent as punishment. It was my fault," I said.

"Why am I not surprised, Walker?" he muttered, but he was smiling for the moment. When we finally reached Signe's door, he turned a more serious expression toward us. "She's been quite ill of late. Be gentle with her."

"We will. Thank you," Odalis promised. With a nod, he knocked and turned the knob, showing us that it was not locked. He left us to creep into her rooms, which had a lingering bitter smell that was reminiscent of strong healing herbs meant to be applied as poultices or consumed with strongly flavored broth.

Signe rested in her fur-draped throne of a chair, her weathered face peaceful for the moment before she stirred awake with a low cough. "Who goes there?" she rasped.

"It's me, Instructor. Sivana Walker," I said. There was a brief sizzle of flame before Odalis handed me a lantern to set on the low table by Signe's side.

The elderly woman eyed me sternly. "You look like an eldrafn chewed you up."

I winced. *Nice to see you too, Instructor.* "That's not far from the truth. I have something for you, though."

I placed Revna's new egg in her hands. "Is this…?" She sucked in a breath as it rocked sharply in her palm. "It's not the egg I gave you, but it *feels* like my beloved Revna."

"She's going to look a little different, but it's still her," I assured her.

The three of us leaned in as a sharp *crack* heralded a tiny beak breaking through the shell. Signe didn't help the little creature hatch but held the egg so we could all watch the baby within shift and push and stretch until she'd created a hole to flop through.

I don't know what I expected, but I realized Signe held a hatchling bird, wet and red from exertion. Signe had me retrieve a cloth and carefully placed the eggshell pieces aside before drying off Revna, who turned into a fluff ball of white down. While her eyes were tightly shut, her mouth was open and twittering squeaky strains of birdsong.

"What a blessing," Signe said, cupping Revna to her heart. A tear track marked both her cheeks.

My chest was full of emotion to see this task through to a successful conclusion. A reunion after fifty years, with Revna rising again to a new life in her old rider's hands. I exchanged a smile with Odalis, who rested a hand on my shoulder. "I'll explain the rest to her if you want. You look like you need to rest for a week," she whispered.

I handed her the pouch which held the other nine eggs with a grateful nod. "Use my bed," Signe said, pointing to the next room over. "I haven't used it in weeks. I thought I would die in this chair...but not anymore. You have given me a reason to go on, and for that, you have my eternal gratitude."

"The honor is mine, Instructor." I went to go collapse on her bed after one last respectful nod.

ARI and I woke at the same time, when dawn crested the horizon a full two nights later. We shared the same groggy return to a world full of sore muscles and belly-churning hunger. Odalis fetched a bowl of porridge from the morning meal, and I wolfed it down while looking down at the dirt-encrusted leathers I'd fallen asleep in.

"The Lord Gatekeeper has requested you return me to the Church of Mercy as soon as possible," she told me as soon as I came up from my empty bowl. When my eyes widened dramatically, she laughed and patted my arm. "When you're up and moving, of course!"

"*Hopefully no time soon*," Ari commented distantly. Even with so many layers of rock between us, I could feel how he nursed his wing especially. I sent a feeling of intense agreement back over our Link.

"I spoke to the Commandant for you while you were asleep. A really interesting piece of news landed on his desk, and he, uh, wanted some explanation for how you got here from Caershire so quickly." Odalis fidgeted with the cuff of her robes.

"What'd you tell him?" I asked, a little wary.

"That you're here and alive due to the favor of the gods.

And I confirmed that you killed that giant eldrafn." She leaned in and whispered behind her hand. "I didn't actually get to see it, but it was reported to be a fantastic display right outside Caershire. I wanted to make sure you got the full bounty and the credit since there was only one other witness who knows you were there."

"Acton Weslecker?" I asked hopefully. "Do you know if he's okay?"

"Word on the deathways is he won't be quiet about how heroic you were," she laughed. "He's waiting for you at the Church of Mercy alongside...well, I guess my father is more there for me."

Well, there was my motivation to get out of bed, but my brows rose. "Are you allowed to see him again?" I asked. "And, err, can you tell me what a deathway is?"

"There's no rule against it," she said and showed me her wrist. She hadn't been messing with her cuff after all, but adjusting a vine wrapped around her wrist like a bracelet. A single flower was budding and lifting from it. "This is going to be my nightbloom one day. He's aware enough to talk to the other nightblooms, no matter the distance, by dipping into the realm of death. Don't go all pale! It's really cool, I promise."

"There's a soul in that?" I asked nervously, pointing to her vine.

She nodded, smiling fondly down at it. "My old horse, Legend. I can't wait to go for rides with him again."

I gave myself a little shake. There was nothing to be spooked about here, even if it was a matter of death and a Mercy's choice of companion. "Hopefully it's soon," I ventured. I swung my legs off the bed and rose with a groan. "Before we leave, I have to ask Instructor Signe for one last favor."

She was in the next room, still on her chair, with fuzzy Revna flapping her stubby wings. She'd probably heard every word both of us had said but barely looked up from her former eldrafn. I wondered what kind of bird she'd grow up to be, because she was entirely too solid to become a living storm, but for now, she was an anonymous baby bird with a chubby belly.

"A favor? Name it," Signe said casually.

"You are aware that the other eggs were eldrafn that died in battle recently?" I began. She nodded once. "Well, one of their riders survived. I would like to return his egg to her, but I will have stipulations. She may know something I want the king to hear."

Her attention flicked to me. "How did she survive the fall?"

"A rozash rider caught her. She wasn't happy about it," I said.

"Did you hear what tribe she was from?"

"Icefang, I believe. She had two white fangs tattooed on her cheeks." I mimed their placement on my own cheeks.

Her answering nod seemed approving. She peppered me with more questions and, in the end, made a stipulation of her own. Solfrid could have Hvitorden back if she also assisted Signe in finding a rider for Revna. "I suspect she will be quite willing to be involved in the process. Any true eldrafn rider would do what they had to for a second chance with their beast."

Just like you, I thought, nodding as well. She entrusted me with the white egg, which was warm but quiet. "I'll let you know how it goes," I promised.

CHAPTER 34

THE KING'S MERCY

I took the opportunity to bathe while Ari dove beak-first into a pile of fish. It was a blessing to chase away the last of the chill lingering on my skin with warm water. I stayed in front of a mirror, taming my hair one brush stroke at a time and inspecting every inch of it. The Mother's protection was gone, leaving me with frizzy locks of orange-red that fell past the line of my shoulder blades.

She'd warned me this would happen, but it'd been a part of me for so long that I found myself missing the streak of white. I was ordinary again. Worse—plain, with chapped lips and wind-bitten cheeks, my skin starting to crack painfully with the lack of care it'd received in the last few months followed by the icy deluge of air that'd flowed over my face chasing the Kingmaker.

This face would have to explain to King Cortes why I was delivering his daughter to the Church of Mercy *again* and how I'd come to be at Fortress Aerie when I should've been standing alongside Weslecker to describe the Kingmaker and its death.

This person in the mirror was the Chosen of Lord Orion. From here on out, I would speak for him and ensure his gryphons were treated with the respect they deserved. I needed to do something about my appearance, to scrub off the softness of youth still clinging to my cheeks and straighten my spine if I wanted to be taken seriously.

I needed Mother and Rissa. The former would coach me again through the proper bearing for all my important events, and the latter would be more than happy to teach me how to use her numerous cosmetics and little tweezers and curlers. But in the meantime, I borrowed a pot of ointment from one of the ladies also preparing for the day alongside me and cringed from my skin burning after application.

I made my way to the mess hall at about half the speed I used to dash through these halls. The specter of memory followed me, reminding me that I'd served a punishment duty alongside Feyring to paint the stretch of wall to my left a different shade of gray, then later ordered to strip off several layers of paint from other punishment duties to do it again more evenly.

Korvic had waited at the doors of the mess hall one evening when I was running late, tapping his foot nervously as he glanced over his shoulder to see if any of the officers on duty had noticed him. "Thanks," I'd whispered.

"Didn't want you to get locked out," he'd muttered back, scuffing his foot. I'd been one of those rare moments without his sarcastic front, and I wore a bittersweet expression as I passed through the open threshold now. I missed both of them with sudden, piercing intensity.

I imagined them in the next life, Feyring chattering the tale of everything Korvic had missed—Operation Redhead and our trip to the Iceberg, especially. Korvic would've wanted to be there along with the rest of us, making his little comments that it was just like us to get disciplined as a group.

"Well, you'd be right," I said to myself.

The real crime was that neither of them had lived to see

the end of the war. I hoped they would receive a posthumous promotion to the rank of Knight-Lieutenant so they would not be immortalized as mere Squires in the Hall of Graduates. They deserved nothing less.

The mess hall itself seemed larger than I remembered, a cavernous space currently being buffed and cleaned by a crew of maids between breakfast and the boisterous event that lunch usually was. I spotted Odalis and Ari near the kitchens, talking to a gray figure. I nearly groaned. Of course I wouldn't get through this visit without making eye contact with the Commandant, who had Night lounging by his side. As I approached, she released a great yawn, peering up at me with sleepy yellow eyes.

"Good morning, sir," I said out of long habit.

A brief smile cracked his strict bearing. "Good morning, Squire Walker," he replied. "It feels like just yesterday I needed to remind you that the Academy is not an inn."

I was chagrinned in a way only the Commandant could inspire. "However, I can clearly see that the gods were involved in some way." He gestured to my hair as he spoke. "The Mother truly gave you a violent task?"

My gaze slid to Odalis, who nodded encouragingly. "It's more complicated than that, sir. Lady Nilara made new lives from the Kingmaker's death. Since those lives now reside with Instructor Signe, I figured you should know," I said.

His brows knitted closer together. "We're not sure what they are yet, but they're not eldrafn. They are a new kind of blessed beast to replace eldrafn," I added.

His skepticism remained high. "I will need to speak with Signe," he replied. "We are equipped to care for gryphons, not…"

"Some kind of bird. I imagine we'll know what they are when Revna grows up," I said.

"Revna," he echoed in shock.

I brightened, happy to know he recognized the significance of that name. "Yes, sir. She's back with her rider at last."

"But she is not an eldrafn anymore?"

"No, sir. The gods have given her a new body and intend for her to take a new rider. That person will have more work ahead of them," I said. "Until then, the new beasts need a place to grow and find riders. Where better to do this than the Academy?"

He dragged a hand down his face, stretching his cheeks. "Squire Walker," he deadpanned.

"Yes, sir?"

"I'm so glad to hear that you and the princess are going to see King Cortes when you leave. You get to explain all of this to him."

"*Try it again,*" Ari encouraged when the Church of Mercy's distinctive spires were within sight. He flew lower and slower than usual, arguing that if we *had* to make this flight right now, it would be on his terms.

"*Good evening, King Cortes. It is a pleasure to see you again,*" I said to him in my practiced formal tone.

"*Such a lie,*" he snorted. I knew he daydreamed about biting the monarch for yanking Lord Orion's necklace away from me.

My composure broke with a little giggle, and I glanced over my shoulder to see how Odalis was faring. She rode tandem confidently, her fingertip currently brushing over the swaying bud rising from her vine bracelet. The wind had her Mercy cloak fluttering behind her in rippling waves.

She wore a serene smile, the kind of self-assured look she'd never had in her former life as a princess. Maybe she was deep in conversation with her budding nightbloom or just peaceful with the knowledge of the reunion to come.

"Maybe the king will not want to talk to me," I said, turning back to our destination. *"Not when he has Odalis back."*

"Then how will he acknowledge the great heroes, Arimus, Walker, and Zaveri?" he asked with a grand lit.

"Gods, Ari. Is it wrong to hope he won't make a big deal of it?"

"Yes! I want a parade in our honor and buckets full of gold."

"What would you even do with that much gold?"

"I guess I'll give it all to you and hope you'll spend it on the lifetime of salmon you owe me," he said.

I was still chuckling when we landed, though he wasn't completely kidding. He deserved a reward for flying past his limits and risking his health to give us a chance to kill the Kingmaker in the first place. It was for him that I squared my shoulders in front of the cathedral doors to the Church of Mercy and wore my best fake smile when a hooded Mercy spotted us and went inside.

The King emerged alongside an armed entourage of guards and gryphon riders, some of whom I recognized from the First. A hint of fine cologne wafted past me before he had Odalis in his arms, tugging her to the tips of her toes. I looked away to give them a moment of privacy, hearing the emotional quality in the king's whispers.

My gaze landed on a dark gray shape wiggling out from the back of the crowd before running straight at me. Ironfeather skidded on his back paws so as not to knock both of us over. *"I knew you were alive!"* he exclaimed. He curled his neck around me when I hugged him around his shoulders.

He backed away to give his rider room with me next. I met Weslecker's green eyes, dancing in the sunlight and let a bit of tension fall from my shoulders. We closed the distance between us, and soon his lips were on mine, erasing all thoughts until someone cleared their throat nearby.

He cleared his throat too and brushed a few stray flyaways behind my ear. "Your task is finished," he said.

"Thanks to you and Ironfeather, yes."

"Please, it was all you and Ari, and I made sure the king and his court know it." He patted my shoulder and indicated someone else skirting the crowd of the king's protection. "This person I found soliciting a ride to Caershire may have helped too."

"Zizi!" I exclaimed, hugging her next. She smiled without showing her teeth, wearing a mantle of fatigue with her mark still a dull scarlet on her cheek.

"The official records mark me as an assist to the kill," she said.

"There's already an official record?" I asked.

Weslecker nodded. "Tell you later," he said under his breath, straightening to salute.

I saluted with him on pure muscle memory before I realized King Cortes had parted from his daughter to approach us. "At ease," he said. "If it isn't Sivana Walker and Arimus, my saviors."

"Good evening, King Cortes. It's a pleasure to see you again," I said just like I'd practiced.

"Please, no need to be so formal. Let us retire to somewhere more private. Bring your pyrojack friend and your..." He eyed the protective way Weslecker shadowed me and breathed something akin to a sigh of relief. "The young nobleman with you. The accommodations here are quite excellent."

We followed him and Odalis into the church, with Weslecker and Zizi flanking me. "Isn't that because they're supposed to be your last?" she asked behind her hand.

"Let's not remind the king of that," he said.

I was too busy admiring the mural that decorated the entry hall in shades of black and white, with green popping here and there. It was an abstract blur, a violent streak here with what looked like a knife in one corner, a hooded figure in another. If we weren't heading for a private audience with the king, I would've lingered to see what story this art told.

Instead, I let myself get ushered into a private dining room and set up a comfortable pile of cushions for Ari with permission to strip them from the couch closer to the fire. Ironfeather settled on top of him, much to my gryphon's grumbling, and groomed his neck feathers and ears with a cheerful chirp.

We had a quiet dinner, and as promised, the food was quite outstanding, especially after the diet of rations I'd been on. The king was more interested in talking to Odalis at first, which suited me fine, as I caught up with Weslecker and Zizi on what had happened after I was teleported to Fortress Aerie.

"Some of the court came out of their bunker to see what the noise was about," he told me. "Everyone was awake after the massive explosion that came from the Kingmaker's death. When I shared what'd happened and why, a head count was ordered. Almost all of the court heeded the king's order to evacuate."

"Except my son, Isaac, and a few of his closest political allies," the king himself put in. "After reading the many reports on his activities of late, I couldn't help but find it incredibly suspicious."

I nodded, unsurprised at this news.

"I put out a royal decree for his arrest. Word arrived just ahead of you and my daughter that he waits for his trial in his chambers in Kaiamear." He passed a mug between his hands, his sausage-like fingers tracing the pattern of swirls upon it. This victorious moment was delivered with heavy reluctance. "The trial will be a private affair. I would like you to attend, Sivana."

"Yes, Your Majesty. When will it be?" I asked.

He circled his hand in a frustrated gesture. "After I meet

with the remnants of the Rathi coalition that murdered Valentino. The ink on their surrender must be dry before we celebrate our war heroes, such as yourself. We must mourn our losses, and only then should we pursue retribution."

Slowly, a more pleasant expression erased the resigned air he wore like a mantle. "I intend to announce you as the next Hero of Altare, Sivana. Thank you for your service to your country."

This definitely had Ari's attention. His head popped up from his cushions, and he made a soft croak. "Yes, and your gryphon as well," the king said, holding his belly with a brief bark of laughter.

"Your Majesty, that is too much. The gods—"

"For better or worse, they have put you in my path to challenge and change my ways," he spoke over me. "Had you not killed that abomination of an eldrafn, I wouldn't be here today."

"But..." I wet my lips, regrouping as Weslecker squeezed my hand and Zizi forced a smile. "I had help from Acton and Zizi. They should be recognized as well."

"They will be. We've already spoken of reward money, and they will both receive a Gilded Combat Cross, the highest award I can give aside from Hero of Altare. This way, I can announce you as a Chosen and give you the proper honor to ask a favor of me in return."

I reset my hanging jaw with a snap. With the shock of the announcement, I'd forgotten the age-old tradition he mentioned. Heroes of Altare were given the honor for a service to the country, which meant they could ask for one big service in return. Almost anything was on the table—land, wealth, fame.

"Congratulations, Sivana!" Odalis exclaimed.

"You deserve it," Weslecker agreed.

I flicked a guilty smile at Zizi, who waved it away. "I'll

find my own way to stand beside you someday. It'll be Walker and Zaveri before you know it."

"I have no doubt," I answered with relief. "Well, Your Highness, I already have something less urgent to ask for. I would like to return home with the army—there's a prisoner of war I believe you should meet."

"Of course," he said with a regal nod.

"And now, you should know what the gods wrought in the wake of the Kingmaker's death," Odalis said.

"Kingmaker," the king echoed.

She nodded. "That's what the gods started calling it, after Sivana thought of the name."

Together, she and I told our increasingly amazed audience about the birth of the new race that would serve as Lady Idunn's blessed beasts. The one thing I didn't share was that I had a cream and white egg secured in a warm pocket in my flight jacket, ready to return to its rightful rider.

CHAPTER 35

THE ROAD HOME

"Most people would be thrilled to become a Hero of Altare," Ari reminded me as he and I rode on the deck of a fishing barge that we'd paid to carry us north until we were close enough to Inisthwaite to make the rest of the flight there. Weslecker, Ironfeather, and Zizi had insisted on accompanying us for the journey.

"I just don't know what to ask for," I confided. I'd gotten up at the crack of dawn to pace the limited deck space I could while the crew continued their jobs around us. We'd mostly paid to be on the barge too while it cast its nets further out to sea than usual.

"That doesn't mean you wish away the opportunity," he pointed out. *"We earned it."*

Yes, but I was about to be announced as Lord Orion's Chosen alongside receiving the award, which would be a part of an event no one wanted to miss. At least, that's how Heroes of Altare were announced during my childhood, and I doubted the king wanted this to be a small affair with how much he was personally affected by the Kingmaker's death.

And if I was to have only one big favor done by my request, what should I ask for? I could become a noblewoman of status, with the kind of wealth that would make marrying into Weslecker's family a done deal. My distant noble heritage would not impress a Duke and Duchess otherwise, and that was a hurdle I needed to cross if I wanted anything serious with him.

But marriage was still a far-off dream compared to the problems before me. Zizi still didn't have Starfall back, and her magic was returning with force, first warming the mark on her face and beginning to rekindle the embers in her eyes. She'd never have a stable life without the rune on that staff, held by another Hero of Altare.

Yet if I asked for Starfall to be returned to her, then I wasn't doing my duty to the wild gryphons who'd flown to our rescue over Manarfell. I just hoped, in my absence, the soldiers hadn't forgotten that they had Lord Orion's protection and weren't to be messed with or harmed.

"You have time to decide. Just like you picked your mate," Ari put in.

I felt the strain of yearning from him. His beak was pointing somewhere north, drawn like a magnet to his other half. *"And you have picked yours?"* I asked.

"Not officially. If only my rider would stop dragging me everywhere," he grumbled good-naturedly. He tilted his head to bunt my side, and I moved into the motion so he didn't head-butt the air blindly.

"Blame the gods," I replied.

"Why? I have a perfectly good Sivvy to blame," he snickered.

I just laughed, accepting the nickname as my due and looking forward to seeing Puzzlebox again so she could crow it with joy. But first, we had to visit the Iceberg before I reported in at Manarfell and inevitably was put to work getting the war machine properly packed and turned around for the journey home.

Our prisoners of war would stay that way until a proper treaty was signed, which meant I found Solfrid of the Icefang

Clan in her cell, her head resting listlessly against a wall. Her amethyst eyes flashed defiantly when she realized I stood on the other side of the bars with my gryphon. Weslecker and Zizi were with Colonel Gladden, distracting him with a signed decree from the king for this woman's release and immediate summons to Kaiamear.

"Your people won. Did you return to gloat?" she asked.

"Despite how we've met, I don't believe we're enemies," I said, ignoring the weak, mocking laughter that escaped her lips. "Because I've come with a gift, in exchange for knowledge of how my crown prince betrayed us all. You asked for Hvitorden or your scarves for it, and I decided to deliver."

I pulled the cream and white egg from my flight jacket, cradled carefully in my palm. She sucked in a breath and shot to her feet, jamming her hands through the bars. Since she was bound around the wrists, she didn't get her fingers far. I stepped back with a *tisk*. "I'll let you have him, but you must agree to a few things," I said.

She straightened with a glare. It seemed there was some steel left in her, after all. "That doesn't look like it would be his egg," she replied. "Let me touch it at least and know you are not playing a trick."

I only let the pad of her fingers graze the shell, knowing I had to show a strong front to this woman, else she'd agree to nothing. Her pale face creased with shock, hands flexing as a little zap of white lightning passed between her and the shell. "It *is* him," she muttered.

"It is," I confirmed.

"Name your price, then." She rotated her hand impatiently, palm out.

"Your information in exchange for the egg. But you won't be telling just me. His royal father is quite interested in hearing what the crown prince promised your people. After this, you will be released and escorted to Kaiamear to tell your story," I told her.

She considered, tilting her head. "Is that all?" she asked shortly. In a flash, she reminded me of her goddess, just as brusque as her.

"Hvitorden's soul is in this egg, but he will hatch as a member of a different race of Idunn's blessed beasts," I said. I didn't have time to give her the whole story, but she nodded with a grave expression, listening intently. "You are needed to help find riders for this new race, which means you must work together with Signe. If you accept this egg, you must live in Altare alongside her for a while."

She released a huff. "Fine. Is that all?" she repeated.

"I have your scarves, but they're not with me right now. I'll give them back to you as soon as I can," I promised and pressed Hvitorden's egg to her palm. She withdrew into her cell with it, holding it between her palms with a few whispered words in her mother tongue.

"You may want to hide the egg when they come release you from your cell," I suggested.

"Thank you...not-enemy," she replied, barely looking up from its shell.

"It's Sivana," I reminded her.

She nodded. "I shall not forget it again. I will see you at the trial."

As expected, when we finally arrived at Manarfell after our stop at the Iceberg, I was immediately scolded after reporting in by the Marshall, then congratulated for a job well done, then given a duty to help pack up the camp.

More notably, I was in charge of the wild gryphons, who were quickly becoming a nuisance as the untouchable ones sent by Lord Orion and protected by his Chosen. Not only had no one attempted to tame them since I was gone, they'd become like lords and ladies, lounging around while the humans and tame gryphons labored around them. They accepted food readily, though, going through fish by the bucket full.

Puzzlebox was amongst the wild flock when I approached them, squeaking, *"Sivvy!"* and tackling me to the ground in her enthusiasm.

"Hi, Box," I laughed, winded and a little achy from that collision with the ground.

"Where'd you go?" she asked, settling on my chest to peer down her beak at my face.

I ruffled her soft neck fur and resigned myself to lying on the cold ground for a while. *"Oh, you know, just helping Ari be a hero."*

"Ari has such a nice dad," she twittered.

I blinked, wondering if we were thinking of the same gryphon. Roshawk himself came limping over after a minute, when Valtora rushed ahead of him to nuzzle their son and pick at the feathers at the base of his wing. She soon shooed Puzzlebox away and took her place, weighing down my front with her bulk and nuzzling my cheek carefully. I watched the white gryphon press against the skylord's side and twitter happily when he draped a wing over her.

"That's a side of him I've never seen," I commented to Valtora.

"He knows what she is and thinks it's shameful she's been pressed to fight," she replied. *"Before you ask, gryphons born with her condition are called cloudlings. They spend their days tending to the hatchlings of the flock since they are forever young at heart."*

I smiled broadly. *"There are more like her?"*

"My love has two cloudlings in his flock. He's prepared to drag Puzzlebox out of the military so she can join them," she said. From her tone, I felt she agreed with my unspoken thought that that might not be the worst outcome. But only if Sharde could join them somehow.

"Skymother? You still want me to call you that, right?"

"Definitely."

"Um, could you let me up?" I asked, wiggling uncomfortably under her.

She tapped the blunt dome of her beak on my forehead. *"No. Every time I let you out of my sight, you and my son are off courting danger. This gives me some peace of mind."*

"Okay, Skymother. Just wait until you hear what we accomplished."

It was safe to say that Valtora didn't let me up for an hour after I told her the whole story, both proud and horrified we'd come so close to death in the service to the gods. She only stood when Weslecker came looking for me and pushed her beak close enough to his face that he balked.

"This is your maybe-mate?" she asked me.

"Uh, yes," I replied.

"Hmm, he will do. You will have beautiful chicks together," she declared.

Face burning, I promised to find Weslecker later and excused myself from them both by going to pay my respects to Roshawk from a few feet away and made my way around the camp, talking to each wild gryphon and reminding them of their manners. By evening, they were diving the cold ocean, skimming for fish to eat that they caught with their own two talons.

I realized again the power of communication as the days passed and the army boarded the naval vessels for the ride home. Through me, the wild gryphons knew when it was time for them to flock on top of one of the ships, much to the staring of the crew.

I saw very little of Ari during this time, as he was deeply interested in staying by Sunset's side. Honestly, I was just as scarce, caught between my duty to the gryphons, my desire to be with Weslecker, and evenings sitting around the fire pit in the squire puddle. Staring into a fire was how Captain Cherin found me, since he and Tempest had been busy with their own important tasks.

"Heard you killed the big one, Wild," he said, one of few who used my new call sign.

"Yes, sir. With the grace of the gods and some help."

"I see this." His single eye was fixed on my hairline. "I'm glad you didn't make me regret letting you chase it."

"Me too," I said wryly.

"Have they told you what's next?" he asked. I thought he was talking about the Hero of Altare ceremony, but it was just a rhetorical question. "Our time together draws to a close. All squires will be promoted in Kaiamear in front of the populace as part of the celebration that awaits us. I intend to give you a full recommendation to be announced as the Ace of your year group."

My startled feelings reached so deep I felt Ari probe our Link. *"I forgot about the Ace award!"* I exclaimed.

The number one cadet of their year group, the Ace gained a prestigious award and a leg up on their peers by being the very best. My father was an Ace, which had led him to an illustrious career until the moment he'd resigned as Commander of the First.

"Well, we were a little busy trying to stay alive," Ari pointed out.

"Thank you, sir. That's a high honor," I said aloud while sending a feeling of agreement to my gryphon.

His answering smile was tight. "I've heard that things back home with the Seventh are rocky at best. Wrath lost a lot of credibility when it came to light that he'd stolen glory from you."

"Oh?"

"Because it's not the first time. Most of us can recount a time Commander Wrath fudged a report to make himself look better," he scoffed. "I spoke with Exquisite recently, and it sounds like he's about to take an early retirement since the top brass have begun sifting through all his paperwork and aren't too happy with what they're seeing."

I kept a cheer trapped behind my teeth, but the news couldn't be more welcome or happen to a *nicer* person. "I've heard that Paragon Hughes may be involved," I said.

"Oh, he definitely is. Nothing happens to Commanders and above if the Paragon isn't involved. It seems you have friends in higher places than I would expect," he said, putting a heavy hand on my shoulder. "I wanted to ask if you could put in a good word of your own for me."

"You would like to be the next Commander?" I asked, nodding when he did. "I couldn't think of a better person after your leadership during both battles over Manarfell. Exquisite didn't see nearly the same amount of combat as you and Tempest, either."

"Much appreciated," he replied. He spent a couple more hours in the squire puddle, grabbing the canteen being passed around and taking a hearty drink before passing it around me. I was his squire for a short while longer, after all.

WE TRAVELED at the speed of the army, walking our way down to Kaiamear over the course of several weeks. Our leadership wanted everyone to return at the same time, which kept the gryphon riders grounded. The best news was that climate grew more bearable with each passing day, and it became more a leisurely time with friends and chores rather than a grueling slog toward the next battle.

It also gave Valtora the time she needed to finally have the plumage to take flight again, and many of our gryphons disappeared into the sky to join the wild ones celebrating around their matriarch. They flew circles around our army, creating displays of aerial prowess that had most villagers cheering as we passed through.

Before our drafted men returned to their families, we were all to report to Kaiamear to set things to rights. Wages were promised after the parade and celebration in our honor. It made even the weariest souls crack a smile to know that days of festivities awaited. The squires were also promised pay equal to what a Lieutenant would receive, awarded after the king knighted us in a special ceremony before an audience of citizens.

The only person who skipped the march home was Prince Mateo, who flew ahead to attend to his father and his duties at court instead. I figured we would see him again during the parade, as each flight was to take a lap around the city, flying the Altarian flag and the flight's colors.

I wondered if the king was already teaching Mateo what he'd need to know as the new crown prince. He was now the only royal worthy of inheriting the crown, a duty I doubted Mateo was enthusiastic about. Perhaps that reluctance would help shape him into a better leader.

Cherin drew me aside when we were within a couple days of arriving in the capital. He handed me a rolled-up flag. "Command wants you and Ari to fly with the wild gryphons like you are your own flight. You might be the only person capable of keeping some discipline in their ranks."

I snorted out a little laugh and confirmed it was an Altarian flag he'd handed me. "They do what they like, sir. I just keep it from becoming full chaos. But I will let Valtora and Roshawk know."

I didn't share that, in handing me a flag and instructing me to make the wild gryphons act like a flight, he'd given me an idea of what to ask the king for after I was declared a Hero of Altare.

But first, I sought out Ellie to walk with her that afternoon to tell her my budding idea. She adjusted her glasses with a thoughtful quirk to her mouth. "Sounds like you're thinking too small. Why ask the king for a couple grains of rice when you could have a whole plate full?" she reasoned. "What you're really wanting to do is change the whole gryphon knight corps."

"How they treat gryphons, at least," I said.

"That's everything, then. Top to bottom. The best place to start for something like that is at the bottom, though, which is the Academy. Here's how I'd change your request…"

CHAPTER 36

WHAT COMES AFTER

A cluster of four gryphons leaned over the diagram I'd scratched into the dirt with the toe of my boot. Ari sat beside me, a silent observer through my vision.

"*Impressing all those humans is foolishness,*" Roshawk said first.

"*If we want to be seen as a group worth respect, we have to do it,*" Valtora countered.

Reyos had his blue feathers fluffed out in amusement. "*Flying like this is impressive to humans? Don't we travel in what you're calling a V-formation?*" he asked.

"*It's more about discipline,*" said Sunset. "*Humans also find it really impressive if a group of soldiers march together, putting their paws down in perfect sync.*"

I wasn't too surprised that Roshawk was opposed, even with Valtora pressing to his side, grooming his neck until some of the tension left his body. "Just think of it this way—all the crowd will see is a cloud of gryphons if you fly together like you usually do. Your flock is some fifty-strong. Don't you think each individual should be able to show off a bit?" I reasoned.

"*Perhaps,*" he said grudgingly.

"*Sivana, maybe my mate could be convinced if you rub some of the stiffness from his side,"* Valtora suggested and nipped his scruff when he warbled a distinct denial.

By this point, I'd at least introduced most of his flock to human touch, showing them that it wasn't something to fear. Roshawk remained apart from that, too proud to accept a massage for his old lightning scars or for the few new ones crisscrossed over top them that were too deep for the healers to mend completely. He limped like a gryphon double his age yet was proud to bear the marks of two dead eldrafn.

Something private passed between the two gryphons, ending with Valtora proclaiming aloud, *"I insist."*

"I never thought I'd see the day," Ari remarked as we watched Roshawk carefully fold his limbs and lie on his side. The older gryphon's tail lashed, and he watched me with a leery eye as I approached. Around us, the other beasts gathered to watch.

"Could someone fetch me a grooming kit?" I asked. I smiled to myself as the three wild gryphons glanced between themselves before Reyos heaved a sigh and trotted off.

Most of my new feathered friends didn't want human tools anywhere near them, but Roshawk needed the oils and salves alongside a good brushing in those areas he was no longer flexible enough to groom himself. A startled exclamation from one of the camp's caretakers preceded Reyos's return with a kit clamped in his beak. I took it and knelt before the beast, nearly as tense as he was.

"First we take the dust off from all this traveling," I said, quite deliberately showing him the broad brush that was gentle on fur and feathers both.

"I thought this was supposed to be a quick rub-down," he muttered.

"It'll feel much better if you're clean first."

I could feel his discomfort and impatience through the grooming, made most acute when I tackled a few of the knots in his belly fur. I smiled to myself; Ari disliked being groomed there as well. Valtora murmured encouragements through it all until I finally rubbed a medicinal salve that was scented with a bouquet of wildflowers between my hands. It would've been better to introduce this to his scars earlier, but better late than never.

Roshawk lifted his beak, smelling the flowers. He grumbled in displeasure from the first pass, which I kept quick and light. When the flash of pain settled, he relaxed again and let me press my palms further into his hide, painstakingly rubbing away some of the accumulated pain and stiffness from decades of maneuvering around his scars.

I stopped when he was stretched out in contentment, his fierce eyes lidded and his side bearing a dull shine from the salve absorbed into his skin.

"See? Clever little human hands," Valtora said while sending me a pulse of motherly love over our Link as a thank you.

"Not terrible," he concluded. *"I guess I'll try to get the flock to fly in formation. Would humans be simple enough to be impressed by one giant V-formation?"*

We would find out soon enough, after one more day's march. Kaiamear's bells rang in a merry jangle of celebration. The wild gryphons were to fly at the end of the gryphon knight corps's section of the parade, with Father, Howl, and Cyclone joining me as the only gryphon riders amongst the formation. They were supposed to fly with the Third, I think, but Father had to lead us, as Valtora was Matriarch, and Howl and Cyclone simply followed what he did.

What I wasn't expecting was for Valtora to take over the idea of a giant V-formation and make it something slightly different that excited the flock as a challenge. We assembled on the grassy rise next to the great road leading into Kaiamear, and I followed Valtora curiously as she nudged beasts here and there until she was satisfied.

I tried to trace the pattern she'd arranged eight gryphons into on my palm. *"Imagine a standard V-formation but with the two at the back of the wings hanging back more,"* Valtora explained. *"Add three more gryphons to make a second point. We'll make a chain through the sky. Now* that *will impress the humans…if all of the flock follow directions."* She snipped her beak toward one of the younger beasts, who was already stepping out of line toward one of his friends.

"Even if it's not perfect, it's still going to be impressive. We're over double the size of a standard flight," I pointed out.

She bobbed her head in agreement and then chased me back to my place in the formation, right off her left wing. Howl would be off Ari's left wing, while the right side would be Roshawk closest to his mate and Cyclone behind him. It was wild gryphons from then on.

Ari twittered a greeting when I touched his wing to let him know I was standing next to him. *"Ready for this?"* I asked.

"Quite. You know, I've always wanted to be on the ground for parades I have to attend," he admitted. *"We practice and coordinate formation flying, but we never get to see it."*

I pet his wing idly as we waited. *"When I watched parades like this, I always wanted to be in the sky instead,"* I said. *"How funny!"*

He nibbled and tugged on my braid in return, pulsing a feeling of agreement. We waited a while for the horns to signal for the higher-ranked flights to take to the air.

"That's our signal. Let's be at the ready," Father said, swinging himself into Valtora's saddle. She turned around and sent out mental instructions that had some of her more impatient beasts scrambling to their paws.

I climbed Ari's saddle one-handed, holding the Altarian flag. Excitement zinged through me as, one at a time, the flights ahead of us took wing, to the distant roar of a crowd we could hear from here. A male voice spoke above the people, as it was customary for a man with a particularly dignified voice to name each flight and squadron as it passed the common folk. I wondered what he'd say about us.

Workers wearing palace livery were soon motioning for us to take to the sky. Valtora flexed her wings, which was followed by the feathery rustle of dozens of wings extending at the ready. She led us into a running takeoff, rising in altitude sharply to clear the city walls and wind the chain of her flock around one of the ringing bells.

It was like flying face-first into a wall of noise. The citizens formed two waving, screaming rows on either side of the main thoroughfare, and they seemed to undulate like the sea when I let the wind unwind the Altarian flag and flapped it high above them.

At least I could hear the announcer, voice magnified to boom over the city. "And last, but not least, our newest flight of wild-born gryphons, led by Commander Nathaniel Walker and his daughter, Squire Sivana Walker!"

I jolted in surprise to hear my name and the answering call from the crowd as we flew overhead. Fingers pointed as the chain of gryphons went on and on, and I resisted the urge to turn my head to see if the wild ones were minding their Matriarch and not breaking formation. We flew our lap around Kaiamear, and I grinned at the turnout. Last time there was a parade like this, I was one of the specks down below, shading my face as I tried to pick out individual gryphons by the underside of their plumage.

It was a good feeling to be recognized. I knew Ari wasn't quite so excited since we knew now that the palace was extending out our victory celebration to encompass a full week. For the moment, I just wanted to enjoy a feast and some acknowledgment of the sacrifices we'd made for the people of Altare.

My family was given its apartment back in the palace. I didn't ask questions, not when Mother and Rissa appeared from the crowd. Mother had taken off the glamor changing her features, smiling broadly as she and Father embraced for longer than was comfortable for Rissa and me.

"Nate's coming too," Rissa told me as we studiously looked anywhere but at our parents' reunion. "You know how he gets with the cloud candy."

"He better be getting us some, too," I laughed.

We waited at the doorway, considering the apartment was empty of any of our things except what we would carry in. It was bittersweet to know we were merely lent this space for the duration of the festivities, until the military made a final determination as to where Father would be assigned.

I broke into a broad smile when Nate stumbled his way down the hall. I knew his orange head of hair anywhere, even if his face was obscured by a fan of cloud candy in every pink, purple, and blue shade they had. He wore an apprentice's robe and had a wand secured in a pouch on his belt now.

I crushed him into a hug once he'd distributed the candy. "When did you get so tall?" I laughed. He'd exited the gawky early teen phase without me noticing, his shoulders broader but still slouched. He'd traded pimples for a sprinkle of reddish hair on his upper lip but still had his goofy, carefree smile.

"Sometime while you were fighting, I'm sure," he replied.

We passed Nate around for hugs before facing the door as a unit. Father turned the knob and let us in. The Crown hadn't been so cruel as to leave us with a series of blank rooms, though. There was basic furnishing and even a pile of cushions within the room I used to share with Rissa, looking like it was meant for a gryphon. Ari would be happy if he wanted to be parted from his parents and Sunset up in the old gryphon stables.

I let a wad of cloud candy melt on my tongue, savoring

the sweetness with a smile. It felt like things were finally going our way.

I GOT myself a private audience with the king in his office, flanked by Valtora and Roshawk, with Ari guided in behind us by Sunset. It was amazing how responsive he was now, as I'd never gotten such a quick summons from a royal before, save for Isaac when he knew he had me caught in his web.

"Good evening, Your Majesty," I said, saluting him. He acknowledged me and didn't get up from his padded chair in front of a massive table absolutely covered in a drift of what must've been important papers. "I have come to tell you my request as a Hero of Altare early. The wild gryphons have some demands, and I think you'll find my idea will make everyone involved with the care and raising of gryphons very happy."

He steepled his hands before him and raised a brow. "Oh? This is quite unusual, but nothing about our acquaintance has been ordinary, has it Miss Walker?"

"Indeed, Your Majesty."

"Well, go on. Let's hear this idea."

I took a deep breath and wet my lips, tamping down my anxiety when Valtora brushed against me, lending me a jolt of her steady strength. "Your Majesty, the gryphon knight corps has a problem that's been left to fester. Our beasts are just not having children like they used to. Because of this, to keep our numbers high, we've been taking more and more wild beasts from their natural habitat and gentled them to become our mounts."

Roshawk breathed a low growl, glaring at the king like this was his doing. For his part, King Cortes listened impassively, his expression a practiced neutral.

"Through speaking with Lord Orion and the experiences I've had with the wild gryphons, I've learned that we are doing irreparable damage to them by poaching their family members. Gryphons form Links with each other just like they do with us, and once two gryphons are Linked as mates, they are a pair for life. It is exceptionally rare for either to take another mate, even if they are separated for years. Such a thing is common now, as brooding females and babies are the prime targets for our tamers to bring in. This happened to Valtora, one of our prime gryphons, and her son, Arimus. As you recall, both served in the First."

"I recall," he replied.

"In the meantime, Valtora's mate, Roshawk"—I gestured to the scarred male—"took no second mate in over twenty years. Fate reunited them, and now he would like to remain at Valtora's side."

He eyed Roshawk dubiously. "I'm sure we can find a suitable rider for him somewhere."

I put my hand on the male's shoulder before he could snarl, enduring a half-hearted snort aimed my way instead. I let go of him quickly. "No, Your Majesty. He wishes to live alongside Valtora without becoming a tame gryphon, as do a number of the wild gryphons that make up the flock that flew to Altare's defense over Manarfell. Those beasts are the wild mates and family members of *our* gryphons, convinced by Roshawk to take up a duty to protect and reunite their broken families. This is where my idea comes in."

The king stroked his bottom lip thoughtfully, nodding. "I believe I know where this is going. Proceed."

"What if we made it possible by establishing a new flight under the umbrella of the Second, which is already in charge of training and taming. A Wild Flight, where the families of our gryphons can live in harmony with a number of properly trained gryphon riders. We could build a comfortable place for them to live close to Fortress Aerie so they can come and go from the wilderness of their old homes as they please.

"If they choose to live with us, they get fed, groomed, and medicated. We would also need to give our tame beasts leave time, especially around mating season. But the gryphon knight corps was decimated from fighting the Rathi, so any couples we reunite with this program may choose to help us repopulate with new babies."

"It will be hard to spare the men for that, Sivana," he said.

"I understand, sir. And I'm sure some of the wild gryphons would prefer to follow their mates wherever they may fly, as long as they're promised that no human will attempt to put a saddle on them or limit their freedom. That brings me to the last part of this idea, which will involve reforming part of the Gryphon Rider Academy process."

I fidgeted with my fingers behind my back. This was the big ask, the full plate of rice Ellie had encouraged me to turn the idea into.

"This new Wild Flight will need a place to live close to, but not included in, the Gryphon Rider Academy. Somewhere where they can be sheltered from the elements, safe and secure to raise their young. A sanctuary, if you will. We could name it after Lord Glorium, the honored demigod mount of Lord Orion." I thought that would be a nice touch for the beautiful beast.

"There, the babies can live with their families for a year. Gryphons are currently bonded when they are very young, and the wild ones believe that is wrong. If the Crown grants me this idea, they also would like the age of first Link to be raised to one year, when a yearling is old enough to make an informed choice for themselves, not only about who they want as their rider, but if they want a rider at all."

The thoughtful smile beginning to crease the king's mouth vanished. "Why would we give them the option after we devote the resources to raise them and care for the wild ones?

Especially after building an expensive sanctuary for them to live in?"

I was expecting this reaction and breathed in deeply. "Because, Your Majesty, it may not seem like it, but gryphons are just as intelligent as we are. The goal is to establish a partnership as equals and have a host of cadets at the Academy for a year who interact and befriend the young beasts to earn their status as a gryphon rider. It's past time we stopped taking advantage of Lord Orion's blessed beasts."

The king stirred, sitting up straighter. "Gods, that's unsettling," he muttered to himself. The glare of a brief flare of magic passed from his eyes, and I realized Lord Orion had shown his approval of my words. King Cortes pinched the bridge of his nose, spending the next few moments in contemplation of his desk.

"You have spoken, and I've heard you, Chosen," he said finally. "I will inform Paragon Hughes and the Academy's Commandant that there is a new flight in need of manpower. The funds for your sanctuary will also be allocated."

"Thank you, Your Majesty," I said amidst the victorious caw and cry of the gryphons around me.

"I wasn't finished," he said.

"Me neither, Your Majesty. If I may bring one more problem to your attention?" I asked hopefully. A hint of annoyance crossed his face, but he motioned me onward. I told him a brief version of Zizi's story about Irene and how she'd acquired the corerune to create Starfall. I hoped I wasn't overstepping, because the king looked increasingly displeased.

"You understand this is a serious allegation against a fellow Hero of Altare?" he demanded.

"Which is exactly why I believe it's never been looked into, Your Majesty. Especially since the victim of this mess is a Lithosian immigrant. All I'm asking is that you help in any way you see fit," I said, putting my palms up.

"I'll see what I can do," he replied stiffly. "If that will be all, then?"

"I believe that is all."

"Great." His response was quick. I'm sure he'd be happy to have me and my gryphons out of his office posthaste. "I was going to say, there is only one person I trust to lead the Wild Flight endeavor you've asked for and ensure its success. And that would be you, Sivana. Congratulations on being the first appointee."

CHAPTER 37

GRADUATION

My success still had me buzzing with a mixture of excitement and anxious energy. Me, essentially a Commander of a group that would never obey the orders of a human if they didn't feel like it. The king left the details to High Command, though, and I was sure I wasn't about to be promoted to the same rank as my father right away. My clorets were stacked on a future where I had the responsibilities of a leader with the rank and pay of a Lieutenant.

After days of feasting and celebrating, I found myself waiting in line with my fellow squires to step into one of the administrative rooms in a different wing of the palace. Weslecker had his arm around me, but we kept the private whispers and giggles to a minimum with the way some of our peers eyed us. Both of our gryphons were elsewhere, enjoying a more restful time in the stables.

"Hey, lovebirds," Sharde said, fitting himself into line in front of us, to a complaining noise from Barlowe a few people back. "Word is that we're getting our pay, plus any bounties we've earned, and our final ranks."

"No wonder this is taking forever," Weslecker sighed.

Sharde grinned and snapped his fingers. "Exactly. Just

wait until we graduate tomorrow in front of everyone. I guess they're saving which flight we're assigned as the big reveal."

"I think I made a problem for them," I admitted. My closest friends knew all about the Wild Flight I'd requested from the king, plus the sanctuary where the gryphons would live. As I fluffed up Puzzlebox's soft mane and tickled her neck, I secretly hoped she and her rider were not assigned to Final Flight, like Sharde had long strived for, but mine instead.

"Hey, Sharde—get in line like the rest of us," Barlowe called loudly.

My friend brushed him off with a dismissive wave. "Please, you know they're going to give me a handful of bronze clorets for my service and tell me I'm ranked last."

"So you could hear in the back of the line," the other young man complained in a more nasally tone than usual. Sharde pretended not to hear him, and soon he was the next squire to step into the office with his gryphon.

A familiar face stepped into the front of the line, his dark eyes darting between Weslecker and me. "Hey, stranger," Weslecker said, clapping Mateo on the shoulder. "Where've you been?"

Mireille edged between me and Weslecker, insisting on gaining my attention for a good scratch on an itchy part of her neck. She bunted my chest with a friendly trill. *"I've missed you, baby girl,"* I said privately.

"I've missed you too, Sivvy. Mateo's princely duties are so boring," she sighed.

"No, please. I just want to talk to Sivana for a second," Mateo was saying when I glanced up, realizing that Sharde had already left the office and one of us was up next. The prince gestured Weslecker in and, once the door was closed behind him, turned to me. "You and him, huh?"

"Yes. For a few months now," I answered, suddenly feeling awkward. Mateo had missed most of that time.

He was suddenly looking everywhere but at me. "I'm, ah, happy for you both. Acton's had a crush for the longest time."

I felt badly for him, saying gently, "It was mutual, but the Academy being as it was…"

"Of course," he blurted. "Look, I wish you both all the happiness if it becomes something serious. Maybe it's silly, but I thought…" Color rose to darken his bronzed cheeks. "Anyway, I'm glad for another reason." He drew me aside from the line and dropped his voice to a whisper. "Father has informed me ahead of Isaac's trial that he already knows that he wants me to make me his heir. He wants me to consider the possibility my hand will be matched to a political marriage."

"Of course," I echoed, but that didn't make me feel any better. Even though he and I hadn't worked out as a couple, I still wanted him to find someone else who could love him for his steady strength and his moral compass that always seemed to point the right way, even if he couldn't always act on it. I forced a smile as I whispered, "You will make an excellent king one day."

He immediately clutched the ridge of his brow. "Father warned me that everyone would start complimenting my every fart the moment his decision was announced. Please, as a friend, promise you'll always tell me the truth even if I do someday become king," he murmured.

I did the one thing I imagined would become off limits when he became crown prince. I hugged him, patting his back as I promised. "And I'll always be your friend, even if you get a big head from sitting in your extra-large chair."

Mateo hugged me hard in return. The way he responded to a casual, friendly touch made me think he needed a hundred more moments like this one. "Thank you," he said.

We parted and were back in line when Weslecker exited

the office, grinning broadly. "I think I have good news," he said.

I let Mateo go ahead of me and smiled. "Oh?"

"The Commandant and a couple of our instructors are in there. They conducted a short interview about what flight I would like to be assigned to, based off a list of ones I qualify for." Weslecker was practically beaming. "They're looking for a junior staff at the Academy to help train what they expect to be the largest class in a long time."

"Whoa, outstanding news. Did you remind them how excellent a swordsman you are?" I asked.

He was nodding and opening his mouth to respond to the positive when there was a commotion of raised voices from the office. The door was ripped open abruptly. Mateo stood at the threshold, gesturing for me to come in with a sharp flick of his wrist. Exchanging a glance with Weslecker, I stepped forward and flinched when the prince slammed the door behind us.

He pointed at me, saying heatedly, "Tell her what you just said to me."

The Commandant sat behind a desk, with Commanders Falirin and Rudrick to either side of him. They didn't look all that pleased. "No amount of grandstanding will change our opinion," the Commandant answered.

"She is to be declared a Hero of Altare in front of everyone," he said. "She deserves to be Ace!"

"And you know the king's decision about your status," the Commandant said, hardly blinking. "Which means you will be the Ace."

Oh, Gatekeeper take me. I was clued in now about their argument. "Since he's going to be crown prince—"

"No," Mateo said over me. "I don't want preferential treatment! I was barely on the Storm Front, while Sivana and Acton killed the gigantic eldrafn that almost wiped out my father's court. How could you say I deserve to be Ace compared to that?"

"There is plenty of evidence of divine intervention in her big accomplishment. Not to diminish you, Squire Walker." The old gryphon rider nodded my way. "Becoming a Hero of Altare is her accomplishment, but Ace will be yours. As our future king, you will always be ranked first, Your Highness."

It was the first time I'd heard the Commandant defer to Mateo rather than treat him like any other cadet. "Well, then I demand you give the title to her anyway. I *know* I don't really deserve to be first, and so do you all," Mateo asserted while pointing to the other instructors.

"My decision is final," the Commandant replied, deadpan.

"It's really okay," I said in an undertone to Mateo. I rested my hand on his shoulder and smiled when he turned my way. "They're right. I did have divine help and shouldn't be qualified to be a Hero of Altare because of it. You're an outstanding gryphon rider in your own right and deserve acknowledgment too."

The anger in Mateo's face faded to a resigned expression. "At least tell me she's second place," he said.

"She is," the Commandant confirmed.

"I suppose it is good enough. I will take up the matter with my father." Mateo shrugged me off and went stomping out of the office.

"Close the door, would you, Squire Walker? We might as well review your file since you're here." Sighing, the Commandant shuffled some folders around. "As I just said, you will be announced as the rank two graduate of your class. Congratulations on everything you've accomplished to get to this point."

"Thank you, sir," I said, shaking off the negative feelings that'd left in the wake of Mateo storming out. Ari must've been napping, as I didn't have him in the back of my mind also pushing for us to gain this title in addition to the one we'd be given soon. We'd never expected to rank so well, and I was happy to hear Ari and I had done better than his first showing at the Academy with Alamid.

"I hope you understand, about the Ace title. The prince will not be able to budge us on this decision," the Commandant continued.

"I do understand, sir. I am content with what I have."

Mateo had been rank one, the Ace-to-be, from the moment our ranks had been revealed. I should've known the title would be his no matter the circumstances. Reality bent for the power of the Crown. We'd never know for sure if I was truly deserving of the title with that in mind.

"As you definitely should be." He quirked his mouth as he flipped through my file. "Several incidents of insubordination and acting against orders. Your superiors forgave a lot of behavior that'd bury you in demerits in my Academy. That being said, you are credited with an assist in killing the Earl, and your file says you've already received your portion of the bounty from that."

"I have, sir."

"We had no bounties for confirmed kills or assists of rozash, as we weren't expecting them on the Storm Front. Your mentor estimated you may have struck the killing blow on two and assisted in the deaths of a dozen more. He has recommended that you be assigned to the best possible flight, but word has reached us that the king has already appointed you to a new project called Wild Flight that will be attached to the Second. We will come back to that in a second.

"You have also earned the bounty for killing the eldrafn you've named the Kingmaker, an abomination of the Knight and the King eldrafns combined. We went ahead and gave you the bounty for both, with a portion removed to pay Squire Weslecker and the pyrojack Zuri Zaveri for their assistance in the task. Here is that, plus your wages."

He gestured to Rudrick, who flipped through a few envelopes and handed over one with my name on it. I opened it and peered at the bank note enclosed, signed and insured by the Crown. My eyes just about bugged out of my skull at the written sum.

"Congratulations," Rudrick said, grinning. "You're a wealthy woman now."

"I...thank you." I didn't even know what to say. They really should've handed the coin to the Churches of Orion and Nilara, but they were handing it to me instead, and I wasn't going to say no. I could do a lot of good with the money.

"Since we don't need to ask you about which flight you'd like, we can skip ahead of the interview," Rudrick said. "You'll be leading Wild Flight, as the only rider the wild ones will even listen to."

The Commandant cleared his throat. "However, the specifics of the new flight will not be something I will decide," he said. "I am quite pleased to inform you that I will be retiring. My last day on the job will be after I introduce my successor to the position and its responsibilities."

"Wow. Congratulations, sir," I said. What outstanding news for him and Night.

"I've just received confirmation that the new Commandant will be none other than your father."

I sucked in a hard breath. "Truly? He's receiving a promotion?"

He nodded, smiling in his strict way. "Night insisted we pass the position to someone with an accomplished female gryphon who can catch any wayward cadet. She knew Valtora was a Commandant's gryphon the moment she caught you after your...incident last year."

Slowly, I was staring to beam. "Yes, sir! She's an outstanding choice for the job. And she will keep the wild gryphons in line when Wild Flight and its sanctuary are established close to the Academy. It couldn't be more perfect."

"Ah, about that," he said. "All I'll say is that you have an upward slog to get Wild Flight established and honored by the rest of the corps. Your briefing with the king appears to be an idealized version. Just the idea of getting building materials for a sizable sanctuary will be a logistical nightmare."

"Of course, sir. I understand it will be difficult to establish, but I believe it will be worth it." And with my father as Commandant, we could make real change happen within the Academy together while the sanctuary was being built.

"I wish you luck," he said with a nod. "You're dismissed for now. Oh—one more question, actually. If we were to assign approximately four more people to Wild Flight, who would you want them to be?"

Ari was still fuming when we attended our graduation. We stood along with the rest of the room, though, when instead of a grand speech, Paragon Hughes himself took the voice amplification device and had us bow our heads in prayer to the Gatekeeper. He wished for the safety and protection of nearly two dozen Squires who hadn't made it to see this day, all posthumously knighted and immortalized as Lieutenants for their service. I breathed out heavily when Korvic and Feyring were named and honored.

"Gatekeeper protect you always," I murmured. The air in the room was solemn as chairs shuffled and everyone was seated.

The group a year ahead of us graduated first, so we got to see how it went. Other than the fact that our graduation was held within the palace ballroom, with an audience of hundreds seated around us, it was similar to what I remembered from my first year. Graduates were called up one by one, from the last rank to the first.

The Paragon read off a list of a squire's accomplishments and awards, then the squire knelt before the king to be knighted and officially appointed to his new flight. Each knight was then given a shield, painted with the crest of their new flight alongside their personal symbol.

I was overjoyed to see Valentic declared the Ace of his year, cheering and whooping after his knighting alongside a number of my peers. I doubted I was the only one imagining an alternative world where it was Victor Callan up there instead, but he was gone and his bullying a thing of the past. Instead, his beautiful gryphon was draped over Ari, clucking quietly as she soothed him down from his annoyance at our rank.

We sat between Mateo, who spent most of the ceremony with his arms crossed and a scowl on his face, and Weslecker in third place. I shifted with anticipation when our peers began getting called up, well aware of who I'd asked to join me in establishing Wild Flight.

The Paragon consulted his notes as Sharde stood next to him at attention alongside his gryphon. "This year group's first graduate is Noah Sharde and his gryphon Puzzlebox, ranked twenty-one of twenty-one. It should be noted that sometimes the qualities of character in a gryphon rider do not translate to glory. Squire Sharde displayed great skill in tending to the gryphons around him, making sacrifices along the way to ensure that his beast reached this graduation stage and a safe appointment in…"

I held my breath when he paused.

"Well, he wanted to be in Final Flight, if you would believe it. Straight to retirement." The audience chuckled as the Paragon spoke, and Sharde grimaced. "But we've decided his destiny belongs in a different direction. He will be joining a new venture instead, a partnership between the gryphon knight corps and our gryphon allies that we are calling Wild Flight. Congratulations, Squire Sharde. Step forward and be knighted."

Sharde broke into a smile as he turned and knelt before the king for his knighting.

Weslecker leaned over and whispered behind his hand, "You wouldn't have something to do with that, would you?"

"I warned the four people I recommended for the job. The Commandant said we couldn't be in the same flight, by the way, else I would've put your name forward too," I told him quietly. "With me in Wild Flight and you in the training half of the Second, hopefully we'll both be living in Fortress Aerie."

"But with separate assignments, so we won't be fraternizing. Perfect," he said and leaned over to press a quick kiss to my brow.

I held my breath several more times through the ceremony. When Credell came up as rank number seventeen of twenty-one, though, he was also assigned to Wild Flight. As was Pereyra, rank fifteen of twenty-one. Biggs was smiling hopefully as his accomplishments were read when he stepped forward as rank ten of twenty-one before he, too, was assigned to my new flight. Four of four of my requests, granted. I deflated with relief. As long as Weslecker wasn't unexpectedly assigned to a combat flight, I was getting everything I wanted.

Before I knew it, I was giving his hand a squeeze as his name was called. The crowd had a smattering of applause when his many combat accomplishments were read and the Paragon pinned a Gilded Combat Cross on his uniform for his assist in killing the Kingmaker.

"We will not be letting talent like Squire Weslecker go so easily. He has been selected to serve as a junior instructor in the art of war at the Gryphon Rider Academy. Congratulations, Squire Weslecker. Step forward and be knighted."

I could've cried I was so happy. Mateo nudged me. "Everything you wanted, eh?"

"Yeah. But wait…where are they assigning you?" I asked.

He smiled and shrugged. "I guess you'll just have to find out, Walker."

A soldier was gesturing for me to come up to the stage next, so I parted from him uncertainly to guide Ari into position next to the Paragon for a listing of our accomplishments. "Sivana Walker and her gryphon, Arimus, ranked two of twenty-one, has overcome several unique hurdles to stand before you today. You would have to be as blind as her gryphon to not know she is the first female graduate of the Gryphon Rider Academy."

The audience interrupted him with a brief round of applause. I struggled not to crack a smile as I stood there at attention. "Yes, yes, I agree. I am also happy to be the first to say that the king has signed a decree allowing more women to walk in Squire Walker's footsteps." He waited out another wave of cheers and clapping, much more enthusiastic with what a huge breakthrough that was. What a huge *change* that was. I couldn't help showing my teeth as my spirits lifted to new heights.

Before he could be interrupted again, the Paragon read the same list of kills and assists the Commandant had confirmed earlier. "For her many accomplishments and her gods-given talent with the gryphons, Squire Walker has been selected to lead Wild Flight and represent our wild-born allies. She will also be honored as our newest Hero of Altare tomorrow as we continue celebrating our victory over the Rathi." The audience was cheering again, going wild, so I was probably the only one to hear him say, "Congratulations, Squire Walker. Step forward and be knighted."

I turned and knelt before the king, who christened me a new knight with gentle taps of his sword. "I humbly proclaim you Dame Sivana Walker. Rise, new Knight-Lieutenant," he said formally.

I did so and saluted him. "Thank you, Your Majesty."

He inclined his head. "Thank *you*, Chosen. Take good care of my son."

I was puzzled by that as I accepted my new shield from a waiting soldier and returned to my seat. My friends hadn't flashed their shields at me, so when I turned mine around while listening to the short list of Mateo's wartime accomplishments, I hummed in surprise. It was painted with the gryphon rampant of Altare on a blue field, like a modified flag. And in the corner glimmered gold paint—my personal symbol, in the correct color.

I was still grinning down at it when Paragon Hughes announced, "We thought long and hard about where to place the Ace of this year, considering his status, and decided his leadership will be greatly appreciated in Wild Flight."

"Oh, you sly king," I said with a little laugh. King Cortes and the Paragon had assigned Mateo as far from combat as possible. Wild Flight was suitably prestigious as a new placement for graduating cadets, but we had our core element of five gryphon riders. We could do without him when he was announced as crown prince and forced to attend to his royal duties.

In the meantime, our shields matched the one given to Mateo, though his was suitably royal with a white field.

"Ready to do this again tomorrow, soon-to-be Hero of Altare?" Weslecker whispered.

"Gods, I hope the ceremony is really short," I replied. "I've had my fill of recognition."

"Too bad," he said lightly, tapping me on the nose. His green eyes danced with happiness, a glow many of our fellow cadets shared in the wake of learning their new assignments.

CHAPTER 38
NOT MY SON

Ari thought I was ridiculous, but by the time I was announced as a Hero of Altare in the throne room, I was past done with the ceremonies and the recognition. It was becoming embarrassing to be recognized so many times for a feat I'd had so much help in completing.

Luckily for me, the king had made the actual ceremony an intimate affair with his court and my family and friends in attendance. He'd placed a medal around my neck, which I was authorized to wear with my uniform. One side of the medal held the symbol of Altare, and the other face was engraved with my name.

More specifically, Sivana the Wild, how I'd be remembered when they finished making a *statue* of me to place in the Hall of Heroes. I was so grateful I was simply uncomfortable. They definitely didn't need to do that, but everyone else who'd had one of these awards placed around their neck also had their likeness and accomplishments immortalized there.

"Now, if you would all excuse us," the king said to our audience. "The people will want to see their newest Hero of Altare, but we will be addressing them this evening from my balcony. We have some business to attend to first."

We do? I nearly blurted it out, but Mateo was a few paces away, gesturing urgently for me to stay quiet. *Okay, then.* I followed the king to a side exit as the small gathering started to disperse, but I wasn't the only one confused, judging by the murmuring following us. Mateo fell into step with me as we walked toward the administrative wing. I had my hand on Ari's shoulder, helping steer him through the narrow hall and around other people coming and going around us.

"What's happening?" I asked him in an undertone.

"Father's decided to move up Isaac's trial. It's happening right now," he whispered back. "That way, when he presents you to the city as the newest Hero of Altare, he can also tell the people about the results and…err…the more uncomfortable decision made in the treaty talks. It'll be a bad news sandwich, and you're the good stuff in the middle."

"You couldn't have warned me earlier?" I hissed.

He put his palms up. "Father just told me about the treaty. Who knows, it might be received well."

My brows tightened. What could've been decided that'd be received as bad news? We'd won. The Rathi tribes owed our nation reparations for the many deaths we'd suffered from fighting out a war that they'd started.

We were stepping into a large office, else I'd have asked. Prince Isaac himself sat at the head of a long table with a number of people already seated. I was surprised at least half of them were Rathi, not just Solfrid sitting free with her hands folded on the table. I'd sent her scarves back to her via a palace page, and she wore one around her neck in a colorful loop, leaving her pale lips free to speak her knowledge.

Isaac was unrecognizable in plain clothes, looking leaner and far crueler with his fine royal veneer removed.

"Let us get this unpleasantness finished with," the king said. A servant pulled out the chair on the other side of the table for him, and I took a free seat next to Mateo while the

Commandant and Paragon Hughes also found a place alongside a few other officials I didn't know.

"This is a sham, Father. Why have such a private trial of unfriendly faces?" Isaac asked. He put on his most cultured tones and straightened in his chair as much as possible with the restraints securing him to it.

Ignoring him, King Cortes said, "We are gathered here today to hear the evidence that my son Isaac…" He cleared his throat, giving his head a swift shake. "That this man before us has deliberately started a war through his actions, committing acts of conspiracy and treason. I alone will be the judge of his guilt, as the only man in the realm capable of judging the deeds of a crown prince."

Gods. I felt a sudden stab of sympathy for the king, who looked like he'd rather be anywhere else. I didn't judge him for wanting to rip this wound open fast.

One of the officials stood. "I have been selected to help the king conduct an impartial trial. In the interests of expediency, we have gathered together everyone with a significant personal account of the crown prince's actions. We will begin with our new Rathi allies."

To my surprise, we had full representation of the Rathi tribes we'd been at war with, each a leader, though some looked awfully young. The son of the last Bloodrapids Clan chieftain was a gawky, pimpled teen, but he still stood to speak. I noticed the man representing the Icefang Clan wouldn't look at Solfrid. Maybe she hadn't had a chance to tell him about Hvitorden—or he hadn't cared.

Some of the Rathi didn't speak our language. Solfrid acted as a translator in that case, helping tell the narrative that the tribes agreed on together and that she backed up with her own story.

"I served as a messenger for the Icefang Clan, sneaking into and out of your capital to speak with the crown prince and then share his words with my tribe and our allies," she said. "I give you my word that everything these men and women have said is true. He promised us a portion of land in exchange for picking a fight with Altare. He shared the weaknesses of your people, as well as caches of weapons, armor, and several variations of your battle plans over the course of the war. He told us we wouldn't have to fight to the bitter end and that he had a plan to become king. He promised that we would be rewarded for backing him, yet it was a lie. We suffered greatly because of him."

"We regret," said the Bloodrapids teen through a thick accent.

"We regret our trust greatly," Solfrid echoed in agreement.

Isaac drew himself up. "Father, are you really going to believe the lies these barbarians dare to breathe in your presence?"

"Mind your tongue, oathbreaker," Solfrid said harshly.

The official gestured for her to sit urgently when her balled-up fist began to spark with her volta magic. "May I remind all in attendance that the crown prince still deserves the respect of his position until the king makes his decision?" His suggestion was a timid squeak in the face of Solfrid's fury, but she threw herself into her seat before she did something she may regret.

"*I was hoping she'd hit him,*" Ari commented in a bored tone.

"*Me too,*" I admitted.

King Cortes sighed heavily. "All right. We have heard the Rathi's side of events. Let's have the rest." He gestured to the official with a meaty hand.

With a nod, Isaac's friends stood next, talking around the issue at hand to mention how Isaac had been beginning to court Princess Erimin in Lithos. Eventually, one broke and blurted, "What I know is that he plotted to have a martyr die to inflame the people's sensibilities. For a while, it sounded like he was talking about the death of the lady gryphon rider."

"Let's hear from her," the official said, nodding to me.

I stood, feeling my knees waver at the look of death aimed my way from Isaac. "That is true," I said, proud of myself for speaking clearly, not hint of a stutter in front of the man that would've celebrated my untimely death. "I have much to share, actually. The crown prince owns the *Kaiamear Gazette,* which took great interest in me during my first year at the Gryphon Rider Academy. He helped shape a favorable reputation for me amongst the public."

The Commandant and Paragon exchanged a nod and stood. "We would like to assist Lieutenant Walker in explaining the extent she was manipulated," the Paragon said. King Cortes inclined his head. "As the king is aware, she made an extensive report to her Commandant when the pressure grew too great for a mere cadet. He has already reviewed her words, but they bear repeating now."

Together, the three of us told the assembled group everything. The secret meetings, the double-speak, and the secret shared from a heartbroken Sunset's memory about the truth of the conspiracy that'd gotten her rider murdered. "Finally, Your Majesty, I would be remiss if I didn't share that I overhead the crown prince's final words to her before she went to war," the Paragon said.

I hadn't realized Paragon Hughes had overheard it and was keeping the knowledge to drop at this crucial moment. "He spoke the true name of the Gatekeeper, cursing her before she was about to ship out to war."

King Cortes reddened. "Is this true?" he demanded across the table.

"Father, you know I would never..."

He slapped his hand on the table. "I raised you better than to *ever* speak the Gatekeeper's name. One of my most trusted men said you have done this, and I am forced to believe him over your continued lying and denials."

Isaac's expression tightened. "I should've opted to have her killed, just like you wanted. She's been nothing but trouble."

"On the contrary, she saved my life and that of my *trusted* officials, who hid with me at Caershire. You and your friends —" The king gestured to the men who'd spoken well of Isaac. "—weren't there. Care to explain?"

Isaac remained mute.

"Can *anyone* explain that mystery to me?" King Cortes demanded.

In the silence that consumed the room afterward, one person stood. "I believe I can, Your Majesty," Solfrid said. I sat, as did the two elder gryphon riders, as the proud Rathi woman lifted her chin. Her father had whispered something in their language which had her nostrils flaring. "I can only venture my hearsay, as I am aware that Emil of the Bear River Clan was meeting with your...crown prince separately from me. He was the rider of the eldrafn you keep calling 'the King.'" She spoke the name with scorn, while I latched on to the clan name she spoke. Could the King have been born of the storm that'd killed Revna and crippled Signe?

"Emil desired something more. His eldrafn was at the end of its life cycle, too old and large to live much longer. I would not be surprised if he made a separate deal for power once his eldrafn began its life cycle anew," Solfrid concluded.

"Is this true?" the king asked his son.

"Of course not, Father. This barbarian continues to slander me, and I'm shocked you're considering believing her," he answered.

"An honorable eldrafn rider would never lie," Solfrid said, instantly bristling with offense.

"Explain how the Kingmaker knew to attack Caershire, then. Explain how its rider knew where it was," the king pressed. Isaac remained silent. "The gods take you, boy! Answer me!"

"Might I suggest some truth serum to loosen his tongue, Your Majesty?" interjected the official leading the trial.

Isaac smirked the moment before King Cortes said, "Yes, I think it is time." He gestured, and a servant stepped forward from the wall, bearing a platter with a single, tiny cup studded with a glitter of gems.

Isaac's expression screwed up. "But Father, it is the law of our land that any member of the royal family is entitled to a trial free of truth serum," he protested.

"Tell me why you weren't at Caershire," the king repeated.

"I...I was held up by my duties!" A bead of sweat dripped from his hairline as the servant stood over him, platter held out. The presiding official had moved across from her, hand extending toward the cup. "Father, don't do this. I've taken vlorine flower serum. I'll die."

For a moment, King Cortes faltered. His arms fell to his sides, and his jaw went slack. He glanced around the assembled audience with a gauging eye before inspecting Isaac with a narrowing of his bloodshot eyes. "You're lying," he said, making another gesture. "Guards! Make sure he drinks the serum."

A pair of guards peeled from the wall where they'd been standing at attention unheeded. One quickly grabbed Isaac's shoulders, and the other pried his mouth open as he made sounds akin to a dying animal. I winced even as I found it hard to look away as the official gingerly poured the serum down Isaac's throat.

A pin could've dropped as the guards released Isaac and he slumped in his chair. *"Gods, he might be dead,"* I thought to Ari. Had I really just watched the king condemn his son?

"I don't think so. I can hear him breathing," Ari said.

In a few moments, I heard the scrape of his breath too, and

the sigh that filled the room with relief as Isaac raised his head with the woozy smile that matched the feeling truth serum inspired, like stuffing one's head with carefree cotton clouds.

King Cortes stood, gesturing for us to remain in our seats. "Son," he said. Isaac nodded in the slowest motion. "My first-born son, Isaac Alonso Cortes. Was everything said in this room true?"

"Yes. Well..." he drew the word out. "I only sent a few letters to Princess Erimin. She wasn't all that interested."

The king was visibly trembling. His fists were propped on the table like they were the only thing keeping him upright. "You truly plotted against me?"

A flicker of self-preservation passed over Isaac's expression, quickly doused by the truth serum's effects. "Ye... Yeeeessss," he admitted reluctantly.

"You began a war with the intentions of using it to humiliate me."

"Yes."

"You manipulated a foreign coalition to kill your own brother." Pain soaked each word. I gripped the edge of the table, tears pricking the corner of my eyes. *Make it stop. You have the truth you need. Don't make it worse with the details,* I wanted to say.

"Yes," Isaac said. He jerked his shoulder and then laughed down at his arm, bound to his chair. "To be fair, I didn't want to. Things got messy in my contingency plan quickly."

"You didn't want to," his father repeated. "You didn't *want* to be a kinslayer."

"Does anyone?" Isaac asked dreamily.

Solfrid repeated the question under her breath in a mocking echo.

The king took a great, shaky breath. "One last question. You spoke the true name of the Gatekeeper?"

"Only a couple times, when it is deserved."

His father's shoulders heaved with a stifled sound. "I have heard enough. I have been willfully ignorant to your actions for too long, and for that, I take full responsibility. You have proven to be a kinslayer and a heretic who has spoken the true name of the Gatekeeper." He pointed an accusatory finger across the table. "I don't even know who you are, for you are surely not my son. As of this moment, you are disinherited and banished to the North Tower to await your execution."

Isaac's eyes widened despite the serum. "Father, you can't be—"

"Get him out of my sight!" King Cortes roared. The pair of guards freed Isaac from the chair and grabbed him, hauling him out of the room while he began to scream and thrash, begging for mercy.

The king hid his face in his sleeve for one long wipe. "We announce Mateo as crown prince tonight. You are all dismissed," he said from between his teeth.

I wasn't the only one realizing the sensitivity of the king's mood and beating a hasty retreat. The unpleasant echoes of the former crown prince's shouts had turned to desperate sobs that I could still hear. I turned to Mateo, who was pale with shock. "So, err..." What did I even say after that display?

"Are you going to ask me about the treaty?" he asked, practically pouncing on the idea. Anything but talk about what'd just happened, I supposed.

"Yeah. Sure."

He motioned I follow him down the hall. I kept a hand on Ari's side to keep him with us through the unfamiliar stretch of space. "You see, the Rathi didn't have enough wealth to pay us. They had almost nothing at all—which is why they wanted land so desperately as to trust my former brother."

When he saw me wince, he added, "That's right. If my father can disinherit him, so can I. Isaac saw that war with the

Rathi was inevitable, so he offered them what they needed, and they jumped. When Father heard about this during the peace talks, he decided to embrace the spirit of change and offer them Altarian citizenship in exchange for ceding their lands to us. Any Rathi living in Altare will be put to the task of rebuilding, but with how many may be moving here, it might not take all that long."

"Wait—you think that will be taken as bad news?" I asked.

"Do *you* really want Rathi neighbors?" he countered. That definitely gave me pause. "Exactly. Even you, one of the most accepting people I know, hesitates at the idea. It's like if Lithos conquered us tomorrow and told us we're all Lithosians now. It won't be a smooth, loving integration of cultures when we've been at war for so long."

"We're talking the difference between half a year's war with the Rathi and several years' worth of war with Lithos," Ari pointed out.

"Enemies are enemies," I said. *"And the Rathi killed two of our friends and countless others."*

"Well, maybe the Rathi will prove to be good neighbors," I added aloud after a pause.

"Maybe. We are the victorious nation here as well. As soon as my father delivers this speech, the lower Rathi Islands will be no more. Their frozen soil will be Altarian." He forced a small smile. "I'll drink to that. And I'm crown prince, I'll drink if I want to."

CHAPTER 39

HOUR OF THE GRYPHON

I MISSED the envelope when it arrived at my family's temporary quarters, but Rissa was waiting with bated breath for me to open it once I returned. It was heavy and addressed to me with the finest calligraphy.

I removed a card made from heavy paper with a pearlescent sheen and the perfectly penned note was an invitation to dinner with none other than the Duke and Duchess Weslecker in a fortnight at their main estate.

"Well?" Rissa pressed, her hands clasped together and a twinkle in her eyes.

I could face down death on gryphon back any day, but the idea of sitting down and having a conversation with the ultra-rich parents that'd been distantly involved in Weslecker's life made me break into a nervous sweat. I passed her the invitation, and she made a shrill sound that had our mother come running. "Look, look!"

She gave it to Mother next, who smiled and nodded in approval. "Rissa, we've got work to do," she said.

"We sure do." Rissa was already looking me over head to toe. "You've got to be beautiful for the speech tonight! But first, can we just take a moment to acknowledge that I was right about who you were going to pick?" She beamed at me.

"You thought I'd choose Acton?" I asked.

"Uh, clear as day! When you came to visit us and told me about him and"—she glanced Mother's way—"the other one, it really sounded like the wind was blowing in that direction. I'm really happy you picked Acton."

I smiled to myself. If she approved, I knew I'd made the right decision. I let Mother and Rissa haul me off to the bathroom mirror to touch up my hair, makeup, and uniform, and while they fiddled, I shared what I'd seen of the trial in a rush so quick they had me repeat it.

"Hmm. Then the former crown prince is dead," Mother had said, accompanied by the *tisk* she usually reserved for me. "To be disinherited in such a way. The king would have him executed swiftly, before he changes his mind."

"I feel badly for him," I'd admitted. I still did as I stood behind him in my best uniform, pressed and cleaned of even the smallest speck of lint. My new medal gleamed like liquid gold in the soft light of evening where it graced us on the royal balcony.

Mother had shined the medal meticulously for me. "Sivana the Wild," she'd read from its face, shaking her head before smiling at me fondly. "I know you didn't pick this, but it's perfect for you."

I supposed I'd created a sort of reputation for myself, but I didn't feel as fierce as the untamed gryphons I'd befriended as I shifted on that balcony between Mateo and Ari. A number of uniformed men like Paragon Hughes and well-dressed advisors formed two solid rows with us behind the king. It was a larger than I expected to accommodate all of us, with a grate forming a U shape that overlooked the palace's main courtyard.

People were still flooding in, and we were high enough that they looked akin to specks drifting together to listen in shoulder to shoulder to a rare direct address from King Cortes. He waved occasionally but mostly stood there waiting with both his hands wrapped around the railing.

There was a new slump to his shoulders, a burden of guilt and sorrow he'd probably carry for the rest of his life. *"I think it's asking too much of him to address Kaiamear after the trial,"* I said to Ari.

He pulsed a feeling like a shrug. *"I was under the impression it had to happen. Don't feel too sorry for him. It wasn't all that long ago when he was trying to have one of us murdered."*

"I know, but..." I shrugged too. *"The Mother calls on us to forgive those who have seen the error of their ways and atoned."*

"Be careful, or I'll ask Glorium what he thinks."

I stifled a laugh. Knowing him, he'd probably appear in person to gleefully proclaim the beginning of his own book of scripture. That was one way to upstage King Cortes. Mateo elbowed me with a discreet glare.

"Sorry," I whispered. He had to be a bundle of nerves, too. This might be the first time his father had pushed him into the public eye. In a way, he was now the king's only child, with Odalis wearing the Gatekeeper's gray. I could sympathize with how much pressure that had to be.

At last, the king held up his arms for silence. Hundreds of faces turned upward as a servant handed him a voice amplifier. "People of Altare, lend me your ears. We entered a difficult time together after a coalition of Rathi struck a mighty blow to blacken the eye of our great nation, but I am delighted to say that we have recovered our dignity by returning victorious."

He paused, letting the audience cheer. The officials around me applauded politely, and I joined them a heartbeat later.

"The brave men and women of our military were victorious despite great odds. Each of the vicious, monstrous eldrafn our enemy wielded against us fell. Their god-blessed berserkers engaged an army that couldn't be bested by sheer strength. We must give thanks to the soldiers who stepped away from their families to fight for their nation and to the gryphon riders who kept the skies safe.

"We give thanks to our newest Hero of Altare, who not only singlehandedly killed the largest eldrafn Altare has ever seen, but also challenged and changed long-held beliefs by yours truly. Give a warm welcome to newly knighted Dame Sivana Walker."

I stepped forward amidst a deafening wave of noise from the crowd, stepping into place next to the king. *"Okay, it feels solid,"* I told Ari after I shook the railing. He leapt up and curled his talons around it, and if I thought the crowd was loud before, they truly went crazy at the sight of my gryphon.

"And her gryphon, Arimus. A proud representative of his race, who was key to Sivana's every success. All of her heroic deeds wouldn't be possible without him, and they did it all while navigating the unique challenges of his blindness," the king added.

"I believed, like many of you may have, that a woman could not be a gryphon rider. I am not too proud to admit that I was wrong, as Sivana has earned a place in the Hall of Heroes and a title of 'the Wild' after..." He listed my accomplishments in an echo of his earlier speech in the throne room when he first put the medal around my neck.

"She will be leading and representing the wild gryphons that flew to our defense during the war. It is the gods' will..." He took a deep breath, looking me in the eye. I nodded, trusting him to announce it if it was truly time for the public to hear it. A murmur rose from the assembled crowd and several arms were pointing to a glimmering figure flying our way. The king didn't seem to notice, starting to say, "As the..."

Glorium swooped overhead with a whistling laugh, blowing my hair sideways as his rainbow flight feathers caught the light mere feet from the balcony. *"Chosen of Lord Orion!"* he crowed loudly at the same time as the king said it.

"Did you call him?" I asked Ari immediately as Glorium flew a few loops over the crowd.

"Maybe," he twittered.

The king set the voice amplifier aside for a moment. "Is this your doing?" he hissed.

"No, Your Majesty. But that is Glorium, the demigod I was telling you about," I whispered back. "He loves attention."

I intended for that to be an understatement, but Glorium had his fun and flew away, leaving an awed crowd waiting to hear more.

Clearing his throat, the king picked up where he'd left off. "Finally, I would like to officially announce that I have approved the Gryphon Rider Academy to accept applications from girls who dream of riding a gryphon of their own." He stopped there and chuckled as the audience reacted. He'd definitely known this would be the most popular part of his speech, even if the news had leaked a few times during smaller gatherings over the last week.

I smiled with pride. "It's a big leap in the right direction," I said, careful to lean away from the voice amplifier.

He lowered it away from his lips again. "Well said, Chosen." He inclined his head in a nearly deferential way. "Go switch places with my son. It's time."

I waved to the audience in farewell and helped Ari down from the railing, meeting Mateo's eye on my way back to my place. He nodded and stepped forward with a quick glance at Mireille. Not to be outdone, he helped her take Ari's place, and she visibly preened at the wave of attention.

"It is truly the hour of the gryphon, and the gods clearly agree," the king said. "We must not forget the brave souls who would bond with one and ride to battle on their back. My son Mateo has done this and returned from war the Ace of his year, the most skilled rider of his year group." We applauded politely again, and Ari groused privately over our Link.

"Due to an unfortunate series of events, I must share that my eldest son has acted out of accordance with his role as crown prince. He has lost his chance to succeed me, which means we must welcome Mateo as my new heir one step from the throne."

I held my breath and listened to the crowd, gauging how loudly they applauded. Some folks would ride the excitement of this big gathering and clap and cheer no matter what, but it did seem like there was a lessening of enthusiasm in the wake of this announcement. Isaac was a popular man, with a following I was carefully excluded from. Who knew how many would be furious to learn that he'd been swiftly disinherited and executed for his plotting?

However, that was it. Short and sweet, without the bloody details. If we were lucky, the common Altarian would think Isaac moved to the countryside for a quiet life in the lap of luxury as a disgraced royal.

Mateo returned to my side and breathed a tense sigh. "That went better than I expected," he whispered.

"Yeah. You'll be fine," I whispered back.

He tilted his lips doubtfully. "We'll see."

"Finally, good people of Altare," the king was saying. "In the wake of their defeat, the Rathi coalition have surrendered a portion of their islands to us. Our enemies have become our allies. Do not be surprised if you see heads of white hair among the crews working to rebuild the port cities across our coast. Many Rathi are proud to call themselves Altarian and hoist our flag after a lifetime of barely scraping by over barren land."

Again, we applauded, and the king brought his speech to a close by inviting the crowd into the palace for one last feast. Mateo went to his father's side and rested a hand on his shoulder while the gathering dispersed.

"Well, you got your wish. It's over," Ari teased. I hung there for a moment uncertainly before joining the shuffle of people off the royal balcony, letting the Cortes family have a more private moment.

"Is it?"

"This is *the last feast, and you endured being shown to all of Kaiamear. Now we can leave at first light for Fortress Aerie like you're dreaming of."*

"True. You're going to be carrying extra bags, by the way. Even though Rissa's staying at the temple here in Kaiamear, Mother wants to move all her things." And despite selling much of our family's furniture and valuables, Mother still had a lot of things.

"That's fine. It's just one trip," he said. Over our Link, I knew he was looking forward to what came next as much as I was, but for different reasons. A certain maroon and red Skymother dominated his thoughts. *"Okay, yes, I can't wait to settle with Sunset."* He pulsed a warm feeling, like the settling butterflies of a deeper infatuation. *"You'll be happy. We've discussed the possibility of chicks when the season comes."*

I stopped dead in the threshold to the great dining hall to gape at him. "You have?" I half-gasped, half-demanded.

"Well, yes. Why not have a bouncing red chick or two after everything we've been through?" he reasoned.

I clutched the medal around my neck, pressing it over my heart. "I'm going to be a gryphon auntie," I said gleefully.

He murred, bunting my thigh. Then he pushed, making me take a step toward the table reserved for us, plus our friends and family, since we were guests of honor tonight. *"Human auntie. And when you have chicks, I'll be the gryphon uncle."*

"Wait, wait, it's way too early to talk about that," I protested privately. I hadn't even braved the meeting with Weslecker's parents and endured what I expected to be an intense inspection and judgment from them.

"Just making sure we establish the titles right now for when it happens," he said with a whistling laugh.

I paused to say hello to a smiling woman with the same sienna-toned skin as Biggs, who bounced a baby in her arms who already had a soft head of curls and big, sweet eyes. "Hope you're having a lovely evening, ma'am," I said.

Biggs himself was out of uniform, playfully chasing a couple of his giggling younger siblings around our table. One of Pereyra's many cousins had joined them.

"Oh, yes. I'm glad they're getting all this energy out, too," she replied. "We're heading home tomorrow. Don't be a stranger, all right?" She'd already invited me to visit her corner of Altare any time as a thank you for making sure her son was assigned somewhere safe after his time at the Academy.

I'd met most of my friends' family at this point. Credell's parents weren't a surprise, both quiet, obviously hard-working folk who'd left their family farm in the hands of his older siblings so they could come to Kaiamear. He resembled his father most distinctly, another tall man with broad shoulders who also bent his knees automatically to bring him more in line when talking to shorter people like me.

Pereyra's family was scattered all over, but they'd come in force to support him and witness his knighting. They'd folded Weslecker and Sharde into their celebrating since neither young man had their family come visit. None of the family had batted an eye when Zizi and her parents joined them each night. I loved the Pereyras already and sat with them while waiting for my own family to arrive to the feast.

They'd also shown great compassion for a grieving Missus Feyring since she'd come to Kaiamear before an official from the gryphon knight corps could present her with her son's shield and the final wages he'd earned. She'd chosen to stay and solicit any stories we had of her talkative son, smiling wistfully through each one. "I'm just glad he had such a good group of friends to get into mischief with," she kept saying. I hoped our stories gave her some feeling of closure.

Ellie slid into the seat next to mine. "Do you have room on your gryphon for one more back to Fortress Aerie?" she asked.

"Yes," I said, cocking a hopeful look her way. She mirrored me with a giggle.

"I may have convinced the new Commandant that if the gryphon knight corps is expanding, maybe the fortress had room for one more new idea," she told me.

"I'm sure it was an outstanding idea," I said. It was from Ellie, after all.

She adjusted her glasses and nodded. "Of course. The military still needs its engineers and logisticians. Where better to learn such things than a military academy? We're just making it official since I was only learning in Fortress Aerie because my family couldn't afford a seat at one of the universities or finishing schools.

"My idea was that anyone with an academic scholarship and the interest could come learn for free as long as they joined the military for a few years after they finished their schooling. Since learning isn't free, they could pay it back by guaranteeing they wouldn't take the knowledge and disappear. Your father liked it as long as I stayed to help coordinate it."

"That sounds familiar," I commented.

"Yes, but I'm not going to be an instructor yet. I'm still learning and growing my skills, so I'll take classes and help coordinate everything as my actual job." She beamed. "It sounds like a lot of fun! And did you know there are a lot of rooms available that can be turned into space to home more cadets and scholars alike?"

"I'm glad. It sounds like there's going to be a lot more activity around the fortress once we return," I said. "But the best part about all this is you'll still be an honorary Kite Flight member and with Sharde."

Ellie blushed, her shoulders wiggling with happiness. "Yes, precisely."

"Any chance of a proposal soon?" I whispered behind my hand.

Her color deepened a shade. "I hope so."

I hugged her briefly, full of joy that both of them would be going back to Fortress Aerie with me. Fate may take them away someday, but for now, we'd be starting our jobs off in the same place. Taking the first steps to modernize the Academy, in fact, carrying our hopes and dreams to a better future.

I reached down to scratch Ari behind the ears, sharing a pulse of affection over our Link. The one thing I was sure of was that we would only make this future possible together.

Weslecker approached the boy sitting on the other side of me and tapped his shoulder. "Excuse me. I'd like to sit with my lady, if you wouldn't mind."

Ellie cooed quietly and fanned herself. I turned and kissed him after he settled in the space the boy vacated, playfully adjusting the Gilded Combat Cross on his uniform while he palmed my medal and traced the words on its face. "You know, you're going to have a wild gryphon try to bite this if you wear it every day," he said.

"I had the same thought. It's shiny and dangles if I bend. Do you think the Crown will make replacements?" I asked.

Around us, our friends and family were settling as the first course was served and beverages were poured by a veritable legion of palace servants.

"They had best invest in making you a few, at least," he said. He palmed the goblet of the juice served before the wine was poured later in the evening and raised it. "I would like to propose a toast."

I lifted my goblet as he tilted his my way with a warm look. "To Sivana the Wild, newest Hero of Altare."

"Here, here!" exclaimed a few of the Pereyras. We took a sip of our drinks together.

My father, who'd been shuffled into a seat close by, raised his goblet next. "To new beginnings!" he exclaimed.

I murmured agreement and drank to that before making the next toast. "And to Wild Flight!"

SIVANA AND ARI'S **adventure will conclude in Gryphon Rider Academy 4: Wild Flight!**

INTERESTED IN MORE? Join my newsletter as one way to get access to a bonus scene from this book! Sign up on my website.

STAY up to date with Gryphon Rider Academy and the Altare world by joining my Facebook group: People of Altare! In this community, we'll talk about fantasy book releases, share fun posts, and have the occasional giveaway.

PLEASE REMEMBER TO REVIEW! Reviews help other readers find stories they may love. Consider leaving a review for Gryphon Rider Academy 3: Storm Front on Amazon and other websites.

ALSO IN THE ALTARE WORLD

ROYAL SPY INSTITUTE

Join an unlikely crew of five misfits and a mouse as they strive to become one of Altare's newest elite spy teams. Heists and adventures await!

The Gilded Wolves meets Six of Crows in this YA fantasy series in which a former thief uses her skills to become a spy. If you like clever heroines, strong friendships, and found family, then you'll love Royal Spy Institute!

- See Royal Spy Institute on Amazon -

ABOUT THE AUTHOR

Elise Hennessy is an author of young adult fantasy full of adventure and found family. She holds a master's degree in journalism and enjoys crafting unique stories. When Elise is not busy writing, she's trying to reduce her prodigious TBR list. She lives in Texas with her family and is owned by two cats.

Find out more about her books at: www.elisehennessy.com

www.ingramcontent.com/pod-product-compliance
Lightning Source LLC
Chambersburg PA
CBHW061541190726
48289CB00004B/1125